Wild Thing

Kim Cormack

Mythomedia Press 2754 10th Ave
V9Y 2N9 Port Alberni, B.C

Acknowledgments

Thank you to my children, friends and family for understanding the endless hours I spend in front of the computer writing. A special thank you, too Haley McGee, Leanne Ruissen and Tasha Lee for your beta reading and editing expertise.

A Letter To My Readers

Your awesome reviews and uplifting words keep me writing full steam ahead even when the going gets tough. I appreciate and love you all. I hope to keep you with me on this wild and crazy ride for many years to come.

Kim Cormack XO

Children Of Ankh Series Universe

C.O.A Series

Lexy's Series

Wild Thing
Wicked Thing
Deplorable Me

Kayn's Series

Sweet Sleep
Enlightenment
Let There Be Dragons
Handlers Of Dragons

Owen's Series

Bring Out Your Dead

Prologue

Some people are born into this world kicking and screaming. They calm down and manage to find a way to fit into society. They have a mother and a father or perhaps only one of those two. Alexandria Abrelle was the name that appeared on her birth certificate. Lexy had never known this girl. She'd come quietly and subserviently into the world, born to a mother, in a coma during her gestation. She was taken from her mother's womb as she slipped away into her next life.

Lexy had been living in group homes and foster care for as long as she could remember. There had only been a few that felt right, but either she'd outgrown them, or perhaps, they just hadn't wanted her anymore. She'd never been given a reason. When it came time to leave the last home she'd been at for a few years, she decided to run away with some of the older ones. They were all tired of allowing someone else to control their lives. They'd planned to hitchhike across the country. It seemed like a brilliant idea at the time.

She had been reborn in a place far worse than any version of hell, one could imagine. After many years lost in places void of humanity, Grey found her and introduced her to a partially immortal family. She'd been saved in so many ways by the Ankh. They were the family she'd always been destined to find. They would teach her to embrace the Dragon that resided within. She would learn that both the dark and light were equally important. Lexy would learn of necessary evil.

4

Chapter 1

Lexy's Story

The Year 1967.

She'd been astonished by the size of the moon that night. At only eleven years of age, Lexy was easily impressed. She was an adorable mass of freckles with wild crimson hair. She'd spent years wearing braids to avoid lice. Her first order of business once on her own was to swear she'd never wear braids again. The fear of having bugs in her hair stayed with her, making a ponytail the preferred option. She'd been living in group homes and foster care for as long as she could remember. There had only been a few that felt right, but either she'd outgrown them or they just hadn't wanted her anymore. She'd never been given a reason. When it came time to leave the last home. She decided to run away with a few of the older ones. They were all tired of allowing someone else to control their lives. They'd planned to hitchhike across the country. It had seemed like a brilliant idea at the time. Once hunger became an issue, the group changed. They'd all had their basic needs attended too and hadn't known what it felt like to be hungry. Soon, they were stealing and beating up hitchhikers as a mob. She'd tried to talk sense into the self-proclaimed leader of the unwanted children. It hadn't gone well. His name was Martin. He'd gone from being a mediocre big brother figure to a horribly abusive one. She'd dared to question his rule and he'd given her a black eye. The group left her by the side of the highway.

She sat in the dirt, watching them walk away, knowing she should run to catch up. *It wasn't safe to be alone, but it also wasn't a good idea to go with them.* She let them leave, deciding to cut across a field and travel the back roads. The dream was to find a family in a small town who wanted a little girl just like her. It felt freeing to yank her hair loose of its restraints as she strolled through the orchard full of apple trees. *She hadn't eaten anything solid in days. She was starving.* Lexy ate five or six apples before she caught sight of the quiet country road of her fantasies. Half a dozen apples hadn't done much to stop the loud grumbling complaints from her stomach. She contemplated staying put. It was a warm night. She could eat a few more, close her eyes and drift off to sleep in the field. *It was tempting.* She looked down at the grass strewn with rotting apples. *It wasn't safe.* Creatures would be showing up to eat the branches cast-offs. *This was a bear smorgasbord. She'd likely end up the main course to the apple appetizer if she fell asleep out here in the open.* She spit on the barbwire fence to see if it had a current. Her spit hadn't sizzled so she touched it with a finger. *It was fine.* She crawled through it, carefully. She felt the sting of the wire slicing her hand, where she'd parted the fence to shimmy through. Lexy glanced at the trail of blood and licked it off. It kept bleeding. She pressed two fingers against it and held them there until it stopped oozing. She blew on it as she strolled down the side of the road. It started seeping, she wiped it on the corner of her shirt. Her thoughts on a solution to her bleeding hand predicament halted, as she heard a vehicle spitting up gravel in the distance. She'd better keep walking. *There must be a town close by. The car was driving somewhere.* It drove right past her and disappeared into the backdrop of the night sky. She caught a glimpse of the woman driving and felt sad she hadn't bothered to pull over to ask if she needed help. Her eyes began to tear up and she blinked it away. She did need help, but she didn't cry. She'd stopped crying a long time ago. Once she'd realised, her tears were pointless. After the third or fourth home didn't want her anymore, she stopped crying. Her feelings had never mattered to anyone. She wandered down that unpaved back road for a while longer before making the decision to start looking for somewhere to sleep. Utterly exhausted, she searched for a reasonably secure, temporary shelter. There appeared to be nothing, but apple orchard in every direction. If there was a town up ahead, there would be sparse traffic at this late an hour. She was exhausted, when an old pastel blue truck pulled over for her. The man had a couple of large dogs in the cab. She decided only a nice man would allow his dogs up front instead of making them sit in the back. He politely explained the reason why there was nowhere for her to sit up front. That should have been a hint. She was too tired for rational thought. She had already convinced herself of his love for his dogs. He offered her a ride in the back of the truck and told her he could only take her as far as the nearest town. *That was exactly where she wanted to go.* She felt the temperature drop, rather suddenly. She embraced herself; crossing her arms, briskly rubbing the goose bumps on her exposed skin. She felt uneasy. Her stomach knotted, as the stranger jumped out of the truck. He opened the tailgate, sat down, and asked her if she would like some hot chocolate? He passed her a thermos. Once again, she felt a sense of foreboding, and chose to ignore it. He looked harmless. He appeared to be nothing but a meek, frail looking elderly man. She convinced herself to ignore the impulse to run. Lexy took a sip of the hot chocolate. The heated liquid slid down her throat with the pleasurable sensation of much needed warmth after the sudden chill. She glanced up, and he didn't appear to want any. She took another big gulp before trying to pass the thermos back.

He assured, "That's okay dear. You can have it all."

She gulped down the entire thermos, without giving it much thought. It calmed the complaints from her grumbling stomach. She felt relaxed and ready for a nap. He offered her a blanket from the front seat, giving the explanation that it would probably be chilly riding in the back. The blanket smelled of mold, but she accepted the simple act of kindness from the stranger. Her eyes began to feel heavy. It became impossible to keep them open. She lay down, wrapping her body in the gamey scented blanket. She drifted off to the slamming sound of the driver's side door.

Lexy began to stir...*She couldn't move?* Her wrists and ankles were bound. She couldn't see anything. She was inside a strange scented sack. She could see the outline of dark shapes through the material. It was a familiar scent, but she couldn't place it. *She shouldn't have left the group. What had she gotten herself into?*

She heard a voice say, "It's not awake."

Another voice responded, "Put it in the barn."

Lexy squeezed her eyes shut. *It, they were referring to her as, it. This was not a good sign; even the homes where she'd been neglected had called her by name. She'd never been referred to as, it. She felt groggy, unusually so. Had she been drugged? She was so stupid. Why had she thought a stranger would be kind to her?* She played dead as a Clanking noise was followed by the sensation of someone yanking her from wherever she was and dropping her with a thud onto the ground. It painfully knocked the wind out of her. Her chest burned. She knew she had to stay silent, her lips were trembling as she blinked away her tears. She had the sensation of being dragged and heard the music of wind chimes, combined with muffled voices. She tried to make out what they were saying, but was abruptly yanked and dragged again, with complete lack of care across uneven ground. She willed herself to remain silent each time her head and neck jolted violently. The dust from the ground filled the bag and it took everything within her to keep her breathing shallow. *A voice whispered, 'Be quiet. Be still. Say nothing. Do nothing.'*

A man's voice hollered, "Put it in stall 11."

Why were they calling her it? Her heart palpitated with fear as she tried to keep herself calm. *The voice in her mind whispered again, 'don't let them know you're awake.'* It sounded like someone was unlocking a door. This was followed by a creaking noise. She heard the muffled sounds of animals. The neighing of horses blended seamlessly with the clucking of hens. They started towing her again. Lexy was doing her best to remain limp. Suddenly, the ground changed beneath her. *She was relieved.* It felt softer, and a little prickly. They stopped dragging her, and the stillness was followed by a door being slammed. *They'd left her somewhere. What were they going to do to her? Why hadn't she stayed with the others?* The voice in her head continued to be her guide, assuring her that if she managed to remain calm, she would survive. *She wasn't sure who or what this voice was, but she was grateful for it.* On a few occasions when she was certain she was alone, she attempted to struggle free of the ties that bound her, realising quickly that there was no point. *There was no escape. Each time she lost it a little, a voice in her head began to whisper calming words of assurance.* They left her tied up and sensory deprived for days, with no food or water. She could barely manage to work up the saliva to swallow. *She knew she was dying of thirst, but her inner voice told her to remain silent.* It whispered, *if they wanted you to eat, they would have fed you. If they'd wanted you to drink, they would have brought you water. They're testing you.* Lexy spent her time listening instead of seeing. She should have been listening before she drank from that thermos. Now that she had nothing but time to listen. She also had nothing but the time to recall the events leading to the predicament she'd found herself in. *Why had she taken hot chocolate from a stranger? She knew better. She'd felt it. There had been a chill in the air, and an ache in the pit of her stomach. She hadn't listened, but she'd seen it coming. She had the time to dwell on it while sensory deprived. She was willing to do anything to survive. If only someone would acknowledge her existence.* She'd do anything for a glass of water or one of those apples that she'd been eating right before she made what she suspected would end up being the biggest mistake of her life. She would do anything for fresh air. She was aware that she was going to die without water. *Why kidnap a girl and leave her in a burlap sack to die? It didn't make sense. Perhaps this was a test of obedience.* Some form of instinct was instructing her from within. She had no choice but to repeatedly soil herself. The scent of her filth was not only overpowering but humiliating. She wished she had something to hold onto. The memory of a mother's embrace or words of adoration. All she had was this instinct to keep quiet, remain still, and wait. Her stomach had ceased to complain. It stopped speaking aloud and started cramping. Her head felt like it was about to explode. She was in excruciating pain. She knew she was close to dying. Nobody would mourn her passing because nobody had ever cared about her. Eventually even her soul altering headaches ceased to be a problem. Everything became quiet within her. She listened to the chorus of animal sounds, until she slipped into a dreamless slumber. Somebody kicked the bag. She lay limp inside of it, opening her eyes.

A voice said, "Girl…You dead?" They roughly booted her again.

She groaned in response to the agony in the small of her back. The material in front of her face was clutched and a knife was plunged into the bag, narrowly missing her eye, grazing her cheekbone. *This was it. They were going to stab her right through the bag.* She held her breath. The light filtered in through the hole that was being sliced. She took her first breath of fresh air in days. The euphoric sensation of fresh air in her lungs, was short lived. A man with the darkest eyes she'd ever seen and a long-jagged scar, running the length of his cheek scowled at her through the slice in the bag. He began to gag from her scent.

He glared at her with contempt and hissed, "You're disgusting." He tore the rest of the bag away, used the knife to cut the ties that bound her and warned, "If you attempt to run. I'll gut you like a deer and enjoy it." He spat on the ground by her and walked out leaving the door wide open.

Lexy didn't move. *He looked like someone that could gut her like a deer, without giving it a second thought.* The man reappeared and placed a metal bucket on the ground. Then he left, locking the wooden door behind him. She took in her surroundings for the first time.

A snide voice spoke from the other side of the door, "You have half an hour to eat the contents of that bucket. That's when I take it away."

Lexy crawled towards the bucket, too dizzy to attempt to stand. She probably couldn't have made a run for it even if she hadn't been terrified. She looked inside of the tarnished metal bucket. It was the most disgusting concoction she'd ever laid eyes on. She needed a drink first. Her throat was on fire. There was a long wooden troth full of water with flies and other miscellaneous bugs floating on the surface. She was too thirsty to think about that. Lexy cupped her hands and tried straining the insects to get a clean looking handful of water. She drank the first handful and started to choke, spitting it all over the stall. A sense of desperation took over. *She had to get the water down. She had to eat.* She placed her whole face into the troth and gulped as quickly as she could. She threw it up, and without missing a beat tried again. This time it stayed down. Then she made her way back to the bucket and attempted to lift it. It was too heavy for her to move in her weakened state. Lexy put her hands into the bucket, a small eyeball of an animal popped through her fingertips. She started to cry and removed her hands. *She was starving. She had to do this.* Slowly, she sank them back in, searching for something edible. She found some sopping wet chunks of bread and closed her eyes, gagging as she ate them. She found an apple core and ate it in its entirety. The door opened, startling her and the man with the scar took the bucket away without speaking to her. Her stomach grumbled as she looked around the stall for something else to eat. She ended up drinking more putrid water from the troth. She tried to keep it down, but it spurted from between her lips. Lexy buried her vomit under the hay. A few hours passed by with no more visitors to the small stall she was being held in. Lexy was startled as someone chucked an apple into the stall and slammed the door. She scurried over and grabbed it. Then she moved back into the far corner against the wall. It felt safer there. She could see the door. She ate the entire thing and began to feel a little better.

The door opened again, and the same silent man placed a steaming hot bowl of water in front of her. An elderly woman shoved past him and ordered her to take off her clothes. *Why wasn't the man leaving?* He leered at her, standing in the doorway.

The woman said, "Either I clean you, or he does. If your soiled clothes aren't off in one second, I'm leaving the job to him."

Lexy's eyes blurred with tears as she took her shirt off and attempted to remove her soiled pants. They were stuck to her for she'd been relieving herself in them for days. She had only underwear on, because she was still flat chested. The humiliation she felt was all encompassing as she lowered her stained underwear to the stall floor. Lexy stood there, covering her body with her hands.

The elderly lady told the man to leave and closed the stall behind him. She slipped on some gloves and plunged a rag into the steaming water. She hissed, "Get over here. I don't have all day."

Lexy obediently came closer and the lady cleaned her thoroughly. The water was painfully hot, but Lexy said nothing. She was grateful to be granted this small dignity. Another sour looking lady appeared with another bucket of water and began to wash her hair, without speaking a word to her. This lady threw a towel in front of her. Lexy grabbed it and dried herself off. Once she was dry, the lady tossed a dress at her. It was quite obviously a dress for a child. It was meant to be worn by someone much younger than she was. She obediently slipped it over her head, noticing a stain that appeared to be blood around the lacy white collar. She shivered as her mind absorbed the gravity of the messed-up situation, she'd found herself in. This was probably a child's blood, judging by the size of the garment. She kept her mouth closed and allowed the depravity of it all to sink in.

Before the elderly lady left, she instructed, "Do what you're told. I'll bring you a delicious meal and fresh water at dinner. If you disobey, they will kill you. There are no second chances in this place."

Lexy wiped the tears from her eyes with one of her hands and shuddered. They would kill her; she didn't doubt that for a second. Whatever she was told to do, she would do. She wanted to survive. They left her alone for a little while. Lexy touched the stain on the white lacy dress. She wasn't the first girl they'd done this too. *How long had she lasted? Had she died inside that burlap sack? Had she never taken the first breath of air? What was her name? Where had they found her? Had she been picked up by the side of the road, just as she had? Had she been drugged with hot chocolate? Had they grabbed her from her parent's front yard? Why was this happening to her? Hadn't she suffered enough in her 11 years of life?* She had the promise of food; of proper nourishment but only if she did what she was told. *What would that be? Who were these people and why had they taken her?* She leaned her head back against the wooden wall, closed her eyes and took a deep breath. *It took a moment to realise she'd been given the gift of fresh air. This was something she'd never known was a gift. She'd always taken it for granted. She decided then and there that life was a gift. She would do whatever she had to do to keep her life.* She ran the lacy material between her fingers. *She would do whatever she had to do to keep her blood from staining this dress.* She noticed something carved into the wall and crawled over to sit in front of the peeling wood. *It was a picture, obviously drawn by small child, perhaps the little girl that had worn this dress before her.* Lexy ran her finger over the child's drawing. She breathed a sigh of relief, knowing the child had at least made it out of the burlap sack. *Why was this happening to her?* She decided to crawl around the room and search for more pictures. What she found was more disturbing. It was initials and names of well over a dozen children. They must have all been held captive in this stall. She felt the urge to go to the bathroom and decided to ask. Lexy knocked on the back of the stall door and said, "Excuse me, I need to go pee." The stall door opened and it was the same man with the scar on his face. He was carrying a white ice cream bucket.

He placed it on the floor in front of her and asked, "Is it number one or number two?"

Lexy politely replied, "Number one."

He handed her a few squares of toilet paper and said, "Holler when you're finished."

He closed the door and she heard it lock with a click. Lexy squatted above the bucket and made a valiant attempt to go. She felt like she was being watched still and it was hard to concentrate. It was difficult to squat when she'd been tied up for so long. Her legs didn't appear to be working properly. Eventually, she managed to go. She used the couple squares of toilet paper and placed them in the bucket. Then she stood up on wobbly legs and made her way to the door. She knocked on the back of it, and said, "I'm done." The door opened and he took the bucket away, returning in a moment with the emptied bucket.

"This is for next time," he explained as he passed her half a roll of toilet paper and curtly added, "Make this last."

Lexy replied, "Thank you," but he was already gone. She sat back down in the corner of the stall and felt a moment of peace, knowing she'd be granted a few small dignities. She surveyed the room for small holes in the wall. *It still felt like she was being observed. It was a strange feeling.* She knew somebody was there even though it made no logical sense. She couldn't hear anything outside the stall, but the rustling and chattering of the barn's inhabitants. Remarkably calm, she dozed off and was awakened by the latch on the other side of the stall as it began to rattle, announcing someone's entrance. The man with the scarred face strolled in.

He abruptly grabbed her by the arm, hauled her to her feet and announced, "It's time to see what you're worth."

He towed her by one arm out of the stall, through the barn and out into the daylight. She'd been in the burlap sack and then the dim light of the stall. The sensory deprivation she'd been submitted to, made her overwhelmed by the sunlight. She squinted as he dragged her towards an old rickety looking farmhouse. She felt a sick feeling in the pit of her stomach. A sense that something horrific was about to happen. Her heart began to race as he harshly towed her up the stairs of the inconspicuous looking rustic house. Her skin began to crawl as she saw a crowded kitchen area full of men with dark eyes just like the one with the scar that had been tending to her basic needs. He abruptly released her arm. She had to fight the urge to run as he shoved her into the crowded room. She wanted to disappear inside of herself as they touched her hair and made her open her mouth so they could see her teeth. She felt like livestock. A disgusting smelling, sweaty, hairy man yanked her scarlet hair and she started to tear up. She searched the crowd until her eyes met with the elderly ladies. The lady who attended to her earlier was upset. *This wasn't a good sign.*

The elderly lady made eye contact with her as she inconspicuously brushed past. She placed a crushed flower in the palm of Lexy's hand and whispered, "Eat this."

She walked away left her standing there, clutching the crushed-up flower. That was when Lexy noticed the man who had been driving the truck.

He rose to stand and began to speak, "Place your bids face down on the table."

They kept touching her, yanking on her hair and shoving her. While they laughed and ridiculed her, until it crossed her mind once again to make a run for the door. A voice in her mind whispered, *'don't run, eat the flower.'* She was wise enough to know escape would be impossible. There were too many of them, the odds were not in her favour. Lexy placed her hand in front of her mouth, pretended to cough and swallowed the flower.

The men began to cheer. One marched over and declared, "You're mine."

What? Her vision began to waver. She felt unsteady on her feet as she hesitantly followed the man to a room in the back. She kept looking behind her expecting somebody to intervene. *This wasn't really happening.* When she should've been most terrified, she felt a sense of complete and total relaxation take over. *She wasn't afraid anymore.* Her vision wavered again. He shoved her and she fell, landing somewhere soft and everything went black.

She awoke in a bed of hay in her stall with the sense something horrible had happened. She couldn't recall what it was, but it hurt everywhere. Looking at her arms she saw bruises on her wrists. *Had she been tied up again?* She noted she had the similar wounds on her ankles. She felt uncomfortable. She glanced down; blood was trickling down her legs. *Was she having her period? One of the older girls she'd been travelling with had told her all about it.* She crawled over to the half a roll of toilet paper she had hidden in the corner and used it to clean up. She sensed it was more but couldn't allow it to cross her mind. *If she didn't think about it, then it didn't happen.* She was thirsty. She turned around and noticed that a bucket of fresh water had been placed by the door of her stall and beside it was a mug with a handle. She was quite relieved to drink from a cup. It was such a silly thing to matter. She dipped the mug into the water and drank from it, noticing once again how bruised her wrists were. It looked like rope burns. She wondered if she'd had them since she'd been hogtied and just been too out of it to notice it earlier. Her eye was sore and her vision was a bit blurry on one side. She tried to get a look at her reflection in the silver bucket. One of her eyes was almost swollen shut. *What happened to her?* A voice inside her mind whispered, *you don't want to know.* The latch on the door jingled, announcing the arrival of someone. Lexy scurried to the far side of the stall and in walked the elderly lady who'd given her the crushed flower. She was carrying a plate of mashed potatoes, vegetables, and roast beef, slathered in gravy. Lexy began to salivate at the sight of it. She knew this lady had helped her. She'd taken pity on her and given her something to make her forget.

The lady bent down and whispered, "I keep my promises." She passed her the plate and instructed, "Always keep one of those flowers on you. Hide it somewhere. I've left some under the hay in the left corner of the room. Once they're gone, you're on your own. That's all there is and I won't be around much longer."

Lexy whispered, "Where are you going?"

The elderly lady whispered, "Don't you worry about that, just enjoy the meal." She abruptly turned around and left the stall, swinging the door shut behind her.

Lexy stared at the plate. *Was it drugged? It seemed too good to be true. In her experience, she needed to be cautious of anything that felt that way.* She dipped her finger in some gravy and licked it off. *It was delicious. It didn't taste drugged, but then neither had the hot chocolate.* They hadn't given her any cutlery so she used her finger to sample a little more. She had little to be afraid of now, instinct told her the worst had already happened. She took two fingers like a spoon and started eating the meal, picking up the vegetables with her fingers. Her body had needed the vegetables most of all. Her stomach was practically singing. The stall door creaked and the lady reappeared with a clean dress and a wash basin. *Why did she need to wash?* She glanced down at the bloodstained dress and decided she wasn't going to look. *She didn't want to know, not for sure.*

The lady said, "If you're in a lot of pain, you can take a tiny piece of one of those flowers and eat it. It might help. You will need to pick and choose what you'd most like to forget. If I were you, I'd save the flowers for something worse. I promise you, there will be something. This time when you wash up, don't dump out the water. From now on make sure you always, save everything they give you until you know they are bringing you more."

Lexy nodded as she ravenously scooped the entire meal into her mouth with two fingers.

It was half gone when the lady looked at her and warned, "If you eat that meal too fast, you'll lose it. You'll throw the whole thing up. Your stomach is probably still too sensitive to eat quickly. I'd save a little for later if I were you." The elderly lady almost smiled at her before she left.

Completely ignoring her, Lexy scarfed the entire plate down in record time. She leaned against the rough slivered wall and placed both hands over her bulging stomach. She should clean herself up just in case somebody came and took away the bucket of hot water. She needed to sit here in peace for a second. She didn't want to move. She didn't want to try to remember what happened or feel anything except the sensation of having a full stomach. A small silly victory that didn't matter at all. The lady had almost been nice to her. She had the sense she'd never see her again. Lexy glanced down at the blood pooling on the straw in front of her. *She was bleeding a lot.* She took the washcloth and cleaned the blood off her legs. Her heart tightened in her chest and she felt an overwhelming sense of shame. When she took off her dress to change into the clean one, she saw what had been done to her. Her stomach was black and blue. There were what looked like bite marks on the top of her arms and her thighs. In that moment she felt her heart begin to solidify. She felt it turn to stone. If she ceased to care about her physical self, nothing could hurt her. She was going to survive. She was going to do whatever she had to do. She recalled what the elderly lady said about where she'd hidden the remaining flowers. They would be her salvation for a little while. Lexy found the flowers beneath the hay, just where the lady told her they'd be. There was also a loaf of bread hidden there, along with a jar of what looked like peaches. Her instincts had been correct. The elderly lady never returned to her stall. Lexy continued to eat a flower each time they brought her to the farmhouse. By the time she began to recall the details of the abuse, she'd become used to it. It had become a part of her daily routine. She glanced at the doors as they led her to the farmhouse each day. Sometimes she heard crying coming from behind one of them. Lexy didn't cry. She knew better. She showed them no emotion at all. It was usually only a matter of days from the sobbing to the late-night shrieking, followed by gunshots and raucous laughter. The unnamed man had given her an explanation, they didn't know how to behave. Lexy knew her place. She did what she was told. She was always quiet, and obedient. When her meal arrived, she was grateful. It was always a bucket of putrid sludge. Sometimes a moldy loaf of bread was tossed into her stall. She tried to hold on to the memory of that roast beef. She thought about it as she ate the grotesque compost like sustenance. She tried to pretend that was what she was consuming. The abuse she endured took many forms. She would go to a place within her. A place where she was safe and nobody could hurt her. She was beginning to lose track of time. She'd counted screams and gunshots for a little while, scraping a line into the wood as a memorial for each unnamed girl that hadn't been strong enough to withstand the abuse. *Sometimes, she wondered if they were stronger than she was. Perhaps, she had this all wrong. Maybe staying silent was a weakness not strength.* Once she'd experienced the truly horrific, Lexy was certain it was only a matter of time before they'd come into her stall late at night to put her down like the wounded animal she'd become. She was a voiceless damaged being that allowed her body to be defiled daily because she was afraid. The gunshots and shrieking had become more frequent and she understood, it wouldn't matter how well she behaved. It wouldn't matter what she allowed them to do to her. Eventually, she would die. This was the reason she made her first attempt to escape. Lexy was being walked towards the farmhouse. She struggled free from her captor's grasp. She could remember the feeling of her bare feet as she sprinted across the overgrown pasture. She ran against the wind, with her dress whipping at her thighs and her hair rippling behind her. Cut, bleeding and bruised, she'd fled with all the fight that remained within her battered body. She darted and wove through the trees, trying to avoid the shots that whizzed past her. They hunted her down as though she were wild game.

Lexy dodged between trees, attempting to use them as a shield. Then she found a tree large enough to conceal her for long enough to take a deep breath. She started to run again. She had no idea where she was running to, or how she would find someone to help her, when it seemed like everyone for miles around was in on the dark acts that were happening on this farm. She panted as she ran on aching legs. Eventually, the pellets began to hit their mark. They riddled her with pellets until her skin burned as though someone had lit a match and set her ablaze. A few welts became a dozen and then hundreds. She kept running with everything she had, as fast as she could. Lexy bolted blindly, wildly through the brush as they riddled her flesh with pellets. They'd been chasing her for hours. They were toying with her. There was too many of them. She'd never had a chance. Exhausted, she could no longer find the strength to carry on. She dropped and curled into a fetal position on the ground to show them she'd surrendered. Someone started kicking her repeatedly, insulting her. One continued to shoot her at close range until her mind wouldn't allow her to undergo one more second of senseless torture. Shock set in; her breathing slowed. She stopped wincing with each shot. Lexy drifted off inside of herself to the place she often went, during her daily visit to the farmhouse. It was on this occasion that Lexy received the ultimate punishment for her attempted escape. She could remember the sensation of being dragged for a time with her head flopping around, scraping on the ground. She was then lifted and tossed into the well. Her ankle snapped during her descent into darkness. She surfaced in the water as light flickered from above revealing the sick version of hell she'd been tossed into. She'd been abandoned, amongst floating rotting corpses, decomposing in rancid well water. There was a moment of panic, followed by horror. She now understood what happened to the bodies. It filled her with a morbid sense of resolve. This was her fate. She would decompose in this rancid gelatin with the others. The strong, the weak, it had never mattered who they were. In the end they were all here rotting in the bile. She was left in that place of putrid violation until she was nearly dead from exposure and infection. She was starving, mindless from her solitude with the dead. She wasn't sure how long it had taken her survival instincts to kick in. It forced her to drink from the slimy bloated corpse water, during her grotesque fight for survival. The last breath of what made her an individual shut off. They eventually realised she was still alive and came to remove her from the well after almost a week submerged in her own rancid personal hell. She'd said nothing of her ankle as they yarded her out of the well with a rope. She'd braced herself for the excruciating pain of that first step but felt none. She'd been afraid to look at it. She'd held her breath on her walk back to the barn. Her bone had been exposed, only a week ago. She casually glanced down and noticed her ankle was healed with no sign of the protruding bone. They walked her back to her old stall in the barn, without touching her. She was pruned, and waterlogged. Her features were disturbingly distorted. One of the men commented on how disgusting she was before he left. She didn't care. She was something, and grateful to be out of the well even though she'd taken the smell of the decomposing corpses along with her. The man with the scars on his face brought her a bucket of hot water and told her to strip. She took off every stitch of clothing without question, right in front of him. Nothing mattered now. He was so disgusted by her bloated state that he turned away. If she stayed like this, it would only be a matter of time before they put her down and tossed her back into the well with the other repulsive things. The scarred man brought her three buckets and told her it would save time. Within a few days, she was almost back to normal. She felt emotionally vacant and somehow, peaceful. They came for her on the third day and brought her back to the house. She was able to withstand each depravity by forcing each stomach churning act out of her mind. It felt like she was slipping further and further into a dark abyss from which there would be no return.

When they led her to the house each day, she stared at each door. Pretending she didn't hear the muffled cries of the other inhabitants of the dark farm, removed the guilt. She felt removed from everything now. Only a few nights later, she was on her bed of straw, trying to tune out the commotion. Lexy opened her eyes, to the pitch of a female voice shrieking, followed by a shower of gunshots. She curled up into the fetal position and went back to sleep without a problem. She was one with the straw floor. Nothing was happening. It didn't matter anymore. Weeks went by and they'd stopped coming for her every day. She was unceremoniously tossed dried bread and given a bucket of water daily. Other than that, she'd been left alone for a while. She played with wood bugs and spiders to pass the time. One large spider in the corner of the room offered her quite a bit of entertainment. She would help it, by tossing other insects into its web. She'd dispassionately watch them be wrapped in silk and eaten, until the nameless man noticed her watching it and took off his shoe and squished it. One day her stall was just left open. She got up and wandered out into the barn. The man with the scar casually wandered over and handed her a shovel. The first thing that came to mind was that they were going to make her dig her own grave. She hesitantly took it from his hand.

The man smiled and remarked, "You might as well make yourself useful. The others have gone hunting. Clean the stalls and feed the animals. Do not attempt to leave this barn. Do not go outside."

She spent most of her day inside the stall, being allowed out to work whenever her door was left open. Nobody had to tell her what to do, she knew. As soon as her chores were done, she went back into her stall obediently and closed the door behind her. One day she ventured to the doorway when it felt like nobody was around. This door was also unlocked. She didn't touch the door. She didn't want to tempt fate. *Where would she run? She had nowhere to go.* She strolled back to her stall and noticed an axe. Knowing it would be ridiculous to bring an axe to a gun fight she ran her finger across the blade. It was so sharp that a line of blood seeped from her fingertip. She placed it in her mouth. When she looked at it again, it appeared to be healed. Her mind was playing tricks on her. She rubbed her fingertips together. She would die here eventually, she knew this. She'd accepted this as her fate. She wouldn't be worth much to anyone. She had nothing left inside to give to anyone. She'd disappeared a long time ago. She knelt before the blade of the axe and it crossed her mind to take her demise into her own hands.

A voice loudly scolded, "Go back to your stall. This is not the end of your story."

Moderately concerned her grasp on reality was gone, she rose to her feet and looked around the barn. There was nobody there. *That didn't sound like the voice in her head. She was losing her marbles.* She went back to her stall and closed the door behind her.

Another week passed by and the group came back from their hunting trip. She understood what they meant by hunting. They'd gone hunting for people. Lexy had been sitting in her stall when she heard the commotion of their arrival.

She heard a girl's voice say, "No, no. Please don't. I'm Okay." Followed by a few deafening gun shots. Lexy didn't even flinch anymore.

Her door opened and they tossed a burlap sack into her stall with her, and said, "You get some company." The bag was whimpering. Lexy poked the bag with her finger.

The bag spoke in a crackly baby voice, "I'll be good. I'll be good, I promise."

What did they want her to do? Did they want her to open it? Lexy opened the bag and inside of it was a child, much younger than she'd been when she arrived. They hadn't bothered to tie the little girl up. She was afraid; she had every right to be.

The little girl whispered, "I want my Mommy." The child flung herself into Lexy's arms.

Lexy wasn't sure what to do. The child was sobbing and clinging to her for dear life. She was uncomfortable. *What was she supposed to do?* She gave the child's head a few firm pats and spoke, "Do you have a name?"

The little girl gave her a strange look and whispered, "Charlotte."

Lexy began to relax. She held Charlotte in her arms and stroked her hair as she sobbed for her mommy and daddy. Lexy's heart had only been a functioning organ used to pump blood until this point. She wasn't sure what to say or do to console a child. Once you were here, there wasn't anything to do. You did as you were told or you died. The girl that was executed ten minutes ago was evidence of that. She wanted to tell the child everything was going to be okay, but it wasn't going to be. Her heart tightened. They were going to do horrible things to this little girl, and there was nothing she could to stop it from happening. The embrace had gone on too long. Lexy was feeling uncomfortable. She gave her a few awkward pats on the head and urged, "You have to be quiet. You heard them shoot the girl that was with you."

The child began crying harder, "They killed her?"

Lexy had no idea what to do so she went with the truth, "She's dead. They shot her. Did you know her?"

Charlotte whispered, "She was my babysitter."

Lexy never had one of those. She questioned, "What's a babysitter?"

"She watches me when my mom and dad go out at night," Charlotte explained.

Lexy replied, "She's not a very good one if you ended up here."

Charlotte nodded in agreement. She asked, "What is this place?"

Lexy didn't bother sugar coating a thing and she said, "You're in Hell." She dug under the straw and found it.

They'd thrown a comb into her cubicle a while back. She began to comb the child's hair. She seemed to be soothed by this act. The door handle jingled ominously. She had to warn her. This child was too young to survive the beating and week-long submersion in the well. So, she did what an elderly woman had done for her. She told her what she would have to do to survive.

Lexy whispered, "Don't ever fight back. Don't try to run. Do what you are told, and they will bring you back." She had no will of her own left at this point. *She was an empty shell void of the part of her soul that gifted compassion and empathy...Or so she'd thought.* Hearing cries of pain coming from the six-year-old child made her cover her ears and curl up into the fetal position. *There was nothing she could do.* Eventually, they brought the haunted version of Charlotte back to the stables. Lexy scurried away and sat on the opposite end of the small enclosure with her knees against her chest. She kept her eyes squeezed shut. *She couldn't look at Charlotte. Words felt useless.* When she finally ventured to open her eyes, the little girl was sitting on the opposite side of the stall with her knees against her chest, staring at her. She didn't appear to be bleeding. Lexy had never felt more grateful. They stared each other down for a few minutes without speaking. Something horrible had obviously happened but they'd spared her from the worst on this first day of confinement. Lexy whispered, "I'm sorry that happened to you." She met Charlotte's penetrating stare and whispered, "If you try to get away, its worse."

The door creaked open and the man with the scar summoned Lexy. Obediently, she got up and went with him. She heard Charlotte sobbing as they took her away. Lexy followed the nameless dark eyed demon of a man up the rickety stairs of the house that had become her own personal hell. She stepped through the threshold and into the kitchen where dozens of depraved eyes awaited her.

Her original captor declared, "You are sixteen-years-old. Normally, I'd sell you off at this age or dispose of you, but the men like you. This is the only reason you live past today. I suggest you keep that in mind while you're tending to their needs."

Lexy nodded in silence. *Her mind was still trying to process the amount of years she'd been held there. She'd been barely eleven when she'd arrived in that burlap sack. She'd been in hell for five years.*

As the months went by, Charlotte tore down her walls, and touched what was left of Lexy's heart. The child had an unbeatable spirit. Her inner light was so strong it couldn't be extinguished by the likes of this place. She continued smiling in the face of the unthinkable. She carried on each day, always finding reasons to laugh. Lexy would brush Charlotte's hair, each night. She'd listen attentively to the stories of her family and the house with a bright yellow door. It felt like she'd known her brothers. After Charlotte was finished telling her stories, Lexy could almost feel the sensation of riding Charlotte's bike downhill with the wind blowing through her hair. Charlotte had been snatched out of heaven and delivered into the bowels of hell. Yet she continued to smile. It was inspiring. She was a miracle with her tales of purple bikes with baskets and streamers. She had parents who loved her because she was an angel. Lexy began to emulate her life, imagining that it had been her own. She told her stories of an old boat shell her father had made into a sandbox for her and her brothers to play in. When the family went camping, she had an orange sleeping bag and a green tent. The stories all contained little things, beautiful moments of an ideal existence. There had been laughter and love in the household Charlotte had grown up in. She had a golden retriever named Freckles, some goldfish and she always fought with one of her brothers. The brother named Max. He told her she was a pain in the butt and her real father was the mailman. Lexy hit the point where she spent all day waiting for a child to return from the house to tell her stories of what childhood was supposed to be like. She'd grown far too attached to the child. She had told her little blessing to accept what couldn't be changed. There wasn't anything they could do about it.

This was the absolute truth in Lexy's mind. She wasn't sure how long it had been until Charlotte had tried to fight back for the first time. She had warned her repeatedly against fighting back, but it was human nature. Charlotte was returned to the stall one evening, severely battered and bruised. The child's small face, so swollen that it was unrecognizable. Blood trickled from the corner of her mouth. Lexy had been told that she had a week to fix her. In one week, Charlotte would be put down and Lexy would be joining her at the bottom of the well. He left her there to tend to the mortally wounded child. She stroked her hair and touched her disfigured face. *Lexy's heart was attached to only one thing; it had begun to beat for reasons other than blood flow.* Lexy had always had a fantasy of one day finding a way to free them both from captivity. In the fantasy, her parents were so grateful that they decided to love her too. They took her into their home. The house with the yellow door and puppy named Freckles. This version of freedom had only been a dream. She bathed the child and cared for her for a few days, feeling something close to what she imagined love felt like. Charlotte's fever began on the third day. It was a severe burning heat that she could feel without even touching her skin. Beads of sweat formed on her forehead as her body made a final attempt to fight a losing battle. She overheard someone mention calling a doctor in a conversation outside of the stall. She knew that they were not talking about a doctor for Charlotte. Lexy had never seen a doctor. A foreign word to her for she had never been cared for, cherished or loved even enough to warrant hearing the word spoken aloud in her company. They obviously could never call a doctor for an abducted child, held captive as a slave, and whipping post, locked in their barn. She spent the rest of the day stroking Charlotte's hair, trying to sooth her. She was so weak. Lexy was afraid to even think the words. She knew what was happening to her friend. *Charlotte was dying.* She splashed the water that had been given to her for drinking water on the child's forehead and tried to pour some into her mouth. Charlotte was too weak to swallow. Her throat ached for her own thirst to be quenched, but they had only given her enough water to sustain one person. *She could suffer. She didn't want Charlotte to suffer any more than she had to.* Her owner had stuck his head into the stall that evening and saw the state that Charlotte was in. He stated aloud that she would need to be put down. Lexy knew what that meant for she had seen them put a horse down. *A horse with a broken leg; which was why she had never uttered a word about her leg, after they'd freed her from the well.*

She hadn't cried in the last few years of her captivity at the dark farm. That night, she cried for Charlotte. She cried for the yellow door the child would never open. She cried knowing the last thing Charlotte would see was the view from the bottom of that well. The last thing she'd feel is her body floating amidst the putrid scent of decomposing corpses. She knew they were going to kill her too, but she didn't care. Perhaps, it was time. Time for them both to be set free. Lexy stroked Charlotte's hair and laid her head on her chest. She listened to her laboured breathing which steadily slowed to randomly timed shudders. Lexy began to pray for the first time in her life, "Die before he comes back. Please, die before he comes back. Be at peace. No one will ever be able to hurt you ever again. I'll be with you soon." She monitored Charlotte's breathing as it laboured and continued to slow. "Please Charlotte…Please. You must go. I'll be right behind you." Tears were streaming down her face, obscuring her vision. She blinked them away as she stroked the child's perspiration dampened hair. Her heart began pleading with everything she had left inside of her. *Please, let Charlotte slip away peacefully in the midst of a beautiful dream. Don't let this happen to her. They can kill me. Take her. Please, save her.*

Lexy stroked her hair and whispered, "You have to let go, Charlotte. Please, just sleep. I'm going to be right behind you." *It would be better for her to die now. It would be better to be shot quickly like that wounded horse. Better than to take one more second of the abuse her tiny body had been forced to endure.* Charlotte's chest shuddered, one last breath. The child exhaled one long deep breath to the sound of footsteps approaching. Lexy glanced up at the doorway as it opened. Three men were standing there with shotguns. Lexy knew what was happening. These men had probably paid for the opportunity to kill her Charlotte. This was wickedness viler than any she'd ever known. *It didn't matter. Her Charlotte was gone. She was safe in the arms of the angels, and nobody could ever hurt her again.*

Her keeper noticed Charlotte was dead and declared, "Sorry men, it looks like we're going to have to change the game. It can't run away. It's already dead."

He picked up his rifle and shot the angel point blank in the face, defiling her vision of salvation. Charlotte's brains splattered, covering Lexy's face and clothing with matter. It came from a hidden restrained place deep inside as she stepped outside of herself and began to scream. The men looked thrilled as Lexy came to life. She shrieked with everything she had left inside of her. Her adrenaline raced as her blood coursed through her veins. She screamed again with her hands covering her eyes as if she could shriek until it could be unseen. She screamed long and hard, allowing all the rage, every ounce of despair, to rise, and fuel her being.

"I have a new deal for you boys. You paid for an experience. I'm going to give you one. You have a ten count to run before we kill you girl. These aren't pellets. One, two…" He began counting aloud.

It took Lexy to the count of four to realise they were going to shoot her. She bolted out of the stall. Her brain didn't want to operate. It didn't even want to function in her grief. She smelled Charlotte's blood. She could taste it on her lips. Her gag reflex kicked in and she fought it. She burst out of the doors of the barn. Outside were half a dozen men, waiting with rifles aimed at her, pumped up for the hunt. There would be no sport as the first one jumped the gun and shot her. Lexy stood there stunned. She looked down at the red pattern on her sparse worn clothing as it expanded on her stomach. She reeled backwards as the chorus of men began to laugh. They shot her repeatedly, but she didn't feel anything after the second bullet. She stood firmly in place and lifted her arms towards the heavens as though she were an angel attempting to take flight. Lexy closed her eyes amidst the multitude of voices. Her passing had come as salvation, and at last she was free.

She awoke to find herself in the grass outside a simple house with a yellow door. In the yard Freckles frolicked. The door opened and Charlotte, a healthy vibrant six-year-old leapt into her open arms. It was a beautiful reunion as they held each other and laughed. Lexy felt joy, unlike anything she'd ever felt in the brutality of her short painful existence. Charlotte asked her to come inside and stay for a while. They embraced again and Lexy followed her friend into the house that she had only heard stories of. Her heart almost exploded with joy as they both walked through the yellow door. At the kitchen table sat a woman dressed in white. The woman was so beautiful; purity flowed from her pores. Lexy was sure she was an angel.

"I've been waiting for you," she greeted.

Lexy sat down at the table beside her. The breathtaking lady reached over and touched her arm. Warmth Lexy had never encountered travelled throughout her body until happiness and calm filled her being. Lexy Abrelle was finally at peace.

Chapter 2

The Retribution Of The Dragon

Lexy opened her eyes, gasping. She inhaled a mouthful of the water from the well and began to choke. *What in the hell?* It took her a moment to realise what this meant. *She was alive.* She stifled a scream as Charlotte's body bobbed up to the surface beside her. Half of Charlotte's face was concealed by the putrid bile, and decomposing flesh water. Her one visible eye, wide open and glazed over. *She was gone. It hurt. There was too much pain. Her heart hurt.* She wanted to claw through her own chest cavity and remove her heart to stop the anguish. Her heart grew heavier, and heavier until the agony of the child's loss ceased to matter, and she felt nothing at all.

She felt her body for injuries. Her memory was full of scattered visions of graphic violence. *They told her to run. She'd been shot...so many times. They must have thrown her body in the well.* Her recollection of the events that led to her submersion triggered a seething rage within her soul. *They had to die. They all had to die.* Something inside of her was taking control. Vibrating with all-encompassing power, she clawed her way out of hell towards the promise of flickering light. As her rigid fingers clutched the top of the well, she recognized the pivotal moment...She was being reborn. Her hands curved around the mouth of damnation, she effortlessly pulled her body over the ledge and crawled out of the womb of the devil without breaking a sweat. This was her rebirth into the land of the living. She stood there surveying the quiet, isolated surroundings. The sounds of livestock in the distance drew her gaze as she grabbed an axe from beside

31

the woodpile. *She had no fear. She was what people should be afraid of.* She walked to the barn and ripped the lock off the stall where she'd been held captive for five long years. A new girl even younger than her Charlotte was huddled in the corner, sucking her thumb. Lexy stood there with axe in hand. The child scurried away, terrified. Lexy's face softened a touch as she vowed, "They will never hurt you again, I promise."

The child with brown pigtails got up and inched closer. She froze and lisped, "You smell bad."

"I can only imagine. Go hide. I'll be back for you," Lexy sternly instructed. The child missing both front teeth grinned. She motioned for her to hide and left her cowering in the far corner of the stall. *They are in the farmhouse. This will never stop.* She stood on the grass before the rickety stairs to the house. *This was a horrific place. The residence of her nightmares. Retribution would be hers.* She scaled the steps, axe in hand and turned the knob on the door. She heard muffled voices coming from the kitchen. *You must put an end to this evil place.* Fury climaxed as the axe swung on its own and limbs flew. *She was both judge and executioner to the damned.* Their essence and innards painted the walls a sick shade of burgundy. Feeling nothing, she snatched the keys to the truck off a hook in the kitchen and stepped over the pieces of her captors. Covered in their blood, with jingling keys in hand, she strolled back to the barn. *She'd made a promise to a stranger. A child that now symbolized the one she'd been unable to save.* She was covered in blood as she entered the stall, but the little girl took her hand without question. She imagined it was Charlotte, she was leading out of the barn, towards the truck parked by the house. She'd just rid the world of evil by doing evil. She felt no guilt, no shame for how dark she'd become while wielding that axe. Lexy opened the door and motioned for the child to get into the vehicle. She didn't speak to her; in her mind she was still pretending it was Charlotte. Lexy walked around and slipped into the driver's seat. She knew where the key went, that part was obvious. It took her a moment, staring at the steering wheel and stepping on the pedals a few times. Once it began to roll forward, she figured out how to drive rather quickly. She drove for hours with the child in silence. Lexy glanced at her and for a split second, it was Charlotte. Then the mirage of what should have been clicked back to reality. She'd fallen asleep, she looked peaceful. Lexy hadn't looked in the mirror, until now…She glanced at her reflection, knowing she couldn't be seen in public like this. She pulled over on the side of the road and began searching for something to wipe the blood off her face. She would need water. She hopped out of the truck, rag in hand, and shimmied down the small hill into the ditch by the side of the road. There was a small amount of water in the bottom of the ditch. She dunked the cloth and wiped the blood from her face and arms. She cupped her hand and took a drink, parched from her murder spree. Then she climbed back up to the truck and sat down in the driver's seat. Lexy glanced into the mirror. She'd done alright with only a cloth. Her clothes were still covered in blood though. She stared at the sleeping child for a second, before turning the key in the ignition. The engine began to hum and chug. *That doesn't sound good.* Lexy chose to ignore it and kept driving, in search of a larger town. They passed a sign that had the symbol for a police station. She turned off the highway towards the town. It didn't take her long to find it, but she obviously couldn't go inside. She'd delivered the child to safety. She woke the child with missing front teeth and said, "You'll be safe now. She pointed to the lighted building. "Go inside. Just tell them what your name is, and where you're from. They'll find your mom and dad."

The little girl gave her a giant toothless grin and asked, "Don't you want to go home too?"

Lexy felt her stone heart twitch. She replied, "Someday, maybe I will." She nodded at the child and the little girl grinned once more before running towards the lighted building. *She had to leave.* Lexy turned the key…*Nothing. The truck was dead. Shit, she had to get out of here.* Lexy grabbed the bloodied cloth and brought it with her. She sprinted away from the truck down a long dimly lit alleyway, darting between buildings and into the wooded area on the edge of town. She continued to run through the forest, until she was certain she wasn't being followed. She would have to stay out of sight until she found clean clothes. Something to wear that didn't make her look like she'd been on a murder spree. The first order of business was finding a place to rest her eyes for a while. She made sure she was well off the beaten path before taking cover between the branches, in the center of a thick prickle bush. Knowing, even though they would be able to smell the scent of her blood, almost anything wild would have second thoughts at slicing themselves up to get to her. Her eyes had grown so heavy she could barely keep them open. She curled up into the fetal position, watching the cuts on her hands heal as she drifted off to sleep.

She awoke with a start. Unsure of where she was for a minute or two. *She'd escaped from the farm. She had saved a child. She was free. It was a new day, night? It was still dark outside, even though it felt like she'd been asleep for a long time. Was it the next night?* Her stomach began to complain. *That was the first order of business. She needed to eat.* She began to pick blackberries from the bush that she'd been sleeping in. They were still green but she didn't care. *It was better than nothing.* She walked back to town through the woods, with only instinct to guide her, seeing the lights through the trees in no time. She entered the town under the cover of darkness, staying in the shadows. With an overwhelming urge to check on the child, she walked over to a display case of newspapers, and looked at the date. *She'd been held in captivity like an animal, for five years.* It had been five years since she'd seen a newspaper or walked down a street. She had nobody, and nothing except for the knowledge that she had brought that little girl back to her parents unharmed. *What if she hadn't?* These thoughts had been flickering in her mind ever since she had dropped her off at the police station. She had to know for sure that she was safe before she could bring herself to leave town. Lexy found a dress in a donation bin outside of the local church and cat food on a few porches. It was protein and it eased her rumbling stomach. Lexy dug through trash for sustenance and checked the headline of the local paper each night for a week. *No headline read, 'Missing girl found.'* She made her way through the shadows, peeking in windows, and searching houses in the small rural town, under cover of darkness. An uneasy feeling haunted every waking thought. At the end of each night, she found herself standing across the street from the police station, starring at the door. The rose brick building seemed less ominous as the sun began to peak over the mountains. Once she'd searched each home in the area, until instinct prompted her to go to the local cemetery to check for freshly dug graves. *Sane people didn't endeavour to visit graveyards at night. Nobody was going to accuse her of being sane.* Lexy walked past headstone after monument, reading stones. *Marcella was five. Laurel was seven. There appeared to be a theme. She counted thirty graves for children that had died in the last ten years. That was impossible in a place this size, wasn't it? Maybe there had been a school bus accident of some kind? You couldn't kill this many small children without the government noticing, could you?* She wandered down the row of children until she came across a freshly covered unmarked grave. *What was her plan now? She hadn't thought that far ahead. She would have to dig it up in order to know.* She wondered if she had enough time before daylight. She stood there before the mound of dirt. *Maybe, it was better if she didn't know? Maybe, she should just walk away. She could leave right now, and never know for sure. She could pretend that the child was at home. Imagine, she was safely tucked under covers in her bed. She needed a shovel.* Lexy scanned the cemetery in the visually impairing darkness and saw a small shed in the far corner of the grounds. She ran to the shed. It was locked. What was left of the hollow shell that once was her heart needed to know the child she'd saved wasn't buried in that unmarked grave. Her adrenaline rushed. She tore the door right off the hinges, grabbed a shovel, darted back across the graveyard and began to dig. Lexy tossed the dirt off to the side and kept going in a frenzy. By the time, she hit a hard surface with the shovel, the sun was beginning to rise. Light trickled its way across the gravestones towards her as she leapt into the hole, landing with catlike agility on top of the box. She hesitated before opening the lid. *This was probably going to be some old dead body. The child she'd saved wasn't going to be in here.* The sky began to light up as she took a deep breath of moist morning air. Her breath was visible as she opened the coffin. On a bed of silk was the child she'd saved. Her hands clawed above her face and nails were missing. Her tiny fingertips were crusted with blood. Her mouth contorted with slightly open lips that revealed her missing front teeth. The white material on the interior of the coffin was shredded and streaked with dried blood. *She'd been buried alive.* She noticed something in the casket. It was a walkie-talkie. She grabbed it and pressed the button. *The batteries were dead. Someone had been communicating with the terrified child as she suffocated.* She placed it in her pocket and whispered, "I'm sorry. I thought they'd take you home to your family. I should have stayed with you." *Lexy decided at that moment that she would never again make a promise she couldn't keep.* She had delivered this child from one version of hell into another. She'd needed to protect her. She hadn't succeeded in that endeavour, but she would seek vengeance, for her. Lexy tried to lower the child's arms and close her eyes, but she was stiff. She was a statue symbolizing the terror she'd endured during her final moments. Lexy closed the casket and reburied the grave as quickly as possible. She was sweating and covered in dirt, but she did not cry. She wasn't sure she was capable of it. She'd cried the last of her tears for Charlotte. This was the first time she'd permitted herself to be out in daylight. She sat in the grass in front of the nameless child's unmarked grave. She needed a name on the stone. Lexy wished she'd known her name. The sun was shining on her grave. Lexy would not leave this place until she'd named the child, marked her grave, and given her soul vengeance. She grabbed the walkie-talkie, rose to her feet and said, "I'm sorry, I won't let them get away with this. I know a promise from me isn't worth much. So, I swear on my soul. That is all I have left." Lexy walked away from the unmarked grave. She needed sleep, and a few batteries. She would find a change of clothes. *There was no rush. She had nothing else in her agenda but vengeance.* Tomorrow night, she would use the radio to call the twisted son of a bitch that buried alive, her one chance at redemption.

She walked back to the barn she'd been staying in. A stray dog missing patches of fur stalked her back through the woods. *The Shephard mix was as hungry as she was. Unspoken understanding passed between them.* She came across a blackberry bush, popped some fruit into her mouth and tossed a few into the Shephard's. *Dogs eat berries?* She picked mushrooms and tossed some into her companion's mouth. They walked together until they came across an apple tree. She grabbed a few and ate them but what she needed was protein. She saw a backyard through the bushes with an almost empty clothesline. There was a towel on it. No cars were parked in the driveway. *She had an idea.* She raced across the yard and peered in the basement window. She checked a few more, the house appeared to be empty. Having an unsupervised childhood, she knew how to pop out a window. She gently deposited it on the grass. She crawled into the basement and lowered herself noiselessly. The unfinished basement had a washer and dryer, and numerous crates of random crap. She opened the dryer, pulled out jeans and tried to put them on, but they were far too snug. There was nothing else in the dryer. She would have to sneak upstairs and check out the closets and drawers. *It was early in the morning. What if they were still asleep?* She almost soundlessly scaled the stairs, gently twisting the doorknob. It creaked and she winced. She had a feeling each step she took was going to create a sound in this old house. She entered the cramped hallway and it groaned in protest to her presence. She gingerly pushed open the door to one of the bedrooms. The bedding was tossed and there were blood spattered sheets. A pool of blood stained the hardwood floor beside the bed. She had a hunch the people who lived in this house weren't going to be returning anytime soon. She left the room, there was one more place to check before she could be certain she was alone. She carefully opened the next door and it was only a small bathroom. Staring at the closed shower curtains she knew what she had to do. She moved them aside seeing no shadows. The bottom of the tub was caked with dried blood. It had been there for a while. She relaxed as she walked back to the bedroom and opened a closet full of clothes. She chose jeans that looked just a little larger than the ones she'd tried on downstairs. She took a blouse and jacket. She tossed the clothes on the bathroom floor and turned on the water in the shower. After rinsing out the tub, she took off her soiled clothing and stepped under the spray. It had been many years since she'd had a shower. She'd bathed using only a small tub of water for years on the dark farm. Lexy squirted shampoo into the palm of her hand. She raised her cupped palms to her nose, inhaling the scent, before she began to scrub her ratty uncombed mass of hair. Lexy closed her eyes, feeling the steady rhythm of the spray against her skin. She soaped herself down and rinsed, until the water circling the drain was crystal clear. She stepped out of the bathtub and searched under the sink for toiletries. *There was a pack of unwrapped toothbrushes and toothpaste.* It was a heavenly feeling to do the simple acts of routine. She tried to run a comb through her hair, it was too far gone to attempt to salvage. She cut her hair to just a touch below her shoulders with scissors from the vanity. Now, she was able to brush her hair. She used some lotion, powdered her feet and put on the clean clothes and jacket. After pocketing the toothbrush, paste and a small bar of soap, she found a toiletry bag of makeup. She'd never used it before. She shoved the lipstick in her pocket, grabbed the brush and brought it into the bedroom with her. She needed a bag. She found a backpack in the closet and put the brush, and a change of clothes in it. *These would be coming with her.* She looked in the mirror on the armoire and smiled. She looked like a different person. She put some red lipstick on and stared at her reflection. The last time she'd gazed into a mirror she had the body of a child. She now had the body of a woman. It was as though time had leapt forward and she'd been none the wiser. She shoved the walkie-talkie into her bag and wandered downstairs feeling calm. She was emotionally tuned out, but clean. *She couldn't recall the last time she'd felt clean.* She resisted the urge to sprawl on the couch. *Maybe there was something to eat?* Lexy stiffened as she opened the fridge and saw human body parts encased in cellophane. She stepped back and closed the door. There was something staying in this house, slowly ingesting the inhabitants, limb by severed limb. Curiously enough, she wasn't disturbed. She was detached from everything. Most people who looked inside of a fridge and found body parts would freak out. She was merely irritated. *It meant she couldn't stay.* She took some canned goods. As she searched the kitchen drawers, she shoved a can opener, spoon, flashlight and various batteries into her backpack. *It was time to go.* She proceeded down the stairs, leaving the way she'd arrived, climbed back out the window, replaced the glass and bolted back into the forest on the outskirts of the property. Her stray companion awaited her return. They travelled together through the forest until they came to the farm she had been sleeping at during the day. There was activity outside. Men coming and going from the barn. She'd thought was abandoned. *Damn it... Where was she going to sleep? She wasn't going to be able to function much longer without it.* Her wayward friend bumped into her, leaping to get her attention.

Lexy murmured, "I guess you wouldn't know of a safe place to sleep?" *She was speaking to a dog.* She smiled at herself. The dog ran ahead of her on the path. She followed him further into the dense brush. Her canine companion really did look like he was trying to lead her somewhere. She'd been following her overly excited friend, wandering into the middle of nowhere for a good half an hour when they came across a cave. It had an extremely narrow entrance. They both just barely made it through the opening. There was no way a full-grown man could make it into the hole. *This would be safe enough.* She took the flashlight out and gazed around the cave. This was some creatures burrow. At least she knew that something was not going to be very big. She peered into the bag and took out a can of chicken. She opened it and laid it in front of her scruffy new friend. She got another one for herself and they ate together. He'd definitely earned his meal. She grabbed the towel that she'd stuffed in the bag earlier and she laid it out. The second she laid down and closed her eyes she drifted away into a deep slumber.

She awoke with a start. *Where was she again? She was in a cave with a stray dog.* The scurrying noises in the absence of light would have scared most people. Lexy was emotionally detached from the idea of fear. She suspected she wasn't afraid of anything anymore. She ran the comb through her hair. *It felt good to do the normal daily rituals. She was going to put the last remaining piece of the dark farm to rest tonight, and then she would start a life somewhere new.* She yanked the walkie-talkie out of the bag and rooted around for fresh batteries. She stared at it for a moment, contemplating several different versions of what she wanted to say.

Chapter 3

Any Last Words?

She pushed down the button and spoke, "I know what you did to the child. I'm coming to kill you." All she heard in response was a crackling sound on the other end.

After an extended silence, a female voice replied, "Who is this?"

Lexy had not expected that plot twist. It was a woman's voice that answered. *She'd been expecting to hear her captor from the dark farms voice. That voice was seared into her memory. It had been male hands that left a scar on her soul.* Lexy responded, "My name is Lexy Abrelle. I found the child in the graveyard. I'm coming to kill you." She heard laughter on the other end.

The voice cackled, "Don't you need to know where I am first?"

"I already know where you are," she calmly replied.

The voice responded, "I'll be expecting you."

She leaned back against the wall of the cave and stared at the walkie-talkie in her hand. *She could have taken them by surprise. Why did she have to go and announce the fact that she was coming? The woman that answered the radio sounded human. Maybe they were a town of cannibals? She would need to travel light.* She left everything in the cave. She shimmied through the narrow exit into the light and sprinted through the woods towards the small local police station. Her canine companion kept pace. In her hand she held only a kitchen knife. She arrived at the station and all she could think about was the feeling of crawling out of that well on the dark farm. The memory kept playing on a twisted repeat, until she felt herself succumb to the fury. She didn't hesitate tonight. She walked straight through the front doors and up to the counter. The station appeared to be empty. *This was strange.* One lady sat alone at the front desk. *Something was off. She could smell it in the air. It was a fragrance her mind was fighting to place, a metallic scent.* Memories shifted through her mind and sorted themselves until it clicked. *It was the scent of blood.* Her pulse began to race even though her expression remained calm and emotionless.

The lady behind the counter enquired, "Is there something I can do for you?"

Lexy replied, "You can tell me what you are. I'd like to know what I'm dealing with."

The lady grinned and her eyes became an odd hue. She leaned across the counter. Her fingernails began to grow. Lexy felt her pulse race again. Her heart began to wildly thump within the confines of her chest. *It wasn't palpitating in fear. It was pounding with excitement. She'd played a victim to monsters in their human form, but this was something more.* Monsters were not just tales that children told to scare each other around a campfire. They weren't stories passed from one child to the next, about noises in their closets. Monsters were real and one was standing at a desk changing into its true form right before her eyes. *It was amazing. She wasn't afraid. She was intrigued.*

The creature cocked its head and responded, "Why would I bother to explain what you cannot even begin to comprehend?"

Lexy swung her knife, stabbing the blade directly through the center of the being's clawed hand. Securing her palm to the desk, her gnarly fingers twitched and clawed in protest. The lady flailed around as she tried to scratch her with nails from her free arm. Lexy punched her in the face with random precision, knocking her out cold. *It had been much easier than imagined. Battling monsters was a piece of cake.* Lexy wheeled the whole chair along with the unconscious secretary to one of the cells, sent her rolling into the area of confinement and slammed the door behind her. She wandered around the precinct, to see if there were any more hideous being's hiding in wait. She opened the door to a room with a few large tables, a microwave and a fridge. Inside the fridge, she found pieces of what she guessed were the actual police officers. She strolled around for a while longer before picking up the phone to dial out. *There was no tone. The phone lines had been cut. What was this?* She heard the front door ding and decided to just go with it. A normal looking man walked up to the front desk.

She met him on the other side and said, "Can I help you?"

He grinned at her and replied," Yes, you can help me. I'm absolutely starving."

She watched his teeth grow into rows of jagged razor-sharp fangs. His body bulged out and morphed to create what might have been a terrifying moment for somebody else. Her mind ran through the list of known things that go bump in the night. *This was nothing she'd heard of in any tale.* She took him out before he even had a chance to think of retaliation. By the following morning, Lexy had a jail cell full of creatures, and not a scratch on her. It had been a simple feat. She wandered into the holding area with matches in her pocket, lugging two full red containers of gasoline and sighed, "Any last words?"

The secretary hissed, "The Legion of Abaddon will be roasting marshmallows over your corpse within the week!"

Lexy replied, "I find that hard to believe. I just took out twenty of you without a scratch. You were remarkably easy to subdue. Just in case you think of something you need to say after I leave. I'll extend you all the same courtesy you extended to the little girl you buried alive." Lexy tossed the walkie-talkie into the cell and poured gasoline on the floor. It travelled down the grooves in the tile and pooled beneath the frantic creatures. She provoked, "This floor is really uneven. Would you look at that? It all pooled right under you guys."

One of the creatures screeched, "You're going to burn in the bowels of hell for all eternity!"

Lexy grinned and taunted, "You first." She lit a match and dropped it on the floor. It travelled a rapid path through her liquid vengeance. They were all shrieking, lost in their excruciating fiery demise. Lexy strolled coolly out of the station, gripping the other walkie-talkie tightly in her hand. *She had a feeling that everyone in this township had been replaced by a sinister entity.* She left the walkie-talkie on the ledge of the fountain in the center of town with a note placed strategically underneath it. The letter read, Dear Legion of Abaddon. I left a walkie-talkie in the cell when I burned them alive. Just in case your friends had any last words, but I didn't stay. I wasn't interested in hearing them. I hope you have a clear picture of what I will do to you when I find you. She signed, Lexy Abrelle on the bottom of the note.

Lexy watched from the outskirts of the wooded area as a gathering of people arrived at the tail end of the blazing inferno that had once been the local authorities. She witnessed a man pick up her letter. He read it aloud to the group of bystanders. He laughed, folded the note and placed it in his pocket. *There were strange unknown factors at play. Things she could not even begin to fathom. Why had she written her name on that note? That was utter insanity. This man didn't appear to be collecting evidence for a crime scene. They were probably monsters too.*

A whole Clan had been sent to do something Lexy had done without messing her hair. This note, along with the flaming jail cell full of Abaddon she'd left in her wake was where the stories of Lexy's superhuman ability in battle had begun.

Lexy raced back to the cave. In her nostrils, the scent of smoke still lingered. She understood that she must put as many miles as her feet could handle between her and the town as quickly as she could. *She felt more secure travelling under cover of darkness.* She frantically gathered up the contents of her bag. Her canine companion had tossed them all over the cave. He was still poking at her backpack as she hurried to shove everything back inside. Her new friend began assertively pushing at the backpack with his nose and a can of chicken rolled out. She remarked, "You'll need a name if you're coming with me. You like chicken so much. I'll just call you Chicken. You and I don't have time to eat. We need to leave."

Chapter 4

The Leader Of The Pack

It was only a matter of weeks before the first Clan was sent to claim her. She hadn't exactly been flying under the radar by exterminating a farmhouse full of evil and a corrupt population of a town. Lexy Abrelle had been kept in captivity for far too long. She would not allow herself to be claimed. She was a separate free entity. Lexy did not require help from anyone. The first Clan that arrived had been Triad. They would not be successful in marking her Triad. As a matter of fact, Triad and the Legion of Abaddon would come for her over a dozen times in the months to come. She took them on, all by herself. *No one was going to take her freedom, not now.* She kept moving, opting to live off the land for obvious reasons. Along the way, she picked up a few more strays. They travelled as equals. Three dogs soon turned to half a dozen and then to twenty. They would hunt at night together and provide meat for her. She would often awaken to a pile of rabbits. Lexy would take one, skin it and cook it over the fire. She'd eat only what she needed to survive, and then give the rest back to her partners. She'd find them extra treats in cabins and homes along the way. In return, they'd guard her while she slept. Lexy would feel safe each time she closed her eyes. She knew her only chance at peace was to settle down with her pack, far away from civilization.

The rag tag group continued travelling north until they stumbled upon an abandoned cabin deep in an isolated area. An area where it would take serious effort to reach her. She'd hoped everyone would just leave her alone. She kept herself busy, endeavouring to bury the dark instincts flickering within her. This cabin in the middle of nowhere became her home for years. She was alone with her canine pack. It was a peaceful period. One day the snow began to fall. The biting chill of the air prohibited her from leaving to hunt with her pack that day. She sat around reading, bored stiff. Due to her lack of appropriate footwear, she was stuck indoors. She had to rig herself up something to wear on her feet for the winter months. Finally, her pack returned with rabbits and other gifts in mouth. Chicken had not returned with the pack. He'd probably become caught in one of the traps, she'd set before the blizzard. Lexy put on layer after layer of men's clothing, and rigged up insulation for her feet, using the rabbit pelts. She ventured out into the frozen world, following the others until her feet pulsated and throbbed with pain. By the time the group found Chicken. It was obvious, he'd lost too much blood. *Her friend was nearly gone.* She removed the trap and tugged her friend onto her lap. He had been with her since the beginning of her new life. She stroked his matted fur and spoke softly to him. When he began to go, she hugged him tightly and begged with him to stay with her. It was then that she felt the warmth travel from her body to his. This was the moment she discovered her ability to heal the wounded members of her pack and not only herself. Food became scarce as the long, frigid winter months dragged on. They went from being the hunters to the hunted. The larger animals of the wilderness became drawn to the warmth and the smells of the cabin. During that winter, they fought off many cougars and bears. It became apparent that there was nowhere safe. Lexy would always be somebody's prey. Her loyal pack kept guard over the cabin at night. It was difficult for her to rest knowing, a few of her friends vanished each week, taken by something in the night.

By the end of the month, her pack had been cut by twelve. They were starving and down to only eight. She'd noticed a few of them staring at her. Her friends were dangerously close to becoming her enemies. Once you've seen the wild eyes of starvation, you recognize the signs. They were at the tipping point of crazy. Her pack was beginning to leave her, emotionally. Each time they went on a hunt she feared two things. Her first fear was that they wouldn't return, and she'd be left all alone. The second fear grew stronger with each passing day. The fear they would turn on her and she would be forced to kill them. She sensed this was inevitable. Lexy slept with one eye open, knowing she wasn't safe with the pack anymore. She was the next logical source of meat. One evening after the pack had left to hunt, it happened. She was drifting off to the sounds of her growling stomach, when she felt a chill in the air. A draft was coming from somewhere.

A voice inside of her mind whispered, *Wake up Lexy. Something is amiss.* She opened her eyes, sat up straight on the bunk and smoked her head on the ceiling. Lexy always slept on the top bunk. This bought her the second that she needed to focus. The front door was wide open. *Why was it open? She was certain she'd closed it. Maybe she hadn't shut it properly?* She swung her legs over the side to jump off the bunk. The second that she did it, she knew it was a bad idea. Teeth sunk into the flesh of her calf. She was dragged from the top bunk. It was on her in a flash. She didn't have time to collect her thoughts. She held the jaws away from her throat. *It was one of the missing members of her pack.* The dog was rabid, slobbering, snarling, it snapped and gnashed its razor-sharp teeth. It bore into her soul with wild eyes of insanity. *Would the pack that she adored be the weapon of her destruction?* Lexy's eyes widened as another one of the dogs that disappeared during the long winter months rushed at her through the open doorway. This one was rabid too. Three more of her missing pack entered through the door, poised to block any attempt at escape. Another one attacked, tearing into the meat on her leg. She felt an explosion of energy. With a blinding mixture of fury and disbelief, she swung her hand in the air. The canine sailed across the room into the wall. It hit the floor whining, sprawled on the ground. The dogs shifted their attention to the wounded pack member and tore it apart. They devoured him alive. Lexy hurled the stray that had her pinned at the ceiling with such force she heard his bones snap. The canine that once protected her was killed instantly. She proceeded to off each one of her rabid former companions. One by one, they fell.

In the morning, she sat slumped in the corner with the door still wide open. Her mind shut down. She could smell nothing but the scent of dead things. The violation that polluted her heart, kept her from healing them. She awaited the return of the loyal part of her pack. They left the night before to hunt. When, they didn't return the next morning, she knew, she couldn't allow the meat to go to waste. *Not when they were all starving to death.* She shut her emotions down. Lexy skinned and prepared her companions over the fire. She knew she should make use of their pelts. She couldn't imagine a scenario where she could wear her friend's skin. *They hadn't been evil, they'd gone mad. There was a difference.* She cut the meat into slabs and buried their bodies in the woods. She marked their graves and opted out of saying a few words. They'd attempted to eat her. She returned to the cabin expecting to feel the shame and guilt of having to face the rest of her pack. Not one returned, not even Chicken. She would spend weeks searching relentlessly, leaving each day at sunrise. There was not a sign of them anywhere. They had disappeared. It was strange because not only were they gone, but all the larger forms of wildlife. There were still birds, crickets, and squirrels. The deer and elk had vanished. Her natural predators had also disappeared. They'd probably moved on after picking off all of the larger wildlife. Once the weather became warmer, Lexy sat on the porch every evening willing her pack to return.

She spent six months after that alone in the wilderness. Each day she went out and hunted for her food, scouring the area for her pack. By this point, she knew they'd been killed. By the time it crossed her mind to go back to civilization. She was afraid to. She had been left alone for too long. Looking back to that time, she realised it was the only thing she'd ever been truly afraid of. She was leery of humanity. *She may be alone out here, but nothing was coming to kill her anymore.* Without the pack to occupy her mind, she began to lose her faculties. With nothing to do but replay horrifying images in her memory, she relived these dark events daily during her solitary confinement. The only reason she retained a semblance of sanity was by reading the crates of books she discovered in the root cellar. Whoever occupied this cabin before her had a love of the written word. They also must have had children who were home schooled. There were multiple textbooks on every subject. The other books varied from Romance to Sci-Fi. She found it hard to relate to the romance novels. The second a love scene began she'd fold the corner of the page, close the book and put it aside. She didn't want to know about that, it brought her mind somewhere dark. It triggered memories she'd been attempting to bury for a long time. Instead, Lexy read about pirates, aliens, spies, detectives and dragons. There were even some children's books. Those she couldn't relate to, for she'd never had a childhood. *They didn't make sense.* There were also some personal items left behind in boxes in the cellar. She found a family portrait and wondered who they were? The image was of a man, woman, and two small boys. On the back were the names Margret, Donald, Troy and Colin. *Where had the other clothing gone?* She'd searched for it, but there had been none. *What had happened to the family?* She only found men's clothes and everything was far too big to fit her. She'd worn it in layers during the winter, but women's clothing, even the children's, would have come in handy.

She read the novels by the light of the fire until a folded-up newspaper article fell out of one. The article was about a house fire that claimed an entire family. A copy of the family portrait was in the box used in the article about their loss. *Why had that portrait been saved in a cabin in the woods? It looked like something that would have been gracing the walls of the home that burned to the ground. Maybe there was more than one copy? She'd been reading far too many detective stories.* The article said the father had been away on a hunting trip. He'd returned home to find his family and home gone. This must have been the family cabin. He'd come out here to live after the fire. That was how the newspaper article found its way into one of these books. She decided to do some more searching through nooks and crannies. Lexy was looking for a hint of foul play. According to the books, murderers liked to keep souvenirs. She searched the cabin from top to bottom and found nothing. Realising she had too much time on her hands and an overactive imagination, she let the premise of foul play go. The family died. The father hadn't come back to the cabin in years. He probably moved on with his life and left the memories of his family in this place. There was a box that contained soap, shampoo and a few blankets. Lexy had run out of soap and hygiene products a long time ago, she was long past caring. The cabin had no running water. There was a creek outside, it was her only source of water. In the winter months, when the creek was frozen solid, Lexy gathered snow and boiled water over the fire. She needed water to drink and to wash, but it took effort. She didn't bother cleaning herself for weeks on end. What was the point of that? She was alone. There came a point when she ceased to care about anything but food. She stopped reading, grooming or thinking about anything, but the search for her next meal. She'd been alone for so long by the time she stumbled across her first human. Lexy had become a wild thing.

Chapter 5

Contemplating The Merits Of Cannibalism

Lexy had been checking traps for hours that day. She'd found nothing in them in weeks. *She was starving.* Something had rid the entire area of wildlife. She had been living off anything she could find at that point. Mostly rodents, bark and bugs. She hadn't spoken a word or used her voice in so long that she'd almost forgotten how to articulate one. She had caught something large. She heard it cry out as the trap snapped down on it. She was so hungry her stomach was rumbling with excitement as she came upon a sight she had not expected to see. There was a man caught in one of her traps. She stood there watching it squirm and curse. She inaudibly contemplated the merits of just cooking it and eating it. *Who would know?* It saw her standing there, and it spoke to her.

He said, "Hey lady, Yes, you with the crazy hair. Can you let me out of this trap? It really frigging hurts."

The sound of his voice was appealing. He had a strange accent. Lexy squatted in front of him and freed him from the trap. She could barely understand what he was saying, but she enjoyed the sound of his voice. She stood up and just wandered away. She had to find food. She was starving. He followed behind her and continued to talk.

"My name's Grey. I've been searching for you. You are one hard girl to locate," he pestered.

Lexy stopped walking and swung her stick at him. *She needed him to go away. She didn't want to answer him. Why wouldn't he just go away? She wanted to eat him. Why was he pushing his luck?*

52

She kept walking away from him. He hobbled along behind her. His leg was quite obviously broken. He didn't complain about it. He just kept rattling off words at her, talking her ear off.

Grey said, "Are you hunting? Checking traps for meat? You don't really want to eat trail kill, do you? I know where we can get real food, stuff that tastes good."

She swung around and scowled at him. *He was beginning to annoy her.* She started to run, dodging roots and vines. She moved swiftly through the rugged landscape with the agility of someone who had memorized where each root lay underfoot. She knew the layout of the land. This was her territory. She heard him hollering behind her. She'd thought she'd had lost him but not quite. She stopped along the winding unmarked trail to check traps, finally finding something. She wasn't in a hurry, the boy was injured, and there was no way he'd keep up with her. She walked the rest of the way, prize in hand. She didn't hear him calling after her anymore. *Maybe he died? Maybe something else ate him?* She flung open the door to the cabin and trudged inside. She had caught only a small squirrel, but it would be enough to tame the desperate sensation of starvation. She started a fire and began to methodically skin the squirrel.

The front door opened, startling her. Lexy grimaced, clutching the knife in her hand. She rolled her eyes. *This guy just didn't give up, did he?*

She cleared her throat and spoke for the first time in six months, "Get out."

Grey chuckled, "She speaks. I wasn't sure you knew how?"

Lexy repeated her last command, "Get out."

He grinned at her and teased, "We're in the middle of bloody nowhere. Where would you have me go? I thought backwoods hillbillies were supposed to be hospitable?"

Lexy scowled, she was pretty sure he'd just insulted her. She was confused by this guy. He obviously wasn't used to taking no for an answer. She decided to keep cooking the squirrel and ignore him. She wasn't afraid of him. It didn't even alarm her when he shut the door. Lexy knew she could take him.

Grey announced, "This door doesn't have a lock? I'm not out here in the middle of nowhere all by myself. There's probably more than one Clan out here. They're all searching for you. Listen, I really like Ankh, and I really don't want to be taken by Triad. That would be a fate worse than death. I know you think I'm just some idiot that followed you home. I'm a nice person. At least I try to be a good one. You can't hide out here anymore. They know where you are. This cabin isn't going to be hard for anyone to find."

She could sense that he was telling the truth. She wasn't leaving this cabin though. This was her home. She wasn't afraid of Triad. She'd dealt with them on numerous occasions. She took a bite of the squirrel meat and offered Grey some in gesture.

Grey said, "Thank you ... I'm not all that big on squirrel. If you're hungry, I know where we can get something to eat. Proper food that actually tastes good."

She was amused by this guy. She was glad she hadn't killed and eaten him. His voice was very calming. She ripped off a piece of the squirrel meat and walked over to where he was standing. He was balancing on one foot, injured quite badly. She had only ever fixed herself and some of her pack. She'd never attempted to fix a human. She held out a piece of meat and he politely took it. She knelt in front of him, knowing he could easily hurt her from this vantage point if he wanted to. She looked up at him as he politely put the meat in his mouth. He smiled at her as she touched his wounded leg. She felt the warmth travel down her arms and into his broken limb. He was healed instantly. She glanced up and smiled at him.

Grey whispered, "You're a Healer. That's what your gift is called. Do you want to see what I can do?"

She stood up and nodded her head. Grey strolled over to the fire that was almost out. Only a few embers of red remained. He stared at the embers and raised his hands. They grew to a raging orange and yellow inferno. *He had fuelled the fire with his mind. It was amazing. She felt her heart flicker with something strange. She finally had someone that she could identify with.*

Grey said, "I lost a lot of blood. Do you have any water? Do you have anything to drink?"

Lexy took a glass from the cupboard. She walked over and scooped a full ladle of water out of the pot. She held it towards him.

He politely said, "Thank you."

There was something about his eyes. The sound of his voice was music to her lonely soul. She didn't want to be away from this person. She wanted to be wherever he was. Lexy was aware that perhaps it had just been so long since she had been in the presence of another person that she had attached to the first person that had spoken to her. All that she knew was that she felt foreign warmth inside of her heart. She raised her hand to her chest. When she noticed Grey watching her, she lowered it quickly. She had a weird panicked feeling in the hollow of her throat at the thought of him walking out the door without her. If she stood her ground, he was right. Triad would come. No, she couldn't stay here. Her place of emotional solace would be violated.

Grey began to plead with her, "I know you don't have a reason to trust me. I can try to explain what's happening. There are three Clans of people like us. The Clans are called Ankh, Trinity and Triad. Clan Ankh is my Clan. They're my family. I don't know anything about Trinity. I know Triad is somewhere nobody wants to end up. Let me take you back with me. Come with me to Ankh, I promise you I will always be your friend."

Lexy stared into Grey's eyes and wondered if you could make your place of emotional solace a person? She nodded and whispered, "I'll come."

Grey appeared to be relieved. He grinned and said, "You won't regret this."

He held out his hand towards her. She didn't understand what he wanted. To take someone's hand was not a built-in instinct for her. Normally this was an instinct that you had as a child. You took your mother's hand when she held it out towards you. Maybe Lexy had known this but she had forgotten in the midst of attempting to block the bad thoughts. She needed to block the memories of the dark farm, at any cost. There was a look in his eyes that she couldn't place. Grey appeared to be upset. His eyes were glossed over and damp. One tear escaped and began to travel down his cheek. She reached out and touched it out of curiosity. She rubbed it between her fingers and stared at it.

Grey asked, "How long have you been alone?"

Lexy, still staring at the moist tear, continued to rub it between two of her fingers.

Lexy glanced up and met Grey's eyes and stated one word, "Always." It was a word that spoken aloud threatened to break an unbreakable heart, and by the pained expression on his face that one word had reached out into the space between them and touched his.

Grey held his hand out once again and said, "You will never be alone again."

He smiled and leaned close to her. He touched her hand and nodded. He was going to show her what he was asking of her. He laced his fingers through hers. The warmth from his hand seemed to flow straight to her heart and something strange happened. Her eyes began to leak, just a little. Lexy blinked and her vision cleared.

She bit her lip and whispered one word in response, "Grey?"

He smiled and said, "Yes, my name's Grey, and your name is Lexy right?"

She gave him a peculiar look because that wasn't a question, it was a statement. She knew what his name was. Grey was the name of the person that promised her she would never be alone again. She could tell from his expression that he had every intention of keeping that promise. She had to find her comfort zone with her voice again before he thought she was a caveman. She smiled. She reached up and touched her own cheek with her free hand in reaction to it. Grey started to laugh. He squeezed her hand and Lexy knew that he would never let it go. She thought about the stories that she had read. If she wanted to pass for somewhat normal, she'd have to remember how the people related to each other and try to assimilate. Lexy wished she'd read the romance novels. She wished she'd pushed past the uncomfortable spots. *She was going to need to read more books. A lot of them...*

Chapter 6

Drunken United Fronts

They sat down across from each other at the rustic table. Grey put his arm down and the table almost tipped over. Lexy rarely used the table. She'd never bothered to fix it. Grey noticed something behind her.

He hopped up and walked across the room. Grabbing it off the top shelf, Grey asked, "Do you know what this stuff is?"

Lexy shook her head to either side. He was holding a jug of golden liquid. *She wasn't in the habit of drinking things if she didn't know what they were. It smelled like something you clean with or put in a car. A foul scented liquid.* She had left it alone.

Smiling, he stated, "This is whisky. It's super old whisky at that." He grabbed two glasses and poured some in each and passed one to her. He announced, "This will put some hair on your chest."

Lexy frowned as she took the glass from him. *She didn't want to have hair on her chest.*

Grey chuckled, "I meant that figuratively. This will make you feel all warm and fuzzy inside."

Lexy wasn't sure that was any better. Was warm and fuzzy inside a good thing?

He smiled at her, nodded, taking a swig from his glass. He gasped, "That's damn strong whisky."

Lexy watched Grey drink the amber liquid and survive. *He seemed to want her to try it.* She sniffed the glass, grimaced and went for it. Lexy immediately began choking and sputtering it all over the table. The warmth of the liquid travelled all the way to her stomach from the small amount that stayed down.

Laughing, Grey urged, "Try it again. This time don't spit it all."

He took another sip from his glass and grinned.

She did the same. *That went down much better. It was almost good that time.* She stared across the table at Grey. He finished his and poured himself another. She finished hers. *It felt like they were playing a game.* She gave him her glass to refill.

Grey winked at her and teased, "You don't seem all that scary to me. Are the stories about you true? Did you really kill ten Abaddon without breaking a sweat and burn them alive in a jail cell?"

Lexy felt extremely relaxed. *She couldn't stop smiling. She wasn't used to smiling.* She placed both hands on her cheeks. *They felt hot.*

Giggling, she corrected, "Twenty." She took another drink from the glass. *She wasn't used to laughing either. It felt amazing. She had feelings.*

Intrigued, he enquired, "Is this the first time you've had alcohol?"

"Yes," she confirmed. Grey snatched the glass out of her hand. *She was even more confused?*

He sighed, "I'm such a bloody idiot. Do you think you're drunk?"

Lexy knit her brow. *She had no idea what he was talking about? She felt great. She felt way better than she had in a long time.* She shrugged because she didn't know what he meant by that.

Grey stood up and remarked, "Maybe our time would be better spent attempting to prepare you. When we leave this cabin, there's going to be a fight."

Lexy smiled because in her life there was always fighting. *This was not a bad thing. This was her favourite thing, nothing she needed preparation for. She was looking forward to the fight. Didn't he find the idea of a fight exciting too?* She bit her tongue and remained silent. *She loved the way this whisky made her head feel. It felt pleasurably numb.*

Grey went to get the pot of water. He filled her cup and urged, "You should have a glass of water. Whisky can give you a nasty headache, especially on an empty stomach. All you have in yours is a little bit of squirrel."

She smiled as her inner dialogue reminded her that she could have eaten him instead of the squirrel. *She would have had a full stomach and no hangover.* Grey poured water into her glass and she drank it. He poured another and she drank that too. He did the same for himself. *He didn't know that cannibalism had crossed her mind as an option to their blossoming friendship. She would probably leave that part out when recalling the day, they met.* Grey was nervously pacing around.

He asked, "Do you have a bathroom?"

She pointed out the window. There had never been a bathroom inside of the cabin. There was an outhouse. A bear pushed the outhouse over and it crumbled into pieces, leaving only a deep hole in the ground. She still used the hole and then covered it with a board when she was finished. *It left you feeling a little exposed while you were trying to concentrate. She wasn't about to go into detail with Grey about how she had a safe number two. She wasn't going to speak more than a couple words at a time until she felt comfortable that she would be able to speak properly. She didn't want to sound like an ogre. She knew she probably looked like one. She hadn't seen her reflection in a long time. She was willing to bet she was scary unkempt. He was squirming. He obviously had to go badly.* Lexy blurted, "Number one?" *There, she'd spoken two complete words.*

Grey chuckled, "Yes, just number one."

Lexy grabbed a bowel from under the sink, gave it to him and stated, "Here."

Confused, he enquired, "Isn't there somewhere private to do this? I'm sure you don't want me exposing myself to you this soon?"

She pointed to the closet. He sheepishly grinned and wandered over opened it and shimmied inside. There wasn't enough room for him to close the door. Lexy looked away.

She wandered over to the window to give him a little privacy. She noticed movement in the bushes outside. Lexy was a hunter by nature. *They were here.* She made eye contact with a Triad. *She'd killed that one before.* Lexy cocked her head. It was amusing to her that they just kept trying. Grey came out of the closet and raised his eyebrows, pointing at the large bowl he'd relieved himself in. She raised her finger and in absolute silence and pointed outside. She pressed her lips together. If he innocently tossed his pee in the bushes where the Triad was hiding, she was liable to go from never laughing, to busting a gut. *Grey, please, do it. Toss your pee in the bushes on the left.* Grey opened the door and tossed his pee at the bushes where Triad was hiding. *It was like he could read her mind.* He closed the door afterwards. She covered her mouth to stop herself from laughing.

He made a funny face and asked, "What's so funny?"

Lexy casually replied, "They're here." She ventured to speak a few more words and it went off without a hitch.

Grey peered out the window and responded, "I don't see anything, but they probably are here. It would be funny if someone was hiding in the bushes where I tossed my pee."

She nodded in response and bit her lip.

"You're drunk. Look at how you're standing," Grey teased.

She obviously couldn't look at how she was standing? You couldn't look at yourself? The cabin floor wavered under her feet again. She stumbled to the table, placed a hand on it to steady herself and announced, "I like whisky."

Fascinated, Grey pestered, "This is incredibly bad timing for you to learn you love whisky. I hope you can still fight."

She grabbed the knife from the table and threw it with impeccable precision. It stuck into the wall a few inches from his head.

Grey winked and provoked, "I hope you weren't aiming at my head, you totally missed it."

It was a tossup between the whisky, Grey in general, and him innocently tossing a bucket of pee in the bushes making her cheeks hurt.

He plucked her knife out of the wall, walked it over, and handed it back. Grey instructed, "Try to follow my lead. If it's Trinity out there, we will live. If it's Triad out there, we're in deep shit. Trust me; it's a fate worse than death to become Triad. Try to stay together, we'll keep each other safe. If we work as a team and make it back to Ankh, maybe we have a chance."

She would keep him safe. He made her laugh. She wanted to stay wherever he was. She planned to help him get back to his Clan. She hadn't been able to get either of the last people she'd tried to help back to their families, but this time she'd make sure it happened. She smiled at Grey. *She didn't follow anyone's lead when she was fighting. It was all instinct.* She turned to take a last look at the rustic cabin that had been her home for a couple of years. *She was ready to leave now. Grey had given her reason to go.*

Grey questioned, "Are you ready?"

Lexy replied, "Always." *It was the same word she'd used when talking about being alone. She was always alone. She was also always ready.* He caught the deep significance of the word as their eyes met. Grey held out his hand and they stepped out of the cabin as a united front. *She'd dealt with Triad on many occasions. They would have an organized assault planned. They'd permit them to leave the cabin.* A slight breeze whistled through the trees and the birds ceased to chirp. The crickets paused their tune. She felt Grey squeeze her hand. Lexy didn't exhibit a touch of fear, all she felt was anticipation. She detected the whizzing of a knife as it travelled through the air towards Grey's chest. Lexy placed her arm in the blade's path, shielding him from the knife. It went through her arm. Grey had a second of panic. She beamed as she yanked it out. Her arm healed instantly. She launched it back, impaling one directly in the heart as he came at them. *The Triad were coming from everywhere, all at once. How many of them were there?* They duelled side by side. Lexy was laughing and flinging men back into the bushes. She'd been repeatedly stabbed, but it didn't slow her down. *Grey was impressive. He was stronger than she'd thought he'd be but he couldn't heal.* Each time she was wounded, she recovered almost instantaneously. *He was nearly ready to collapse. If she healed him, she would accompany him on the forest floor. They would have her too, nobody would rescue either one.* She observed Grey go down out of the corner of her eye. Three Triad kept her occupied and when she swung around, Grey had been taken. *They'd been keeping her engaged so the others could snatch him.* Concern fluttered in her chest. *She seldom panicked about anything. Any sort of emotional attachment would be tricky. It had been a long time since she'd felt any form of affection for anyone. It had happened immediately with Grey. She would have to reclaim him from the Triad. She wasn't going to let him lose his family.*

The crickets commenced their chirping. The birds began to twitter as though they thought the unrest in the woods was over. The turmoil in the wild was far from over. The fight had only just begun. Lexy ran to catch up with the Triad, but not through the central path. She moved through the bushes through the prickles, and skunk weed. She slipped in a creature's hole, wrenching her anklebone. It snapped as she went down. Once she saw visible bone pierced through her skin, she knew the injury would slow her down for at least twenty minutes if she didn't help it along. *She didn't have that kind of time to spare.* She glanced at her exposed ankle bone, snapped branches off a bush, laid them on either side of her ankle and took off her shirt. She wrapped it around the branches and compressed it with everything she had to help her body set her ankle faster. It was excruciating but she couldn't cry out, for there was surely more than one Clan out in the bushes searching for her. *The last thing she needed was for the other Clan to find her while she was healing.* She heard Grey's words in her head. *Grey believed being Triad was a fate worse than death. She had something to fight for now. She would fight for his freedom.* She unwrapped her ankle and it was healed in record time. Lexy didn't bother putting her shirt back on. She pursued the Triad noiselessly in the shadows as they endeavoured to hike out of the forest.

Chapter 7

Certifiably Insane Redheads

Lexy knew the area like the back of her hand. She easily managed to get far enough ahead to move snares into their path to use as traps and patiently waited in the shadows for her prey to be subdued by their own lack of caution. Under cover of darkness, the hidden traps began snaring prey. The clicking noise of each one closing on limbs, followed by startled howls, allowed her to keep count until she was confident the traps had all been used. Lexy stepped out of the veil of trees making her presence known. Emotionally disconnected from their plight as they flailed in anguish, her stomach rumbled. *She entertained the thought. Grey was unconscious. It was convenient. She'd just take him with her when she was finished dealing with the Triad.* She stepped over the ensnared men and stopped by the one who wasn't shrieking. He smirked as she approached. This sparked the need to assert her dominance. *He wasn't afraid of her. She was a little disappointed. None of them smelled of urine. Grey must have missed the guy in the bushes. What a shame, that would have made for a comical moment. She'd killed these men before. The cocky one, was their leader. She'd have to make sure he understood who was in charge.* She squatted by the leader and taunted, "You found me."

The wounded man cracked the world's cheekiest smile and teased, "I'm impressed. You can speak. I wasn't sure you knew how."

She knew how. She just usually chose not to. For lack of having to, sometimes it was difficult to find the right words. She planned to ease back into it but everything from his disdainful gaze to his

64

mannerisms made her want to kick his ass. Lexy provoked, "If I haven't spoken to you in the past it was because I deemed you unworthy of the attempt." *That whole sentence had come out exactly as she'd wanted it to. She'd read a lot of books during her, self-imposed exile.* Impressed with her ability to recall unused vocabulary, she strutted over to a wailing Triad, removed her blade, clutched his hair and silenced him by coldly slitting his throat. "Far too scrawny. Not enough meat on his bones to bother dragging him back to the cabin," she commented and moved on. *Her eyes kept darting back to their leader to see if he was afraid.* She whispered in the next Triad's ear, "You should be more than enough meat to sustain me for an entire winter." Thoroughly entertained by their horrified faces, she pressed her blade against his throat and declared, "I'm going to have to string you up in this tree and bleed you out first." *If she hadn't wanted to save Grey, she probably would have strung them all up and bled them out. Starvation was an evil thing to have dancing around in the back of your mind.*

They watched in horror as she grabbed a rope from her pack, swung it up around a tree branch, bound his feet, and yanked him up into the tree. *Hanging by his ankles, with one of his legs broken must be excruciatingly painful.* Lexy didn't bring it up as she slit his throat. He squirmed and became calm. Wandering over to each one, she commented about how scrawny they were before taking them out where they lay ensnared by her traps. She released the dangling man she'd bled out. He dropped to the dirt with a thud. *Each move she made had been for one reason and one only, to terrify the leader of the Triad into believing she was going to bleed him out and eat him.* Lexy crouched in front of the leader of Triad and asked, "What is your name?"

"It's Tiberius," he answered.

He was remarkably calm. What she'd done to his men hadn't even fazed him. Lexy enquired, "Aren't you afraid of me?"

Captivated by her, he provoked, "A little but honestly, I'm still trying to figure you out. I'm a thousand years old. I've been starving before. I understand how one would resort to the act of cannibalism. What I can't figure out is why you would agree to go with this Grey kid willingly to Clan Ankh, when you are so obviously meant to be mine?" Lexy was intrigued by his delusional statement. She cocked her head and sat down in the dirt just out of his reach. *A thousand years old my ass, did he think she was born yesterday?* She sparred, "What would make you think I was meant to be yours?"

Tiberius teased, "You are a certifiably insane red head and that's kind of my thing."

Tiberius had made the wrong move. He'd brought a hint of sexuality into the conversation. She was years away from not having the instinct to kill any man that spoke to her that way. Lexy knew she was a wild thing. Her hair a pile of matted scarlet and her body odor was undeniably fowl. She'd been running through skunk weed for hours. This probably added to the potency of her extreme lack of hygiene. *She didn't care.* Lexy crawled towards him on her hands and knees like a deranged untameable beast. Tiberius pulled something out of his pocket and tossed it towards her. *It was a chocolate bar. Had he just thrown a chocolate bar at her? Did he think he could placate her with candy?* It had been years since she'd tasted chocolate. She remembered how delicious and decadent it tasted. She had found a few bars in homes as she passed through towns on her travels into the wild north. Lexy tore the wrapping off with her teeth. She was just about to take a giant bite when Tiberius grinned and gave his plot away. *It was drugged, wasn't it? How do you capture a person that is slowly starving to death? You offer them something incredibly tempting and you drug it. She'd been down this road before.* She ripped the bar in half and offered it to one of the only live Triad ensnared in her easily detected traps. He didn't want to eat it. She pressed down on the trap. He screamed and ate what she'd given him, to stop the torture. He passed out within seconds. Lexy shook her head at Tiberius. She opted out of speaking to him again. *Why wasn't he afraid of her?*

Tiberius teased, "You can't blame a guy for trying? That Grey kid can't handle you. A part of you has to know that." *He wasn't remotely afraid of her. She wanted the leader of the Triad to fear her. Lexy knew she must look like a monster. Tiberius wasn't afraid of monsters.* She announced, "I not only plan to kill you, but I want to make good and sure you feel every excruciating second. I'm going to hang you in one of those trees and bleed you out. Would you like that?" A glint of something she couldn't quite place flashed across his expression.

"Enough of that pillow talk. You're nothing but a tease," Tiberius flirted.

He whispered something else. She couldn't quite make it out, so she leaned in closer. He lunged forward and stabbed her in the stomach. She hadn't bothered to take away his weapon. *She didn't care if he stabbed her.* She smacked his hand away, removed the knife in her gut without the smallest sound of discomfort and healed almost instantly for she was a Healer. She held his knife within his reach to see if he was stupid enough to grab for it. Tiberius stared into her eyes with unwavering calm. *He was just like her and that knowledge fuelled her overwhelming need to dominate him. It was a territorial feeling. She wanted this man to fear her. She wanted him scared to death so he never tried to assert his dominance over her again. How was she going to terrify someone who faced her with unwavering awe? She had an idea.* She ran her tongue slowly up the length of the blade, not understanding for an immortal as dark as Tiberius that was practically a marriage proposal. *He had an agonised expression, she didn't understand. What did she have to do, pluck out his toenails?*

In awe, he whispered, "You're a magnificent creature."

She knit her brow. *What in the hell was wrong with this guy?* She took her blade and slid it slowly right through the center of her palm. Blood seeped out of the incision as she pulled it out and it healed instantly. Another attempt to frighten him and all she'd managed to do was accidentally ply him with more innuendo. He was grinning at her. Lexy probed,

"You can't hurt me, Tiberius. Why do you keep trying? I love the way it makes me feel."

With a pained expression, Tiberius licked his bottom lip, bit it and gasped while staring like she was the main course at dinner. He sighed, "Honey, you just keep adding to the list of reasons why you're meant to be mine."

She was completely confused. Almost to confused to kill him. What was going on here? What in the hell was wrong with this guy? No matter what she did he was not the least bit afraid. This was going to call for drastic measures. She took the rope and tied his feet. He chuckled and looked at her as though they were about to play a game.

Tiberius naughtily instructed, "Make sure you tie my hands too."

Lexy shook her head. She hadn't planned on tying his hands, but it was a good idea. She took off her last baggy layer and his eyes lit up. She was wearing a thin worn out tank top that was completely see through. Disassociated from her sexuality, she didn't notice nor did she care. She bound his hands so tightly it cut off his circulation.

Tiberius remarked, "Not that this isn't totally doing it for me, but sweetheart you seriously need a bath. This is a little tight, but I'll play along."

Was he seriously complaining that she bound his hands too tightly? She was about to kill him, and he still thought this was a game. When she tossed the other end of the rope into the tree, she saw the lightbulb turn on over his head. She straddled him backwards to release the trap from his leg. He sat up as she released the trap and looped his bound hands around her neck. She struggled for a second then noticed he was quite obviously enjoying the situation. *What in the hell was wrong with this guy? He was sick in the head.* He squeezed her throat, but she could tell he was only toying with her. He could have easily snapped her neck.

He loosened his arms just enough for her to be able to breathe as he seduced, "Do you really want three of my Triad to watch."

She almost smiled but stopped herself. *This guy honestly thought they were mutually flirting. Normally she would have just killed him and been done with it, but his stupidity was so astounding, she couldn't resist the urge to play with him.* Lexy whispered, "Do you want me to take care of them first? I don't care if they watch me finish you off."

Tiberius mischievously vowed, "If you come with me to Triad, I might just have to marry you. Well, after I give you a bath and find out what you look like."

Lexy didn't know how to participate in the dance between a woman and a man. *Honestly, she had no clue if he'd just insulted or complimented her. He both repulsed and intrigued her with his words. There was something else. He made her heartbeat faster.* Her body reacted to his closeness, piloted by primal instinct. *Tiberius made her feel dark. She'd always been afraid she was meant to be a dark thing. Not that she was turned dark because of circumstances, but that she'd been born this way. She had been trapped in the darkness for too many years. If she went with Triad, she knew she would never find her way back into the light.*

She had a vision of a childhood not her own and saw herself riding down a hill on a bicycle with shiny streamers flickering. At the bottom of the hill was the house with the yellow door. It beckoned her to enter it. A family awaited her. She glanced at Grey's body. *He'd spoken of family and friendship. He was the owner of the voice that she'd instantly attached to. He was her yellow door.* Lexy rested her head against Tiberius, allowing him to believe he'd gotten through to her. As he relaxed his arms, she slipped out of his grasp and yanked the other end of the rope. She pulled him upside down and tied the rope off. He dangled upside down, swearing at her because she'd tricked him. His expression changed and he began belly laughing. "Nothing personal, but I'm going to have to say no to your marriage proposal," she sparred. Before he could recant, she slit his throat.

He gurgled his attempt to take it back and save face.

"I only left your men alive, so they could watch me kill you," she taunted as the life drained from Tiberius and the light left his eyes. She grabbed one of the Triad by the hair and said, "There is blood all over the place. I'm going to have to take off now before starving wild animals show up to finish you guys off. Maybe you'll get lucky, I haven't seen anything bigger than a squirrel in six months."

Reviving Grey proved to be more difficult then she'd imagined it would be. She needed time to regain enough energy to heal him. She carried Grey over her shoulder for miles through the uneven terrain. Until she couldn't endeavour to carry him for one more moment. She began to drag him, utterly exhausted. She had no steam left but knew where they could hide. She would use all she had left to drag him to safety. After another hour of doing the impossible, she dragged him into a cave she'd come across many years before. Lexy closed her eyes. She'd need a short nap, before healing the boy she hoped would be her friend.

Chapter 8

Yellow Doors

Lexy awoke with a start. It took her a second to remember where she'd ended up. She was in a cave. She had taken a short nap. She was in close confines with a boy. She scurried away from him. She was sitting too close. Lexy picked up a stick and thought about poking him with it. She wanted him to wake up so she could hear him speak again. Then she remembered that she fell asleep before she'd healed him. She put down the stick. She still had work to do. Lexy scooted up beside him and touched his wavy blonde hair. It was soft, a completely different texture than the dog's fur. She felt her own matted mass of hair and decided that hair felt much better when it was shorter and clean. She was curious about a lot of things, and he was out cold. She had spent two long years in only the company of canines. She leaned over and smelled his neck. His scent was miraculous. She was now even more aware of the nasty stench that must linger around her. She smelled his skin again and smiled. She would need to bathe as soon as she could manage it. She had to heal him. She would have to stop smelling his skin once she did that. She knew it would be a creepy thing for Grey to wake up with her smelling his neck. He was a person not a member of her pack. She placed her hands on his chest and felt the warmth move from her own body, as it travelled down her arms into him. She felt a bit lightheaded and then there was nothing.

Time flashed by and in an instant, she heard a familiar voice and it caused her to open her eyes. She sat upright and noticed Grey sitting against the wall. *He was watching her. He had obviously been waiting for her to awaken.*

Grey whispered, "You saved me."

"I couldn't let them take you," Lexy replied.

He teased, "That was a whole sentence; I think you might have been holding out on me."

She sensed the relief in his voice as she explained, "I didn't have a reason to say a word, for a long time. I was just working my way up to it. I was also a little afraid everything would come out wrong."

Grey said, "Thank you for coming to help me. I know you didn't have to."

What a silly boy Grey was with his intoxicating accent and unknowing words. She knew he was going to drag her out of the emotional void she was trapped in. He may save her life. She was depending on him to bring her with him to be a part of this family that he felt so much for. She could see what he would mean to her even through the darkness. Lexy divulged, "Yes, I did."

Grey enquired, "Why?"

Lexy confessed, "You are my yellow door." She knew it sounded all kinds of crazy.

Instead of questioning the meaning of her words he did something unexpected. He held out his hands in the darkness and vowed, "I'll be your yellow door. Whatever you need me to be. I will be that for you."

She knew this was the truth. He had found a clear path into her wounded dark heart. He'd convinced her he wanted to be her friend. As he took her hands the darkness within her vanished and it was like someone turned on a joy receptor in her soul. He'd lured her out of her Dragon's layer and charmed her with the melody of his words. She would go anywhere he asked. *He'd calmed her Dragon with the touch of his hand granting her peace. Grey knew what it felt like to set his life aflame.* They left the safety of the cave and began searching for the rest of his Clan.

Lexy attempted to lead Grey out of the woods. If the birds were tweeting and crickets were chirping, Lexy knew predators were scarce. Even though, she'd eaten the occasional bird and random cricket. They never treated her like a predator. Their footsteps cracked twigs, but Lexy knew they couldn't take the path. *This wasn't the time for the obvious route. The easy road would be blocked, as in life. Off the beaten path was the way to go.* Lexy couldn't help but ask, "Where are they? I thought this Clan was supposed to look out for you?"

He answered, "They sent me in to the woods to find you, all by myself. They held the other Clans off long enough for me to have some uninterrupted time alone with you. The Ankh should be waiting for us, somewhere around the abandoned ranger station. Do you know where that is?"

Lexy forgave his admitted untruth. The Ankh had clearly trusted Grey enough to send him into the woods alone. The ranger station was still quite a long way from civilization. She asked the obvious question, "Why would they have sent you into the woods all by yourself to find me, knowing the other Clans were going to be there?"

"The Oracle told them to do it," Grey explained. "The usual excuse for most Clan actions. Our friendship is destined to happen. The Oracle said you'd come willingly with me, and only me."

Lexy knew that was the truth. She hadn't known why, but she'd known she could trust him. They heard shrieking, and the crickets were silenced. She'd caught someone else in one of her traps. *He would have been dinner.* Her stomach growled loud enough for Grey to give her a peculiar look.

Grey grinned and said, "Hungry?"

She answered, "Hungry enough to eat a Triad." He shot her a funny look. *He wasn't sure if she was being serious. She was a little serious.* She pictured him scolding, *take that Triad's leg out of your mouth.* She giggled and glanced at her walking partner. *He looked more than a little concerned. This was probably the first time anyone had brought up cannibalism in casual conversation. She imagined it wasn't a regular occurrence in a land where people weren't starving to death. Even another person was appetizing in her current state.*

He asked, "You're not going to eat me, are you?"

"Not anymore," Lexy teased.

Grey chuckled, "Good to know." He grabbed something out of his pocket and handed it to her.

He had a bar made from what appeared to be nuts and cereal. He'd been holding out on her. She ripped it in half and offered him half.

He refused it and assured, "It sounds like you need it more than I do." *She didn't worry about Grey attempting to poison her. It hadn't even crossed her mind. Her instinct was to trust him.*

He kidded, "I hope that granola bar bought me a little more time."

She couldn't help herself. Lexy casually replied, "I wouldn't have saved you if I were still planning to eat you." Grey didn't say anything back. He kept walking beside her, shaking his head, smiling. *He was a weird guy. He thought she was kidding about the whole cannibalism plot.* She trudged through the bushes, consciously keeping her footsteps in time with his. *She wasn't sure why she was doing it. Perhaps it was to fit in.* The awkward silence had gone on for too long. She stuck her tongue out at him. He knit his brow and returned the gesture. She felt peaceful. They hiked through the brush for another hour without even the hint of another Clan. *Had they just given up? She didn't think they would give up that easily. Maybe they were regrouping?* Through the tree, she pointed at the old abandoned ranger station. *Grey seemed relieved. She wasn't sure what her feelings were at this moment. She liked Grey. What if the others weren't like him? What if they were like Triad?* She stopped walking.

Grey questioned, "Are you okay?"

She felt panic shiver through her body and fought the urge to run away.

"I know the Oracle is right about us. You look bloody terrifying. You haven't bathed in months and you're absolutely covered in blood, but I feel safe with you. On my life, I'll never hurt you. I will be your yellow door. Whatever that means…I will always be your friend," he vowed as he extended his hand.

Lexy felt her urge to flee subside as she took his hand and they stepped out into the clearing together. She saw a group of people. There were four of them. A dark-haired boy and girl were gawking at her. Their perfection was intimidatingly unnatural. The other guy had blonde hair and a welcoming smile. There was another girl with long wavy chestnut brown hair. *She had the gentlest eyes she'd ever seen.* Lexy continued watching her as the group approached. She avoided eye contact with the two stunningly beautiful ones. *She wasn't sure what it was, but their exquisite beauty felt like a trap. She felt drawn to them. They were birds with distracting feathers. She had to practically force herself to look away.* She kept her eyes focused on the girl with the gentle doe eyes and resisted the urge to bolt as the four grew closer.

Grey squeezed her hand and introduced her, "These are my friends. Jenna is our Oracle. I told you about her. The blonde guy beside her is Orin. That's Frost and the other girl is Lily. Everyone, meet Lexy." They all smiled in greeting.

Lexy felt overwhelmed. Her days were filled with monotonous nothing but checking of traps during daylight hours. Her only acts of humanity were in passing time with the words of books, and the sight of a crackling fire at night. *Perhaps this was the reason she still had the ability to articulate a reasonably intelligent sounding sentence.*

The guy that had been introduced as Frost said, "We haven't seen the other Clans at all. Did you run into them?"

Grey replied, "You could say that. I'm not sure what happened. They made short work of me." He squeezed Lexy's hand again and added, "Lexy saved me from Triad. They had me. She found me and saved me."

With a knowing smile, Jenna said, "Thank you."

This day had been too much for her introverted self. The girl that hadn't spoken to another human being in two long years. She was like every other wild thing, afraid of being caged. She knew these people didn't want to hurt her. They wanted her trust. Her eyes darted to each of them and then back to Grey. He squeezed her hand and she realised he hadn't let it go. *There was a large part of her that wanted to remain a wild thing. This part wanted to snatch her hand away from Grey, and escape into the bushes to freedom, as an untameable creature.* The voice in her head told her if she kept holding his hand, she could still be saved from loneliness and her demons from the dark acts plaguing her.

Grey gave her hand a gentle squeeze sensing her distress and assured, "It's Okay, Lexy. They are the good guys."

She looked at her hand and examined the thin thread that held her to him. *How was she still holding it? Why had she come with him? She didn't know. This was something she'd never experienced before.*

Jenna said, "You just stay with Grey. Keep holding his hand. You can take your time to trust us. Take all you need. We do have to get out of here though."

Grey led her towards a truck parked around the side of the station. He held her hand and explained, "We have to put some miles between us and everyone else. The rest of the Clan is waiting for us. Please, trust me."

It was a truck. Of course it was a truck. Orin got into the driver's seat and started the engine. Grey motioned for her to get into the cab beside him. The others all got into the back. *This was a different situation. There were no dogs. No foul scented blanket. No thermos of hot chocolate.* She noticed the uncomfortable look on Orin's face as he crinkled his nose and rolled down a window. *She was the one with the foul scent this time.* She knew this and was thankful the driver hadn't voiced it. She heard a few hoots and laughter coming from the back of the truck. Lexy had a hard time resisting the urge to grin as the passengers bounced around the back while they drove down the severely degraded gravel road. They were being flung around like rag dolls, laughing. The sound of their laughter was putting her at ease. Orin and Grey were both howling as the others bounced around. Lexy couldn't help but notice that the beautiful Lily was about as joyful as a cat thrown into a bathtub. The vehicle stopped moving for a second before pulling out onto the highway. Everyone released a simultaneous sigh of relief. They drove until the scenery changed to prairie and the land became flat. She watched the sun begin to set far off in an endless field. Time for her was confusing. A day could disappear so quickly that she would feel like she had just watched the sunset only a few hours before. Her eyes became heavy and she tried to fight it. She watched the endless fields until they melted into a flat line and disintegrated into nothing.

Chapter 9

Feeding Dragons

Grey's voice whispered against her hair, "Wake up, Lexy."

She opened her eyes. Feeling exposed, she glanced down to see what she was wearing. All she was wearing was a tank top that didn't belong to her and some shorts. *She felt strange. She was clean.* Grey was sitting beside her on the bed.

He held up his hands to signify surrender and tried to explain, "We had to clean you up. Jenna and I did it. She did the bathing part. I thought you might not want me to see you naked. We borrowed clothes from the other girls, along with deodorant and perfume. You were out cold for a long time. The blood caked all over you just wasn't sanitary. If I put you into the bed all covered in it. The hotel staff would have been suspicious."

Lexy stood up, she felt her hair. It was shorter, much shorter. She gave Grey a peculiar look.

He explained, "I couldn't get a brush through it. I think it looks good though."

Lexy felt disorientated as her feet hit the hotel room carpet. She looked down and even her feet were clean. *Her toenails had been cut and polished. What in the hell? Her fingernails were trimmed and polished.* She stared at her hands and then felt something weird and constricting. *She was wearing a bra. She'd never worn one before. She didn't like it.*

Cautiously, Grey enquired, "I hope you're not upset."

Lexy asked, "Did you drug me?"

He replied, "No, I didn't drug you."

Somebody drugged her. She wouldn't have slept through all of this if she hadn't been drugged? It had been years since she'd seen her own reflection. She felt like a monster. Did she look like one? Looking into Grey's eyes, she asked, "What do I look like?" He escorted her to the bathroom. There was a sink and a mirror. It had been a long time since she'd seen running water. She twisted on the tap and smiled before she glanced up at her reflection. *She hadn't seen this girl in a long time.* She ran her fingertips across her face and smiled. She ran her tongue across squeaky clean teeth.

Grey explained, "That weird taste is baking soda. You have great teeth. I don't think you even need to go to the dentist. Maybe it's a Healer thing?"

Lexy bit her lip and looked at Grey in the mirror behind her. He was worried. He thought she was going to be angry. She should be. She was confused. He'd taken care of her. For that part, she was grateful, but some parts of his explanation didn't make sense. *How had she slept through the whole thing?* She flinched when people tried to touch her.

He grinned from where he was standing behind her in the mirror and said, "I'm sorry, I had to cut your hair. It'll grow back."

His smiling face disarmed her. The calming effect he had on her was undeniably strange. Lexy responded, "No, I like it like this." Grey smiled.

He probed, "Are you still hungry?"

A little confused, she replied, "You know I am, but I'm not as hungry as I was. Why is that? Did I eat something?"

"No, but do you remember Orin? He's the guy that was driving the truck," Grey explained. "He's a Healer, just like you are. He gave you some of his energy. I think that's why you slept for so long. Your mind must have been in desperate need of a good long comfortable sleep."

Why would I need to be healed? She looked into Grey's eyes. *She could almost hear his mind pleading with her to stop asking questions. His mannerisms alone showed that he was extremely nervous. She always noticed fear in an adversary. She did not want to think of Grey as an adversary, but his story didn't make any sense. She kept sleeping while they bathed her and brushed her teeth? While someone painted her nails?* Lexy absorbed her surroundings. His account hadn't made sense, but the fact that they'd cared for her made her chest ache. It was a foreign sensation. *Grey had taken care of her.* She had a vision of combing Charlotte's hair. The child she'd cared for. *Charlotte was gone.* She wondered if her body was still floating at the bottom of that well. then remembered that Charlotte's body didn't matter. She was happy and free from pain. Lexy had a moment in the light. She knew that there was a place of calm and beauty. She'd been there. Lexy began to wonder if returning to that place was possible, after everything she had done. *Could she still find that place of light? Could she free her heart from its painful shell? Could she ever allow herself to care for someone as much as she had cared for the child, she'd lost? That remained to be seen. She knew one thing for sure. She knew that she could care for this boy named Grey. She knew he cared for her.* He'd omitted part of the story. He'd lied by omission, and that was still a form of deception. Grey passed her some thongs to slip on her bare feet. He opened the hotel door into another world. Heat rushed in. *Where were they?*

Grey announced, "The others are waiting for us downstairs in the restaurant."

Lexy peered out of the door. The hotel was surrounded by a sandy parking lot. The grains were picked up in the slightest touch of a breeze. It was a magical contrast to the stifling heat. She descended the stairs after Grey. *They appeared to be in the middle of nowhere.* There was nothing as far as she could see in every direction. Absolutely nothing but a vast wasteland of sand. She'd only ever read about the desert. She had seen it in magazines when she was younger. *How did they get here? She must have been asleep for a long time.* The sun was a sweltering looming giant. *They were far from her cabin in the woods.* She followed Grey down the cement sidewalk to the restaurant. The door jingled as they entered. The scent of delicious food accosted her senses. The hum of voices was all around her, she felt the urge to panic again. Sensing her apprehension, Grey took her hand and led her to a table full of wide-eyed Ankh. *Why did she still hold his hand with this feeling of blind trust even after he had proved himself untrustworthy?* She accompanied Grey towards two empty seats beside Jenna. They sat down. Feeling out of her element, Lexy didn't make eye contact with any of the curious eyes. She just stared at the empty place setting in front of her. She hadn't used cutlery since she was eleven years old. She would remember what to do.

A male voice addressed her from across the table, "My name's Markus. I'm in charge of the Clan. I'm also the one that marked both of your hands. I have been looking forward to meeting you both. Lexy and Arrianna, welcome to Ankh."

Lexy hadn't noticed anything. *Marked her hand?* She glanced down at her hand and saw the mark of Ankh on her palm. *When had he done that? Something fishy was going on here.* She looked over at the other girl Markus had spoken too. She appeared to be equally confused. She was also staring at her hand.

The girl that had been referred to as Arrianna questioned, "I'm not Trinity anymore?"

"No, you're Ankh now," Markus responded.

Nervously, Arrianna stammered, "When did you do this to me?"

The waitress arrived at the table. Markus changed the topic, "Order anything on the menu. Anything you want."

Lexy felt her inner predator whisper, *sit down, shut up and pay attention. You are hungry, eat first, ask questions later.* She opened it up and looked at the pictures. *Everything looked good.* She glanced up at the girl named Arrianna. She was staring at her menu. Her inner turmoil, clearly visible.

Grey greeted her, "It's a pleasure to meet you Arrianna." He reached over to shake her hand.

Arrianna didn't play along. She left Grey hanging with his hand in her direction. The other new girl remained motionless, silent. She felt a kinship with the girl who was trying to be strong. She didn't know what to do with the urge to bond with her. Everyone else started to order. She listened to what they were having. She liked the sound of Frost's order. It was enormous and he ordered a beer with it. When the waitress asked her what she wanted. Lexy pointed at Frost and quietly said, "What he's having." He'd ordered the biggest grossest cheeseburger on the menu with everything but the kitchen sink on it with a side of fries, onion rings and a beer.

"You might get sick," Grey cautioned.

Lexy glanced at Frost. He assured, "I have a feeling she'll be fine."

He nodded his belief in her ability to consume the same gross amount of food. Lexy smiled at Frost and glanced around the table. *It felt like everyone was staring at her again. Why was everyone staring at her? Oh...Yes. She knew why. She didn't look like the missing link anymore.* She quietly took in the faces of the people she was sitting with. Lexy glanced down at her hand again. Her mind whispered, *leave it alone.* She was too hungry to leave the table. Lexy suspected, she'd be pissed when someone told her the story of how she'd acquired the mark on the palm of her hand. The waitress strolled over to the table, bringing Frost's meal first. He motioned for her to serve Lexy instead. The waitress placed the enormous plate of food in front of her. Lexy just stared at it. *Nobody else had been served. She didn't want everyone to be watching her. This made her uncomfortable. She felt like she was a wild animal sitting at a table pretending to be civilized. She was a wild thing. She knew this about herself.* She looked around the table slowly. *Were there other wild things sitting at this table, attempting to be civilized? It had only been days since she'd seriously contemplated eating a person. Now, she was worried that she might not remember how to use cutlery. Was she even supposed to use cutlery for anything she had ordered?* She glanced up and felt Frost's eyes on her. He winked and she had a feeling he knew what she was thinking about. He picked up his burger and took an enormous bite. The sauce dripped down his chin and Lexy smiled. *It didn't matter how messy you were when you ate. This was a relief.* She took a bite of her own burger and her taste buds began to sing. *Real food, this was real food.* She finished off the entire burger along with the mountain of fries. She then ate the onion rings so fast that everyone else was not even halfway through a meal, half the size of hers. *She was still hungry.* Frost winked and handed her his onion rings. Lexy looked up at him and smiled. She ate all of them. He was grinning at her across the table. Frost ordered two giant chocolate milkshakes from the waitress. When she came back, he passed one to her. She took a trial sip. *It was delicious and cold.* She drank it too quickly. *Her brain felt like it was about to split in two. What was this?* Arrianna reached over Grey and touched her arm. Lexy stiffened for a second, until she realised the girl was trying to help her pain, not stop her from eating.

Arrianna explained, "That was brain freeze. You get it when you drink cold things too quickly."

Lexy looked at Arrianna. Her mind urged, *Smile at her. She is in the same situation as you. She just spoke to you. You have to say something back.* With her mouth full, Lexy valiantly forced a smile and mumbled, "Thank you." *They made her say thank you on the dark farm for everything.* Her mind drifted back to the vile place, adrenaline kicked her in the gut, rather effectively stopping the thoughts from creeping in. Her inner Dragon began to claw its way out from under the surface of her skin. Lexy massaged her arm and fought the urge to bolt from the restaurant. *There were too many people in the room. She was suffocating. She couldn't breathe.* Grey casually touched her shoulder to talk to her. She shifted in her chair. *People had to warn her before they just reached out and touched her. Dragons tend to bite unwanted fingers right off.*

Grey whispered, "Are you okay? Are you starting to feel nauseous? I'd be in the bathroom heaving over the toilet if I ate what you ate."

Grey could breathe fire, but he seemed far too kind to be a Dragon. He wasn't capable of understanding that what she needed could not be quenched by food or kindness. The fury was always there. It laced the blood that flowed through her veins with venom until it began to flow out of her pores and explode from the surface of her skin. She could only stop her mind from thinking about the things that poisoned her for a little while. She shut her eyes and took a deep breath. In and out, in and then out. She attempted to make her inner Dragon fall asleep. Under her breath Lexy said, "I'm fine."

Chapter 10

Bad Ass Destinies

One of her hands was resting on the table. She took note as Jenna's inched closer and didn't jump as Jenna placed her hand on top of hers.

Jenna whispered, "Learn to love the Dragon, I can teach you how to control it."

Lexy didn't need to look into her eyes for she felt the truth in her words. Her Dragon disappeared with only a touch from the Oracle's hand.

The moment was broken when Frost leaned across the table and reminded, "You forgot to drink your beer."

Lexy picked it up, looked at the cap and tried to put it in her mouth to bite it off.

Grey's eyes widened, he stammered, "No, no. Don't do that Lexy. I'll open it for you."

Uncomfortable, Lexy looked around the table. *She'd put it in her mouth without thinking. It was an uncivilized thing to do.* She'd been cleaned up and was doing her best to act tamed but she could tell some of them still saw her as the wild thing she'd become while left to her own devices.

Grey opened it and sweetly whispered, "I just didn't want you to chip your teeth."

Lexy sniffed it, crinkled her nose and looked at Frost for guidance. He was grinning at her. She took a sip and almost spat it out. *This stuff was horrible.* Frost had already ordered another one. *It must be a normal drink. He seemed to like it.*

Smiling, Grey whispered, "If you don't' like something, pinch your nose when you drink it and it won't taste as bad.

People will see that you don't like it, but you'll realise why other people do, once you drink the first one."

Lexy didn't plug her nose as she downed the whole bottle. *It was way better than the whisky Grey had her sample a few days back. She had a hunch that this beer was sort of like whisky.* She sat there listening to the animated conversations going on around her. Enjoying being a fly on the wall, she began to unwind. Another beer was placed in front of her. She picked it up and sipped it slowly, listening to the chatter. *Once she'd finished the fourth beer, she was in a far better state of mind.*

Markus chose that moment to explain, "I was the one who branded you Ankh. We were told to sedate Lexy before trying to touch her. I broke your necks to seal the deal, while you were asleep. Grey and Jenna cleaned you up. Orin healed you. Arrianna, we claimed you the same way, out of convenience. I'm sorry to be this blunt. We know you would have listened to logic but Lexy wouldn't have given us a chance to explain. I know you've been through this before when you were claimed by Trinity. It won't be the same here. We're not coworkers. You're not just Healers to us. You aren't a commodity to be gained. That mark on your hand makes you part of our family. We are different. We're a family in this Clan."

He'd said the magic words. They were a family. Lexy did not react. Frost ordered her another beer. *She was part of their family. She had always wanted to be part of a family. Jenna had told her she would teach her how to control her Dragon.* Her demeanour changed. *They had two Healers already. She would not have to hide her Dragon with the Ankh. Markus wanted the Dragon to be a part of his family. Jenna wanted her to embrace her inner Dragon. She wanted her to learn to love it.*

Visibly upset, Arrianna declared, "I'm not sure how to respond to that logic. You broke my neck while I was asleep? This was necessary? Thorne asked me if I wanted to become Trinity. I was given a choice."

With a patient smile Markus countered, "In a perfect situation that is exactly how it's done. Mark my words.

Thorne, would have snapped your neck and brought you with him no matter what your answer had been."

"Maybe, I guess I will never know," Arrianna muttered.

Lexy found herself fascinated by Arianna's open mouth policy. *She was bolder than she'd first appeared to be.* She drank her beer quietly and watched the unfiltered scenario unfold.

Grey assured, "I have only been with the Ankh for a few months. Markus is telling the truth. They are a family. We have duties, but we also have fun."

Glaring at Grey, Arrianna probed, "So, you think watching whole families being slaughtered without warning anyone is fun?"

This girl was determined to pick a fight with someone.

"That's not all we do," Grey sighed.

"Oh, you're right, if they survive the blood bath, they get the opportunity to be taken away from everything they know, under the guise of us offering them protection. Maybe they'll even be drugged and have their necks snapped?" Arrianna provoked. She raised her glass, looked at Markus and mock saluted, "Lucky us."

Markus chuckled, "That is only part of our duties, a small part. You are seriously determined to hate me, aren't you? Were you really that attached to Trinity? Tell you what; I'll give you back to them in two months if you don't like it with us."

Arrianna called his bluff, "I know you're lying to me. You already told me the choice scenario was bullshit."

Ankh's leader stood up, placed his hand with the symbol of Ankh on his heart and swore he'd bring her back in two months if she didn't want to stay. The table full of Ankh looked confused. Markus baited, "Satisfied?"

Arrianna provoked, "Why do I have a feeling you rarely leave anyone satisfied?"

There were a few snickers. *Why were they laughing?*

Biting his tongue, Markus glared at the feisty ex-Trinity. He glanced around the table; the giggles ceased.

The others respected Markus but Arrianna didn't find him the least bit intimidating. Markus sounded like a leader, but he didn't have the appearance of one. She'd seen what her options were. She'd spent time with Tiberius. She was prepared to give this a chance. She studied Grey's expression. *He looked mortified by the other new girl's behaviour. She liked this Arrianna. She was a little bit of a badass.*

Looking directly at her, Markus enquired, "Do you have any smart assed comments you'd like to add?"

No, she was fine. Lexy casually asked, "Who do you want me to kill?" Half of the table choked on their lunch. Frost was giggling.

Grinning, Markus stated, "You don't have to kill anyone today."

She was meant to be a weapon. She wasn't upset by this revelation. She knew who she was inside. Markus expected her to be angry. They'd killed her in her sleep for safety reasons. It was good to know their leader wasn't a stupid man. They had to take her by surprise. Her blood pressure began to rise. *She wasn't upset. Why was she feeling like this?* Her heart was pounding. Her skin shivered goosebumps across her flesh. *What was this?* It clicked and she knew what was happening. *Arianna's anger was affecting her. The Dragon wasn't asleep anymore. Arianna's insolence and bitterness towards Markus had awoken the beast. She wasn't going to be able to hold it in. She had to get away from the table.* Lexy stood up and looked at Markus in a panicked state. Then it happened, the flickering of the emotional switch in her brain. Right before the desensitizing filter slid into place, it always felt like she was standing outside of herself watching. She was about to lose the ability for rational thought. *It always made her feel uneasy before the numbness of nothing. She had to get out of the restaurant. She needed to leave. Tick...tick...tick,* she could hear the ticking of the grenade inside of her. *She was almost ready to explode.* Lexy coldly stated, "You were right to kill me while I was asleep. I would have killed every one of you, without flinching. I wouldn't have been able to stop myself." Grey grabbed her arm to calm her. *She was going to have to explain her adverse reaction to physical contact before she cleaned his clock.* Glaring at Grey, she icily disclosed, "Even you." Without bothering to excuse herself, she left the table. *Just five more seconds. She would be away from the Clan.* Lexy escaped the diner in search of fresh air and all she found was steamy, dry hot air. This made her livid. She bolted out into the wide-open span of desert, sprinting until she came across a large cactus with sharp spikes. She impaled both of her hands on the needles. The pain calmed her down. She yanked them off, healing almost immediately. Lexy stood in the sweltering heat as droplets of perspiration trickled down her forehead. She heard a faint rattling sound. Beside her thong adorned feet was a rattlesnake. She noticed it a moment too late, it sunk its fangs into the meaty flesh of her calf. She didn't even flinch. She bent down, grabbed it by the rattle and shrieked. In her unravelled state, she repeatedly whipped the reptile against the prickly cactus. She swung until the snake was in shreds. She was holding only the end. There was nothing left but chewed up snake meat. She heard someone clear their throat. She whirled around. *It was Grey, Arrianna and Jenna.*

Arrianna ribbed, "Remind me to never make you angry."

Wild-eyed, Lexy stood frozen in place, holding the snake carcass.

Jenna offered up a plan, "If you kill one of us and heal us, you will calm down. Your gift is too powerful. In the beginning, our gifts are like addictions. We must learn to control them. Grey and Arrianna are the other parts to your whole. You three will be tested together. Grey, you are fortunate. Healers always go into the Testing Enlightened. Arrianna and Lexy will be at full force, when you're at your most vulnerable. It is Lexy that will be your trio's champion. It will be her ability to turn off her emotions that will save you all. Arrianna, your emotions are too volatile. It's not your fault. You wear your heart on your sleeve because of your Empath ability. The Empath gift will help you three know what people's true intentions are. The Testing will be particularly emotionally taxing for Arrianna. Arrianna, you may think you were better off with Trinity. I'm an Oracle. I know why you're upset. He wasn't even one of your potential soulmates. You didn't love him."

Arrianna rebutted, "I would have."

Jenna casually corrected, "He would have been nothing but a waste of your time. You are supposed to be right here, right now. You three have a destiny. You develop something incredible. Our Lexy has an inner Dragon. She's your trio's brute strength. Arrianna, your internal compass will guide the way. Grey is the tether. The tether is an essential role. Grey's a Firestarter. He hasn't been Enlightened and already has this gift. His ability to put the fire out is going to be the gift that means the most. Grey, you're the only one that can even them out, the emotional and the emotionless. Right now, Lexy's Dragon needs to be tamed. You three must decide when to tame it, and when to set it free. She must discharge energy in order to tame it. She needs to heal someone…Watch this."

Jenna flinched as she impaled her own hand on the needles of the cactus. She offered her wounded hand to Lexy.

As Lexy her Jenna, she felt the rage disappear. She exhaled and admitted, "That helped."

Jenna announced, "Follow me. I have something to show you." She began to walk into the desert and the trio followed, without question.

Chapter 11

Tales Of Ankh

They continued to walk into the desert together with no idea where they were going. They followed Jenna blindly into the searing heat of the afternoon sun until Grey began to stagger. He dropped to his knees in the sand. A dry powdery mist rose around him. Lexy held out her hand. He looked at her and hesitantly took it. She helped Grey to his feet, healing him. He gave her a smile of gratitude.

Grey, finally steady on his feet, continued to walk for a few minutes before asking the question they all wanted to know, "Where are we going?" Jenna didn't answer she simply continued to walk in the sweltering desert sun.

Arrianna teased, "Do you even know where we're going?"

Jenna winked and laughed, "Sometimes the most incredible journeys start by simply putting one foot in front of the other and walking in the direction that you want to go."

Lexy was tired enough to not feel psychotically volatile about their unplanned excursion into the middle of nowhere. *She would be fine if Grey dropped from exhaustion every half an hour.* They approached a single rock in the middle of the desert. There was a buzzard sitting on it. *He was obviously waiting for the stupid people wandering alone in the desert to die.*

Staggering as they approached the stone, Grey leaned up against it to balance and stammered, "How am I supposed to keep up with these two?"

Jenna laughed and disclosed, "You don't have to keep up. I have it on good authority that neither one of these girls will ever venture to leave you behind."

In a delirious state, he sighed, "I think Arrianna hates us, and according to you Lexy is a Dragon."

He turned to face Lexy and mumbled, "Are you going to turn green and scaly? Don't Dragons eat people?"

Jenna grinned and assured, "Neither of these girls are going to eat you... anymore."

Grey slurred, "Well, isn't that comforting."

Lexy smiled as Grey dropped into the sand again.

This time Arrianna stepped in and asked, "Can I help him this time?"

Lexy, feeling reasonably even keeled, nodded at her and replied, "Go for it."

Arrianna knelt beside Grey. She shook her head and healed him. He opened his eyes with his head still on Arianna's lap.

He teased, "Awe... I'm touched. You don't hate me."

Arrianna tossed Grey off her lap into the sand. She got up and brushed herself off. Lexy was able to read between the lines. It was as though she was able to understand the secret language that existed between these two people. Arrianna didn't want to like Grey, but she did.

Jenna stated, "I'm about to show you something that will change your perception of everything." She placed her fingers underneath the edge of the stone. The sand slid away to reveal stairs that descended into the desert floor.

Arrianna whispered, "This is cool. I've never seen one of these."

"Azariah has always taken good care of us. Follow me, it will all be much easier to explain once we're inside," their Clan's Oracle explained.

They descended into the darkness and it was much cooler. It was a comfortable temperature once they had climbed down the flight of stairs. Lexy knew she was meant to be here with the Ankh. Without a doubt she had followed

Jenna. It was too dark to see where they had ended up at the bottom of the staircase.

Jenna asked, "Grey, can you light the torches as we get to them? The others will be meeting us here soon."

They made their way down the long dimly lit stone and clay corridor. They came to a large open space with cushions on the floor and carvings on the walls. The carving on the wall was of three men and one girl.

Jenna began to tell a story, "A thousand years ago breeding with mortals became illegal under immortal law. The premise being that too many halfblooded immortals were being created through the indiscretions of the gods. The first large scale Correction happened in Rome. I was a part of that Correction. Seventeen children were hidden in a crypt by one of their parents under instructions from Azariah. Azariah was one of the Guardians that did not agree with what the immortals were planning to do."

Jenna pointed at the wall and said, "These carvings over here tell another tale. This is the story of The Brothers of Prophecy. Three partially immortal brothers were in love with the same girl. The youngest brother had been her best friend all her life. They were the same age. They thought they were in love. He would have been the logical choice to marry, but her father decided she should marry the oldest brother. He was kind and dependable. The youngest one was a bit of a loose cannon. The middle brother had been taken away to train as a soldier when he was only nine but he came back to attend his oldest brother's wedding. The second he saw her, it was a done deal for both. They tried to run away together but lost each other during the mayhem of the first large scale Correction. She ended up with the other two brothers and her father. The middle brother, ended up being the one to find the seventeen children, saved by Azariah that day. We were hidden in a crypt. The middle brother swore that he would take care of us and the first Clan of Ankh was created. We would then be taken to the in-between. The girl would be injured while on the run with her father and his brothers. She'd end up in the in-between with us. We would have a chance to grow up protected. We'd be taught to fight. For nearly one hundred years, we'd live there untouched and unbothered by the outside world. Until one day, she disappeared. She'd been drawn back to the land of the living and deposited into her semi mortal shell. We would all go back with him to try to find her. For almost a hundred years the girl's father and Frost's two brothers had been waiting for her to rise.

She'd accidentally used Frost's name. He'd given her his food. She didn't see him as the fatherly type.

Jenna winked at her and then began to speak again, "The girl, wounded during their escape from Rome, had been hovering somewhere between life and death. Her mortal shell preserved in a tomb. Just in case you haven't figured it out yet the other two brothers were named Tiberius and Thorne. The three of them, along with the injured girl had made it through the crypt to another continent. They settled in Mesoamerica. Each brother believed that when she awoke, it would be him that she'd chose. The other group had also been gathering immortal children. Travelling back and forth to save as many halfblooded immortals as they could. They had a rather large settlement by the time she arose. They hadn't known she'd been with Frost the whole time. The group hadn't been granted passage to the in-between, for they had not been saved by Azariah. They had saved themselves. By the time Frost was allowed to come back with the full-grown children of Ankh to find her, it had been years. She'd believed she would never see him again. They could not hide their involvement, of course, for they had been together for a hundred years. Tiberius and Thorne, enraged at Frost's betrayal, parted ways. Tiberius and Thorne split off from Ankh. Before Tiberius left, he erased the girl's memory and swore his allegiance to the dark Guardian Seth. Together, they created Clan Triad. Infamous for his pranks, Seth visited the girl and implanted thoughts in her mind. She would always feel like Frost wasn't the right one. Their connection would always be missing something. They'd be drawn together as though they were magnets, but she'd never be able to love him as she once had. Seth released a spiritual affliction within her and made Frost the only cure. Frost would be bound out of duty and love to never leave her side. Yet, he would never be able to be with her. Each time this ailment occurred, they'd have to erase her memory again. Her own father had her spelled to make sure that no matter how obvious it appeared to everyone else, she would never be able to see the truth. She could never know who she really was. Seth, the constant prankster, would add things to the pile every time Triad got their hands on her. The games they'd played with fate backfired on Tiberius. She couldn't remember what they meant to each other as children either. Karma is, in fact a bitch."

Jenna paused to make sure everyone was still following along. They'd been hanging on every syllable. It was like a fairy tale. There was good and evil. There was even a princess.

She continued to speak, "At one point, Tiberius captured her and Triad had her for several years. She began to fall in love with him again, in the absence of Frost. Tiberius wasn't enough for her either. Every spell or curse of dark purpose has a price to pay. Tiberius couldn't have Seth take her affliction away without it causing her memory to return. He kept her, even though she wouldn't be able to love him properly in return. When her curse surfaced, he was forced to return her to Ankh. Tiberius loved her enough to let her go; knowing Frost was the only cure to what ailed her."

Arrianna remarked, "I've heard a bit of this story, through the grapevine, while in Trinity. Thorne's not big on conversation from what I've seen. He seemed like a pretty decent guy though."

Jenna replied, "He is, I have nothing bad to say about Thorne. Sure, we're on opposite sides, but it's only because we must be. When Thorne became the head of the third

Clan, Trinity. He didn't stay involved in the whole Brothers of Prophecy feud. He just moved on with his life. Thorne's the ultimate serial monogamist. Frost and Tiberius opted for a different route and became playboys of epic proportions. The girl they moved heaven and earth for became the Bermuda triangle of relationships. It's a long story but stay in Ankh long enough and you'll figure it out."

Grey chuckled, "Frost appears to be quite content with his playboy of Ankh status.

Arrianna sighed, "Frost is undeniable man candy."

Jenna chuckled, "That he is."

Grey groaned, "Seriously girls are we really going there...Man candy? Everyone knows the girl you keep mentioning is Lilarah. Markus is her father, and he took over for Frost as the head of the Clan for some reason."

Jenna replied, "If you were paying proper attention to the story. You'd understand why we omit her name while telling it."

Grey said, "I've personally heard that story fifty times."

Arrianna asked, "You obviously like Thorne. If he doesn't care about the Lily thing, why is Ankh still fighting with Trinity? A thousand years is a long time to carry on having a pissing contest over some girl."

"I wish it was up to us, but it's not. There is a Guardian for each Clan. We follow orders and do what we're told. We have jobs to do. We help maintain the spiritual order of things."

Arrianna reached up to touch one of the carvings on the wall, and Jenna snapped, "Don't touch that." She sheepishly stepped away from the wall.

Lexy found herself fighting the urge to touch the wall. She gave Grey a funny look. He was staring at it too. She had a feeling he was fighting the same strange urge.

Jenna started talking again, "For many years Trinity was the largest Clan. When they began the Testing, Trinity lost over half of their Clan. They were too different, there was too many of them. The group couldn't emotionally attach.

The Third tiers started putting us through the Testing to thin out our population. Well, that's what we thought the Testing was for."

Lexy barely heard what she was saying. The instinct telling her to touch the carving on the wall, was so strong, it was all she could think of. Grey's hand raised to the wall and Jenna smacked it, stunning him out of his trance.

Jenna said, "I said, don't touch the damn wall. You'll regret it. You never touch anything engraved on the wall of an Ankh crypt."

Grey was still rubbing his hand. He was visibly offended that he'd been slapped like a mischievous child. He scowled and said, "Was that really necessary?"

Jenna gave him a flirtatious smile and said, "Absolutely." Lexy kept her lips pressed together, to stifle the smile that threatened to break free.

Jenna continued to speak, "We are not here to mess around. We're here for what's behind that wall at the end of the corridor."

Arrianna became visibly excited. Her lips parted and she gasped, "Are we going to the in-between?"

A voice piped in from behind her, "Where else would we be going?"

Chapter 12

Confined Spaces

Lexy spun around to the sound of Frost's voice. *There he was in all his man candy glory.* A Frost that Lexy now felt a tiny flicker of empathy for. She'd lost someone too. She didn't understand what it felt like to be in love. She couldn't even fathom it. Lily stood beside Frost. She smiled at him, completely oblivious to their journey together. Orin snuck up behind Jenna and hugged her from behind. He kissed her cheek and she started to laugh. Lexy found herself smiling. She wondered what it would feel like to be loved like that. Her heart twitched. She shoved the emotions, born of curiosity, deep down where they couldn't endeavour to sneak up on her again. She couldn't allow her mind to wonder about feelings that she'd never risk having. She felt someone's presence at her side. She knew exactly who it was before she ventured to sneak a peek.

It was Grey. He leaned over and whispered, "Have you ever been in love?"

Did he think she'd lost herself in the wilderness because of a love gone wrong? She thought about it again, realizing that perhaps she'd hidden herself away because a pack of wild dogs loved her more than any human being ever had. She'd felt oneness with them, until they'd attempted to eat her.

Lexy gave him a matter of fact reply, "Nobody has ever loved me." She felt Grey's stare but didn't turn around. She'd spoken of feelings. She couldn't even fathom a situation where vocalizing this wouldn't feel like she was speaking a foreign language.

She heard Grey's voice say, "I will be the person that loves you back."

She heard Arianna say, "I will too."

Lexy turned in the direction of their voices, both touched and afraid of what they'd said to her. They were both staring at her with glistening eyes.

Lexy stared into Arrianna's eyes and stated, "You're leaving us in two months."

Arrianna met her unwavering gaze and replied, "No... I'm not leaving anymore."

Lily squeezed Arrianna's shoulder and said, "I hate to interrupt this love fest, but it's time to go home."

Lexy wandered behind the group as they disappeared one by one through the solid wall at the end of the hall. She turned around to look at Arrianna when it was her turn to walk through.

Arrianna said, "Just do it. Don't think about it. That is the rule of thumb in the Clans."

Lexy held her breathe as she walked through the wall. She entered a room with giant stone Egyptian looking tombs. *What in the hell is this place?* She walked towards one and raised her hand to trace the Ankh symbol that was carved artistically into the lid.

Lily said, "I wouldn't do that if I were you."

Lexy yanked her hand away.

Orin chuckled, "Yes, do try to avoid touching anything with a symbol on it." Orin placed his hand on one of the tombs and they all ground with the sound of stone on stone as they slowly opened. They were empty. *Well, that wasn't very exciting.* She stood there stupefied as the others piled into the tombs. Jenna climbed in one with Grey and motioned for her to join them.

Lexy bluntly stated, "I'm not getting in that." She'd been kept in a stall for 5 years. She was not willingly getting into a confined space. She couldn't do it. *What if this was a trap?*

Jenna held out her hand and explained, "We travel in these to the in-between. You will only be inside of it for five minutes tops. I promise you'll experience more freedom there then you've ever felt before in your entire life."

Lexy watched Arrianna climb in a tomb with Frost and Lily. She stared at the tomb and tried to get in but her mind would not allow her body to do it.

Orin walked over to her and said, "I'm in control of operating them, but on the inside of the lid is a handprint. It's a failsafe switch. You can get out at any time."

Jenna repeated something she'd said earlier, "All great journeys start with a single step in the direction that you want to go."

Lexy closed her eyes and climbed into the confined tomb beside Grey and Jenna. Grey began to stroke her arm gently. She fought the urge to smack or pull away from him. She couldn't pull away. There was nowhere for her to go. She would be trapped. *Baby steps, she told herself. Just take baby steps.* The lid began to close and she squeezed her eyes shut. She wasn't afraid of many things but found enclosed spaces unsettling.

Grey whispered from behind her, "Just breathe."

Jenna said, "Have you ever been on a carnival ride?"

Grey said, "I've done this before."

Jenna laughed, "I'm not talking to you. I know you have. I'm talking to Lexy."

Lexy thought, *I was held captive in a barn stall for five years by sickos. No, there were no Carnival rides in my frigging stall.*

Lexy said aloud, "I've never been."

Jenna sighed, "Oh... Shit."

Grey chuckled, "You can do better than, Oh Shit. Oh Shit, does not inspire confidence."

Jenna said, "Either you will really like this, or you will really hate this part."

Suddenly, a blinding white light began to strobe and the tomb jolted to one side. Lexy's stomach lurched. *What in the hell was that?* She felt panicked. Lexy couldn't see the handprint. There was no way to open her eyes as the blinding light began to strobe. She felt Grey wrap his arm around her; she clutched Grey's arm to her chest.

He chuckled, "I personally can't get enough of this ride." The whole tomb lurched to one side, then there was the stomach-churning sensation of being shot up into the sky. Grey began to hoot with excitement at the top of his lungs. She heard Frost join in. The tomb began to spin upwards and then it felt like it was slowing down. She only had a moment to breathe before the tomb began its rapid descent. They were spinning so fast. As the screaming tomb full of Ankh rapidly descended into lord knows where, she was either going to spew vomit on everyone or pass out. They were spinning to fast. They were all stuck to the roof of the tomb. There were a few jolting movements. She squealed and clung onto Grey's arm. He was laughing hysterically. There was a blinding flash. She felt the sensation of moisture and wind on her skin. Lexy opened her eyes. *Oh Shit.* They were all free falling through the clouds with no tomb at all.

She heard Jenna's voice call out, "Grey, you know the drill."

Arrianna sped past them falling at twice the speed the others were falling at. She shrieked, "They don't do this in Trinity. What in the hell is this shit!" Frost raised both hands above his head and caught up to Arrianna. Through the whipping sound of the wind Lexy could heard Frost yelling at Arrianna, "You have to stop yourself."

Lily hollered at Grey again, "You know what to do Grey. We've worked on this."

Grey began to freak out, "You assholes know I can't bloody stop myself!" He began to flail, it sped up his descent into the unknown.

Lily's voice called out in the whirling sound of air, "Push away from the ground. You can do it!"

Lexy said nothing. She'd turned off her emotions. She was able to take the insanity in without becoming lost in it. She knew what Lily meant when she told Grey to push away from the ground. She'd moved things before, only small things. She couldn't see the ground, she was descending through damp clouds. Once she passed through the clouds, she grinned at the rapidly approaching desert floor. *They must have drugged her again. This wasn't really happening.* She heard the pitch of both Grey and Arianna's shrieks mere seconds before they hit the desert floor. A cloud of sand exploded around them. *It was real...Shit.* Lexy was ten seconds from making her own crater in the desert when she pushed away with both hands, and screamed with such fury, that it slowed down her descent. She hovered in place for a moment, then relaxed, landing on her feet in the warmth of the sand, with legs as wobbly as a baby fawn, she toppled over and still created a tiny cloud of the fine grains around her. Lexy sat there for a second, while she brushed herself off. She was trying to decide which one of these immortal assholes was going to get a punch in the head for this. She hadn't had time to decide which one she was going to blame, when she heard shrieking above her. *Who was falling now? What in the hell?*

Jenna instructed, "I'd move."

At the last second, Lexy rolled out of the way. Arrianna managed to stop herself from falling out of fear of landing on her. She dropped from her hovering position, to the sand, making a puff of grains in the air as she landed on her butt. Frost started laughing. Lexy hissed, "Is something funny?" His chuckles were silenced by her venomous response. She was actively reigning in the need to kick his ass when she heard Grey hollering. *He wasn't going to be able to stop himself.* He hit the ground, about fifty feet away and sand blasted into the air. She glared at Frost. He covered his mouth to stifle his laughter. In a matter of seconds, she heard Grey screaming again. *What in the hell? You must keep falling until you figure out how to stop.* Lexy stood up, walked over and stood directly under him. She placed her hands above her head and made an attempt to push him up. His descent slowed. Grey landed almost gracefully on his feet in the sand, wobbled and tipped over.

Frost chuckled, "That's a first. I can honestly say nobody has ever stopped someone else before."

Arrianna was still sitting in the sand where she'd landed, she was pissed. She grumbled, "In Trinity they give you five minutes to experience the joy of being here before they start messing with your head."

Grey stammered, "Usually, we land feet first here too. We do that crap later. What in the hell was that for?"

Jenna sighed, "Orin probably saw a spider and took his hand off of the tombs."

Lexy caught the humor in Jenna's sarcastic comment. Even though her heart was still pounding in her chest, and the adrenaline still rippled underneath her skin. She stood there and stared at the great wide-open span of the desert. Above her the sky began to swirl with pastels like a water colour painting. *This place was unreal.* She knelt in the sand and ran the grains through her hands. *She was home.* It was the softest most luxurious feeling sand that had ever graced the tips of her fingers.

Arrianna knelt in the sand beside her and said, "If this stuff was in my sandbox as a child. I would have never gone inside."

Grey asked her, "Did you have a sandbox? I didn't have a sandbox."

Lexy realised that her history and how she had come to be a wild thing was a riddle that Grey needed to solve. He wasn't going to stop asking her random things until he pieced together her past. Feeling a sudden burst of hostility, she got up and walked away from the group. She remembered Jenna's words. She needed to use her ability. The more she used it, the more she needed to. Her arms were still vibrating from stopping Grey's descent. She was rather impressed she stopped him. She sensed Grey behind her. Arrianna was also coming. She knew this without looking back. Her heart twitched again. *She wanted them to be there.* They walked behind her in silence. The scenery shifted and they were strolling through the grass together. Lexy turned to see if everyone else was still there. Jenna was with them, but everyone else had vanished. *Where had they all gone?*

Jenna explained, "Everyone has somewhere they like to go while they're here, and none of them need to be here for this next part."

Grey asked, "Don't you have a place you want to go?"

"Not particularly," Jenna countered. "This is more important. I need to keep an eye on you three."

Grey flirted, "What trouble can I possibly find while standing in an enormous field of grass?"

"If anyone can find trouble Grey, I have the feeling it would be you," Jenna taunted.

He chuckled, "You have me there."

Lexy knelt in the grass and leaned to smell it. Grey cleared his throat. She looked up. The three were standing above her wondering what in the hell she was up to. *Mental note...People don't smell grass.* She scrambled to her feet and stated, "It smells like nobody else is around."

He knit his brow and said, "Good to know?"

Arrianna held out her hand as a symbolic lifeline, meant to bring her back into a place of humanity. Lexy accepted it. Grey took her other one. She'd never walked hand in hand with two people. She couldn't explain why, but it felt right.

Chapter 13

Sweet Sleeping

They strolled together hand in hand. *She allowed this, fighting against the instinct to pull away, desiring strength above anything else. She strived to become an insurmountable mountain.* Arrianna warmly squeezed her hand. *She felt confused. She'd built this wall around her heart for a reason.* With each squeeze, her heart twitched and warmed. *With every smile of friendship, she felt something. A touch of fear. They'd see through her inability to be like them and leave her. These two people made her feel vulnerable.* They roamed the expansive meadow until the scenery flashed again. Anticipating the sensation of warm sand between her toes, she felt her heart solidify into a creation of broken glass. With every beat, the jagged edges of her hidden truth impaled her soul. Lexy froze mid step. *She was standing by the well.* The axe with the blood-stained handle lay against the stone. She couldn't move. She couldn't breathe. *This must be the getting to know you portion of their training. They'd see the animal within her. Nobody could love that. No matter how far she ventured from this farm she would always be the monster created within its walls of timber and shame. They would see what she really was. She was a murderer, a psychopath and a victim. She was all three of those things. The most humiliating identity she'd taken on, was victim. She had allowed herself to be one for so long.*

Arrianna whispered, "I feel like we need to get out of here." The Empath within her was obviously reading the horror of this place loud and clear.

Jenna said, "Lexy brought us here."

At the mention of her name, Lexy's adrenaline began to race. She fought the urge to vomit. *She didn't want them to see this. This dark place was her version of hell.* The farmhouse and the barn stood in the distance. The scenery changed and they were standing in the stall, watching as she cradled dying Charlotte in her arms. They heard her praying for the child to die, crying with her as Charlotte took her final shuddering breath. They watched in horror as her captor shot the child in the face. Brain matter blanketed her skin, Lexy shrieked repeatedly. She watched her own expression as the man told her to run. She followed herself outside to the pack of vile, disgusting men, so excited over the opportunity to kill her that they began to shoot her, before she'd even had a chance to run. Lexy watched the other version of herself as they shredded her torso with bullets. She raised her arms into the air, accepting her death willingly. Her body crumpled to the ground; life slipped away as blood soaked the sparse material of her dress. They kicked and spat on her body. One of them urinated on her before the man with the scar on his face knelt, yanked a handful of hair from her scalp, sniffed it and shoved it in his pocket. They dragged her body away. Her own vacant eyes stared back at her. *She hadn't been there for any of those disgusting final acts. She'd been safe, in a beautiful place, with Charlotte in her arms. She'd walked through the yellow door with Charlotte by her side.*

She watched her head scrape on rocks and bounce in the dirt. *What disgusting disregard they had for her five years of sick, twisted services.* Her corpse was tossed into the well, along with Charlotte's. The tiny sliver of light inside flickered and her emotions turned off. Lexy looked inside the well, now simply observing. The rancid scent of decomposing bloated corpses assaulted her senses. *Something was climbing out of the well. It was her.* A gnarled hand with shredded fingernails clasped the lip of the well, as her dark vengeance seeking alter climbed out. She watched the vision as she grabbed the axe and walked to the barn. She followed herself as she made her way to the stall where she'd been held captive for all those years. To everyone's horror, inside was a new little girl. The child scurried to the far corner of the stall. The other version of her promised to be back and told the child to hide. She followed her memory to the farmhouse. Her Dragon self climbed the steps holding an axe. She looked down at the blade and booted open the door.

None of the others entered. They remained on the steps, listening to the deviant inhabitants' tortured shrieks of anguish. Next came the vision of Lexy as she stepped back out onto the porch, soaked in the blood of her enemies, void of all emotion. The Dragon within her had cleansed the area of evil by doing evil. The group could not even manage to comprehend the horror of what they'd seen. Nor could they raise their eyes to meet hers. They followed the blood-soaked vision of Lexy towards the barn, in silence. Her double opened the stall to find the child, as soon as the group walked into the stall, the scenery flashed with blinding white light, and they were all somewhere else.

Nobody's emotions had a second to regroup before it became apparent, they were now somewhere meant for Grey. He held a swaddled infant in his arms. *Why was he holding a baby?* Grey walked up the long dusty drive, towards a small inconspicuous looking house. A worn looking bike lay in the middle of the path. Grey maneuvered around it, holding the baby close to his chest. He whispered to the sleeping infant and kissed the top of its head. The land around the home for as far as one could see had been void of rain for quite some time. Grey was talking to the baby. He paused at the sight of the slightly ajar front door. He tapped the door open with his foot, and it swung open. The scene before them was nothing short of a horror movie. There was blood everywhere. Grey froze mid step, pressing the baby to his chest to shield it from the horrific sight. He didn't call out, as most people do. He carefully, silently followed the trail of blood into a small living room. A women's body lay on the floor. He knelt over a body with the child in his arms and whispered, "No…No. Mom…Mom."

He cradled the sleeping baby in one arm and tried shaking his mother with the other. "Mom, please don't be dead." There was a noise. The muffled sound of voices, from another room. He gently laid the sleeping infant in a heap of clothes in the corner and hid it under a blanket.

What was he doing?

"Please, be quiet," he whispered as he kissed the sleeping infant, and silently rose to stand. Grey glanced back at the pile of clothing on the floor. He grabbed a book off the shelf, taking it with him as he gingerly tip-toed back to the front door. Noise came from the other room. The clashing of dishes and the sound of someone riffling through drawers. A form flashed in his line of sight. He tossed the book down the hall, a scruffy looking man appeared. Grey bravely baited, "Come and get me." He bolted out the door as the man sprinted after him. Grey raced down the dusty path as fast as his feet would carry him.

Lexy could see what he was doing now. *He was leading him away from the baby.* More came from around the side of the house. They were too fast. They were on him in seconds. *He never had a chance.* More appeared, they were coming from every direction. Half a dozen at least with knives.

Grey held up his hands and warned, "I know why you're here. You know what I can do."

They started laughing as one of the men assured, "I'm sure it's nothing we haven't seen before." His assailants edged closer. He blasted the ground with fire from his hands. The dry grass lit up and began to blaze. He whirled around, creating a circle of flames for protection.

The man who appeared to be in charge chuckled, "Nothing I haven't seen before, kid."

The flames kept them at arm's length, but the fire had begun to spread. The grass was too dry. Twigs crackled, the heat around him rose, until he was forced to suck the fire back. Nobody flinched. They tried to approach him again and he lit a new circle of grass. Grey, sweating from the heat, had lit the ground on fire too close to his body. He put it out, by sucking it back, once again. Visibly exhausted, he staggered a bit while glancing back at the house. It took his attention away for the split second they needed. One of them stabbed him in the back. Grey's knees buckled and he dropped to the ground. The group began their brutal assault. He was kicked in the head by one, and in the stomach by another, while disorientated. He passed out.

One of his assailants remarked, "Just to be sure." He stabbed Grey in the thigh. They stood there for a minute before walking around the side of the house. A cars engine began to purr.

That was where they'd hidden the vehicle, they'd arrived in. They drove away, and once it was out of sight, something miraculous happened. Grey had only been playing dead. He opened his eyes and attempted to get up but he couldn't. He laid his hand on his thigh, cauterized his wound and cried out in agony. This was how Grey survived his Correction. He'd lost too much blood. He crawled to the house with his final burst of strength but didn't make it far before succumbing to his injuries. From the tip of his fingers came a small ember. It floated on the wind through the open front door of the house, coming to rest on a curtain. While he was unconscious, another vehicle pulled up the long dusty drive. Lily, Orin and another girl with blonde curly hair hopped out of a truck and ran to his aid. Orin and the girl with the blonde curls carried Grey's body out of the field and laid him in the back of the truck. As they drove away smoke billowed from the house. Everyone's hearts tightened in their chest, for the sleeping infant was still inside. Grey had accidentally lit the house on fire.

The landscape flickered again, and without a chance to take a breath. They group was transported to Arianna's experience. They were by her bed watching her sleep. Arrianna was quite the little princess with her pink canopy bed, and a lacy bedspread. She had shelves of perfectly organized dolls and books. A few articles of clothing had been tossed on the floor. A woman came into the room, picked up her clothes, and bent over to give Arrianna a kiss on the cheek before leaving the room. She left the door open a crack, and a sliver of light travelled in from the hallway.

Arrianna was rolling around restlessly, having trouble sleeping. The group heard a whimper, followed by a hollow thud from outside of the bedroom door. Arrianna was facing the other direction, but her eyes opened. She registered the fear, the knowledge that something was wrong and pulled the covers over her head. The door slowly creaked open, and a man holding a knife, dripping with blood entered her bedroom.

He smirked at the sight of the teenage girl attempting to hide under her covers. He walked to her bed, shaking his head at the trembling lump of bedspread. His eyes were still lit up from the excitement of the kill. He sat on her bed and stroked her form almost lovingly as he toyed, "This won't do, I need to see your eyes." He caressed her again, and Arrianna visibly shivered beneath the comforter. Impatiently, he tried to peel the covers away, but she wouldn't let go. He chuckled, "That's fine. We'll do this your way." He slowly methodically trailed the blade of the knife over the bedspread, until he found his sweet spot.

She gasped as he drove his blade through the covers into her stomach and the mattress behind her. She was pinned, she couldn't move. Arrianna didn't cry, nor did she beg for her life. She clutched the covers over her head. She wasn't going to give him what he wanted. She wasn't going to let him look into her eyes. Out of frustration, her attacker yanked the knife out, to use it again and she rolled off the bed onto the floor. She'd been stabbed, but she didn't miss a beat. He ran around the bed and came at her with the knife. Arrianna kicked him, launching him backwards into her dresser. She leapt up while he was stunned, tossed the lamp from her nightstand at him, and scrambled out her open bedroom window. She rolled down the slanted roof, gripping onto the gutter, she dangled from it, and began to scream for help. Her assailant followed her onto the roof, before he could reach her, she let go, and hit the lawn below with a hollow thud. The neighbours had heard her, lights began to turn on in the surrounding houses, and in moments people were running towards her. The scenery flashed again and they found themselves standing back in a peaceful meadow.

Jenna announced, "You've now seen each other's darkest moments. Your mission is to discover a way to bring each other back from what you've just had the opportunity to relive. The three of you can have the rest of the day to figure out what I mean by that. While you have some free time, might I suggest you try to make a few happy memories."

Arrianna remarked, "Make happy memories, seriously? After what we all just had the opportunity to relive...The opportunity?"

Jenna vanished and the three were left standing alone, strangers in a foreign land. There was a lengthy moment of silence while presumably the other two endeavoured to find words. Lexy didn't have anything to say.

Grey was the first to speak, "How long were you there?"

His question had been directed at her. She had no intention of answering it. There was no point. They had only seen a small touch of what she'd gone through. What they'd seen had barely touched the surface.

"We don't have to talk about it right now," he whispered.

Lexy slowly turned around. *She wanted to do something else. She had no intention of talking about it. The getting to know you section of this training was over.* She met Arrianna's solemn expression.

Feeling her unspoken resolve, Arrianna changed the subject, "Well, that was tons of fun."

"Far too much fun," Grey mumbled.

With empathy in her eyes, Arrianna admitted, "Mine wasn't that bad, in comparison."

"Neither was mine...in comparison," Grey agreed.

What were they getting at? This had been emotionally draining, for them, but it wasn't for her. She had her emotions turned off. It wasn't an issue. They wanted to talk about it and this kind of mushy bonding stuff was way out of her realm of understanding. What just happened was nothing. A rock appeared in the grass by her feet. *Had that been there all the time?* Lexy picked it up, swung back and rifled it into the air. She threw it so far it disappeared from her line of sight. She looked down at her feet. *There was another one. This one was much larger.* She bent down, picked it up and repeated the same motion. Another one appeared. This time it was a small boulder. She picked it up, wound up to throw it and Grey placed both of his hands on it, stopping her. *Was he certifiably insane?*

He asked, "Where are you Lexy?"

She wanted to throw the rock. This was what she wanted to do. She glared at him. Every part of her wanted to rip his throat out with her bare hands…*Almost every part. There was a small part that didn't want to hurt him. This was a new feeling. It was more than that; it was instinct to protect him.* She looked at both of their hands on the stone. *She suspected the Ankh symbol binding their souls created this need to protect these two complete strangers. She didn't like it.* Grey took his hands off the stone. She methodically threw it. *It wasn't nearly as satisfying as the first two times had been. He'd wrecked her zen moment with the ration. Her feelings were coming back at record speed.* Lexy looked down for the next rock and found Grey sitting at her feet.

He looked up at her and urged, "Let's find something fun to do. Unless you want to toss me next?"

He was staring at her all innocently from his place at her feet with a childish grin on his face. He plucked a flower out of the ground and handed it to her. *He was insane.*

Grey teased, "Peace offering?"

Something about him made her feel peaceful. Lexy sighed as she took the flower from his hand. *She'd never been given a flower as a random act of kindness before. Was this symbol that bound them strong enough to drag her back into the light each time she became lost in the darkness? It happened a lot.* "Okay," she compromised.

Grey announced, "Ladies and gentlemen, she's back!"

Chapter 14

Happy Places

Arrianna smiled and asked, "Can I give you a hug?"

Lexy grimaced in response. *She was glad she'd asked her permission before just hugging her. She wasn't in a cuddly mood. To clarify, she was never in a cuddly mood, and could not imagine that she would ever become a cuddly kind of girl.* She blandly replied, "If that's what you feel like you need to do." She allowed Arrianna to embrace her and made a stiff attempt to respond. *The hug went on for too long. It was far too tight. She didn't know what to do to make it stop.* Awkwardly, Lexy patted Arrianna a few times on the back.

Arrianna whispered in her ear, "What makes you happy?"

Lexy replied honestly in Arrianna's ear, "Killing people." Her verbal filter was officially off.

Arrianna abruptly stopped the hug and questioned, "Really? That's your answer to what makes you happy?"

Grey winked and chuckled, "I actually saw that answer coming."

Arrianna appeared to be disturbed by her honesty. *That was the only thing she'd ever done that had given her any sort of pleasure.*

In an obvious attempt to lighten up the conversation Arrianna asked, "What about kittens or puppies? Don't they make you feel happy? Haven't you hugged a kitten and felt your insides get all squishy?"

She had no idea what Arrianna was talking about. She glanced in Grey's direction, hoping he'd decipher the conversation. *It had made no sense at all.*

Grey disclosed, "I can tell you what I love to do. I love to listen to music. It makes everybody happy. It is a proven theory."

Arrianna said, "Alright, we should listen to music. Dancing makes everyone happy too."

Lexy raised her eyebrows at the idea of dancing. Usually dancing was triggered by a feeling of joy while listening to music. Both joy and the opportunity to listen to music had been in short demand in her life. If they wanted to dance, then she would endeavour to watch. A catchy song began to play. Arrianna and Grey began singing at the top of their lungs but were both singing completely different words. They howled laughing and shoved each other in jest. Lexy watched the other two goofing around like a couple of nut bars and for the first time she wished she knew how to have fun. *She wanted to feel what they were feeling. Perhaps, that was the first step.* The next song was "Rock and Roll all Night" They were practically screaming the words. She felt her cheeks tighten. She was smiling as she watched them dancing around together. A new song started. Grey held out his hand to her. She shook her head from side to side to state her case, but he wasn't going to give up. She sensed this dance with him would be a much-needed step towards understanding humanity. *She wanted to allow herself to be in one word...Happy.* She took his hand and stiffly allowed Grey to twirl her around. She even tried to do what he was doing with his feet. Lexy felt something foreign bubble up inside of her, and she wanted to run. He sensed her need to flee, yanked her towards him and held her close. *She didn't want to hurt him so she had to play along.* Eventually her ability to turn off her emotions succumbed to his happy vibes and the sound of her own laughter made her feel almost lightheaded. *This was what the word happy meant.* It was the tickly sensation of the grass underneath of her toes. It was the feeling of completion in the touch of Grey's hand. It was the sound of music. This was her happiest moment to date. She took mental note of it. The three danced until they collapsed in the grass.

Grey looked at Lexy and commented, "I love the sound of your laughter."

There was that word again...Love. Was it normal for people to toss around that word, like it was nothing? I love your laugh. I love to dance. I love to sing. I love to listen to music. Maybe it was normal? She knew she had a lot to learn to pull off normal. She turned to look at Grey. *He was still staring at her. Was she supposed to say something back?* It felt like she was from another planet. An alien being, attempting to decipher what the correct response would be to normal conversation.

She made eye contact with Grey, and attempted to explain, "There are things people do that I don't understand. I now know, about music and dancing."

She glanced at Arrianna and said, "I want to try holding a kitten."

Grey sat up and laughed, "Like this one?"

A kitten pounced on Lexy's stomach. It startled her and she fought the urge to toss it. She sat up and out of thin air, six little fluffy white kittens appeared. They began rolling around playing with each other. At first, she cautiously observed them. They were curious creatures, much smaller than the baby pups from her pack. The pups hadn't lasted long. They were picked off, one by one in the wild. Grey picked up one of the balls of fur and rubbed his cheek against it. He grinned and passed it to her. Lexy cupped the cuddly ball of adorable warmth in the palm of her hands. She stared at it. *She felt awkward, what was she supposed to do with it?*

Arrianna urged, "Pet him. Isn't he adorable?"

Lexy replied, "How do you know it's a he?"

Grey looked between his legs and said, "I can't tell. They're too little."

Arrianna laughed, "I really can't tell either."

Lexy, stiffly held the squirming kitten. *It was vibrating.* She held it up to her ear. *It was purring. It was a pleasing sound.* She held the baby kitten to her chest and began to stroke it gently. *It was so soft.* She found herself grinning from ear to ear. They all sat there, petting the kittens and playing with them for a long time. Until the kittens, tuckered out, piled into a ball and fell asleep. *This feeling of happiness, it was pretty incredible. They'd changed her for the better, with a song, a dance, and a purring kitten.*

"Thank you," Lexy whispered.

With a warm smile, Grey responded, "You never have to say thank you to me."

Sprawling in the grass, Arrianna sighed, "I feel incredible, even after the crap we've gone through today."

On his back beside her, gazing at the sky, Grey remarked, "See, that's progress. If we could have kittens in our pockets, everywhere we went, we'd be set."

"Kittens don't stay kittens for long," Arrianna sparred, smiling in the sunshine.

While smelling a flower he'd plucked from the ground, Grey clarified, "If we could have immortal kittens, riding around in our pockets, we'd be set." He tossed a handful of grass at her.

Arrianna tossed a handful back as she chuckled, "Our enemies would be quivering in their boots."

Feeling the need to continue emulating them, Lexy lay in the grass smiling. *It was only her first fully conscious day with Ankh and she already felt like she belonged with these two incredibly strange people.* She inhaled the fragrant grass, it mixed in an appealing way with the luxurious scent of the flowers surrounding her. She felt safe in this place of dreams, and foreign sensations. She closed her eyes and drifting off into a dream in the land of the in-between.

While she slept, she dreamt of beautiful things. There was no sadness, or isolation in the visions dancing through her mind. She awoke with a sense of calm flowing through her being. Grey's arms were wrapped around her. *This was a bizarre feeling. There was security and warmth in his embrace.* She wanted to close her eyes again, so she could continue to pretend she was still asleep. She listened to the steady rhythmic sound of their breathing and found herself smiling again. *What if this all disappeared? What if this whole thing was only a dream? What if she lost them both somehow? She now had something to lose.* She shut her eyes again as he shifted his arm. Lexy decided then, and there that she'd never allow these two people to become lost. She would keep these two people safe, no matter what the personal cost. Lexy felt a presence and opened her eyes. The other Ankh were standing there watching them sleep.

Frost teased, "Oh, isn't this adorable."

Instantly awakened by the tone of Frost's voice, the other two opened their eyes. Lexy viewed the group and recognized a face that she hadn't seen earlier. *It was the blonde curly hair they'd seen in Grey's past.*

The blonde stranger met her curious expression with, "My names Freja, I'm Ankh. To make a long story short, I went to meet you guys at the hotel. Nobody was there. I ordered a pizza because I hate eating in restaurants alone and had a few drinks from the minibar. I remember feeling drugged, and then Tiberius was in my room, ranting about some Lexy chick hanging him in a tree and slitting his throat."

Frost introduced her, "Freja...Meet Lexy." He pointed at her.

Freja did a slow pronounced golf clap and declared, "Bravo." She went to shake her hand, Lexy gave her a strange look.

"Our Lexy's a little slow to warm up to people," Frost explained.

Freja grinned and said, "Not a problem. We'll get there." She addressed Frost, "My body's obviously a trap. I'm sure Triad is at the hotel waiting for us to come and get it."

Frost sighed, "No drinking when you're alone Freja. It's a Clan rule for a reason."

Freja shoved him and scolded, "I wasn't drunk, you idiot. I ordered a pizza and had a couple of shots, while in a locked hotel room. I wasn't getting hammered, dancing around in my underwear. I closed my eyes for second and Tiberius was sitting on my bed hitting on me, talking about someone he wants rather badly." Frost started to laugh.

Lily added to the comedy by winking at Freja and whispering, "How was he? I've always been morbidly curious."

Laughing, Freja countered, "I was thinking of just going for it but I realised, I'd rather bathe in a tub full of lemon juice and razor blades…forever. All joking aside, we're only here for another hour earth time. The air-conditioning was on, my body's fine. It's actually getting past Triad to my body, that's going to be tricky."

Grey piped in, "So, let me get this straight, the air-conditioning is on and that matters because you want to get to your body, before it starts to smell? What if they report it to the police? Have you guys ever had to go get someone's body at the morgue?"

"He can't do that. It's against immortal law to expose us. They'd also be exposing themselves," Lily explained. She paused for a second before adding, "Triad wants Lexy. They'll just lay low and wait for us to come back for Freja's body."

Lexy noticed Grey's reaction to being spoken to by Lily. He couldn't even look at her. He kept staring at his feet.

Frost whispered in Freja's ear, "He's probably sitting beside your corpse right now, stroking your hair, talking about killing Lexy."

Freja shivered and shoved him away. "That's gross and probably true, but I didn't need the visual."

These people were entertaining.

Curious, Arrianna asked, "Why did they send you out alone?"

"You know the drill. You were with Trinity before Ankh," Freja replied, "All we're allowed to do is scope out the kids before their Correction. Part of the journey towards immortality is how you handle your first death. You must come to terms with it. The more violent the demise, the stronger you become. I know it seems cold to just watch and never warn or speak to them but it's easier if you don't get attached. Most of the time, they don't survive their Correction. You three are here with us but we've lost five others to their Corrections this year. We only have a year left to train you three before the next scheduled Testing. The Testing occurs roughly every five years, unless the Correction survivor numbers are high. That hasn't happened this time. Only three of you survived."

Grey was still red faced and fidgety. Lexy cocked her head. *What was that scent? She'd done something to him.* Lexy grabbed the raven-haired stunning immortal's arm and sniffed her. Lily played along. Lexy shot her a dirty look. *It was an appealing scent. Too appealing.* Lexy scowled and questioned, "What are you?"

Smiling awkwardly, Arrianna touched Lexy's arm and whispered, "You're not supposed to smell people and then ask them what they are."

Lexy curtly responded, "Why not?"

"It's okay," Frost chuckled. "It's our pheromones." He held his hand out to her. Lexy grabbed it and smelled it. His scent made her feel funny.

Fascinated by her lack of filter, Frost probed, "Do you know what pheromones are?"

"No," Lexy decreed, humorously invading his personal space by overzealously sniffing his neck.

Grinning, Frost explained, "We attract mates by giving off a scent, like an animal in heat."

Lexy nodded, it made sense. She smelled her own hand and said, "I don't smell bad, but not like you." She held her hand up to Grey's nose and ordered, "Smell it."

Grey whispered in her ear, "Don't ask anyone to smell your skin, it's a wee bit creepy."

With an enormous grin, Freja declared, "I like her."

Lexy knit her brow. *She didn't know her. Why would she say that?*

Changing the subject, Lily addressed Freja, "How does the new kid look? Do you think he has a shot at surviving?"

Freja replied, "He is a home-schooled kid, living in a trailer in the desert with his grandparents. There doesn't appear to be an athletic bone in his body. I wouldn't hold my breath."

Lexy understood this conversation. *They must travel from place to place, picking up kids who survive their Correction.*

While placing a flower behind Lexy's ear, Arrianna sighed, "Nice to know all the Clans are the same. They can't kill children, can they?"

"They're not allowed to send anyone until you're over the age of sixteen," Frost answered. "They want you to fight back. They want to see what you're made of. Potential gladiators that want to kill for sport are difficult to find. Killing small children isn't sporting. It took three hundred years before those guidelines were set in place. A lot of small children and infants died before then. They were murdered and disposed of on the word of an Oracle...No offense Jenna."

Jenna said, "None taken, it's the truth. I was both an Oracle and one of those children."

Chapter 15

Love Is A Battlefield

Lexy lost interest and attempted to wander away from the group.

Grey clutched her arm and quietly urged, "I think we're supposed to stay here."

Resisting the urge to bite the hand clutching her arm, she looked into his eyes. *She didn't like it when people stopped her from doing what she wanted to do.* Her need to protect him outweighed the need to kick his ass but this ticked her off. He grinned at her and grabbed hold of her hand instead. The ticking time bomb within her disarmed itself. *How did he do that?* Lexy started thinking about moments they'd shared in the in-between. She eagerly anticipated the opportunity to do those things again. Some kittens and dancing, that's all it had taken to get through to her.

Ending the moment of silence, Freja declared, "We should stop messing around and start training you three. We have a lot of ground to cover. It would suck to have to hunt down my body at the morgue in some hick desert town a couple hundred miles from the hotel." Freja winked at Grey. He winked back and she laughed, "Grey, you're wasting your time. I can see a bad idea like you, coming from a mile away."

"In my experience bad ideas end up being the most fun," Grey baited.

Beaming, Freja teased, "Your seventeen years of experience." She shook her head as she walked away. Lexy observed Frost running to catch up with her. They were whispering and laughing. *She wasn't following this conversation along properly. Frankly, she was a little bit lost. She'd lost her at, Grey was a bad idea…*

Grey hollered after Freja, "I'm almost eighteen!" Freja glanced back and smiled.

What did Grey's age have to do with anything? Everyone was walking away. Everyone, but Jenna.

Jenna stepped in front of the three and ordered, "Follow me. We don't have any time to waste."

They'd just followed Jenna across the desert to an uncertain place. It felt like they were accompanying her somewhere certain, this time. The scenery flashed and they were wandering deep into the forest. When she looked up, all she could see were trees that stretched forever into a faint splash of blue. *This was an intriguing place.*

Jenna began to speak, "This is the practice battlefield. Lexy, I know you don't need a pep talk. To the others, you can't really die here. There's no need to be afraid. You three need to learn to fight as a unit. Try to stay together. Lexy, it's time to wake the Dragon. I'll bet it's out cold after holding those kittens. For the record, that was adorable. It was also a well-timed lesson. You're not always going to have a warning before shit hits the fan. Sometimes, in life, you must go from snuggling with kittens to mass murder. It's an immortal thing. You two have seen a few of the events that created the Dragon. Lexy can turn it on at the drop of a hat. It's turning it off that's going to be the challenge. Learn to control Lexy's Dragon and you three will be the first group ever to walk out of the Testing like it was nothing." Jenna disappeared and they were left standing in the forest alone.

Lexy inhaled the scent of cedar trees and pine needles. She picked up a pinecone, squeezing it into the palm of her hand. *This battlefield felt familiar. It felt like home.* She was excited, but the other two, clearly did not share her enthusiasm. Her mind sorted through the obvious. They had no weapons. They needed to find a weapon. Lexy surveyed the surrounding for potential weapons.

Arrianna picked up a stick and asked, "Do the Ankh use bows? In Trinity we spent most of our time training to use one."

"I've only been in a Clan for a couple of months, and only this one. I have no idea," Grey replied.

Arrianna looked at Lexy and asked, "Which weapon do you prefer?"

Lexy stated, "I don't need a weapon, but you two should find one." *Nobody responded to what she'd said.* She looked at her fellow Ankh. They were too terrified to move, surrounded by cougars. Three of them, and they were enormous. They resembled sabre toothed, prehistoric cats. *Lexy wasn't afraid, but the other two were going to be little help. One cougar each, this shouldn't be difficult?* Lexy indifferently wandered around, picking up sticks as the cougars slinked closer. She handed one to each of her freaked out fellow Ankh. Lexy took in the beasts. Saliva was dripping from fangs curved over the bottom of their jaws. Every move was as calculated as a cat cornering a mouse. Lexy shrugged and assured, "There are only three of them. This isn't a big deal. Don't scream, predators love that. Don't try to climb a tree or run away. This is all about avoiding the teeth and claws. Protect your neck. These are wild animals. They'll want to play with you before they eat you."

Grey stammered, "Good to know. Thanks for the pep talk Satan."

Lexy giggled, *this was going to be fun.* Three enormous felines paced in a circle around the three, stick wielding Ankh. It was going to cramp her style being part of a trio. She wanted to go nuts and enjoy the fight, but she had to think about two other people now. Two people that experienced fear. Lexy announced, "Try to confuse them, long enough for me to kill them."

Arrianna whispered under her breath, "Yah...Not a problem."

Picking up a boulder the size of a basketball, Lexy grinned. *It was time to pick a fight. Speed things up a little.* She gripped the stone in her hands, made eye contact with one of the mountain lions and cocked her head as she ordered, "Use the tree trunks as a shields in 3…2…1…" Lexy wound up and launched a rock, exploding the brain of one. The other two cougars sprinted at her. Lexy dodged between tree trunks, laughing because she'd had no time to bend down to grab for another weapon. She'd never taken it under consideration that they'd choose to only go after her. Grey began hollering at the monsters and Arrianna joined in. They got the creatures attention. The mountain lions spun around to see what the ruckus was about providing Lexy with the split second she'd needed to grab a weapon. In the time it took for a breath, she leapt on a beast. Straddling the massive feline, dominating it like a bull at a rodeo, she swung back and stabbed it in the throat with a piece of wood. It let out a gurgling sound and went limp. The final creature chose that moment to attack with saliva dripping on her face as jaws snapped at her. It took every ounce of her strength to keep the massive dripping fangs from clamping down on the soft tissue of her throat. Her Clan members charged at it, wielding their sticks as swords. They hollered, throwing things at it, until it became annoyed enough to turn its attention away. With only a split second to act, Lexy leapt on it with her full weight, pinning its neck between a raised root and her body. The wild thing began to struggle. *This wasn't going to work. She wasn't heavy enough.* She'd dealt with acts of dominance within the pack. Both feline's and canine's alike use the throat as their preferred kill zone. With both hands and the full weight of her torso in use, she did what she had to and bit into the creature's jugular… It stopped fighting. She was between a rock and a hard place. She knew the creature had only paused long enough to determine whether she could do what she was threatening to do. Out of nowhere, Grey leapt on top of her. She felt the cat's neck snap and its body went limp. She hadn't intended on tearing its throat out with her teeth, but with Grey's sudden weight, it happened, accidentally. Warm blood spurted from the exposed vein into her face and Grey's. He rolled off her onto the ground beside her, gagging. Lexy began choking and coughing up blood. She spit a mouthful into the dirt and stood up. Using one of her hands to wipe the blood from her mouth, she attempted to calm her ragged breathing. *Adrenaline was still pulsing beneath the surface of her skin. She was far too amped up. Something else was coming.*

Grey wiped the thin spray of blood from his cheek and said, "I'm so glad you're on our side."

Sickly pale, Arrianna whispered, "Hold that thought, it's not over."

Arrianna obviously felt the same sense of impending doom. Lexy loved this. The other two appeared to be dealing with it. The sense of approaching danger was exhilarating. There would always be danger. It was never going to be out of their lives, deaths, or whatever the hell this version of their existence was. Lexy whispered, "I say you learn to love it." The three of them backed up against each other, holding their makeshift weapons out in front of themselves for protection. They each surveyed the span of forest. A mass amount of large beige creatures were slinking their way through the thick foliage towards them. *There were too many. There was no way to fight them all. There were dozens of them. This was amazing.*

Grey gasped, "It's impossible."

Lexy grinned and countered, "Completely impossible, isn't it great!" Her pulse sped up as adrenaline commenced pumping through her veins, in preparation.

"We can't win," Grey stammered.

Lexy couldn't wipe the smile off her face, even for Grey. This was incredible. A battle with impossible odds. This was what she was created for.

Arrianna looked at Grey, and then into Lexy's eyes as she nodded and decreed, "Then, we die like badass superheroes."

This became their call to arms. They would die like badass superheroes on a hundred occasions over the following two weeks in the in-between, during increasingly messed-up scenarios. Each time they endured a version of death, a more severe one would occur. They would be killed by impossible things. They'd be attacked by monsters that didn't exist in the real world. They'd fall and they would be buried alive. They would suffocate and freeze to death. They'd be hunted by drugged arrows and impaled by spears, all by the hands of their own Clan. The trio would be taught to use a sword. Lexy proved to be skilled at everything. She realised by the end of the first week that her ability to harness her fury and rage was an incredible gift. She always retained a flicker of light, just enough to find her way back to the two Clan members that created it, within her. There were moments of joy. Arrianna taught her to swim and Grey taught her how to look for beauty. They rode horses and danced in a meadow full of monarch butterflies. After these flashes of happiness, they continued to fight, until the three understood they could never die.

After two weeks they returned to the land of the living and only two hours had lapsed. They were ordered to stay inside of the crypt. The rest of the Clan needed to go find Freja's body and lead Triad away.

Lexy was so exhausted. Her eyelids were so heavy, they felt weighted. She was the first of the three to find a reasonably comfy spot on the dusty pillows on the floor. She felt Grey snuggle up with her. He shifted as Arrianna joined them. Lexy didn't have to turn around and look. *She could sense it when they were all together. They were her new pack.*

Chapter 16

Contemplating Cannibalism 101

Lexy awoke to the sound of breathing. She lay in silence, listening to the soft soothing rhythm of her friend's peaceful slumber. Grey's arm was draped around her. She didn't want to wake him, so she gently lifted his arm and slipped out from under it. She sat there, against the wall for a minute, watching them sleep. Jenna wasn't with the group. Lexy wandered away in search of her absent Clan member. It only took a moment to find her. She was standing in the main chamber with her face inches from the wall and a palm flat against it. *What in hell was she doing?* Lexy moved towards her, to get a closer look. Jenna appeared to be asleep standing up. Lexy touched her arm and visions of violence flooded her mind. Lexy yanked her hand away, severing the psychic connection. Jenna's eyes were open. Her pupil's vacant and foggy white in colour. She was clearly in the middle of something messed-up. *Was she in trouble? Had she touched the wall by accident?* The carvings told the story of Ankh. She found her eyes drawn to the stone. Unable to look away, she was tempted to touch it. Her hand rose as if by its own accord.

Lexy's hand was a hair from touching it when she heard Jenna's voice say, "I wouldn't touch that."

Lexy snapped out of it and said, "You're awake."

Jenna replied, "Well, I guess I should explain myself. That had to look creepy. I have visions and most of the time they happen while I'm awake."

"Not a problem," Lexy remarked. "I'm a little under sensitive."

Jenna replied, "Just a tad."

She really wanted to touch it.

Lexy's hand rose to touch the wall again and Jenna smacked it, laughing, "I'm dead serious. Don't touch the damn wall."

Smiling, Lexy sparred, "Don't smack my hand."

Jenna grinned and countered, "Don't make me." She sat down on one of the puffy pillows on the ground. It released a cloud of dust into the air, and she coughed a few times.

Lexy's stomach complained, she was hungry. She knew they hadn't planned to be stuck in the Ankh crypt. She didn't even want to say the words out loud.

Appearing to read her mind, Jenna answered, "No, there's no food in the crypt, and I can't go outside to hunt for anything until they're gone. The visions are crystal clear. I can't leave, not even for a second."

This was inconvenient. She'd only had a chance to eat one meal before they'd gone on that little trip to the in-between. Lexy had been hungry before, she understood the gravity of the situation. *They'd better not be stuck in here for long. She wasn't a fan of enclosed spaces. The walls were already closing in on her.* Lexy sat on the stone floor, next to Jenna. She didn't speak or attempt to question anything.

Jenna placed her hand on top of Lexy's and attempted to explain, "I've already seen your reaction to being stuck in here. You must stay calm for as long as you possibly can. Do this as a courtesy to Arrianna. If you start to lose it, we'll have to send you and Grey back to the in-between. You'll be together, but you'll be sacrificing Arrianna. A Healer must stay behind to operate the tombs. I know you've become close. Starvation is an evil beast, as you well know. Arrianna made the decision to stay with Ankh for you, Lexy. If you don't need her, she'll try to go back to Trinity. If Arrianna leaves this crypt and makes it back to that hotel. My version of your future is null and void. She'll leave if the two of you go into that tomb together and she stays out here starving. I've seen it. This claustrophobia you feel may kill all three of you, but only if you allow it to. The three of you only survive the Testing if you are together. Those are the cold hard facts."

She understood what Jenna was saying. It was her turn to make a sacrifice. It was her turn to try to find the ability to comfort her Clan members in a situation that was familiar, only to her. She had seriously contemplated eating Grey. It felt like a lifetime ago. The weeks she'd been on the rollercoaster of violence and bonding had altered her. She cared about Arrianna. Jenna would know what starvation was all about after a thousand years of life. She would reign it in. She'd have to leave her emotions on for Arrianna. She walked back to where the others were sleeping.

Jenna chuckled from behind her, "Nobody gets to eat Grey."

Lexy grinned, hesitated and then kept walking. *She'd never eat him now.* It was a strange feeling to know someone was always capable of reading your internal dialogue. Her inner dialogue was remarkably messed-up. For several years, all she used was her inner dialogue, rarely attempting to speak aloud. The others would catch up to her level of crazy. In a week, they'd all be starving, and their sanity would be hanging by a thread. She wandered over to the others. They were still sleeping. Lexy observed their peaceful slumber for a while, knowing neither one had ever undergone the slow, excruciating act of starvation before. *She could try to persuade them that this was just another method in which they needed to learn how to die? In the in-between, there had been no retreat but here there was an escape. It was right out that door, and into the desert. They looked so peaceful.* She'd take a thousand knife wounds over the slow, steady aching demise of starvation. *Did they care about her enough to stay when they had the opportunity to leave? This was a test. Did she care about them enough to be able to reign in her panic over the enclosed space, she'd be forced to spend the next week in? Was their attachment to each other strong enough, after only two weeks and a bit of Clan voodoo?*

Arrianna opened her eyes, looked directly into Lexy's and said, "What's wrong?"

Without a speck of emotion, Lexy began to explain the situation, "We could be in here with no food for weeks. We do have water. When the opportunity arises, Jenna will go out hunting. She can only go when her visions say it's safe for her to leave us. None of us can leave. If even one of us leaves, the others will die during Testing." She could have just as easily been talking about the weather.

Arrianna declared, "Well, doesn't this suck. We can do it."

She didn't understand. She'd never starved. She had never felt the anguish of it. She would know. By day three, if Jenna couldn't venture outdoors to hunt for food, Arrianna would understand.

Grey opened his eyes and repeated her words, "We can do it." He sat up, wiped the sleep from his eyes and groggily assured, "We can do anything, we're badass superheroes. How bad can it be?"

They explained the situation in detail. He wasn't concerned, having never starved before. She suspected Jenna knew the torment of starvation for her lack of wanting to speak about it.

The first two days in self-imposed exile were spent telling the stories of their mortal lives. Lexy opted out of giving them any details regarding hers. When the headaches began, they drank water until it no longer helped. Trying to keep their minds occupied, Jenna showed them visions of the past in a pool of water like a movie. It was an incredibly cool talent. They had to fill the time, for being stuck underground within a crypt was painfully monotonous. On day three their stomachs cramped and the panic set in. Lexy knew this feeling all too well. Their bodies were beginning to rebel. Grey started pestering Jenna about being able to go somewhere else within the tomb. Arrianna was a Healer. When Jenna explained that Arrianna and Jenna couldn't go with them, he understood. The mind splitting migraines intensified, followed by incapacitating dizziness. Everyone's blood sugar had become dangerously low. On regular intervals, Jenna stood at the same place in the crypt and stared at the wall. Lexy watched her, willing the ability to hunt tonight to creep into the visions. She watched her eyes shift from white to their normal hue and she saw the disappointment. Irrational thoughts began to slip into her mind. *She could sneak out of here and catch something in five minutes flat. Nobody had been able to take her before. Why would they be able to now?* She was a hair from breathing Dragon fire all over Jenna and forcing her way out, when she realised what she was doing. *She was the one with the background in starvation. If she was here, how close were the others to busting their way out of this place? She was still capable of rational thought. This was good.* She sauntered down the passageway until she located the others. Arrianna was doubled over, in agony. Grey's eyes were charged with his inner fire. Their tether was beginning to loosen. Lexy's body grasped what this state was. She'd always been starving for something. There had never been a time when she hadn't had a hunger in the pit of her stomach for food, warmth, or a companion. *She had water and three companions.* She was starving, yet grateful for what she'd received. Her time in the cabin, was still vivid in her memory. The years on the dark farm, successfully held her emotions at bay. *If there was ever a moment to open up and talk about what she'd left unsaid, it was now.* She left and came back with a goblet of water for each of them to drink. *They were all a second from making a run for it.* Lexy began to tell her story, "I was eleven years old when I ran away with a bunch of older kids from our group home. I had a disagreement with the makeshift leader of the group. He hit me and left me by the side of the highway. I could see them walking away. I probably could have caught up, but they were doing these horrible things to people. I was afraid we'd get in trouble. I knew I'd be better off on my own. So, I left the group, and the highway, thinking if I took a backroad it would be safer.

I cut through this field. I was starving, wandering, with no idea where I was headed. I was walking through this enormous orchard full of apple trees, in those last moments of freedom. I remember how large the moon looked that night. The feeling of the rotten apples as they squished underfoot. I was so tired and there wasn't anywhere for me to sleep. If there had been, I might've stayed right there until somebody showed up to chase me away. I started walking down this backroad, under the illusion that if I made it to the next town, someone might help me. I heard a vehicle coming. That first one drove right past me, but the next one stopped. A pastel blue truck pulled over and in it was a man with a bunch of friendly looking dogs riding up front. I remember feeling like this must be a nice man because he loved his dogs enough to allow them to ride up front with him. He offered me a ride in the back. I remember rationalizing it. It was just easier for him than displacing his dogs. He shared his thermos of hot chocolate and ended up giving me the whole thing. I was too hungry, and exhausted to question it. I was a kid, I thought maybe he felt guilty that I had to ride in the back of the truck. I remember staring at the size of the moon in the sky and waking up with no idea where I was. I was in a bag, my wrists and ankles were bound. I knew I'd been drugged. I was taken to a stall in a barn, they locked the door behind me. That's where I lived. The first time they took me into the house. I had no idea what to expect. There were a bunch of men. This old lady snuck me a yellow flower and told me to eat it. It drugged me and I blacked out. I woke up, back in the stall, bleeding. On some level I knew what happened to me, but if I didn't remember, I could pretend it wasn't real. They brought me to that house every day. Eventually, I tried to fight back, and got away. A group of men hunted me down, shooting me with pellets. I remember how much it burned. They dragged me to that well after they caught me. When they finished beating me, they tossed my body into it. My leg broke on the way down. They told me that this was where the bad children on the farm went. I was kept in a well full of half submerged, decomposing bloated corpses for almost a week. I'd heard screaming at night, followed by gunfire. I knew those girls were the bodies in the well. I went somewhere inside of myself. I found a place to hide. All that was left of me after that week, was the skin I came in. The scent of that well, stayed with me. Every time they made me do unthinkable things, I shut my emotions off, and went back into that safe place. I would have done anything to never go back there, and I did. I never said no. I never fought back. Years went by like that. I went from the barn stall to the house, until I didn't even have a soul anymore. I was just this empty emotionless shell.

One day, they showed up and tossed a bag in my stall with a little girl in it. She was only six years old and her name was Charlotte. They'd taken her babysitter too, and already executed her. I let her out of the bag. She kept hugging me and telling me she wanted her mommy and daddy. I didn't even know how to respond. She asked me where she was, I remember telling her she was in hell. I wasn't capable of hopeful thoughts anymore. At that point, I was little more than livestock. I didn't have the desire to escape. Where would I have gone? Who would have wanted what was left of me? She'd been there for maybe half an hour when someone showed up to bring her to the farmhouse. You had to do what you were told or you'd be executed and tossed into the well. There were no second chances. I told her to do whatever she was told to do. I didn't want her to be executed and disposed of as garbage. I knew once she went into the well, she'd never come out. I knew this because I never came back out.

When they brought her back, I knew they hadn't done to her, what they'd done to me. She was only six, she wouldn't have survived it. I never asked what they did to her. We never talked about what happened there. She was only upset for a little while on that first day. Charlotte was only ever upset for a little while. She had this unbreakable spirit.

Charlotte had hope in her eyes, she was always smiling. She told the most beautiful stories. Those stories became my dreams. She had a golden retriever named, Freckles and a house with a yellow door. She had a bicycle with shiny streamers on the handles. Charlotte used to tell me about what it felt like to ride that bicycle downhill. I'd just comb her hair, and we'd talk about how her life used to be. Each time they came to get her and bring her to the farmhouse. I knew what was happening to her. I'd shut my emotions off. I knew we couldn't get away. You did what you were told or you died. I'd accepted my place. They started leaving my stall wide open each time they took her away. They knew I'd never run away and leave her behind.

One day she didn't come back until nightfall. They brought her back, so badly beaten, she was almost unrecognizable. They gave me a few days to fix her. They said, if she died, I'd be joining her at the bottom of the well. I tried my best to save her. She got so sick, she was burning up. I heard them talking about putting her down. I began to pray for the first time in my life. I prayed she'd slip away while in the middle of a beautiful dream. She would go someplace far better and she'd be safe. Nobody could ever hurt her again. She'd died, by the time they came for her. I didn't care if I died by that point. I was already gone. Three men walked into the stall and one of them said, they were going to have to change the game because Charlotte was dead. He shot her in the head just to be sure, and something snapped inside of me. I started to scream. I screamed for every time I should have and didn't. He ordered me to run, the plan was to hunt me. I ran out of the barn and a group of men began to shoot me. I remember standing there as they shot me. I raised my arms to the sky and willed my suffering to be over. It was for a bit. I embraced Charlotte and we walked through the yellow door together. Then, I woke up in the well. You both saw what happened after that. You just didn't know the story behind it. Well, there it is. That's all of it." She'd gotten through to them. The sounds of their stomachs had been silenced. Grey's eyes were full of agony, not anger. Arrianna's hand was covering her mouth.

Looking into Grey's teary eyes, Lexy disclosed, "Grey, when I said you were my yellow door, that's what I meant. You're what home means to me. I knew what you were to me, even then. Arrianna, you're my bicycle with streamers. You are the one who can teach me to take that emotional journey downhill. I see who you both are to me. You've taught me so much already. I'll teach you both when not to feel. I want to lose my mind in this enclosed space. It reminds me of that stall. The reason I haven't is because I can't risk losing either of you. I know you're both starving, but I've been starving for months not days. I need you to stick this out with me. I promise no matter how dark it gets in the future, I'll guide you through it. I just need you to promise me, you'll help me find my way back into the light when it's all over."

Completely forgetting the torment of starvation, Grey scooted over and took her in his arms. She let him. With her head resting on his heart, she could hear the steady rhythmic thumping. He stroked her hair and kissed her head. This would be the first of a million times he kissed her there.

Arrianna shuffled over to join their embrace and whispered, "I'm not worried about the Testing. We can survive anything together."

Chapter 17

Bugs, Lizards And Birthdays

There was a noise. They glanced up and Jenna was standing in the doorway with a dead lizard in her hand. While they were talking, she'd snuck away and caught something.

Jenna held it up in the air. She declared, "I caught a... No idea what this thing is called."

Their first meal in three days was a desert lizard. They cooked it with Grey's flame and split the sparse amount of meat. There wasn't a lot, but it was reasonably satisfying. Jenna disappeared every night and returned with the desert's offerings. It kept them reasonably sane for a couple of weeks. After that, the days began to mesh together and the premise of time was lost.

Lexy awoke the next morning to find Jenna glaring at her. *What now?*

Jenna questioned, "Are you already eighteen?"

Lexy groggily responded, "I'm not sure, I've lost track of time."

The Oracle's eyes lit up as she explained, "Your Clan is permanent once you're eighteen." She asked Lexy for the hand without the Ankh symbol. Lexy held it out and Jenna twirled her gold Ankh symbol ring to face inwards. Jenna warned her, "This might hurt." She pressed the ring against her other hand and nothing happened, no sizzling flesh, no pain. Jenna grinned and declared, "Well Miss Lexy, you're officially Ankh."

"Hey, wait a minute, my eighteenth birthday was only a month away," Arrianna revealed.

Jenna signalled for her to hold out her symbol free hand. She barely touched it and Arrianna's flesh began to sizzle. She said, "Not yet. I should have been marking the floor to keep track of the days. I didn't think we'd be in here this long. I'll check again tomorrow."

With those words, hope returned for all of them. Jenna started to laugh, "That's why Markus said he'd return you to Trinity if you wanted to go back in a couple months. What an ass."

Arrianna scowled and said, "I can hold a grudge for years."

The Oracle announced, "As soon as Arrianna's eighteen, we're out of here. We'll order everything on the menu and sleep in a bed. Markus owes me big time so we're also drinking everything in the minibar to celebrate your birthdays."

"My birthday isn't for a few more months," Grey added.

Jenna replied, "Nobody was ever coming for you."

Grey grumbled, "That was sort of mean."

Squeezing his shoulder, Jenna teased, "No need to be offended. You my dear are of the upmost importance to us. None of you come out of the Testing, unless you're together"

The next few days of bugs and snake dinners went down a hell of a lot better once there was an end to their exile in sight. Jenna tested Arrianna's brand each day, until one day no flesh sizzled beneath the golden Ankh symbol. After a whole month of self-imposed exile in darkness, they were finally free. The four stepped out into the desert sand at daybreak on Arianna's eighteenth birthday. Standing in the sunshine was a glorious feeling. They marched through the sand towards the hotel, a symbolic oasis in the middle of the desert. Jenna shoved the door open. The bells jingled to announce their arrival. The jingling of the bells felt more like a victor's trumpet after battle, even though this last battle had no weapons of any kind. It had been within them.

The waitress arrived to take their order. Jenna came up with a reasonable explanation for their dishevelled appearance, "Flat tire." Their state demanded an explanation. They had the food delivered to their room and took turns using the shower. Always the gentleman, Grey offered to go last. The food arrived while he was in the shower. Wearing nothing but a towel, Grey sauntered out, not caring he was in a room full of girls. They all gawked as he hopped on the bed and grabbed a hand full of fries. He was a tad exposed.

Clearing her throat to draw his attention, Jenna remarked, "Grey, you don't have any underwear on."

"Starvation trumps manners," he declared, as he ate half his burger in a couple bites.

Lexy thought of Grey's warning during her first meal with Ankh. They were all going to be sick with how quickly they'd ingested their first full-sized meals in a month. She had no intention of slowing down so she opted out of pointing out the obvious.

Jenna glared at Grey until he explained, "I don't want wear my dirty clothes. I just had a shower."

Smiling she disclosed, "Pull out the loose panel in the back of the closet and see if you can find something to wear. That's where we found the clothes we're wearing. We keep a few things stashed in hotels we frequent, for emergencies."

The lightbulb turned on over Grey's head. He hadn't caught on to the fact that they were all wearing clean clothing. He retreated into the closet and came out complaining, "There's only girl's stuff in the bag."

"We just spent a month underground. Put on some lady's underwear and a damn dress, nobody cares. I'll take our clothes to the lobby. There was a sign by the desk for laundry service.

He slipped on white cotton bikini briefs. Always the comedian, he strutted out to show off what he had on and

138

chuckled, "Ladies underwear is so comfortable." He began dancing to induce laughter.

They were all far too hungry to catch the joke. Jenna rolled her eyes and sighed, "You know those leave little to the imagination." The comment caused both Lexy and Arrianna to look up and catch sight of Grey's shenanigans. Jenna shook her head and teased, "You'd better hurry up. Lexy's going to eat everything."

Lexy glanced up and dropped the fries in her hand back onto the plate. She gave Grey a meek look and apologised, "Sorry, I wasn't thinking."

Arrianna laughed and said, "I'll order more burgers."

He grinned as he bent over and grabbed the handful of fries, Lexy dropped. Grey walked away, wiggling his back side. He rifled around in the bag and chose something to wear, reappearing wearing a kilt. It would have been passable, if it wasn't barely covered his behind. It was far too short, dangerously so. A Scotsman by heritage, he had no problem owning the kilt for a night. They slept on real beds, waking the next day with clean clothes, and full stomachs. They hadn't dared touch the minibar after their stomach's comically loud complaints over the introduction of solid food.

Another week passed by before their Clan returned. They had been forced to travel halfway across the country to lose Triad. Tiberius's messed-up obsession with obtaining Lexy for Triad had been extremely inconvenient. Trinity also caught up, delaying their return. It was too late now, both girls had been sealed to Ankh. Neither one could switch Clans.

Chapter 18

Even Dragons Are Capable Of Personal Growth

Over the next year Lexy would slowly become the girl with a voice. She'd keep her hair shoulder length and her lipstick brilliant red. She'd become a force of nature, with a purpose. Arrianna would teach her how to use her emotions. She would stay close to Grey, always. She was never far from his side. The Clan would teach them how to die, and how to deal with impossible situations. They had accomplished a lot, in only one year. When the year was over, all three, felt quite secure in their ability to survive almost everything. Lexy wasn't too concerned about the Testing. She knew all she had to do is keep the two people she'd grown to love by her side. *How difficult could that be?*

When they arrived at the last stop before the infamous Testing the first order of business was to run a final redo of their Sweet Sleep. This was the first act in quite a while that had given Lexy pause. *How much would they see?* She'd told them what happened but hoped they wouldn't see it. *To know they'd seen it with their own eyes, would be humiliating.* They'd all seen her in full Dragon form on numerous occasions. They had no secrets from each other. They'd seen her swinging the axe and witnessed the blind rage she was capable of. Whenever thoughts of the dark farm surfaced, she'd make eye contact with Grey and allow her adoration of him to quiet the screaming in her soul.

Only a few members of the Clan would be present to witness the final redo of her Sweet Sleep. Orin was one. She liked Orin and she didn't venture to use the word like in reference to many people outside of her trio. He'd always been kind and patient with her. After witnessing her darkest day, he couldn't maintain eye contact with her. It felt like he was staring at her naked form. He could see the shiny green scales beneath her skin. Jenna knew everyone's secrets, for there was never anything that could be hidden from an Oracle.

Once they finished the final redo, there was only a short while to emotionally recuperate before they had to attend a banquet with all the other Clans. A temporary cease fire between the three Clans had been called. The elders were leaving them alone for a whole week to attend something called, "The Summit."

Arrianna dressed her and did her makeup. Barely recognising herself, Lexy stared in the mirror. She was wearing a short incredibly tight teal green dress.

"You look stunningly beautiful, Lex," Arrianna whispered. *She felt beautiful, but overt sexuality still made her uncomfortable. Men would look at her. She didn't want to stand out of the crowd.*

Grey knocked on the door and said, "Are you two ready to go?" Arrianna opened the door and Grey's lips parted as he took Lexy in. He'd been rendered speechless.

Arrianna preened, "Doesn't she look beautiful?"

Grey couldn't stop staring at her. Arrianna socked his arm. He said, "Yah...Yes. She does."

The three left the camp site and strolled down the trail. Lexy removed her heels and carried them in one hand.

Grey poked her and warned, "You should put those heels back on, you'll have dirty feet."

She hadn't thought of that. Balancing against a tree, Lexy wiped one of her bare feet on her dress.

Grey chuckled, knelt before her and slipped her heel on her foot. He whispered, "I'm fairly certain Cinderella never wiped her feet on her dress."

Lexy teased, "Cinderella's imaginary, and there's no such thing as Prince Charming."

Grey sparred, "I'd like to think I'm somebody's version of Prince Charming."

Lexy brushed off her other foot and slipped her shoe on. She brushed off her dress and said, "You look alright in that suit."

With smiling eyes, Grey replied, "You look alright in that dress."

Arrianna sighed, "You know what would be alright. It'd be alright if we could get there while they're still serving dinner, I'm absolutely famished."

They followed the directions on the barely legible wooden signs. They arrived at the rustic log cabin hall, standing side by side as a united front, unsure of what to expect. There was a receiving line at the front door. Frost, Tiberius and Thorne stood side by side. *There they were, the infamous, Brothers of Prophecy.* One by one, they greeted everyone as they entered the hall, with Markus as the designated referee. Lexy wasn't shaking anyone's hand.

Frost mouthed one word, "Wow," as he stared at her.

Tiberius met her icy expression by openly gawking at her, taking in her legs and dress, stopping at her eyes. She felt her pulse rise as the blood rushed beneath her skin. *This wasn't going to be easy. She really wanted to murder him.* She hadn't budged from the doorway. It was Grey who noticed first. He strolled over, took her hand and gave her a gentle pull towards the lineup. "I wouldn't do that," she whispered.

Grey leaned over and whispered in her ear, "You'd never hurt me."

Lexy relaxed a tiny bit, he was calling her bluff. *No, she'd never hurt him.* He led her over to Markus and Frost.

Markus took her other hand and said, "Stay away from Tiberius. Try and have a good time tonight."

Markus looked at Grey and warned, "Don't leave her alone for a second. Don't even go to the bathroom. You know Tiberius is going to mess with her."

Grey nodded, laced his fingers through hers and gave her a gentle tug towards the large wide-open double doors that led to the decked-out banquet hall. She went with him, knowing only that she didn't want to do anything to hurt Grey. *She didn't want to get him in trouble.*

Grey glanced at her, squeezed her hand and asked, "How you doing? You feel alright? Any murderous impulses?"

She shot him a dirty look. *Funny.*

"Kidding, I'm only joking," he chuckled.

They found a seat at a long table. He pulled her chair out. She gave him another weird look, before sitting down in the seat.

A waiter asked if she'd like something to drink. Grey answered for her, "Definitely."

Lexy nodded slowly and said, "Yes." She felt eyes upon her. When she glanced up Tiberius was staring. He winked at her. She looked down at her glass of red wine, with such contempt it began to boil.

Grey snagged the boiling glass of wine from in front of her to stop anyone from noticing her lack of control. It burned his hand and he hissed, "Shit, that hurt." He stood up and switched the hot wine with a fresh glass as the waiter passed by. He squeezed her knee and whispered in her ear, "You can't blame Tiberius for staring. You look really pretty, Lex."

It was an intimate gesture. She would have smacked anyone else. She took a drink from the new glass of wine and replied, "Arrianna did it," without making eye contact. She downed her glass of wine. The waiter placed another one on the table in front of her, just as she placed the empty glass on the table.

The waiter placed one in front of Grey and he said, "Thank you."

She copied him, "Thank you." The waiter seemed surprised she'd used manners. Her reputation for being uncivilized had preceded her. She looked at Grey and he was smiling. He knew she was on her best behaviour. He also knew she was still learning how to behave. She may look like a lady, but inside she still felt like a wild thing.

Grey leaned closer and whispered, "We don't have to stay long. Let me know when you've had enough."

She smelled something delicious. The staff was bringing around a cart, placing plates of food in front of everyone. A plate was placed in front of Frost a few seats away and he dug right in, without ceremony. When a plate was placed in front of Grey, Lexy took note of the meal being served. When her plate was placed on the table, Lexy's heart constricted in her chest as she tried to hide her reaction. On her plate was roast beef, gravy, mashed potatoes and a crushed yellow flower. *Nobody else had a yellow flower on their plate.* She shoved her seat away from the table. *What if her food was drugged? Was the wine drugged?* Coldly, she stated, "I need some fresh air." She heard Grey repeating her name but ignored him. *She couldn't breathe. She couldn't breathe…There was no air in the room.* She kept her cool as she fled from the table and shoved her way through the crowded dance floor. She pushed on the door, but something had been placed right in front of it. She shoved it open and stopped cold. A giant sack of potatoes had been strategically placed to block her exit. Lexy swallowed and gave the sack a cautious kick with her foot. Somebody was taking her on a sick stroll down memory lane. She'd better call it a night. It was time to go back to the motor home. She wanted to climb under the covers and wait for tomorrow. Lexy took off her shoes, walked down the stairs and began to make her way down the trail. The crisp evening air began to calm her. She stopped and leaned against a tree, as her mind fed her images of Charlotte's smiling face. She closed her eyes, wishing the thoughts away. *She couldn't think about her. It made her feel things she couldn't allow herself to feel.* Lexy covered her eyes with her hands and whispered, "I'm a Dragon. I don't need to have feelings if I don't want them. I'm a Dragon." She felt the tickle on her skin and took her hands away from her eyes. Thousands of tiny yellow flowers were raining from the sky above her. They were in her hair...all over her body. Her heart sprung to life and began to breathe, even though she was willing it to be gone. It ached and throbbed with the guilt of the brutality she'd been unable to save Charlotte from. Lexy stood with the palms of her hands raised to the sky as the flowers descended from the heavens. *Why was this happening? Who was doing this?* She lowered her hands and began to slowly walk through the yellow shower of shame. *She needed Grey.* She needed him with her, but kept walking to the campsite, knowing he deserved to have some fun. *He couldn't be at her side all the time. He deserved more than a life of teaching her how to be normal. She could control herself for one night, for him.* The flowers stopped their descent from the sky. As Lexy rounded the bend in the trail, she froze. On the picnic table by the R.V was a pile of crushed up yellow flowers and a silver thermos. *What in the hell?* Lexy sat on the long wooden bench. She covered her mouth with both hands and rested her elbows on the rustic table. She wasn't sure how long she'd stayed there, staring at the thermos in silence. Her mind was overflowing with thoughts best left forgotten. She needed to know for sure. Lexy reached for the thermos and twisted off the metal lid. After the shower of flowers falling from the sky, she already knew what it contained. Lexy sniffed the contents. *It was hot chocolate.* Her eyes teared up. *She didn't cry, why was she crying?* She blinked the moisture away and covered her face with her hands again. *Who was doing this? They'd destroyed her Dragon with yellow flowers, a plate of food, and a thermos.*

She heard Grey's voice behind her, "Are you alright?"

Lexy stammered, "The flowers on the trail. Didn't you see them? They are just like those flowers on the picnic table. There was a flower on my plate, only my plate."

Grey tried to touch her shoulder and she stiffened. He took the hint and removed his hand, giving her some space. He whispered, "I didn't see any flowers on the trail. There's no flowers on the picnic table, Lex."

Lexy shook her head and asserted, "They were there, Grey."

He grabbed the thermos, smelled it and went to take a drink.

Panicked, Lexy hissed, "Don't drink that it's poisoned."

Giving her a strange look, he placed it back on the table and said, "Thanks for the heads up." He picked it up again and smelled it. "I'm sure it's fine. I think you might be seeing things that aren't there tonight. Maybe you're having an adverse reaction to the wine or it could be stress."

Lexy smirked and stated, "Fine, drink random hot chocolate left by a stranger on a picnic table in the woods, if you want too."

He winked and taunted, "I will, just to prove nobody is trying to poison you." Grey took a drink from the thermos.

She'd assumed he was joking, until she heard him swallow. *She'd only been eleven years old. That was her excuse.* Lexy shook her head at him and sighed, "Did you seriously just drink some of that?"

Grey flippantly commented, "It tasted fine to me."

Lexy whispered, "I was eleven years old, when I was kidnapped and brought to that farm. I was drugged by hot chocolate. I drank it out of a thermos just like that one."

Grey's eyes widened as he disclosed, "Oh, I thought you made it, and just didn't want to share."

Lexy pointed at the pile of flowers on the table and whispered, "An old lady gave me flowers that look just like those ones, to make me forget."

Grey slipped his hand over top of hers and whispered, "Lexy, there are no flowers on the table. Just a thermos of hot chocolate. It could have been left here by anyone. It's a totally normal thing to drink while camping."

He was trying to talk her out of what she knew to be fact. He looked a bit off. Grey tried to stand up and slumped to the ground. Lexy watched him fall from her seat at the table. She didn't move or try to stop him from falling. She just sat there, staring at the thermos. A part of her thought it would be a great idea to drag him to a bunk in the motor home, go get the thermos, take a drink from it herself and go lay down beside him. *No thoughts, no memories, just peaceful nothing.* She got up, wandered over to his body, crouched beside Grey and stroked his messy blonde hair. *Her yellow door was out cold.* She towed him to the RV, dragged him alongside a bottom bunk and sat down for a second watching him breathing on the floor. *She couldn't leave him there. He'd never leave her on the floor.* She loosened his tie and unbuttoned his shirt a bit so he'd be more comfortable before tugging his dead weight up onto the bunk and tucking him in. Lexy kissed his forehead gently and whispered, "Well, at least now I can go deal with this without getting you in trouble too." *She couldn't allow anyone to do this to him. They could hurt her, but nobody was going to hurt Grey.*

She gently closed the door and walked back to the banquet hall. As she climbed the stairs, she noticed the bag of potatoes was gone. All eyes were on her as she entered the hall right at the end of a speech. Someone she didn't know was standing at the podium. The end of the speech was about the behaviour that would be expected of the new Clan while the others were absent. Everyone was seated, but her. She slinked back into her seat. Once the speech was over, the music started up. She scanned the room, knowing nobody could have arranged for flowers to rain from the sky, but someone could have made her see it. *Could they have made her feel it?* She recalled the sensation of the petals. *This was silly.* She was teetering on the edge and somebody was doing their best to push her. Lexy grabbed for the glass of wine, she'd left on the table and just about took a sip of it, before noticing a yellow flower floating in the circular pool of burgundy. Lexy glanced around the room, looking behind her, she met Tiberius's enormous shit eating grin. *That sick son of a bitch.*

Markus asked, "Are you feeling alright?"

Lexy passed her wine to Markus. He peered into her glass and fished out the yellow flower, visibly seething with anger.

He knew what those flowers were used for. This part hadn't been a hallucination. The flower in her wine was real.

Markus cleared his throat and warned, "It doesn't matter if you missed the speech. I know you got the jyst of it. Leave the banquet if you must Lexy, but don't you dare retaliate. This is what they do. They push the buttons of the ones that have the shortest fuse. There will be a better time and place for those thoughts of vengeance you're entertaining."

With her mind tingling with rage, Lexy snatched her wine off the table and got up with it clutched in her hand.

Markus enquired, "Where's Grey?"

"Grey was drugged," Lexy curtly responded. "He's sleeping it off on his bunk."

Markus glared at her and probed, "Why didn't you just heal him?"

She sparred, "He can't get in trouble for what I'm about to do if he's unconscious, now can he?"

Arrianna leapt up and shoved her way through the crowded dance floor.

"Whatever your about to do, make sure it looks like an accident," Markus sighed.

"Don't ask a Dragon to be a mouse," Lexy countered.

Frost casually disclosed, "Nobody gets entombed for an accident, but accidents happen." He didn't budge from his seat to stop her.

Lexy, abruptly left the table. She strolled past Tiberius on her way to the bar, pretended to lose her balance and dumped a whole glass of wine on him, staining his white shirt. She provoked, "I feel terrible, I'm so clumsy."

No fool, Tiberius slowly unbuttoned his shirt and peeled it off. He tossed it on the floor in front of her and teased, "The next time you want me to take my shirt off...just ask."

Lexy shook her head at him and walked away.

He hollered after her, "Be a dear. Grab me some tonic water from the bar. Oh, wait...and an extra jug of water."

Lexy responded politely, "Sure, no problem. I'll be right back." She strolled away from the table occupied by Triad to the bar and reappeared with a jug of water in one hand and the tonic water in the other. She cracked an enormous smile and said, "Here's the water you asked for, Tiberius." She dumped the entire jug on his head. He was shocked for a second, and then he began to laugh as she placed the tonic water on the table in front of him with some napkins and countered, "For the stain on your shirt."

He called after her, "Not so fast. I was told to give you this."

Knowing she should keep walking away, she paused and took the few steps back to him. He passed her something. Lexy took it from him. She opened her hand to see what it was…It was a little yellow flower.

"For the stain on your soul," he sparred.

Without hesitation, she attacked, knocking him to the floor. Lexy straddled him and wrapped her hands around his neck as he howled laughing.

She hissed, "Do you think rape is funny?"

Tiberius pinched her wrists so she couldn't close her hands. He seductively replied, "You know I'm willing. There's no need to rape me."

Someone had obviously set Tiberius up to look like the bad guy. It was usually him, but not this time.

Frost yanked her off, pulled her to her feet, spun her around and teased, "You really have to stop flirting with him." Lexy drop kicked Frost in the junk. He fell to his knees and groaned, "Oklahoma, Oklahoma."

Everyone started to laugh. Jenna steered Lexy away from the tittering crowd of immortals. *She wasn't sorry.*

Jenna grinned at her and assured, "I'm sure half of the girls in this room have wanted to strangle Tiberius and drop kick Frost in the junk. I don't think anyone's going to turn you in for it."

As Jenna led Lexy out of the building, Grey and Arrianna were walking towards her. *They were pissed. She'd never seen Grey this angry at her.*

Grey looked at Jenna and asked, "What did she do?"

Still trying look stern with smiling eyes, Jenna answered, "She dumped wine and water on Tiberius, then strangled him in front of everyone."

Arrianna remarked, "Is that all?"

Jenna added, "Then she drop-kicked Frost in the…"

Grey sighed, "Go back to the party and have a good time. We've got it from here."

Lexy still wasn't sorry, but she was curious. As they started to walk away from Jenna, she looked at Grey and said, "Why did Frost say Oklahoma?"

When they stopped laughing, Arrianna enquired, "Do you know what a safe word is?"

Lexy blankly stated, "No idea what that means?"

"It's what you say to get someone to stop doing something you don't want them to do," Grey explained, still grinning.

Lexy looked at Grey. *That made sense.*

Arrianna clarified, "In bed."

That dirty piece of crap. On a dime, Lexy spun around and sprinted back to the banquet hall. Hearing the commotion behind her, Jenna turned around and all three of them tackled Lexy before she made it back inside. She squirmed for a minute but didn't want to hurt them so she stopped trying to escape. She decided to seek vengeance on another occasion.

Grey sighed, "Are you done? Can we just go back to the campsite and get some sleep?"

She knew she was in the doghouse with these two. She'd left Grey drugged without healing him, so he couldn't do the job he'd been asked to do that night, as her designated babysitter. She didn't want them to stay mad at her so she replied, "Alright, I guess so."

As they walked away from the banquet hall this time, they both kept holding an arm like she was a wild animal ready to make a break for it. *It was a little bit offensive. She probably deserved it, but it was insulting just the same.* When it became clear she had no intention of going back to the party to kill anyone, they released her arms as they entered the motor home.

"I'm going to make us something to eat. I know I'm starving. Dinner looked incredible, such a shame I didn't get to eat any," Grey muttered.

She knew his comment was directed at her. She said, "I could eat something."

"I ate dinner. I'm okay," Arrianna replied. Grey made sandwiches and Arrianna poured them each a glass of milk.

He sighed, "You realise we're drinking milk and eating sandwiches instead of enjoying that party. What did they say to you?"

Lexy swallowed the bite of her sandwich so she could reply, "Tiberius gave me one of those flowers and told me, it was for my soul, so I strangled him and when he started to laugh. I asked him if he thought rape was funny. He said, he was willing, I didn't have to rape him. Frost pulled me off him and told me to stop flirting with his brother."

"I see what happened. If you'd healed me before you went back, all of that could have been avoided. You know that, right?" Grey explained, with understanding eyes.

Lexy answered honestly, "I was going to do it anyway. I didn't want to get you into trouble."

Smiling, Grey shook his head at her and teased, "You're insane, but I still love you."

Lexy smiled and answered, "I know." She watched him eat his sandwich for a moment, before adding, "I warned you about the hot chocolate."

He grinned and said, "You did warn me. I'll give you that."

As Arrianna walked away, she called out, "I'm going to sleep, I'll be in the back room. Come join me when you're finished.

Chapter 19

Count To Ten

By morning the older Clan members were gone. They found a note on the tiny kitchen table. There was a cabin number. It read, feel free to stay there for the week. The trio packed bags and trudged through the trails in search of the cabin. The door was unlocked so they all jumped onto the bed and sprawled, until Grey's stomach began complaining rather loudly. Realising they were all starving, they cleaned themselves up before making their way to the banquet hall. Everything had been cleaned up from the night before, it was spotless. The tantalizing fragrance of bacon from the breakfast buffet wafted across the room towards her. They scanned the room for a place to sit together, grabbed some plates and attacked the buffet. Lexy scooped a heaping pile of food on to her plate. Everyone else was looking rough this morning.

"Well, at least we're not all hung over," Grey chuckled.

Arrianna grinned and said, "This is true." She popped a whole piece of bacon into her mouth. Lexy sat quietly, devouring her breakfast, avoiding eye contact with the other Clans. They kept staring at her. *Did she have ketchup on her face?*

Lexy looked at Arrianna and whispered, "Is there ketchup on my face?"

Arrianna whispered back, "No ketchup, they're probably just curious about you."

While still chewing, Lexy mumbled, "They're making me feel uncomfortable."

Arrianna snickered, "Well, that's good. Don't you see how incredible that is?"

Lexy scowled at her and said, "Have you been sniffing glue?"

While grinning, Arrianna explained herself, "You're feeling something. Uncomfortable is a feeling, Lex."

Lexy stared at her plate. *This was not the best timing to have feelings. The Testing was coming. They'd all be in there, and certainly not playing for the same team once this weird weeklong cease fire was over.*

Grey leaned over and whispered in her ear, "Talk after you've finished chewing."

She didn't have a clue what he meant by that. Lexy whispered back, "I don't understand?"

Arrianna shook her head slowly, in Grey's general direction. Once again, Lexy felt lost in the conversation, due to her inability to understand the non-verbal cues people used.

A girl with long dark curly hair sat across from where Lexy was seated and praised, "When you kicked Frost in the unmentionables, it made everyone's night."

Unsure of what to say, Lexy stared at the stranger. *She knew her.* If she wasn't mistaken, she'd kicked her ass on more than one occasion. *Why was she being nice to her? Was this a trap?*

Smiling at the girl, Grey answered for her, "I'm sure Lexy would say, you're welcome if her mouth wasn't full."

Lexy didn't understand why she'd say that, but knowing Grey wouldn't lead her astray, she repeated his words, "You're Welcome."

The girl smiled as she introduced herself, "My name's Glory." She held out her hand.

Lexy looked at the outstretched hand with the symbol of Trinity on it, and then at Arrianna. *Was she supposed to shake her hand?*

Arrianna shook Glory's hand first and said, "I'm Arrianna, that's Grey. Lexy can be a little slow to warm up to people, but I'm sure in her mind she's shaking your hand."

Lexy looked down at her plate and smiled. That wasn't even close to what she was thinking. She was fighting the urge to stab the touchy-feely girl in the hand with her fork. The others carried on a perfectly pleasant conversation with Glory, while she stared at her plate, wondering when this charade of pointless friendship was going to end. It didn't, they spent most of the day, lying in the sun together, pretending they were going to be friends. Lexy ignored everything, closed her eyes, and attempted to take a nap. When she groggily opened her eyes, she thought they'd left her alone on the dock. She rubbed her eyes and sat up. Grey startled her as he climbed out of the water using the ladder on the side of the dock.

He crawled over to where she sat and remarked, "Good, you're awake."

She felt funny as he crawled towards her on all fours with pearls of water glistening on his skin. His damp medium length hair was sticking to his cheek. He was grinning as he yanked the corner of his towel out from under her behind. In one motion she snatched a bottle of lotion off the dock and poised to hit him with it.

Grey chuckled, "Hey, calm yourself down. You were sitting on the corner of my towel."

She was sitting on his towel. Lexy mumbled, "Sorry."

Grey grinned and teased, "There's a cease fire. You can't spend your week whipping suntan lotion at people. Count to ten next time, before you react."

She didn't respond. *Arrianna and Grey could correct her behaviour, but if anyone else tried to do it she'd shove that bottle of suntan lotion where the sun didn't shine.* Grey heard her thoughts. He cracked an enormous grin. *She knew she was high maintenance. How could he keep smiling at her as though her behaviour wasn't driving him crazy? How could he care about her when she was an antisocial hot mess most of the time?* He hung his legs over the edge of the dock, and dangled them in the water, patting the wood beside him, motioning for her to come and sit there with him. Lexy sat beside him, slipping her legs into the water.

Grey said, "It feels good, doesn't it?"

Lexy looked into his eyes and smiled. *It felt incredible.* She found herself staring at his lips. A lone bead of water had remained on his bottom lip. It looked like a gleaming pearl in the sunshine. Lexy reached over and wiped it away with one of her fingers. Grey stared into her eyes, confused by the intimate gesture. He licked his bottom lip, and then bit it. Lexy couldn't take her eyes off him for some reason. She felt like she wanted something to happen, but she wasn't sure what it was. Grey's face inched closer to hers. Her heart began to race as she stared into his eyes. He shook his head and looked down at his legs. He cleared his throat, exhaled and scrambled to his feet. *What just happened?* He held out his hand. She took it, allowing him to help her up. She didn't want him to let go of her hand, and then he did. It felt wrong as he released it. It was strange that he wasn't talking to her or looking at her while they walked back to the cabin. She noticed a tiny yellow flower on the path. Lexy purposely crushed it beneath her barefoot and kept walking. *One demon down, a million more to go.*

They climbed the stairs to the cabin they were sharing and Arrianna wasn't there. There was a note on the bed. It read, gone for dinner. They caught up with Arrianna at the banquet hall. She appeared to be engrossed in a conversation with one of the Trinity boys. They filled their plates and found a seat. Grey kept glancing in Arrianna's direction and looking away before she caught him staring.

He turned his attention to her and said, "You don't think she'd go there, do you?"

Lexy looked down at her plate. *It felt like she'd been avoiding uncomfortable situations by doing this move a lot.* She recalled an earlier conversation and had an answer, "I wonder if that's the guy she had a thing with before she was taken by Ankh?"

He spoke under his breath, "Maybe it is."

Lexy placed her hand on his and said, "You've said it twenty times this year alone. People always want what they can't have. Arrianna knows she can have you."

Grey's serious expression cracked into a giant grin. He ribbed, "Are you saying I should go have some fun with another girl and then she'll want me?"

Lexy looked at her plate again. *That wasn't what she'd meant to say.* Grey was smiling now and he appeared to be in a better frame of mind. Lexy said, "If you want to do that...have some fun with someone else. I'll behave myself. I'll be fine without you." This was of course a lie. She'd never be fine without him.

Having heard what he'd needed to hear, Grey hopped up and left her sitting there by herself at the table. She definitely hadn't meant for him to take off before they'd finished dinner. *What did it matter really? She was going to spend it staring at her plate.* She finished eating quickly and snuck away from the banquet hall unnoticed. Lexy decided to go for a little walk. She'd take a tour around the grounds and check the place out. She decided to go back to the trailer for the night. *She'd leave the two of them alone together. Maybe Grey would get what he wanted?* She hit a familiar place in the trails, heard twigs crackle behind her and swung around.

Glory laughed, "Don't attack me. I swear I come in peace."

Lexy shook her head and kept walking. Glory caught up and started to walk beside her without speaking. They approached the motor home. The flowers were gone as well as the thermos.

Glory asked, "Do you want to hang out for a while?"

Lexy stared at her, trying to think of an appropriate response. Both of her feelings police were otherwise occupied this evening. Curious, she probed, "Okay, what do you want to do?"

Glory grinned and replied, "The others are building a campfire. Do you guys have any marshmallows in that RV?"

That wasn't a bad idea. Lexy liked roasting marshmallows on a campfire. She nodded and said, "I think we do. I'll go have a look." Glory followed her inside. She found a bag of marshmallows and tossed it to Glory.

Glory caught it and laughed, "Perfect."

They closed the trailer and began walking back to the beach. The sun had already begun to descend behind the mountain range that surrounded the lake. Glory and Lexy found a spot on a log close to the crackling flames of the campfire. It was strange to be sitting next to a Trinity, even stranger to find her tolerable. Lexy was having an alright time. She was letting Glory do all the talking of course, but she didn't seem to notice she was the only one speaking. Afterwards, they strolled back to the motor home with the sounds of nocturnal creatures in the background. They stood beside the picnic table and Lexy wasn't sure what to say. She wanted to go to sleep. Glory was still standing there staring at her. Glory inched forward and kissed her gently on the lips.

Confused, Lexy said, "Thank you?"

Glory cracked a giant grin and teased, "You don't like girls, do you?"

Lexy innocently replied, "I like Arrianna and Jenna. I guess I like you too. You're Alright."

Glory smiled and replied, "It's okay, I think I get it now. I'll see you tomorrow. I'll try to stop myself from kissing you again. I just assumed, sorry about that. You didn't appear to like guys; I thought maybe you liked girls?"

She needed someone to explain this, Lexy knit her brow, waved and said, "I'll see you tomorrow."

Laughing as she walked away, Glory sparred, "See you tomorrow, heartbreaker."

Lexy went inside, closed the door and stood there for a minute. *Heartbreaker?* A lightbulb went on over her head. *She got it! Glory liked her romantically. She hadn't seen that coming. Although, she never saw anything coming with men either.* She turned around, opened the door and said, "Did you mean…" Glory was long gone. She closed the door and locked it. To be honest, she was flattered. Lexy climbed up on her bunk and snuggled under the covers. *Did she like girls? It had never occurred to her. She thought Glory was pretty. Frost was freaky act of nature beautiful.* These thoughts were not what she needed right now. *She missed Grey.* He would have been the perfect sounding board. *Having him around simplified things for her.* She buried her face in the pillow and smiled. *A girl had kissed her and she hadn't reacted with violence. If a guy tried to kiss her, she probably would have cleaned his clock. She wasn't going to be able to sleep.* She rolled over and sighed, "Damn it Grey." *She needed him to be here.* She wondered what he was doing for a second, and then decided she didn't want to know. The thought of him kissing someone else made her sick to her stomach. Her mind travelled back to earlier that day when they'd been sitting on the dock together. She imagined a scenario where he'd kissed her instead of pulling away. She drifted off into dreams of him.

She awoke the next morning to the sensation of being held in his arms. *She was being held in his arms.* He must have come to find her during the night. She tried to sneak out of bed.

He hugged her tighter and groggily whispered, "How come you came back here?"

She put her head back down on the pillow and whispered, "I thought you wanted to be alone with Arrianna, or someone else."

Grey snuggled into her hair and whispered, "I had a feeling you needed me. You have to know that I'll always choose you, over anyone, or anything."

And everything became crystal clear in her heart…

The rest of the week was spent lying on the beach and roasting marshmallows in the campfire with Grey and Glory. It didn't take long for Lexy to realise that Glory was attracted to the person, gender appeared to be inconsequential. Lexy didn't feel instantly hostile when a girl shamelessly flirted with her. She found Glory both flattering and entertaining.

Glory was aware she wasn't going to get anywhere with her, but she seemed to enjoy watching her attempt to decode the flirtatious behaviour. Arrianna popped in occasionally, but she was otherwise occupied with someone she used to know intimately, as she'd guessed on that first night. Grey could have been running around chasing girls all week, but he stayed by Lexy's side. He was getting a kick out of watching her reaction to Glory's flirtatious behaviour.

On the last evening, the trio sat on the floor of their cabin. They'd been feeling off all day. It felt like something was coming. It was probably the Testing they were being warned about. Knowing they may cease to exist, Arrianna had this idea to write letters to be read in forty years, if they made it out. Grey and Arrianna wrote about their hopes and dreams. *Lexy only hoped for one thing. She hoped she would be able to save them. It wouldn't serve her duty as a Dragon, to sit and write about her dreams for the future.* She sat there staring at her paper after the others had finished. In the end she wrote, *I won't let us die in the Testing. I know I can save them. I hope when the Testing is over, they can save me from myself.* She paused for a moment, looked at Grey and wrote, *I love him. I wish I could be everything he needs.* She folded it up, sealed the envelope and passed it to Arrianna. She taped their words of wisdom under the dresser in the room.

Chapter 20

Badass Superhero

Lexy excused herself, saying she needed some fresh air before bed. She strolled down the trail listening to the sound of the crickets chirping their night serenade. Lexy took a different route this time, following a bunch of fireflies. A giant group. It felt like she was supposed to follow their mesmerizing glow. She came across what appeared to be rodeo grounds. They flew right through the open doors. *How had they missed this place?* Lexy followed the hypnotizing light into the grounds. *She wasn't alone.* Floodlights turned on, temporarily blinding her, before revealing two Clan members suspended on the wall on the far side of circular grounds. *It was Glory from Trinity, and a Triad she'd never met. What in the hell?* Lexy whirled around. *She appeared to be alone.* She ran towards Glory.

Glory raised her head and croaked, "Behind you."

Lexy whirled around, but not fast enough as a fine black mist encased her. Her legs gave way and she crumpled to the dirt.

She heard fighting as she came too nailed to the wall next to Glory. They were all here. Their symbols would have gone off, luring the others into the trap. Grey, Arrianna and others she knew were getting their asses kicked. She noticed the blackened irises on someone she didn't recognise. *It was Abaddon. Had the Testing already started? Saying she was pissed off would be the understatement to end all understatements.* Lexy watched as Grey was launched into the air. His body smoked the side of the stands. Her pulse raced and her breathing became laboured. *Oh no, they didn't.* She tore one of her arms from the wall, it healed instantly. She yanked the nails from her other arm and dropped to the ground. Crouched like a beast, her predatory instincts took over, determining where the weakest Abaddon were, through the veil of rising dust. There were at least twenty. Arrianna went down. Her symbol went off. Lexy sprinted into the center of the battle, snapping necks and tossing every Abaddon in her path into the air like rag dolls. She grabbed one by the legs, propelled him around, using one of their own as a weapon against them. She snatched a knife from another and slaughtered all twenty before half the Clan had a chance to go down. Just as she was about to question the wounded, she'd left breathing, they turned to ash, disintegrating into nothing.

She strolled over to Grey. *He wasn't dead. This was convenient.* She healed him and helped him up. Then she knelt before Arrianna, who was dead. *Shit, there were a few dead ones. She'd have to heal Arrianna first. She was going to need more energy than she had within her.*

Grey held out his arms and prompted, "Go on, I know you need it. Wake me up when it's done."

She took his hands and felt the warmth of his life force travel up the length of her arms into her chest. Ridiculously light-headed, she knelt before Arrianna, laid her hands against her chest and passed on Grey's energy. Arrianna opened her eyes as Lexy's vision wavered. *That wasn't easy. Her limbs felt like Jell-O.* Arrianna grinned and grabbed Lexy's arms, giving her just enough energy back to recover.

Arrianna chuckled, "That's the first time you've brought someone back, isn't it?"

"That wasn't as easy as I imagined it would be," Lexy replied.

Arrianna questioned, "Who did you use?"

Lexy smiled and said, "Who do you think I used?"

Arrianna shook her head and sighed, "Do you realise what you did? I'm never going to be able to shake him now.

He's going to be able to find me in the in-between, even when I don't want him too."

She hadn't known that little tidbit of information. They started to heal the rest, one by one. *Well, there goes her newly discovered fantasy...Crap.*

Arrianna tore Glory down from the wall and began to heal her as she glanced over at Lexy and casually enquired, "How'd they get you up on the wall?"

Lexy had just finished healing the Triad who graced the wall beside her. *She was still pissed off they subdued her with mist.*

As Glory opened her eyes, she answered the question for her, "They used the mist."

It felt like cheating. Lexy scowled as she held her hand out to the nameless Triad.

He hesitantly took her hand and said, "Thanks."

They were all healed except for Grey. She heard someone say it was four in the morning. *They weren't going to get a chance to sleep before the others came back from the Summit.* Lexy knelt before Grey and whispered, "At least you had some sleep. I hope I didn't lose you." She laid her hands on his chest and he instantly opened his eyes. He grinned at her and she knew she hadn't.

They walked back to the camp as a united front. They were all Clan and it didn't feel like it mattered anymore which of the three they belonged to. Lexy, Grey and Arrianna climbed the stairs to the cabin and flopped down on the bed, feeling like they'd only been asleep for a few minutes when someone started knocking on the door. Lexy heard the door open.

Frost's voice boomed, "Rise and shine kiddos. It's time for the Testing." He jumped on the bed and started shaking them.

Arrianna groaned, "No, no. We've only been asleep for five minutes."

Frost kissed her on the cheek, messed-up her hair and teased, "It doesn't matter."

Lexy opened her eyes, scowled and mumbled, "Seriously?"

Frost laid his head down on the pillow next to her and whispered, "Seriously."

Lily cleared her throat to get their attention and announced, "Get in the shower you three, make it quick."

"Alright ladies, you heard Lily. I'm sure we'll all fit," Grey chuckled.

Looking adorably messy, Arrianna sighed, "I'd laugh if I'd had enough sleep to find anything funny."

It only took her a second to get excited about the Testing. Lexy jumped up and raced for the bathroom, laughing as she slammed the door and locked it behind her. She sauntered over to the mirror and grinned. She had blood all over her clothes. They'd been too exhausted in the wee hours of the morning to care. She peeled her clothing off, turned on the water and stepped under the spray. It felt incredible. She showered as quickly as she could, and then hollered at Arrianna. She'd been in such a hurry she'd forgotten to bring clothes with her.

There was a knock on the other side of the door and Grey teased, "Did you forget something?"

"My clothes," Lexy admitted.

Grey called through the door, "Is there something special you want to wear to be murdered in, or can I just grab you anything?"

Lexy grinned, placed her hand against the door and replied, "I'm not sure it matters." A minute later there was a knock. Grey opened the door a crack and slipped her clothes inside. Lexy put on the underwear, bra, tank top and shorts. She towel-dried her hair, walked out and said, "Next." Arrianna shoved past Grey and slammed the door behind her, laughing.

Frost handed her a steaming cup of coffee. She smiled at him, walked over to the front steps of the cabin and sat down. Frost followed her.

He sat down beside her and remarked, "You've obviously had a good week."

"It was a good week," she disclosed. Something caught her eye. There was a tiny yellow flower on the step beside her. She didn't mention it, she just brushed it off with her hand. Glory strolled past with a group of the Trinity. She waved at her and winked, continuing to walk away. Lexy started laughing.

Frost gave her a funny look and provoked, "Trying something new?"

She casually placed her coffee on the step, socked his arm and sparred, "We're just friends."

He rubbed his arm, raised the mug to his lips and remarked, "That's going to be inconvenient."

Inconvenient? Lexy raised her eyes to meet his and asked, "What do you mean by that?"

Smiling, he explained, "You're going to have to fight her…Kill her."

Lexy smirked from behind the mug and stated, "That's not a problem."

Frost shook his head and taunted, "I forgot who I was dealing with."

She took another sip of coffee, knowing she was lying. *She liked Glory. It may be difficult to kill her. She was going to have to shut her emotions down five-seconds into the Testing.*

Arrianna joined them with her cup of coffee and said, "Grey should be quick."

Frost glanced at Arrianna and provoked, "So, Lexy likes girls now?"

Lexy punched him again. This time, he spilled his coffee all over the place.

With knowing eyes, Arrianna taunted, "What about Grey?"

Grey wandered up with perfect timing, "What about me?"

Lexy looked at Grey and said, "Glory just walked by and winked at me. They're just messing with me."

Grey shoved in between the girls and revealed, "It was pretty cute. I think Lexy secretly loved it."

Arrianna smiled and said, "She is hot. I would have been flattered."

Shaking her head, Lexy announced, "Alright, I've had enough of this conversation." She got up and walked down the stairs, away from the group.

Grey chased her down the stairs. He chuckled, "You taking the cup of coffee into the Testing with you?"

Lexy swung around and baited, "You know what…Maybe I am." She kept her serious expression for a second, then passed the mug to Grey and smiled.

Grinning, Grey baited, "Bet you could fight the entire Testing with a cup of coffee in one hand, without even spilling a drop?"

Frost stood up on the stairs and said, "Confidence, hopefully that's a good thing. It's time to go, you three."

They ran back into the cabin to grab their backpacks. Grey put his arm around Lexy's shoulder and gave her a squeeze.

"I wish they'd give us details," Arrianna whispered. "What's going to happen in the Testing? What happens to us if we don't come back out?"

Grey embraced Arrianna and assured, "We have Lexy. We're coming back out."

Lexy had never been worried about the Testing. Not even for a second. She was going to protect them; they were her people. The three, linked hands as they walked down the stairs away from the cabin. The campground sounded empty. A bushy tailed black squirrel darted across the trail ahead. The Dragon sparked from within. There was a time that squirrel would have been lunch. Grey glanced at Lexy. She wondered if he was also recalling their first meal together. Sunlight shone through the trees in the trail leaving visible dust particles dancing in its wake. Visible streams of light escaped from the heavens above to bless them on their way into what had only been described as hell.

Frost stopped walking up ahead and commented, "Well, isn't that pretty?"

They all stopped. The trail before them was strewn with so many yellow flowers you couldn't even see the path beneath the carpet of yellow. A voice in her head whispered, *"It's time to shut down. Kill everything you see. Shut your emotions off."* Grey squeezed her hand. *He saw them too. He hadn't been able to see them last time. He knew what these flowers symbolized for her...The end of her innocence.*

He asked, "Do you know what these are Frost?"

"I don't know, buttercups?" Frost answered as he knelt and scooped up a handful. His expression changed. "These flowers are used as a sedative. There must be thousands on this path. Why would these be here?"

They walked across the carpet of innocence lost. Grey kept squeezing her hand, but he didn't need to anymore. With each step her emotions shut down a little more, soon they would be gone. They followed Frost through the trails towards the Ankh crypt until they reached a small cave that wasn't big enough to fit in.

"I'd move Arrianna," Frost cautioned. She backed up. He reached into the hole, touched something and the ground opened, revealing a set of stone stairs leading underground.

Awestruck, Grey declared, "Now, that's cool. One in the desert and another in the forest."

They descended into the crypt lit by torches, flickering at twenty-foot intervals down a long dimly lit corridor. They could hear voices up ahead and entered a large open area where their fellow Ankh lay lounging on pillows on the floor. They all stood up when they noticed they arrived.

With a maternal smile, Jenna walked up to stand before the three and said, "Are you ready?"

Grey sparred, "Can I say, no?"

Jenna took his hand and whispered, "No, isn't one of your options."

Nervously, Grey said, "I didn't think it was."

Chapter 21

Our World Needs More Dragons

Without speaking, Markus looked at Lexy and nodded. She nodded in reply. He looked at the group and said, "You kill everyone. You're not friends anymore. They've all been told the same. You kill everything that moves. Stay with Lexy, stand back up and keep moving forward. The end of the Testing is the Amber room. Only two of the three Clans, will make it out. The third, will be trapped inside the Testing, lost forever. Don't be the third Clan. We have faith in you. Stay with Lexy. She's capable of leading you through this hell."

Lexy didn't speak to anyone. She said no goodbyes as the others did. There was no need for goodbyes. She wasn't afraid. She felt nothing at all. She was ready to do what they'd trained her to do. She followed the group as they walked through the solid wall at the end of the long corridor without flinching. Grey and Arrianna were behind her, trusting if she walked through, they could.

Their leader instructed, "You must move quickly through each wall that opens. They'll close on you, and you can become trapped somewhere extremely unpleasant. The same rules apply when you're in the Testing." Markus placed his fingers in the ridges on the stone, pushing the heel of his hand flat.

The wall slid open, and they all ran through, finding themselves in another stone room with carvings on the walls. The carvings appeared to be Egyptian. Wall after wall shifted away, until they found themselves standing in the dark.

Markus loudly requested, "Azariah, bring us light." The room brightened.

They stood in a room made of gold. The walls, and the ceiling, absolutely everything was gleaming. Jewels were strewn across the ground: rubies, diamonds and emeralds. Arrianna and Grey gasped, in awe of its splendor. Frost looked at Lily and asked her to place her hands next to his. They lay their palms flat in the handprints on the gleaming wall of gold. The carvings on the wall resembled the two and their hands fit perfectly in the prints. The wall slid away. The group dove through the opening, as it slid shut behind them. Lexy was a casual observer as the other two attempted to remain calm in a room of white nothing. There didn't even appear to be a floor. She waited for the stomach-churning sensation of plummeting downward, but they didn't fall. They stood on nothing surrounded by nothing. With a blinding flash of light, they were standing on the outside of what appeared to be a stone floor hovering in the sky. It shifted below her feet, she spread her legs further apart to regain her sense of balance. Jenna stood before her on the floating slab of stone that appeared to go on forever. Grey and Arrianna were far away. One before Frost, and the other with Lily.

Jenna spoke the words that would become her mantra, "You must give yourself over to the Dragon completely. If you disappear into the Dragon, you will save Grey and Arrianna. All three of you will come back to us. You can't do this halfway. There must be complete and total surrender to your instincts. Our world needs more Dragons."

She glanced in Grey's direction, then at Arrianna. She couldn't read their expressions from this distance but knew they were afraid. She sensed their fear like a toxin in the air. *Other predators would too.* All they had to do was find her. She had complete confidence they could, no matter where she was. No matter what she became. A familiar voice in her head whispered, '*Give them hell.*' The stone shifted beneath her feet, opened and she dropped through. It smarted when she landed, but she wasn't hurt. She looked up as the ceiling closed, with a final glimpse of Jenna's face, leaving her in complete, and total darkness. Sensing danger, she scrambled to her feet. Her stomach tightened as she inhaled the scent of something foul. *She wasn't alone.* Her skin prickled with goosebumps. The room exploded with blinding light. She squinted in the glare. As her vision came into focus, an enormous green razor-sharp tail swung back and at her. *Shit.* Her mind seared with momentary agony, as the top of her torso slid in one solid chunk of meat off the bottom half of her body. There was nothing she could do as the beast devoured her. She was thankful she'd ceased to feel pain. The lights went out, and she awoke in what felt like seconds. Lexy was in the dark again. A warrior, by nature she stayed on the ground, hoping to miss the swing of the tail. Again, the light incapacitated her, and the tail swung before she had the time to react. Her head rolled across the floor. For a split second she was a bystander, hovering above what was left of her as her bottom half was devoured by the monster. The picture flickered, and disappeared…

Gasping for air as she awoke, she remained on the floor. Lexy rolled in what she thought was the opposite direction, until she bumped into something. It wasn't stone. She'd rolled right into the creature's legs. *Shit.* She'd thought by altering her position, she'd be able to avoid the swing of its tail. The light exploded, blinding her momentarily. She froze, with her stomach flat against the floor, breathing light feathered breaths. When the beast didn't move, she suspected it couldn't see her. She slowly shifted, just a touch so she could get a look at the creature butchering her, repeatedly. It was enormous. The monster had shiny onyx scales, a razor-sharp lizard's tail, and the horns of a bull. It was an ungodly creation with clawed almost human fingers. It only had one eye, smack dab in the center of its forehead, reminiscent of a cyclops of folklore. She froze in position, as the lights went off again. Plotting her next move, Lexy crawled along the stone until she was situated behind the beast. Her inner predator whispered, *take out its eye. That is the weakness.* She waited for the flash of disorientating light, scaled its back, and clawed at its one giant orb with her nails. The creature bucked, shrieked, and tossed her around until the jelly from its eye squirted down her hands, as she tore it from the socket. The hideous creature flailed a few times and slumped to the stone, completely still. The light went out again and Lexy wondered if this whole scenario would replay. Alone in the dark with her thoughts for only a second before the wall opened to Arrianna's outstretched hand. Lexy reached for it, Arrianna yanked her through. It took a moment to regain her faculties. She stared down a long seemingly endless stone corridor that faded into black. She didn't much enjoy the feeling of being trapped. *This felt like one.*

Arrianna held up her hand and squeamishly said, "Tell me this isn't eyeball juice." Lexy didn't answer. Arrianna wiped the slime on her white sarong. "This is disgusting."

Grey wasn't with her. Lexy asked, "Where's Grey?"

Arrianna replied, "I have no idea. I can't even believe I found you. I think it's already been a few days."

She'd just fallen through the roof, hadn't she? Confused, Lexy shook her head and corrected, "You mean hours."

Arrianna asserted, "It's been days. The walls shift each time you pass through. The scenery keeps changing. It's impossible to know where you've already been. It feels like you're walking in circles. That's why it took me so long to find you."

Lexy looked at the Ankh symbol on her hand. She traced her finger across it and said, "I'll find him."

Arrianna replied, "There's no point in even looking at it. Our symbols don't work properly in here. A few times mine lit up and flickered, but that's it."

They hadn't moved a muscle, but the walls began to grind. They'd be squished. They were nothing, but bugs under a Third Tier's foot. The one obvious escape route narrowed with each passing second. Lexy ordered, "Run!" The two sprinted, single file. When they reached each dead end, it was as though the walls sensed their approach, and allowed passage. They darted through the last shifting wall, directly into the center of a sword fight. Grazed by a swinging blade, Lexy maneuvered out of the way, spun around, snapped a Triad's neck, and stole the blade from his death grasp. She tossed the sword to a weaponless Arrianna. A fine mist of blood from a Triad sprayed her. Arrianna began to fight as Lexy dodged each sword's deadly swing. She swept the feet out from underneath another one, taking the sword from the stunned girl's hand, by grabbing the sharp edge of the blade. She didn't care if she cut her hands, superficial wounds only ever took a moment to heal. In battle, it wasn't even close to a fair game. Lexy was unbeatable. She sliced, and stabbed her way through the shifting doors, until everyone was lying on the floor, including Arrianna. Lexy grabbed her body and began to tow it away. She felt an odd sensation, a tug followed by a small shock. She peered down at the body she was dragging, her friend turned to dust in her hands. What was left of Arrianna, slipped through her fingertips, and sprinkled on the cold stone underfoot. Frozen in place for a moment, unsure of what she should do, Lexy stood there. A flickering image of her friend appeared, and then Arrianna solidified on the ground before her. *What in the hell?* Lexy helped her up. *They had to get out of here. Grey had to be the priority. If the others all disintegrated, they'd be starting to reappear by now. They didn't have much time.* The two girls ran through rooms, moving swiftly through each sliding wall, until they ran into one with no floor. Lexy only had time to swear, before plummeting into the unknown. The air rapidly warmed. *She couldn't inhale the air.* Overwhelmed by stifling heat, she descended into an approaching glow. *This was going to suck.* She landed in the glowing river of lava, lit up, and burst into flames. There was excruciating pain, unlike anything she'd experienced, and the sweet peace of nothing.

She regained consciousness with the pitch of Arrianna's screams, still echoing in her mind. She moved her fingers. She was lying on something soft. *Dare she open her eyes?* She inhaled the pleasurable scent of fresh cut grass, and contemplated pretending to be asleep for a little while longer. *She had to find Grey.* Lexy scrambled to her feet, ready for anything. She hadn't been ready for the spectacular visual that accosted her senses. There was not a flower on the ground, nor a cloud in the sky. She wiggled her toes in the exquisite teal grass. It was the softest she'd ever had the pleasure to stand on. She appeared to be all alone. *She'd lost Arrianna. How was she looking at blue sky? How was she standing on an endless field of green?* The sky wasn't one shade of blue, it was splotches of various hues. It looked like pieces of a puzzle. Her stomach tightened. *It was too beautiful to be real. This was a visual trap, colourful bait to lure partially immortal fish. They weren't in the in-between. They were somewhere dark, somewhere they were supposed to be fighting their way out of.* She felt Grey's presence before she saw him. She spun around, and in the distance a figure approached. She wasn't sure how, but she knew it was him. He staggered a bit, stopped moving, and dropped into the grass. Lexy sprinted towards him. *What now?* When she reached Grey, he was covered in fire ants. She swept them off with her hands. It burned her flesh, but it was nothing in comparison to the lava bath. The ants disappeared before she'd rid his skin. He was still breathing, but unconscious. She shook him and whispered, "Grey, get up." She lovingly stroked his hair. He didn't wake. She shook violently and hissed, "Greydon, get the hell up. Don't make me smack you." Her effort at pleasantly rousing him hadn't worked. *She didn't have time for this shit.* She hauled off and slapped him across the face.

Grey croaked one word, "Snakes."

What snakes? She didn't see any snakes? Everything was flat and green, with exception to the ant hill he'd been unlucky enough to wander over. Pulling a barely coherent Grey, onto her lap, she whispered, "There's no snakes. Those were ants. Come on Princess. Rise and shine. We have to get out of here." *Why was he so out of it? Her hands were burning.* She glanced at her scarlet palms, something moved under her skin. *This wasn't going to be good.* Her palms split along her lifeline, and hundreds of tiny wriggling baby snakes burst from her palms, travelled up her arms, and into every orifice. They slithered into her ears, up her nose, and squirmed into her tear ducts. She was vibrating with adrenaline, clawing at her own flesh with her fingernails.

"Shut it off," a voice whispered.

They were inside her, squirming beneath the surface of her skin. *She had to get them out!* Their outlines wriggling all over her body. *Get them out!* She chewed the flesh off her own arm and spat a chunk of meat into the grass. The voice screamed, "SHUT IT OFF!" Lexy stopped tearing at her flesh with her teeth and became calm. *This isn't real. There are no snakes under my skin.* She looked at her palms with no visible wounds. Grey was asleep on her lap. As her heart warmed, the creepy sensation of wriggling reptiles beneath her skin ceased. She couldn't help herself, as she gently caressed his hair out of his eyes. *He needed to wake up. She had to save him. They had to find Arrianna.* She stopped stroking his hair and stared up at the endless ceiling of blue, knowing it was all a hallucination. *She was in a colourless crypt of stone, floating in the sky. There was no grass. There was no multihued blue puzzle sky. This isn't real.* There was a blinding explosion of white light, and she was sitting on a chilly stone floor, with him lying across her lap.

"Well, that sucked," Grey croaked as he opened his eyes and sat up.

Arrianna materialized. He leapt to his feet and the two embraced. She was relieved to see Arrianna. *She wanted to be part of their hug.*

"Shut it down," a voice echoed from the walls.

She looked around. *Was everyone else hearing that?* Instinct urged her to listen. *She couldn't be wanting a hug. Dragons don't need cuddles.* She had to cease all physical contact long enough to become the undomesticated version of herself. *She needed to be the wild thing. The girl in the woods, all alone.* Lexy rose to stand, and ordered, "It's time to go."

"I thought I'd never find you guys," Grey admitted.

Smiling, Arrianna corrected, "Lexy found you, I just got here."

He didn't hug her. With a charming grin, Grey sweetly tucked a strand of wild crimson hair behind her ear and stared deep into her eyes with unspoken appreciation. Her heart warmed. Lexy turned away from him to shut it down. *She was going to have do something seriously dark.*

With renewed pep, Grey declared, "Well, how do we get out of this place?"

Lexy vacantly responded, "We're all going to die."

Grey's voice teased from behind her, "I knew you'd say something like that."

He touched her back. Lexy knit her brow and coldly stepped away from him. Her stomach twisted into a knot, and she smiled. Her pulse began to race as a shot of adrenaline shivered through her meat suit. The temperature in hell began to rise. She heard someone vomiting and turned to look. Their internal warning systems were obviously working overtime. They were doubled over holding their stomachs, gagging and choking. Her stomach had given her warning, but not to that degree. *This was a good thing.* She was upright while the others were barely able to stand. Grey dropped to all fours spewing up clear liquid. *It looked like water. This was going to be good.* Perspiration trickled down her hairline into her eyes, Lexy vacantly wiped it away. *Bring it on.* The dull grey walls before the group, became glowing orange and ash. The corridor blistered, bubbling like human skin dipped in boiling water. It lit up with flames and became a raging inferno. Her skin was drenched with perspiration. They could turn back right now and walk in the other direction. That wasn't what they were supposed to do, she could feel it. The raging inferno ahead became a sick display of screaming faces, distorted with anguish.

Arrianna whispered, "Is this what happens to us if we don't make it out?"

Staring straight ahead, Lexy replied, "Probably, failure isn't one of our options." Their next move would be excruciatingly painful, but it was obvious. She'd been told to follow her instincts. She had the overwhelming urge to walk into the hall of flames. Lexy glanced back at her fellow Ankh, and nodded, signalling her intention.

Grey said, "Seriously?"

Arrianna nodded and confirmed, "Badass superheroes it is."

"Or complete frigging lunatics," Grey countered.

Lexy turned away and marched directly into the inferno. Her mind lit up with familiar brutal agony as her skin bubbled and melted away from the bone. Everything went black. She awoke in what felt like seconds, gasping for air. She scrambled to sit up. *She was alone. Had they chickened out, or had they followed her into the fire? She felt sick. What if she lost them? Damn it, her emotions were back.* Lexy's heart leapt as Arrianna's image flickered and appeared in the stone corridor. She was struggling, unable to move her limbs. *This was new?* Lexy stood up for a better vantage point.

A voice prompted, "Walk away."

She couldn't tell whether it was coming from outside of her mind or inside anymore. She was supposed to listen.

With perfect timing, Grey flickered and solidified beside the ailing Arrianna. He groaned, looked directly into Lexy's eyes and said, "Don't you even think about it."

He also appeared to be having a difficult time with his motor skills. They had to be able to keep up with her. When she ceased to care, it would be up to them to stay by her side. Maybe this was the reason, a part of her kept pulling her back? She now cared about things a proper Dragon had no business caring about. Attachment was a tricky beast. Once again, the voice in her head ordered her to leave them on the floor and walk away. She sighed and helped Arrianna to her feet. Her friend instantly regained her balance. Lexy looked into Grey's eyes, took his hand, and helped him up. He was too weak to stand on his own, his body slumped against her.

"Thank you, for not leaving me behind. I know you need to," he whispered as he embraced her.

She stiffened, and he held her tighter. His breath against her hair, the warmth of his bare chest against hers. Each of these things created dents in her armour, and twitches in her heart. He kissed her cheek tenderly, and that part of her that felt something intense for him sparked. *Damn it, Grey.* Lexy pulled away with accusing eyes. She reprimanded, "You can't do that. Not here…not now."

He regained his footing. Still mentally compromised, he teased, "According to Jenna we're all supposed to be capable of going from cuddling kittens to mass murder by now. I know it's selfish, but I needed a hug, and the standoffish attitude is driving me crazy. All I want to do is hold you, until you snap out of it. We are so far past this, Lex. It feels wrong to let you go. It feels like I'm sacrificing you to save myself."

She looked into Grey's eyes, and even though she tried to stop them, her feelings for him registered. *She was supposed to be surrendering to the Dragon within. How would she do this when he could make her step away from the edge of the abyss with the sound of his voice, a gentle kiss, and the touch of his hand? She had to let go of the last shreds of her humanity. What if she couldn't?*

Arrianna looked at Grey and stated, "You have too. You know you have too."

Lexy wasn't sure if what Arrianna said was meant for her, or Grey. Her words worked for both her thoughts, and what he'd spoken aloud.

Grey whispered, "I promise I'll bring you back after this is over." He teared up and turned away.

Arrianna kept eye contact with her and vowed, "Always."

The walls began to shift, they were forced to end their sappy goodbyes and run. They sprinted down the long winding corridors of stone as the crypt continued to move and guide them. It occurred to Lexy that they were merely cattle, being herded towards the next excruciating version of death. She ran ahead of the others, hearing their footsteps as they pursued her, but she didn't look back. *She had to let go.* The walls altered with the grinding of stone against stone, until they ran into a room where Glory was being swarmed by ravenous monarch butterflies. Lexy made no attempt to stop it from happening, the others followed her lead. Frantically shrieking for them to help, Glory swung her arms, until her carcass dropped to the stone. All that was left of the girl that kissed her was a skinned skeleton with some chunks of meat dangling from bones. *Shit, that was impressively dark.* The swarm of carnivorous butterflies came straight at her, Lexy didn't flinch or show an iota of fear. Her brain screamed as the fluttering lovely flesh-eating creatures devoured her, picking her bones nearly clean of muscle and flesh. The swarm moved on to ingest her Clan. She'd stayed alive long enough to hear their high-pitched wails of agony. *She was staying alive longer now.* The lights went out…

Lexy gasped, she heard rushing water. *Was there a river nearby?* Lexy opened her eyes, still in the crypt with no visually appealing mirage. No fields of green or multihued blue skies. For a second, she was almost disappointed. *At least it had been a change of scenery.* Just on the border of the shadowed area at the end of her line of sight she saw water, beginning to pool on the stone floor of the massive floating crypt. *She'd have to be more careful what she wished for in the future.* She rose to stand, ready to meet her fate head on. Water poured in from holes in the ceiling, each one roughly twenty feet apart. *They'd be submerged in no time. Drowning, how bad can this be?* She heard Grey and Arrianna behind her, and once again fought the faint urge to turn around. It wouldn't serve any purpose to watch them squirming from the fear she was no longer capable of comprehending. Nor would it serve her to allow the one fear she couldn't shake to enter her train of thought. She had to get them out of this place. They stood side by side as the water pooled around their ankles, and rapidly rose to waist depth.

Nervously, Grey asked, "How many ways are there to die?"

There were countless endless ways to die, so she didn't answer. She couldn't respond for that might spark the part of her that he owned. The part of her that had no business lingering under the surface of her skin even after she'd given control to the beast inside.

"There are countless, endless ways to die," Arrianna whispered.

Lexy smirked, *Arrianna heard her thoughts like she'd spoken them aloud.* She knew Arrianna understood why she wasn't playing along. She was succumbing to the version of herself that didn't care. Her warped alter ego that didn't love anything, or anyone. The water was up to her neck, and then her feet lost their footing. Lexy didn't attempt to stay afloat. She permitted her body to sink beneath the surface, hovering there in the midst of chaos. Her instincts were usually set on survival, but since she'd arrived in this place, they'd been guiding her to do the opposite. Trust your instincts was playing on a loop in her mind. *A mantra with a purpose.* The bubbles, created by her Clan members flailing limbs, swirled in her line of sight. *They were fighting this version of death. Was it simply because they could? This version wasn't instantaneous, it was drawn out. They had to stop. They'd only win this battle by dying with strength and dignity.* Lexy grabbed onto Arrianna's leg and yanked her under. She struggled and managed to free herself from Lexy's grasp. She grabbed her again, catching Arrianna's attention. She met Arrianna's panicked eyes and thought, *let go. Just let go.* Arrianna appeared to understand, and she stopped struggling. Grey was floating next to her. The option of making it to the surface was gone. Arrianna grabbed ahold of Grey's hand, squeezed it, and stared into his eyes. Without words he understood what she was saying. He allowed the fight to be over. It was beautiful, the way they looked deep into each other's eyes, holding hands until the light disappeared, and their fingers unlaced. *Why was she still alive? She knew why. She'd been entranced by the beauty of their demise. She'd forgotten to let go.* The pulsating burning of her oxygen deprived brain, was replaced with the sensation of being wrapped in warmth as a voice whispered, *Go to sleep. You must sleep.* The visions of dancing bubbles, and angelic floating corpses faded to black.

Lexy gasped and opened her eyes. This time, they were sitting there waiting for her to rise. Lexy sat up and listened for the sound of water. *There was nothing.* This version of death was completed. It was oddly satisfying. Neither one tried to speak to her or help her up. As the stone began to grind, she scrambled to her feet. A half dozen Triad wielding swords attacked. In a flash, Lexy disarmed a few to arm her fellow Ankh. The sounds of clashing swords fuelled her need to feel the warmth of their blood on her skin. The room was covered in a fine crimson mist of by the time the battle ceased, and the Dragon was free.

They darted through gliding walls, gathering small velvet bags containing salt, figs and stones. The group raced through an opening wall and slid out onto the icy surface of a pond.

Grey extended both arms, attempting to balance. He whispered, "Don't move. The ice is going to crack."

The crack was slowly making its way towards Grey. She'd have to speed this up, they didn't have all day. Lexy grinned and stomped, sliding around before attempting to do it again. The ice cracked and separated beneath her feet. Grey started swearing. She heard the others, breaking through the ice, but didn't look. She'd ceased to care about anything except her priority, and that was to kill them all, as many times as the Testing required. Lexy took a final breath as she fell through the ice into the frozen water. The agony of the icy demise was easily comparable to any heat related death she'd experienced. She awoke on the snow-covered shore, confused as to why she was still somewhere cold. *It only took a second to understand what happened.* Grey had climbed out and he was gingerly making his was across the icy pond towards the shore. *Damn it, Greydon.*

Arrianna materialized on the shore beside her and said, "What happens if he misses one?"

Operating on instinct, Lexy signalled for Arrianna to follow her. She casually strolled across the surface of the lake, stopping about five feet from the icy demise escapee.

Grey shook his head, attempting to bargain with her, "Come on Lex. Don't do it. I'll die twice next time."

Silly boy, you can't bargain with a Dragon. Just as she was about to stroll over and chuck him into the frozen pond. The ice exploded around him. A reptilian beast with enormous protruding fangs chomped down on his torso and dragged him into the freezing water, leaving behind a red spray on the ice, and bubbles in the water. A moment later a fountain of blood sprayed up, one of his arms flew out, and slid across the ice. His dismembered arm came to a stop right in from of them.

Visibly shaken, Arrianna remarked, "That was unnecessarily graphic. Mental note. It can always get worse. I won't be avoiding a damn thing."

"Good to know," Lexy said as she unceremoniously shoved Arrianna into the water and leapt in after her. The first version of their icy demise had been quick. Lexy was only submerged for a second, when she felt the excruciating sensation of jaws snapping down on her lower leg. The beast dragged her into the freezing depths. *She'd die soon. It would be over fast.* The creature took her on a swim, broke through the surface of the ice and yanked her out. *Just eat me already we have shit to do. It being far too careful with her. Oh, Crap.* It hauled her to the shore. *Maybe it was saving her for later?* She had a flash of how carnivores in the wild feed their young. *Oh, Shit.* A dozen small versions of the hideous creature raced towards her. The beast had dropped her off as a snack for its offspring. *She didn't have time for this. Normally, she would have been able to fight them off and tossed them away, or torn them to pieces with her bare hands, without flitching. She had a situation. She couldn't move her limbs. It was happening to her now, with extremely shitty timing.* As wild animals often do, they went straight for her neck and stomach. They tore out her intestines and ingested her slimy pale hued innards. *It was painful, but oddly entertaining.* She felt a few hard yanks on her arm, and then watched as one of the creatures walked away with her arm dangling from its mouth. *It was as though she was watching it happen to someone else, it was hilarious.* She felt the same tugging sensation as one ripped off a leg. *This was far too funny. She might be losing her mind. Why was she still alive? It didn't even hurt.* She was pretty sure there was nothing left of her, but a severed head. She was laughing in her mind as a massive set of dripping teeth sunk into her face, and the lights went out...

Chapter 22

Gone

She had the most violent dream. She was slaughtering countless hideous creatures and terrified Clan. It was all visions of blood and chunks of meat. There was so much darkness. She wasn't sure if her Clan was still with her. She'd fallen for days, in a sea of dark things with hollow eyes, and then had a vision of Arrianna standing in a lighted door, pulling her out. Lexy opened her eyes to find herself lying on something soft. *Was it a pillow?* She recalled a baby something strolling away with one of her arms and chuckled aloud. She sat up. Grey and Arrianna were eating a meal and staring at her because she'd woken up laughing. She was in a small cubicle. It wasn't much bigger than the jail cell full of Abaddon she'd set on fire.

Smiling, Arrianna enquired, "Is something funny?"

Lexy was still grinning because she was really lying on a pillow, and for some reason that was hilarious.

Arrianna continued to speak, "Grey carried you all the way here. The last time you reappeared, you didn't wake up."

Lexy didn't make eye contact with anyone as she strolled over to the table and began to eat. There was a mountain of rolls, fruit and figs. What she really wanted was meat. She tore a piece of bread apart with her teeth, it was stale. She spat it on the table, and chuckled.

Arrianna whispered, "Are you feeling alright?" She tried to touch her.

Lexy growled and tried to bite her hand. Arrianna dove out of the way and landed on the floor. Lexy grabbed a plate full of fruit from the table and threw it at her. It smoked her in the head.

Arrianna snapped, "What in the hell, Lex?"

Grey didn't move a muscle to stop her. He whispered to Arrianna, "I'll bring you a plate. Maybe you should go sit over there."

Confused, Arrianna whispered, "Are you serious?"

Without speaking, Grey nodded. Arrianna shimmied until she was out of Lexy's reach, sitting against the wall. He passed her a plate of food.

Lexy bit into a fig and there was a pit in it. She spat it at Arrianna.

Grey whispered, "Be careful Lex. There's pits in some of those figs, there's none in the grapes."

Why was it speaking to her? She didn't want it to talk to her. She was thirsty. She looked up to see if there was anything to drink. Grey carefully slid a goblet of red wine towards her. She scowled, *she wanted water.*

"I'm sorry that's all we have," he whispered. "There's a fountain on the other side of that wall, but the other Clans are here. I'm not sure you want to go out there."

Was she supposed to give a shit? Lexy got up and marched over to the wall. *It didn't open by itself.* Lexy stared at it. This was the first time she noticed the finger indents, and the curved one for the base of the hand. She placed her fingers in the grooves, and the wall slid open. A group of Trinity, including a dishevelled Glory were gathered around the fountain. The second she stepped out, they scattered. Lexy climbed into the fountain and began to drink straight out of it. At the bottom of the fountain was a sword. She stood up, clutching it in one hand, surveying the others. *They appeared terrified. They should be...*After having some fun with her new sword, she returned to the chamber. Her memory was foggy, everything blended together, in macabre flashes of violence. She was covered in blood when she strolled back into the room, after working up an appetite. She sat and continued to eat without chasing Arrianna away. Lexy grabbed a glass of wine, sniffed it and then chugged the entire goblet.

Arrianna whispered, "It has to be you Grey." She gingerly rose to her feet, walked over, and laid her head down on one of the pillows.

Grey casually observed, "You've obviously been busy, and incredibly quiet. We didn't hear a thing."

Lexy tore off a piece of bread with her teeth and chewed it. The loaf was covered in blood. It was dripping from her hands. *She didn't care.* Finally void of all emotion, she was in the state she needed to be in. She picked at the bloody loaf of bread and chucked it. *She needed meat.*

Grey slammed back his enormous glass of wine, looked into his empty goblet and implored, "Don't leave without us...without me."

Her heart twitched. Lexy spoke aloud for the first time in weeks, "I'm coming back."

Inching closer, he touched her hand and begged, "Please Lex, don't go away again. You've been lost in your head for weeks. We've been chasing you, trying to stay close. We need to get out of here. Try to remember me."

Contact with his hand gave her heart a nudge. Memories began flashing through her mind, she casually responded, "I'm not lost, I'm just how you found me. I know who you are, and you know what I am."

He strolled over to where Arrianna was trying to sleep, crouched and began gently shaking her. "We have to go," he whispered.

Lexy shook her head. *They were wasting time with naps and fruit.* She staggered to the wall she'd passed through, feeling light-headed. *This was potent wine.* She placed her fingers, and the heel of her hand in the grooves. The wall ground open to reveal bodies, scattered in the area surrounding the fountain. *Had she really killed them all?*

Grey whispered, "There's gas coming in through that square in the corner." He stepped out of the room and pointed at the visible vapours. Then froze, at a loss for words as he took in what Lexy had done without making a sound.

Arrianna stood beside Grey and said, "She has to want to leave. I don't think she cares. I bet Jenna never saw this coming."

Lexy stepped over most of the bodies, purposely stepping on a few. A couple were dangling over the edge of the fountain, she shoved one out of her way. The other corpse groaned. She smiled, and swung the sword, severing the head. It plopped into the fountain with a shocked expression on its face. Lexy started to laugh. She sat down in the water and bopped it on the head with one finger, and it bobbed around in the water. She picked it up by the hair, cocked her head and stared into the vacant eyes for a second, then rolled it across the room. The severed head left behind a trail of blood. She'd never gone bowling, but she'd seen bowling, and this reminded her of it. Far too casually, Lexy glanced at her two stunned Clan and said, "We should go bowling." *She really didn't give a shit. It was incredibly freeing.* The water in the fountain was tinted red. *She didn't care.* She cupped her hands and drank the blood red liquid from her palms.

Grey wandered over and sat on the edge of the fountain. He watched her in silence for a minute before saying, "I miss you."

Lexy scooped up another palm full of red tinted water, and loudly slurped it, without responding. She lowered her face under the surface of the morbidly tinted water, filled her mouth with water and spit it, at Grey's chest.

Grey didn't flinch. He kept speaking, "We need to get out of here. We need to get back to our Clan. If the other Clans beat us, we'll be stuck in here forever."

Staring into the water, Lexy grinned and began to move her hand in a circle, creating a tiny whirlpool. "The walls are alive. They'll show us the way out, once we're finished dying," she disclosed. Grey extended his hand to her, a gesture of humanity. She ignored him and stood up on her own.

"She's right about the walls. They feel alive to me too. We'd better get going, this place is filling up with gas," Arrianna urged.

Grey wandered to the wall and it slid open. He said, "I guess we're supposed to go this way." He strolled through the opening and started walking down the lengthy corridor. Lexy decided to follow Grey for a change. She could hear rushing water, but there was none to be seen. The ground underfoot flickered. *It was a hologram.* They dropped through the floor of trickery into rapids, travelling through a forest. All Lexy could see was the white foamy surface and greenery as she whooshed past it. Her stomach smoked into a log hidden beneath the bubbling white water. The wind was knocked out of her, she remained slumped against the log, certain this death was not about drowning. There were rocks up ahead. Then a drop off. *A waterfall, how ingenious.* She shot over the edge, watching her Clan vanish into the spray below. She'd hoped the death would be instantaneous, no such luck. The water pounded her against the rocks, and into the side of the cliff bluff, snapping limbs, pummelling her body, but she was still alive. The others hadn't surfaced. *Where had they gone?* Lexy dunked under and saw a couple of funnels of water. They appeared to be sucking the water straight down. She swam towards one, and allowed it to take her, spinning her down into a drain, or chute. She shot down a tunnel that reminded her of something she'd seen on signs by the side of the highway, yet never done. She'd never gone to a waterslide. She whizzed down the smooth rock tubing until the slide split off in two directions, swerved to the left, and began to fall free of the slide. Lexy descended into nothing for quite a while before splashing into an underground pool in what appeared to be a cave. She bobbed to the surface, swam over to a rock, and pulled herself out of the water. She wasn't dead and was no longer injured. Lexy sat there on the edge of the underground pool in near darkness. Above her the torches in the cavern lit up as if by magic. *What fresh version of hell awaited her in this place? Would she be swarmed and eaten? Would she be torn apart? Would the water turn to lava? Did she care? She was forgetting something important.* She scrambled up the side of the rock face to the mouth of the cave above, and stared down a long hallway lit by torches, placed at twenty-foot intervals on either side. She began to walk down the corridor. Flashes of the dark farm lit up in her peripheral vision. Her past played out on the walls on either side of the corridor. The man with the scar opened the stall and looked at her. He'd been one of her captors. She knew he couldn't really be here. She'd killed him. On the wall beside her, a vision of Charlotte skipped away, stopped and knelt to embrace a golden retriever. It was Freckles.

The scarred man strolled up and lured, "Come with me." Charlotte took his hand, stepped out of the wall, and into the corridor. They started to walk away together. *No, don't go with him.* Lexy tried to grab for her, but her hands slipped through her body. *She wasn't real.* Lexy knew this, but in the past, she hadn't done anything to stop it from happening. They disappeared, and yellow flowers began to float from the ceiling. Lexy held up her hands and felt the flowers landing in her palms. Lexy closed her hands and crushed the delicate yellow flowers into pulp. Visions of the cabin, and her pack lit up the walls.

At the end of the hall under cover of darkness she heard growling. Her heart twitched as Chicken stepped out of the shadows. She'd lost her weapon. Her canine companion salivated, gnashing his teeth as he moved slowly down the corridor towards her. He made an odd sound and bulked up, doubling his size. *This was new.* She looked into his eyes; certain it was him. Even if it was only his essence, her companion was still there. She didn't want to kill him. She'd choke him out, instead of finishing him off. Chicken made the sound as he doubled in size, once again. Blocking the entire corridor was a massive rabid beast. The creature twitched, and spider legs protruded from either side of his body. She heard a rattling sound. His wagging tale had morphed into a massive rattlesnake. They stared each other down. Lexy stepped towards him to signify her intention. *It was all or nothing now. She'd never be able to subdue this creature.* She grabbed a torch from the wall and strode towards the beast. About ten feet in front of her a hazy form appeared, then solidified. *It was Grey.* The creature darted at him, Lexy's heart dropped. With the instinct to protect him too strong to ignore, she leapt into action and hollered, "Get down!" He dove out of the way, and she ran right through Chicken, skidding across the floor. *It was another hologram.* She spun around and marched towards Grey. She stood above him, wanting to kick him in the face for bringing her back early. Instead, she held out her hand. He took it, and as soon as he was on his feet, he embraced her. She tried to close herself off from him, but she couldn't. She hugged him back and whispered, "You really have to stop bringing me back."

Caressing either side of her face, Grey whispered, "You brought yourself back. I didn't do a thing."

Their reunion was cut short by the distinct pitch of Arrianna's screams. They sprinted in the direction of her screams echoing through the crypt. When they found her, she was clawing at the ground, flailing around.

Grey tried to help and was shocked by touching her skin. He yanked his hand away and enquired, "Do you have any salt bags left? Should we throw some on her?"

Lexy replied, "No, I don't still have any salt bags. I just went over a waterfall."

Helpless to ease her agony, he asked, "Should we split up and look for some?"

Lexy shook her head, knelt by Arrianna's tortured form and offered, "I'll see if I can calm her down." She placed her hands on Arrianna's chest and attempted to siphon some of her energy. *It was excruciating. She wasn't possessed, this was something else.* Lexy tried to jerk her hands away but couldn't. She gasped, "Grey, you're going to have to kill me." With pleading eyes, she ordered, "Do it." He snapped her neck and her body crumpled on the floor.

Lexy gasped, inhaling the stale crypt air. She was cradled on Grey's lap. He was stroking her hair lovingly.

Upset, Grey whispered, "Don't ever order me to kill you again."

Gazing into his concerned eyes, Lexy whispered, "What's wrong with you?"

He shook his head and said, "You mean besides the fact that I just murdered you, on command?"

"Good, it's not just me," she whispered, feeling exposed in his embrace.

He probed, "Not just you? What do you mean by that?"

Lexy sat up, turned his direction and admitted, "Let's just say it goes both ways." *Arrianna was peaceful now. She seemed different as she opened her eyes.*

Arrianna inhaled the crypt's air, choked and croaked, "That was an epically crappy experience. I think I was just, Enlightened."

Intrigued, Grey said, "You've had your healing ability for years. Do you have anything else now?"

Scrambling to her feet, Arrianna laughed, "I just opened my eyes Grey. Give me five minutes. I feel strong though, powerful. My pulse is racing. I'm practically vibrating."

She'd forgotten a large chunk of the Testing. She wasn't sure if she'd been Enlightened. She'd blacked out for weeks and gone on a murderous rampage, if that counted. The walls on either side of the passageway began closing and they were forced to run. With no time to plot strategy, they sprinted through corridors as the walls shifted rapidly. In a blur of adrenaline and instinct, they darted through a wall as it ground open and found themselves trapped in a room, with no finger ridges or visible escape.

"I have a bad feeling about this," Grey whispered as he slowly spun around.

Arrianna shouted, "Down!" The ceiling dropped six feet in a heartbeat. They were all lying flat on their stomachs, on the stone floor.

Grey laughed nervously. "That was close."

Lexy's stomach turned and she said, "Shit." The ceiling jerked, then dropped, squishing the trio like partially immortal ants on a sidewalk.

Remaining completely still to catch her breath before opening her eyes, Lexy struggled to push herself up but couldn't operate her arms. She made a second attempt and smoked her head on the three-foot-high ceiling. *Ah, Crap. Here we go again. Cue hoard of man eating baby lizard fish creatures.* She twitched her fingers in something gooey. *It was probably the splat they'd left behind after being compacted like cars at an auto wrecker. Where were the others?* It was pitch black. She couldn't see two feet in front of her face. Lexy was dying to call out, but she wasn't a moron. She started crawling forward. *She despised enclosed spaces, hated them with a passion. Damn it, she still had feelings. This was inconvenient.* Lexy heard a loud purring sound. She crawled faster, making it to the wall, her fingertips felt nothing, but stone. She moved as silently as she could manage along the length of the wall. *There had to be an escape route.* She felt the vibration of purring under her fingertips. There was an echoing sound of a cat hacking up a hairball. *What in the hell?* She froze to Grey's muffled cries, and moments later, Arrianna's shrieks of agony. *That demise sounded instantaneous. Why was she postponing the inevitable? The enclosed space and reoccurring emotions were wrecking her badass vibe.* Lexy stopped moving and shifted around to travel in the direction of the purring sound. She couldn't see anything, but cats could see in the dark. She scanned the darkness. Yellow glowing orbs appeared ten feet from her face. She stared into the creature's eyes, without blinking. *She had to die to catch up with the others. Here kitty, kitty. Come and get me.* There was the sound of a cat hacking up a hairball again. A giant splat of something hit her arm. She felt an explosion of intense pain. It began to burn as it solidified. Her arm snapped off at the shoulder. She tipped over, as her shoulder, then her torso solidified. *She wasn't burning, she was freezing.* Her chest seized and the lights went out.

She awoke next to Grey with her head on a pillow. They were in another one of those sleep chambers. She could smell the food. Lexy tried to move. *It was becoming harder to get up each time she went down.* She struggled to get up, and eventually managed to. Arrianna was sound asleep on the other side of Grey. She got up to see if there was any meat on the trays. *Of course, there wasn't.* Lexy ate some fruit and bit off a few chunks of bread. She downed a goblet of wine and decided to refill it with water. *It wouldn't hurt to check the fountain for a sword.* Lexy placed her fingers, and the heel of her hand in the grooves. The door slid open. *She was alone. There was not a soul in sight.* She wandered into the open area by the sleep rooms, surveying her surroundings. *It felt too quiet.* She climbed into the fountain and sure enough, something metal glinted on the bottom. She snagged the sword, as the shadow of something moved behind her. With sword in hand, she spun around and decapitated a gigantic lizard. Its head rolled across the floor. Finding it amusing, she chuckled. *She'd decapitated something each time she'd tried to get a drink of water.* Lexy stared at the lizard, recalling the ones they'd eaten while trapped in the desert Ankh crypt. *There was a lot of meat on this thing. It was huge. She wasn't going to be able to tow the creature to the chamber. She'd have to carve it up here.* Lexy sliced a few large chunks of meat off, to bring back with her. While she was elbow deep in lizard guts, hacking it into transportable pieces, a wall ground open. She was grinning. *She was going to eat something that had tried to eat her.* Triad saw what she was doing and closed their chamber, without even attempting to come out. Her wall ground open, and she glanced up to see Grey standing in the threshold.

"I'm not even going to ask," he sighed, smiling.

It was probably better if he didn't. Lexy lugged the chunks of lizard back to the room. She strolled up to Grey, dropped the pieces on the floor and questioned, "Can you cook this?"

He shook his head, grinned and replied, "I can try." He charred the flesh but couldn't cook it for long because they were in an enclosed space and the room filled with smoke. Arrianna opened the wall to let some escape. When Grey was finished, it looked appetizing.

He carried the slabs of meat to the sparse mini buffet and remarked, "Just don't tell me what it is, and I'll eat it."

Lexy didn't feel like talking. It was highly unlikely she would have brought up the origin of the meat in conversation. She did realise, she was void of emotion. *How long had she blacked out for this time? Had she been on another murder spree?* After eating her fill, Lexy felt renewed interest in escaping the endless corridors of grey. *She'd had some payback. She'd killed one of the dark inhabitants of this hell hole and devoured it. She felt strangely vindicated.*

They sprinted through the maze of narrow winding stone halls. This whole area had paintings on the walls, they knew not to touch any. Grey became Enlightened next as he accidently grazed the wrong wall with his shoulder. He was launched into the wall on other side of the passageway. His body twisted and contorted. He violently jerked around, giving the appearance of someone being electrocuted. They knew they had to wait until it passed. They understood there was no way to speed up the process. When Grey recovered, they carried on dying creatively in increasingly depraved ways.

In time they found their niches. Arrianna gave the trio direction with her empath ability. Lexy led them through darkness as only a wild thing could, with fearless rage, and control over her emotions. Grey became the interpreter between emotional response, and lack thereof. Things became easier as soon as this happened. They kept climbing up, through the ceiling of each room, into the next. Each new room held a more horrifying version of death than the last. Eventually, they all reached the point where their tedious, repetitive demises became nothing. Insignificant moments they were forced to endure for the sole purpose of moving forward. This was when the Testing deemed them worthy of immortality. The trio climbed through the last floor into a room, just as they had thousands of times before. This room had a massive orb of Amber in the center. They'd been going through the motions for so long that when then finally found the Amber room, it was quite anticlimactic.

Chapter 23

New Beginning's

The Ankh rose to their feet and stared at the figurative end of the Testing. *Was this really the end?* Each of their faces registered the same disbelief.

"This must be it. We did it," Grey laughed.

Arrianna whispered, "What if it's too late? What if the other Clans are already out, and we're trapped in here?"

Lexy stepped towards it, nodded at the other two and declared, "There's only one way to find out." She placed her hands on the Amber orb and the others did the same. Her arms attached to the stone, with an unnerving sensation. She was sucked into its core as the scenery exploded with white light. In an instant Lexy was plummeting from the sky into an enormous coliseum full of spectators. Grey and Arrianna were falling beside her. The rapidly approaching sand was red, it looked like they were about to plunge into a sea of blood. The three landed gracefully, side by side in the warm crimson sand.

A booming voice announced, "Clan Ankh." The whole place filled with thunderous applause.

Where had that voice come from? Lexy glanced up at the cheering stands full of people.

They hadn't figured out where the voice had come from when it ordered, "Choose your stone."

Confused, Arrianna whispered, "What stones?"

Suddenly dozens of small rose quartz stones appeared in the sand. Lexy nodded at her Clan. She'd do it first. A part of her feared they were still in the Testing and this was just

a hallucination. She crouched and picked one up. *It was real.*
She rolled the smooth rose quartz between her fingertips.
Their symbol of Ankh was engraved in the stone. *This was
real. They'd done it.* She felt a vibration that tickled her fingers,
and then a sedating warmth. It travelled from the stone in
her hand, up the length of her arm, to her heart. *She'd secured
her place in her immortal family.* Lexy clutched her stone. *This
was what she needed to create her own tomb.* Each member of Clan
Ankh had one. They cheered again. Lexy peered up and took
in the coliseum full of elegantly attired spectators. It was as
though ancient Rome, had been frozen in time.

The crowd applauded again as Grey chose his stone. He
clutched it in his palm and whispered, "This is insane. What
is this place?"

Arrianna appeared to be afraid to make a choice. The
crowd became silent. She bent down, chose her stone and
the place thundered with applause.

The voice boomed, "You are now and forever, Ankh."

Her heart began to palpitate as she sensed a presence. A
real dragon with glistening scarlet scales swooped through
the sky above her. She could feel the force of the air from
its wings. Lexy was completely awestruck, as she rose to
stand. Two magnificent dragons were perched on the towers
of the castle adjoining the coliseum. In her heart she knew
they'd come to see her. She couldn't look away.

Grey grabbed her arm, squeezed it, and whispered,
"Somebody's coming."

Lexy looked away from her scaly supporters. A woman,
in a flowing ivory gown strolled towards them. Lexy glanced
up again, and her fellow dragons were gone. She turned her
gaze back to the lady who had now made her way to the
center of the coliseum. The mumbles from the stands
hushed. Everyone was silent. The woman in off white, raised
her hands in the air, and squealed with an ungodly pitch. The
three clutched their heads as their brains hummed with pain
and dropped to their knees in the sand. Lexy's peripheral

vision flickered, the scenery exploded once more with white light.

In the blink of an eye, she was standing on the glistening white sand of the in-between. This time it was sparkling with diamonds. Clan Ankh, sprinted towards them, with proud smiles, and welcoming embraces. Lexy stepped away, requiring personal space. She watched, Grey and Arrianna as they embraced each member of their Clan. Grey began telling animated stories of Dragons and battles, as though it happened long ago. Lexy found a comfortable position, cross-legged in the warmth of the sand. She scooped up the silky grains and allowed them to trickle through her fingertips. Nobody approached or attempted to speak to her for a while. They just allowed her to be at peace. She stayed there playing in the sand, until she heard Jenna speak her name. She began paying attention to the conversations around her.

Jenna was speaking to Grey as she explained, "Dragons can turn off their emotions. This makes them dangerous creatures in the mortal world. Dragon's need a Handler. Grey, you're the obvious choice." Lexy glanced up at Grey. He didn't appear to understand. Jenna clarified, "Your souls have a connection. That's the reason she went with you and why she always will."

Markus walked up, embraced Grey and declared, "You have some work to do. You must bring her back enough to attend a banquet. She just needs to be passable. They'll make her bathe, and she'll have to wear a gown. You three, will be introduced to Third Tier royalty."

Kicking sand, Grey laughed, "How do you think I'm going to get her to do that?"

Lexy heard everything. *She wasn't bathing, nor was she putting on a dress. It wasn't happening. She was done with that place. She wasn't going back there. She'd also decided she wasn't following any more of their rules.* She watched the others joking around, as though the hell they'd just gone through had been nothing. She stared at the Ankh symbol on her hand and recalled the words. *Ankh, now and forever. She'd been a hot mess during the*

Testing. She'd done her job and led them out. Why were they pushing their luck? Grey sat beside her in the sand. Lexy shook her head and smiled. She glanced up and noticed the others walking away. *They were leaving them alone. Grey had a new job as her keeper. She couldn't be insulted; he'd been doing that duty for quite some time. They'd just made it official.*

He grabbed a handful of sand and admitted, "This just never gets old." He wasn't stupid, he knew what he was up against. Sprawling in the sand next to her, he sighed, "I'm exhausted, Lexy. I know this is the last thing you want to do. It's the last thing I want to do, but we need to do it. You can make this easy on me or you can make it difficult. I'll stay by your side the whole night. We'll leave early."

Lexy wasn't about to change her mind. She sprawled beside him in the warm sand, and stated, "This whole speech is a waste of your time."

"I know it is," he chuckled.

She turned to look at him. *Was he really going to let this go?*

They rested in complete silence for a while before he gave it another shot, "You know we need to do this. You understand it isn't a choice, it's a duty. I know somewhere inside, you still feel that connection to Ankh... to me."

"No, I don't feel anything," she fibbed. She didn't want to do anything but lay here in the sand next to him. *She wasn't going back to that place.*

Grey rolled onto his side, gave her the biggest grin, and chuckled, "You're a liar."

He had this one expression. It was impossible to keep a straight face when he used it on her. She turned away. *He'd made her smile. She was busted.*

He inched closer to see what she was hiding. He chuckled, "You're smiling. You're such a liar. You still love me." He tossed a handful of sand at her.

Her chest tightened, and she knew why. *It was the reason she'd had to fight to let him go during the Testing. Her attachment to him had become more powerful than the Dragon within her.*

Grey whispered, "Please, Lex. I'll do anything you want for a month if you come willingly, and don't kill anyone while we're there."

Lexy laid there for a minute, contemplating her response. *She wanted to be angry. She wanted to stay a wild thing, but he'd done something to her resolve. How did he do this to her?* She set her price and wagered, "A whole year. You'll do anything I want, for a year."

Grinning, he accepted, "Alright, a whole year. Anything you want."

"I'm going to need kittens, and sedatives," Lexy sighed.

Grey teased, "Is sedating the kittens really necessary?"

She gave him a shot in the arm and sparred, "It might be."

Gazing into her eyes, he confessed, "I'm glad you came back to me. I wasn't sure you'd be able to see the bigger picture."

"I'll always come back to you," Lexy vowed, knowing that was true with every fibre of her being.

Arrianna piped in, "Should I leave you two alone?"

Neither one had noticed her standing there. Grey ribbed, "Don't be silly."

Arrianna sighed, "I'm feeling a little left out. It's always been the three of us, and now you guys have the whole Handler, Dragon thing going on. Where do I fit in to the mix?"

Grey chuckled, "You'll always have a spot in my harem."

Arrianna kicked sand at him, as she countered, "I love you Grey, but I wouldn't hold my breath."

The three newest Ankh, spent a week in the in-between time, playing with kittens, watching the clouds drift by and dancing in the sand. They were left alone so they could bring her humanity back. *Truth be told, she'd been back the second Grey asked her to come back. She wasn't sure she liked knowing he had that kind of control over her heart.*

Their peaceful calm was broken by Jenna's voice, "Ready to go?"

Chapter 24

Third Tiers

The group landed barefoot in the crimson sand of the foreign realm, greeted by a deserted coliseum. Grey whispered, "Well, this is way less intimidating."

Lily grinned and taunted, "Oh, you just wait."

A group of what Lexy assumed were palace guards in golden armour marched through the archway and proceeded single file towards where they stood.

The guards split in two groups and behind them was a tiny built man in a flowing fur lined burgundy robe, who spoke with authority, "Now you can put a face to the voice. My name's Audyro, but you can just call me Andy. I honestly don't have the patience left today to correct fifty silly mispronunciations of it." He motioned for them to follow him, spun around and casually strolled back towards the grandiose archway.

As soon as he'd opened his mouth Lexy had known who he was. He was the voice they'd heard when they survived their Testing. He was the announcer. *They were going to mispronounce his name. What an Ass. He was such a jerk.* Lexy was walking beside Frost. He poked her, and when she glared back at him, he made the motion of zipping one's lips on his forehead. *Shoot. He could hear what she was thinking. Why did she always forget they could do that?*

Andy chuckled, "Yes, I'm an Asshole, and you forget because you live in the land where most people have to move their lips to be heard. I have to say something. You, my dear, are a glorious creature. That whole playing with the severed head thing was the funniest thing I've ever seen. Kudos to your crazy. It was most entertaining."

Lexy wasn't sure what he was talking about, but she used her manners and replied, "Thank you?"

Frost couldn't stop grinning at her as they followed Andy through the artistic archway into a hall of stone and marble. She heard him whisper to Arrianna, "Was she really playing with a severed head?"

She didn't look back at the hushed voices but heard Arrianna's reply, "What happens in the Testing, stays in the Testing, Frost."

The group stopped in a large open area full of art. The walls were adorned with magnificent jewel-toned tapestries running down the length of each one. There were incredibly realistic life size sculptures of beautiful women situated in each corner. Lexy felt drawn to one of the statues. She made her way to the stone figure and placed her hand on it. She could sense the energy within. *They were real people. What in the hell?*

Markus leaned over and whispered, "I'm certain the king's ex-wives and female friends would tell you there's situations far worse than being entombed."

She knew that. She'd survived worse while still mortal. Lexy asked, "Why do we let them do things like this?"

Markus pressed one finger to his lips and instructed, "Play along. Do what you're told unless you want to be a Dragon standing in the corner of the room, for all eternity dressed as a princess. I'll answer all of your questions, once we're back home in a safe place."

Flamboyantly, Andy announced, "It's time to make you three absolutely stunning. I personally can't wait to see what you all look like descent." He looked at Grey, winked and flirted, "Especially you."

Appearing to be both concerned and flattered, Grey raised his eyebrows. Arrianna had his back. She laced her fingers with his and provocatively kissed his lips. Stunned as their lips parted, he smiled. *The sight of Grey kissing Arrianna made Lexy feel queasy.*

Making it clear he was spoken for, Arrianna toyed, "I guess we'd better get ready honey."

A half dozen sparsely clothed women signalled for the three to follow them. The survivors of the Testing were led away from the rest of their Clan. Grey and Arrianna held hands until they were out of sight.

He whispered, "Thanks Arrianna, he's an attractive little dude, but I'm not ready to expand my horizons."

Arrianna replied, "I'm under the impression that choices are not really a thing here. Maybe he'll lose interest. If not, I guess you'll be expanding whatever the hell he wants you to expand."

Lexy went from feeling sick to fearing Grey was going to light Arrianna on fire with the expression on his face. Lexy hadn't given much thought to what they'd want her to do. There had been more than enough drama to keep her thoroughly entertained.

"That's frigging hilarious Arrianna. Do try to remember, we're all in the same sinking boat," Grey sparred.

Arrianna placed her arm around him as they walked and whispered, "You know I'm joking. I'm also aware we can handle whatever someone asks of us in that respect. You and I that is…"

Grey's expression changed. His tanned face became sallow. Lexy knew he was thinking about her, mainly because he was staring at her, but it was more than that, she felt his concern. *Yes, sexuality was a firm line in the sand for her, for obvious reasons. Nobody would be that stupid. Apparently, they'd seen her playing with a severed head.* Grey impressed her, by refusing to leave her side, when they arrived at the community baths. *He was taking his Handler duties seriously. She still wasn't sure how she felt about it. Did he control her? Did she control him? Were they able to control each other?* Grey turned away as Lexy slipped out of her sarong, and into the exquisite tub full of red flower petals. He stripped down and slid into the same tub on the opposite side. Their naked bodies were concealed by petals, floating on the surface. It was a surprisingly intimate situation. She lay in the sedating fragranced water, closed her eyes and relaxed. Every so often, her foot grazed his, and it reminded her she wasn't alone. After the most luxurious bathing experience of her life, they were escorted to another room. One by one they were asked to step inside. It was a rather amazing, they were dressed and had their makeup on in minutes. This was where they became separated.

Lexy and Arrianna were led down a long corridor that resembled the inside of an Ankh crypt and ushered past two guards fully armoured in gold, into a room that gleamed. The walls, the ceiling, everything appeared to be made of gold. The two were adorned in jewels worthy of royalty. Arrianna looked stunning in the white gown she was wearing, it was pleated to the floor, floating around her with the smallest movement. Her hair was piled on top of her head. She looked like a princess in a fairy tale. This was the first time Lexy ventured to look at her own reflection. They'd covered her freckles. She had ivory skin, crimson curled hair, with matching lips. She looked like a movie star from a black and white film. She was wearing an exquisite cream-toned lace dress that hugged her curves, a necklace with glittering green stones, and matching earrings. Lexy felt beautiful, and suspiciously calm. *Why was she this relaxed?*

They walked the two girls back down the corridor until they came to a large double door with soldiers standing guard. They stepped aside and opened the door to a room filled with familiar faces. Grey stared at her without speaking until she made her way to stand at his side.

Grey gazed deep into her eyes and tucked one of her curls behind her ear as he said, "You're so beautiful, Lex. I could imagine you walking up the isle towards me in that dress."

She wasn't sure what that meant but she had no urge to stop him from touching her as his hand slid down to the soft exposed skin of her shoulder. He cocked his head and slowly trailed his fingers down her arm.

Jenna stepped between the two and quietly laughed, "So, you two obviously got into the same tub."

The guys looked amazing in gold form fitting man skirts, and bare chests. Especially Grey. He was still biting his lip and staring at her.

Jenna placed a hand on both of Grey's cheeks, looked into his eyes and said, "You've been drugged, my friend. It's probably for the best in the long run, but you won't be much help as a Handler tonight if you don't snap out of it to some degree. You need a glass of wine and some food."

Grey's eyes focused as he whispered, "Really?"

Jenna sighed and told Arrianna to distract him. She whispered to one of the guards. He shook his head and laughed. He walked over to a box on the wall, placed his hand on it, and it lit up with the perfect outline of a handprint. It swung open when he removed his hand. The guard rifled around for a second, then he closed the box and passed Jenna a small bottle.

Jenna strolled over to Grey and requested, "Can I see your hand?"

Grey knit his brow and held out his hand. Jenna took the lid off, inside of the bottle was a tiny dropper. She dropped a pearl-sized droplet into the palm of his hand and ordered, "Now, rub your hands together."

He did as instructed. His eyes widened and he said, "What was that?"

Jenna grinned and replied, "You shared a bath with Lexy. I'm sure her bath had something in it meant to relax her. That tincture will counteract the effects."

Grey looked at Jenna. She nodded her head slowly from side to side. He didn't say the words he was thinking aloud, but Lexy heard them loud and clear. *He'd wondered if Jenna was going to give Lexy the antidote. They'd been worried about her behaviour. They didn't want her to be hostile. The drugged bath had worked out to the Clan's advantage. Of course, someone drugged her bath. Why wouldn't they drug her bath? She wasn't even shocked anymore.* Lexy glanced around the room. All the women had been done up to perfection, the men were dressed down in comparison. The Ankh, in the line had paired up to enter the ballroom. Frost was standing beside Lily. *Those two were freaks of nature.* The double doors were opened and Trinity joined them. They were all now waiting outside an arched entrance. Thorne, the leader of Trinity shook hands with Markus and embraced Lily. He nodded at Frost.

Jenna slapped Thorne's butt and teased, "Aren't you forgetting someone?"

The leader of Trinity gave her a giant hug and whispered, "I wasn't sure we were still doing the hug thing?"

Jenna grinned and whispered, "Orin's not here. Don't worry about it."

Thorne leaned in, and whispered in her ear, "Come find me later." He walked over to Arrianna and embraced her, whispering in her ear, "I'm glad you made it." He shook hands with Grey and then hesitated in front of Lexy. He extended his hand and she took it without thinking much about it. She shook his hand. Thorne walked back to his original place in line and whispered something to one of the beautiful Trinity girls. She didn't blame him for being standoffish with her. She'd massacred his Clan on countless occasions. Arrianna was staring at one of the Trinity. The guy she'd spent all her time with during the week before the Testing. Lexy couldn't recall his name. *Was it Rob, or Bob?*

Grey turned around, met her eyes, leaned in and whispered, "His name's Rob."

Normally she would have scolded him for listening to her thoughts, but she didn't care tonight. *She was definitely still sedated.* The others began to walk in couple by couple. The groups that had made it through the Testing were held back.

The announcer with a thing for Grey announced, "The survivors of the Testing, Clan Ankh." The three of them linked arms and strolled into the room. They maneuvered around a half dozen court jesters having a comical sword fight. The head table laughed, as blood spurted from a dismembered arm. Grey yanked Lexy out of the way and she narrowly avoided the spray. A part of her wanted to go back there and stand in the arterial firing zone. *That felt normal, this fancy banquet did not.*

Grey squeezed her hand and whispered, "That was close." He pulled out a seat for her, then for Arrianna, and they sat down with the rest of their Clan. In front of them, on the burgundy table was an overwhelming amount of food. Her stomach growled, loud enough to make everyone turn and stare at her. Lexy glanced at the head table. *Nobody was even touching their food. She was so hungry.*

Markus sat down beside her and whispered, "Do me a favour, don't even look at the head table."

Lexy reached for a plate of what appeared to be drumsticks.

Jenna whispered, "We're not allowed to start eating until the head table starts."

Well, this was inconvenient. The head table was busy watching court jesters slicing each other up. There was a slit up one side of her dress to her thigh. Grey squeezed her knee. She shifted in her seat, then grabbed him back, missing his thigh. Grey's eyes widened, and he gave her a strange look. She'd accidentally grabbed him somewhere personal. *Whoops...*

Frost saved the awkward moment by bluntly addressing Jenna, "So, what's going on with you and Thorne?"

Jenna shook her head at him and said, "Five years ago, during the last Summit. Orin and I were on a break. I know you haven't missed the testosterone show. Orin starts one whenever we run into Trinity."

Always impressed by blunt honesty, Frost chuckled, "We only ever run into them when they're trying to steal one of our new Clan, or vice versa. I honestly had no idea. My question is why?"

The main table began to eat. Jenna passed the plate with the drumsticks to Lexy as she answered, "He's gorgeous, attentive, it just happened. I could probably come up with a million excuses."

Arrianna smiled at their Oracle and remarked, "It's nice to know you're just as flawed as the rest of us."

Jenna winked and teased, "You don't know the half of it." She noticed Lexy's search for utensils and said, "There aren't any, Lexy. You have to eat with your fingers here."

Frost and Lily were summoned to the main table, and they both placed fake smiles on their faces, and left to go sit with the royalty. Lexy was dying to ask someone why they left.

Jenna passed her a goblet of wine and answered the words she'd left unsaid, "Frost and Lily have to do whatever the royals require of them this evening. If I were you, I'd keep out of the head table's line of sight."

Lexy looked into her glass of wine, picked a few yellow petals out of her glass, and took a drink. *Whatever the royals require of them?*

Their Oracle addressed her again, "I'd also stop taking those out of your wine. I'd just drink it."

Markus bluntly decreed, "Stop talking in code. Tell it to her straight. She's a Dragon, she can take it."

Lexy picked up one of the petals, she'd taken out of her wine, and placed it on the corner of her plate. She looked at it, knowing Jenna always had her best interest at heart, she popped it into her mouth. Grey and Arrianna were extremely inebriated, impressively so. She saw the head table chatting and then turning and pointing at them. *It reminded her of something. A moment when she was eleven-years-old.* It was then that she grasped the situation. Music blared and dancing began. Everyone got up and laughed their way to the open space of the dance floor, except for her. She was the only one that remained seated. She didn't want to look. She snuck a peek at the head table under the veil of her thick luxurious lashes. Nobody appeared to notice her, so she stayed seated, and didn't bother getting up. She took a sip of her wine and watched her friends. Grey and Arrianna appeared to be having the time of their lives. She glanced over when she heard the squeak of the chair being pulled out beside her. It was Jenna. She sat down, grabbed her goblet of wine, and motioned for a celebratory cheer.

They raised their glasses and Jenna suggested, "You should drink the whole glass."

Lexy met her knowing gaze and downed the entire glass of wine. She stared into the empty glass and heard the countdown in her head. 3...2...1...A guard appeared behind her seat at the table and ordered her to follow him.

Jenna whispered, "Don't alert the others. Shut it off."

Lexy slowly got out of her seat and followed the guard through the crowded dance floor of the ballroom. She caught sight of Grey and Arrianna. *They were off in their own little world. Jenna was right. They couldn't do anything about this.* She followed him down a long marble hallway, and through an open door at the end of it. She was led inside and told to wait. Lexy sat down at the small rounded table in front of elaborate golden curtains, encasing a large open window. The top of the window was tinted with stained glass in vibrant colours. *It reminded her of the sunsets in the in-between. She didn't contemplate the idea of escape. These were the immortals that created the Testing. There was no point.* Lexy traced the outline of the goblet with her finger. She picked it up and stared into it. She was just about to touch the rim to her lips when she heard a voice from the doorway.

A good-looking teenage boy said, "You don't have to drink that. I'm not going to touch you. I promise you, I'm not." He closed the door silently and turned around.

She'd seen him sitting at the head table. He was a member of the royal family.

"I'd never force myself on a girl without her consent. I thought I'd take you out of the mix before you ended up in a volatile situation with one of my brothers," he revealed.

She wasn't sure how to respond. Had a stranger just randomly come to her rescue? This was a new experience.

He grinned and hinted, "This is where someone usually says, thank you."

Lexy cautiously said, "Thank you."

"My name's Amadeus, I'm the illegitimate son. I don't have a title." He motioned for her to give him her glass. He walked out onto the balcony, dumped it, and came back to refill it. "I would prefer you to be coherent while we speak. Trust me, you won't need to be drugged. I'm not that guy." The royal passed the glass to her and sat directly across the table. He held up his glass for a toast and gestured his salute, "To avoiding bad things."

She copied him, holding her glass at the same level. He grinned as they clicked the glasses. They both drank and Lexy was relieved. *It was normal wine.* She was curious. *Why would he choose to spend a platonic night with her? Was he trying to lure her into a sense of calm?*

He grinned at her and on either cheek, he had deep dimples. Amadeus appeared adorable and harmless as he explained, "I don't get to meet many interesting people. I've heard some crazy stories about you. Is it true you lived in the woods with a pack of dogs?"

Lexy replied with one word, "Yes."

Amadeus smiled as he sipped his wine and enquired, "Did you really do those things to Tiberius?"

"That depends on what rumor you heard," she countered.

He chuckled, "The one where you seduced him, strung him up in a tree and then killed him in front of his own men." She didn't respond and he said, "I'm just trying to get to know you. Don't you want to get to know me?"

She sighed, "Not really."

Amadeus cracked up and admitted, "Your honesty is refreshing. You'd be surprised at how many women pretend to want me, but they're only with me for an imaginary title. A title I only receive if something happens to three of my brothers. A title I have no interest in."

Lexy took a drink from her glass and asked, "Am I supposed to care?"

Fascinated by her lack of filter, Amadeus chuckled, "I guess you don't have to."

Lexy took another sip of wine and shook her head. They sat there for a few minutes in silence while someone brought in a tray of desserts.

When they left, he suggested, "Try the one with the berries. That's the best one."

There was only one of them. Lexy broke it in two pieces and offered him the other half. He took it and said, "Thank you."

She bit into the delicious creamy creation. *It was the best thing she'd ever tasted.* Amadeus kept smiling at her.

Entertained by her every movement. He held a treat, inches from her lips and urged, "Try this one."

It was a dare. She wasn't sure if it was the wine or the fact that he hadn't laid a hand on her, but she leaned forward and took a giant bite of the pastry he was holding. She closed her eyes and allowed the flavours to swim around on her taste buds.

He kept smiling at her as he whispered, "You've got some right there." He pointed at the corner of her mouth. She tried to lick it off and kept missing. They both started laughing and he motioned that he was going to get it for her. He touched the corner of her mouth with his thumb and wiped it off. He licked off his thumb and she bit her lip. She wasn't sure what it was, but she couldn't shake the feeling that she wanted something to happen. They spent the duration of the night, until the wee hours of the morning having hilarious conversations about nothing important. He offered her the bed to rest her eyes several times, but eventually understood that even though she wanted to trust him, she wasn't built that way. Neither of them slept, they talked until a knock on the door, signalled her Clan's departure.

Amadeus rose from his seat to walk her out and remarked, "That was the most pleasurable night I've ever spent with all of my clothes on." He caressed her cheek, leaned forward and kissed her softly on the lips. She didn't stop him or react adversely to his touch. "See me again in five years?"

Lexy grinned, an honest genuine smile and teased, "If that's what you want, I don't really have a choice do I?"

He took her hand, raised it to his lips and confessed, "I guess you don't, but it has to mean something to you that I wish you had a choice."

It did mean something to her. This whole night had meant something to her. A man had the opportunity to hurt her, and he didn't. It was a life altering experience. She returned to the concerned eyes of her Clan and told them she'd had a good night. She didn't go into detail. She was pretty sure the others just thought she couldn't remember.

Grey spent months glued to her side, wracked with guilt. There was nothing he could have done. Nothing happened but he wouldn't believe her. Jenna had been right about keeping her mouth shut, and quietly sneaking away. Grey would have gotten himself entombed. Her two best friends eventually succumbed to their attraction. Lexy had never minded this for she had no reason to believe that she would ever be a normal girl. A part of her wanted to be the girl that was capable of a having a proper relationship with a man. They were all best friends, and more than anything in this world, she just wanted Grey to be happy; but he had other ideas. *Her best friend was big on self-sabotage.* His relationship ended with Arrianna when he cheated on her with Lily.

Lexy would watch Grey with his always ready heart as he continued jumping into absolutely ridiculous romantic situations. She envied him though, because he still had one to give away. He never seemed jaded by his exploits. He would flit around the Clan, but he would always come back to her when he was truly in need of solace. They were each other's refuge. Every night he'd lay beside her, stroking her hair, telling her animated stories. He made her laugh. This was what love was to her. Sexuality had never been brought into it. She'd always known Grey loved her back. They were the dark and the light, in perfect harmony. Lexy and Grey were a package deal, and because of this, they were requested to do many messed-up jobs together. Abaddon was always attempting to start a plague or possession. The Third Tiers always had a sick sense of humour. Whenever they sent only one of them to do something, it was personal. Grey was sent to correct his own sister. The infant he'd thought he'd accidentally killed by causing a fire during his Correction. She'd survived, but she had never been meant to. She'd been turned by Abaddon by the age of twelve. This was supposed to be against the rules, but somehow, she'd become a demon. A demon named Laura. When it came down to it, Grey hadn't been able do it. He'd set his sister free, only to have the entire Clan sent back to redo the job less than six months later. By this time, little Laura had been on a murder spree and slaughtered entire households. Grey's punishment for his disobedience had been to have his abilities stifled by Azariah. When it was taken away from him, he had an easier transition than most, for he barely used his ability. In their Clan, Grey's most prominent ability was his kind heart, and eternal optimism.

Chapter 25

The One

The bounds of their friendship eventually shifted. That first time with Grey had been both confusing, and beautiful. It was the event that began to heal a part of her, soiled from years of abuse, even though she wouldn't see it clearly for many years to come.

They were in the in-between, training a new batch of Ankh. They'd taken a break, leaving the newbies alone for a while. Grey always seemed to take a trip down the same rabbit hole, losing himself in his guilt. On this day, he'd taken her with him. Lexy found herself standing alone in the torched frame of the house he'd hidden his infant sister in. She walked into the gutted kitchen area, overlooking the span of the yard, behind the house. She'd never seen the barn in her view of Grey's Correction. She strolled through the open door, welcomed by clucking chickens and snorting bovine. Grey was in a screaming match with his sister. During these live action dreams, his ability to light the world ablaze was still at full strength. He lit up the barn and laid his possessed sibling to rest. Lexy stepped out of the shadows, and there he was, kneeling in the ashes. His hands were covering his eyes as he shuddered. *It had taken all he had to destroy his sister.* Lexy knelt before him and wiped his tears away. *She wished she knew how to take his pain away. His heart was so beautiful, why was he always trying to break it?* She whispered, "Look at me, Grey." He removed his hands and stared into her eyes for they were his safe place. Just as his eyes, were hers. Without words, Lexy moved in and gently brushed her lips against his. A brief look of confusion passed between them. She kissed his lips again. He groaned her name and pulled her onto his lap. She straddled him. He parted his lips, and began to kiss her in a way, she'd never been kissed before. Their lips, and tongues moved together, in soul melting seduction. His lips left hers to trail kisses down her neck, as his hands touched her softly, repetitively, until she was shuddering, shaking, and desperate for more. *She wanted him.* She slid her hands across his muscular chest and then lower. He groaned her name, running both hands through her hair, directing her lips back to his. His tongue danced along her bottom lip, nipping at the tender flesh. *She didn't want to think. For the first time she knew what she wanted, and it was him. All of him, in every way.* She was the one in control, it was all her as she slid down on top of him. He groaned her name again. *Every nerve ending in her body felt alive.* She rode the waves of intense pleasure as they vigorously moved together, faster and harder, until they cried out in unison. They clung to each other, trembling from the intensity of what they'd shared. He shifted her around, without moving from within her. She was beneath him, gazing into his eyes. Her heart was nearly bursting with love as her body silently pleaded for him to keep going.

Grey whispered against her hair, "Don't worry, I'm not done with you." He began to move again. She felt something building within her, driving her to gyrate her hips, against him. Waves of blindingly intense pleasure swept her away, she succumbed until her toes curled. She arched her back, and cried out, biting down on his shoulder to stop the sound of her cries. He lost control, pounding vigorously until he cried out her name, and collapsed on top of her. A dark cloud of soot and ash rose around them. They both began to laugh and choke. They lay there as the soot settled. Both were still panting as the shock set in. They'd crossed a few dozen lines.

"That was unexpected," he whispered.

Humming with pleasure, she confessed, "I've never done that before."

He kissed her tenderly on her shoulder and whispered, "I'm honoured."

Lexy smiled at him and said, "What do we do now?"

Grey trailed his finger softly down her hip as he disclosed, "We're not normal people, Lex. We're not living normal lives. I'd ask you to marry me, but I'm pretty sure we're not allowed to be together. We could risk losing what we have. I can't lose you."

Her heart tightened as it began to sink in, rocked by intense waves of isolation. *She was a Dragon and he was her Handler.* Lexy allowed her heart to disappear into the murky depths of her soul. *He was probably right, but it felt like he was trying to debate his way out of a complicated situation. She had to get away from him, but all she wanted to do was kiss him and hold him again. She wanted to carry on where they'd left off.* Lexy scrambled to her feet. With a dull hollow throbbing in her chest, she walked away from him. He called out her name but didn't attempt to pursue her. She glanced back. He was sitting there with his face in his hands. She hadn't succeeded in fixing him, but she'd taken leaps, and bounds towards healing herself. She'd given herself to Grey, and it had been the most beautiful experience of her life thus far. *Heaven help her, she loved him. Whether or not she was supposed to. How would she forget the pleasure of the reckless abandon she'd felt, while in his arms? What would it be like between them now? Maybe there was a way to erase what happened?*

The scenery around her exploded with a brilliant light. The grass disappeared beneath her feet. She dropped to her knees in the sand of the in-between. *If Azariah had summoned her. This was going to be humiliating.* Lexy opened her eyes and looked around. She was by herself, kneeling in a white room. She brushed the sand out of the way to reveal a white marble floor. *It always astounded her when something about her surroundings was altered by someone else's suggestion. This had not been her will...or had it?* She recalled her last thought; *she'd wanted to erase what had happened between them. It looked like she'd erased everything and clean slated the in-between.* She was standing inside of an enormous white cube chamber. She rose to her feet and wandered over to one of the walls. *She needed to touch it. Was this a hallucination? She'd never been in this place before. This was something new.* Each time she thought she was growing close to the walls, they moved farther away. Lexy turned around as she felt a familiar presence. *She'd been right. This was going to be embarrassing.*

The glorious being in the light, Azariah teased, "That wasn't a smart move my child. Whatever possessed you to do that?"

Lexy replied, "A freak act of epic stupidity?"

Azariah winked and said, "Otherwise known as love." She touched the side of Lexy's face and when she removed her finger, it was covered with soot. "Any memory of today's events will be erased when he sleeps. For Grey, being with you was only a dream. You needed to know the joy of loving someone in that way."

Confused, Lexy whispered, "It didn't actually happen?"

Azariah questioned, "Do you wish it happened, even with his reaction afterwards?"

"Honestly, I'm not sure," Lexy confessed.

Ankh's Guardian teased, "I have a good idea. Be sure next time, before you jump the gun."

Lexy felt her face heating up. She knew she'd made a mess of things.

"Theoretically, your physical body isn't here. He's your Handler, Lexy. He won't remember. It was only a dream. A dream with a lesson attached," Azariah assured.

Lexy repeated, "It was only a dream. It didn't happen." She stirred and realised she was in her tomb.

The tomb opened to Grey. He held out his hand and said, "Your chariot awaits. Well, it's more like a motor home, but we can always pretend."

Maybe it really hadn't happened? She took Grey's hand as she knew she always would.

Chapter 26

Moving Forward

Months slipped by, and eventually the Clan separated their little trio for the first time. Markus took Arrianna and a few of the others with him to pick up a teen that survived his Correction. It was pouring outside all day. They'd spent the day in the RV, playing games, and bullshitting about recent jobs. Jenna gave everyone's hair a trim. They'd accomplished a few things, but they were all going a bit stir crazy by dinnertime. It was her turn to make dinner. She started to rifle through the cupboards for ingredients. She was surprised when she actually had the ingredients for what she wanted to make. Grey started cursing and she glanced away from the chicken sizzling in the frying pan. Lily was beating them all, as per usual. They played cards wagering dimes and nickels. Today, she suspected the four were playing for dares. She'd overheard part of the conversation.

Grey slammed his cards down on the table and hissed, "You're such a bloody cheater."

Lily smiled innocently and shrugged as she chuckled, "Pay up boys." Frost scooted up beside her and whispered something that made her grin. Lily announced, "You boys have twenty-four hours. You know the rules."

Jenna padded down the compact hall into the kitchen, and asked, "Twenty-four hours to do what?" Nobody answered. She sighed, "You guys are idiots. You've never beaten her once. Why would you bet on anything?"

Orin sighed, "The tedium of intense boredom."

Jenna shook her head at her other half, then leaned over to smell Lexy's concoction. "What are we having tonight?"

Lexy continued stirring her masterpiece as she replied, "Teriyaki chicken stir fry."

Jenna inhaled the steam, rising from the sizzling frying pan then announced, "It smells delicious. I'm famished."

This was how it was most of the time. They casually spent their time as a group of roommates living in an RV travelling across the country in search of new members. They were sent on the odd Correction, but most of the time the Corrections were done by Markus's part of the Clan. They ate at the table together and afterwards the boys were responsible for doing the dishes. They were whipping each other with the towels, when somebody knocked on the door. *Nobody ever knocked on the door.* Everybody froze.

"Oh, for heaven's sake you bunch of wussies, we're immortal," Lexy muttered as she stomped over and opened the door to find a gorgeous guy standing there. He had the sexiest chocolate brown eyes, matching the rich tone of his skin. *He'd rendered her speechless. She'd never had a physical reaction to a boy like this, it was lust at first sight.*

The hot stranger explained, "They dropped me off, and told me to tell you my name's Tomas. They didn't have time to mark me, because the other Clans showed up. They said you'd explain everything." The entire room just stared at him.

Grey jumped up and shoved past Lexy. He shook his hand and enquired, "I'm curious...Why didn't you run away? I would have ran like I was on fire if someone kidnapped me, and dropped me off with a bunch of strangers."

Tomas shrugged and replied, "Honestly, I didn't have anywhere else to go." He walked past Grey into the room like he belonged there.

"So, nobody told you anything?" Frost asked as he got up and came over.

Tomas responded to Frost's question with a short story that was all too familiar, "Well, this is going to sound completely insane, but a few months ago a group of strangers, broke in my house and butchered my family. I woke up in the morgue. The doctor who was about to do my autopsy, passed out cold."

Lexy grinned, *they always pass out when you wake up in the morgue.*

Tomas continued his tale, "I ran away, because frankly it's a little upsetting to wake up during your own autopsy. I tried to go to a few friends for help and they ended up dead. I hopped on a bus, and went to the city, hoping to blend into the crowd. I was staying at this seedy hostel downtown. Between the noise and the nightmares, I hadn't slept in weeks. I thought going for a walk might help. I cut through the park and monsters started chasing me. A truck full of people pulled over in the parking lot and a pretty blonde said, 'Come with us, or die.' So, I got in the truck. They were giving me a speech about being partially immortal, when somebody rammed into the truck, and it flipped over. The blonde girl yanked me out of the wreckage, stole someone's car, there was a high-speed chase. When she was sure we'd lost them, she dropped me off here. Let's just say, I've become rather open minded."

Frost noticed her openly ogling Tomas, hanging on every word, he chuckled, "Here," and tossed her his ring. "You do it."

Lexy caught the ring in midair and slipped it on her finger. *She'd never marked someone, Ankh.* She glanced at Frost and asked, "Should I do this right here?"

"Do it however you want to do it," Frost replied with a knowing grin. In his mind he added, *don't go too far from the motor home. You'll have to drag his body back.*

Lexy grinned and ordered, "Tomas, give me your hand."

He took her hand, winked and whispered, "Well, gorgeous, if you're planning to give me that ring. I think we should at least go on a date first."

Lexy grinned, flipped the ring around, and branded his palm with the symbol of Ankh. He swore and yanked his hand away. He was staring at his hand cursing, when Lexy casually snapped his neck. She sat down at the table, grabbed Grey's drink, took a swig of it and said, "Well, which one of you is using your tomb for this?"

Orin started laughing, "That was remarkably insensitive. You didn't even ask him any questions?"

"I'll be nice to him when he wakes up," Lexy sighed.

Jenna shook her head at her and smiled. She ordered, "Frost take the body to the back room. Lexy, you go back there and heal him. Everyone else, get out there and pack the site up. We have to leave, right now. We'll eat later."

We can't leave, what about Arrianna? She'll be stuck with the other half of the Clan.

Frost dragged the body to the room at the end of the hall. He hollered, "Lexy, I know you heard Jenna's orders."

Lexy was ticked off. *They were leaving Arrianna with the other half of the Clan. If she used her own energy to heal him, she'd be out cold. If the other Clans caught up with them, she'd miss all the action.* She followed Frost to the end of the hall. *Orin was a Healer too. Why did she have to do it?* She shimmied past Frost in the hall. When their eyes locked, she knew he'd been listening to her thoughts.

Frost whispered, "Maybe there's a reason it has to be you."

Lexy didn't give him a response. She sat down on the floor beside the hot guy's body and stewed. *How long would they be separated from the other half of the Clan?* She heard the door slam a few times, and then the calming hum of the engine. She felt the crackling of the gravel under the tires. *They were really leaving without her.* She pulled her fingerless glove off and stared at her mark for a minute. If their marks hadn't lit up, the others were fine. Jenna was right, they wouldn't risk coming back to the campsite. They'd try to lead the other Clans away. It had never been a big deal to separate from the other half of the Clan for six months, but Arrianna had never been with them.

Lexy stared at Tomas. He'd had a pretty crappy day. His eyes were open. That was the only thing that made him look dead. She took two fingers and closed his eyelids. Now, he looked like he was only sleeping. She slipped her hands under his shirt and laid them on his chest. Her chest warmed as her life force travelled from her heart down her arms and into Tomas. Her eyes grew heavy and the lights flickered and went out...

When she awoke, she found Tomas staring into her eyes.

He whispered, "Did you just brand me, break my neck, and then lay down, and take a nap beside me? Do you realise how messed-up that is?"

Intrigued by his lack of candor, Lexy felt the strangest urge, and allowed it to take hold. She grabbed his shirt, pulled him towards her and kissed him to shut him up. He kissed her back, and it was that easy. Tomas wasn't a complicated guy. Their relationship was all about the quiet moments and late-night rendezvous.

Arrianna was gone with the other half of the Clan for more than six months. They led the other Clans on a wild goose chase until Tomas was of age and couldn't be stolen by another Clan. When Arrianna returned to find Lexy in a relationship with the boy. A guy she'd moved heaven and earth to save, her mind was blown.

Lexy was asleep in Tomas's embrace. Grey started to pound obnoxiously on the door of the motel room they were sharing.

Grey hollered, "Alright Lexy, booty call time is over. We have a job."

She opened her eyes, and groaned before yelling back, "Be there in a few. I just need to get dressed." She swung her legs over the side of the bed and sauntered barefoot to the bathroom.

Tomas groggily mumbled, "Seriously babe? It's two o'clock in the morning. He could have at least tried to be polite about it. Tell him, I'm not a damn booty call."

Lexy heard him but didn't respond. She was already in the bathroom rifling through her bag for her toothbrush. She wasn't going to have time to shower. She put on fresh deodorant, touched up her makeup, and ran her fingers through her shoulder length wavy crimson hair. Feeling passable, she left the bathroom. Grey obnoxiously hammered on the door again. Tomas rolled over, buried his face in his pillow and mumbled, "He's such a pain in the ass."

Lexy didn't respond. *There was no point in defending Grey. He treated Tomas as an inconvenient distraction.* She slipped out the door and tried to close it quietly behind her. Grey was standing there with an enormous shit eating grin on his face. Lexy gave him a dirty look and scolded, "Was that really necessary?" They strolled towards the parking lot together.

Grey shoved her and sparred, "As long as you're just having fun. Eventually this pretending to be a normal girl game, is going to blow up in your face. He doesn't even know who you are." He walked around the truck, opened his door, and then reached across to unlock the passenger side door for her.

She slid into the seat next to him, knowing he was right. *She wasn't going to be able to keep this up.* At least now, she was clear on why he was being such an insufferable douche. *He was worried about her.* He kept referring to Tomas as her booty call because he knew she wasn't going to be able to keep up this facade of normalcy forever. *He knew what she was hiding.* They drove in silence for a while. She stared out the window, just thinking. *She was happy, but Grey was right, Tomas didn't really know her. Grey had been tolerating her relationship. He knew her secrets, and was aware of the savagery, she was capable of. Tomas had only ever seen the toned-down version of her. He was only seeing what she wanted him to see. It was an omission of truth. An omission for personal growth. Lexy wanted to be loved. She knew it wasn't forever.*

Grey squeezed her arm gently and apologised, "I'm sorry I brought it up. Stop over thinking everything, Lex. I'll try to be nicer to the guy."

He'd heard the commentary as her brain allowed the truth to sink in. Lexy opened the glove compartment. There was nothing edible in there. She asked, "Where's the job? Do we have time to stop for snacks?"

He chuckled and dug around in his pocket with one hand on the wheel. Grey chucked a chocolate bar at her and teased," I knew you'd be hungry."

Lexy tore the wrapper off, and then she tore the bar in two, and handed the other half to him. She shook her head and sighed, "You're a funny guy, Greydon."

He grimaced at her use of his whole name and disclosed, "We're doing this one alone. We're going to go scope out a new kid that's scheduled for Correction. We're supposed to hang around for a few weeks. If they survive, we get to them first and bring them back with us."

"You could have told me to bring my bag," Lexy complained. She chucked the wrapper over her shoulder.

Grey pointed to the plastic bag at her feet and scolded, "Come on, there's a plastic bag for garbage right beside your foot."

She loved spending time with Grey. That wasn't the issue. He could have told her they were going to be gone for a while. She could have told Tomas. Was it wrong to want to preserve her fantasy for as long as she could? There was no reason they needed to be the ones doing this job.

Once again, he answered her thoughts and said, "I volunteered, I knew it was the only way we'd be able to spend some time together alone."

Come on Grey. Why did he always do this to her? He wanted to keep her heart with him. He was afraid she was giving it to somebody else. They couldn't be together. He could sleep with Arrianna, Lily, and anyone else that caught his eye, but he couldn't sit back and let her do the same. He was acting like he was jealous. Maybe he was starting to remember? Would that matter? She'd let go of Tomas in a heartbeat if they had a chance to be together. If she knew he wouldn't forget what happened between them...

The truck jerked as he abruptly pulled over on the side of the deserted highway. He glared at her with accusing eyes. "What don't I remember?"

Lexy couldn't look at him. She stared out the window and said, "Just drive Grey. Stop listening to my thoughts and drive. Trust me, it really doesn't matter what you remember. It'll never be allowed to happen. I'd like to see this kid before their Correction. Just drive."

Grey whispered, "Lexy..."

She ordered, "We're not talking about this...Drive." He pulled out and continued down the highway and neither of them spoke. She was afraid to think so she turned on the radio and music blared as they drove down the highway. *She'd let that slip, that was stupid.* She drifted off to sleep to the sound of the music.

Grey whispered, "We're here." He poked her.

Lexy opened her eyes and squinted in the sunshine glaring through the windows. *How long had they been driving? Where were they?*

She heard the driver's side door slam. *Great, he was pissed off? Why was he angry?* She was half asleep still and her memory of the night before was a bit foggy. She tried to stretch while still inside the truck, smacked her hand on the door, and recalled the reason. *She was going to have to deal with this. He wasn't going to let it drop.* The door creaked as she opened it and they were parked in front of a roadside diner. He'd left her in the vehicle and just gone inside without her. *He was seriously choked.* She pushed on the door to the diner and a bell jingled. Grey was seated at the counter instead of at one of the dozen empty private booths. He didn't even want to sit with her. She wanted to go sit in one of the booths but didn't have any money. *She'd left everything she needed back at the motel with Tomas because Grey had omitted the length of time they'd be gone for. He'd only volunteered to do this job with her to get her away from Tomas. Wait a minute. She was the one that should be mad.* She sat a couple of chairs away from him at the counter and he slid something to her. It was a credit card. He held up one of his own, showing her, they didn't need to speak. *Fine then, she wouldn't speak to him.* Lexy ordered her breakfast and started to read a newspaper. *They'd made it quite far the night before. They were in Minnesota. This job was going to suck.*

The waitress asked her if she wanted a coffee. Lexy responded with a polite, "Yes, thank you." She didn't look at Grey, and he didn't attempt to look at her. *This was painfully immature, they weren't really teenagers.* She heard Grey finish his breakfast and leave. The front door jingled. *What in the hell, Greydon? You prissy little bitch.*

The waitress passed her a note and said, "The man a couple seats down asked me to give this to you."

Lexy thanked her and read the note. *Get what you need from the pharmacy and get your own hotel room. I'll meet you at the high school at nine am.* She grinned as she paid the waitress, thanked her, and left. Lexy shoved on the jingling door and squinted as she walked out into the sunshine. She glanced in each direction. Grey was long gone. The truck was also gone. *Of course, he took the vehicle and left. Why wouldn't he? Asshole.* The giant pharmacy sign across the street beckoned her. She grabbed the toiletries she needed and a curling iron. That's what she required to feel normal. She went next door and bought a few changes of clothes. After she had what she needed, she stopped at the liquor store to grab some refreshments and snacks. *She was looking forward to the time alone. The joke was on him, this was exactly what she needed.* She paid for a hotel room down the street, took a shower, star fished out on the queen-sized bed and drifted off for a luxuriously long nap. When she woke up, it was dark outside. She'd spent the whole day asleep. Lexy flipped through the menu on the bedside table, ordered room service and then sprawled out to watch T.V. She tried to watch a show but couldn't stop replaying the conversation they had in the truck. *He was fine with mass murder, but heaven forbid she hurt his feelings. He'd never done anything like this before. They'd never even had a real argument. Never one that lasted longer than five minutes. Why now?* She wasn't sure how late it was when she succumbed to the weight of her heavy eyelids, but it felt like she'd just closed them for a second, when the sunshine started streaming through the sheer blinds. She had to get up and get ready for school. The thought of it made her smile. Lexy never dressed to blend in. She was supposed to, but she rarely did what she was told. She applied her brand-new cherry red lipstick in the mirror and took in her appearance, feeling sexier than usual. Perhaps it was because they were fighting? She wandered down to the diner. Grey was sitting at the counter eating his breakfast. She grinned, *he could have eaten anywhere. He had the truck. He knew she needed a ride, but he was unflinchingly stubborn.* She slid into the seat beside him and said, "How long are you planning to ignore me?"

He took a drink of his coffee and replied, "Omission is a lie. You lied to me."

Shit, then she'd been lying her ass off to Tomas. Grey turned around and glared at her.

"Do me a favour, don't even think about him while you're around me." He shoved his seat out and left his meal on the counter. "I'll be waiting in the truck. Make it quick." He left her sitting there alone. The waitress came to take her order. She ordered a coffee to go and a muffin. *It was like having a psychotically jealous ex that you had to work with every single day. This was the reason they couldn't be together.* She walked out of the diner to the sound of bells and noticed that he'd found a parking spot closer to the front of the restaurant. She pulled on the door and it was still locked. He always unlocked the door. *He'd done it on purpose. She wasn't sure why?* He reached across and unlocked the door for her. Lexy got into the truck and he pulled out before she had the chance to close the door. *He was being ridiculous. Yes, she got the bloody hint. He was upset. Well, she was too, and she hadn't done anything to deserve being on the receiving end of this crap.* They pulled into a parking spot at the high school. She hopped out before he'd parked and left him there. *Ass wipe, two can play at this game.*

Grey called after her, "You don't even know if it's a boy or a girl."

Lexy didn't respond as she strutted away. *She'd figure it out.* She shoved open the school's double doors and surveyed the hallway in front of her. She needed to go somewhere private. She ducked into the bathroom. Lexy placed her hands on either side of her head, and focused. She felt the heat from her Healing ability spark. This would only work for a few minutes, and she'd be exhausted, but it'd be totally worth it to get one up on him. The bathroom door opened, startling her. She saw a faint blue haze around the girl that dove past her, into the stall. She needed to get out into the hallway while it was still full of students. Preparing herself for the trip she was about to go on, Lexy stepped out of the bathroom. The students scurried in packs in both directions, followed by trails of purple, orange, blue, and green. *There she was…a flicker of yellow.* She watched the petite blonde dash into her class. The Aries group usually handled all of their paperwork. She'd been so intent on finding the girl, before Grey. She hadn't even attempted to make her way to the office. The bell rang and she was directed to the office by a teacher. Things were so much easier when Lily and Frost were with them. They had this magical power of suggestion thing. Lexy's abilities in that area were pathetic. She wandered into the office. Grey was already charming the pants off the secretary. She grinned, *he'd been thrown off his game too. He'd forgotten to hide his accent. Grey was an extremely likeable guy when he wasn't being a prissy little bitch.*

He turned around, grinned at her, and shook his head. *Good, she was glad he'd heard her inner commentary. The truth hurts.*

The secretary was a sweet lady. She addressed them both, "You two are siblings then? You sure don't look like twins. Fraternal twins, obviously? You're both in all the same classes. You can help each other find everything. I'll show you where your first class is. We'd better get going, you're already late kids."

Kids, that's funny. They were both older than the secretary. Great, now she'd have to consciously curb her southern drawl and pretend to have the same accent as Grey. They were supposed to be playing twins. Grey's family was from Scotland and they'd moved to Australia before his teens. His accent was impossible to copy. They marched down the hallway following the secretary side by side. She popped her head into their first class, which also happened to be their marks first class. *Damn it, the Aries Group was good.* They both found an empty seat. Grey managed to sit right behind the girl they'd been sent to scope out. He didn't know it was her. A part of her wanted to keep her mind shut and let him figure it out for himself. She really wanted to get back to the others, and out of this tense situation with Grey. She looked at Grey and thought, *it's the girl sitting in front of you.* He turned around and smiled at her. *Maybe if she let him take the lead, he'd stop the insanity?* She attempted to look like she was paying attention. The teacher was staring at her. *He'd better not ask her a question in front of the class.* He asked her a question. Her pulse began to race. Grey piped up and answered it for her. The bell rang and Grey waited for her, outside the door. They followed the girl to her next class while she chatted with her pack of friends. This was what they were supposed to do. They weren't supposed to speak to her. They were just supposed to watch her, see if she survived her Correction, and make sure the other Clans didn't get to her first.

They got into the car at the end of the school day without even knowing her name. It was better that way. Most of the time they died during their Corrections. She was a tiny girl, sometimes the little ones were feisty, but she appeared to be completely unconcerned with her surroundings. *She hadn't noticed them at all.* Normally they would have spent the whole day joking around and taking bets on what her gift would be, today they barely spoke to each other. Not even on the drive back to the hotel. She got out of the truck and Grey drove away. *He must be staying at a different hotel. They'd never had a fight like this.* She watched him leave. She ordered an early dinner and quickly devoured it. Her burger was amazing. Frost would have been impressed. He was the one that was always trying to find the perfect burger. Lexy grabbed her bottle of red wine and poured some into a little plastic wrapped cup from the bathroom. She filled the tub, took off her clothes and slipped into a heavenly bubble bath. She closed her eyes and relaxed in the fluffy cloud of bubbles, she was submerged in. The stress of the day melted away and she dozed off.

She woke up to Grey's voice, "You're not supposed to fall asleep in the bathtub."

She startled and splashed him, "What in the hell? Get out of here. I'm naked."

Grey replied, "I see that, but the bubbles are doing a nice job of covering…most of you."

Lexy shifted the bubbles around to cover everything and said, "How did you get in here?"

While watching her in the tub, he confessed, "I forgot my key, my wife fell asleep, and I can't get into our room."

"Well, you've been an asshole to your wife for days. If I was really your wife, I'd have words with him for giving you the key. Get out of here, so I can get out of the tub," she ordered.

He was dead serious as he countered, "Why do you care? We've seen each other naked. According to your inner commentary, we've slept together too."

"Get out of here, Grey," she whispered.

He sat on the edge of the bathtub and baited, "Do you have any idea how I've been feeling? How jealous I've been over your fling with this Tomas guy. I've been sick to my stomach. At least I know why now." He swished the bubbles out of the way with one of his hands, exposing her breasts.

She whispered, "Stop it, Grey. Don't do this…I'm happy."

His eyes penetrated her soul as he seduced, "Tomas doesn't matter, you know he doesn't…"

"Please leave," Lexy pleaded.

Grey sparred, "Not a chance."

Lexy pulled the plug and sighed, "Then go wait for me in the other room."

Grey stood up, and sweetly replied, "That, I'll do." Obeying her request for privacy, he left the room and closed the door. From the other side, he toyed, "I'm not leaving. I'll be out here waiting for you."

Lexy got out of the tub, dripping all over the floor. She quickly locked the bathroom door. She heard him laughing from the other room.

He chuckled, "Are you planning to stay in there all night?"

She dried off and wrapped the towel around herself. *She didn't have any clothes in the bathroom. Why was he doing this now? She'd finally moved on.* She ran a brush through her hair and left it wet. *She was not going to backslide. She was not going to end up in bed with Grey. Was she supposed to give up the time she could have with Tomas for one night? A night he wouldn't even remember. She might as well get this uncomfortable conversation over with.* She stepped out to find Grey lounging on her bed, drinking a beer, flipping through the channels.

He glanced up and said, "Are you ready to have an honest conversation?"

Lexy grabbed some clothes out of her bag and answered, "In a minute." She disappeared into the bathroom, put on some shorts and a tank top, and reappeared. She strolled over and sat down on the edge of the bed. "Alright Grey, say what you need to say."

He grabbed another beer out of the cooler, passed it to her and teased, "Don't try to take the cap off with your teeth." He chucked an opener at her.

She opened it and ribbed, "You're hilarious. You know I'm far past that."

He took a drink and probed, "Are you far past me?"

She kept looking at the bottle she was holding as she replied, "Yes, I am. I have to be."

He shook his head and whispered, "I don't believe you. Look into my eyes and say it."

She didn't respond, she couldn't...

He paused before asking the question he'd come to ask, "Tell me how it happened. When did we..."

Lexy got off the bed and said, "It doesn't matter. We're not allowed to be together. We can't have that kind of relationship. It was just a dream. That's all it can ever be."

Grey walked towards her and coaxed, "What if I want more?"

Lexy placed her hand against his chest to keep him from coming closer and confessed, "Then I'll give it to you, because I love you, and you'll forget about it in the morning. I'll watch you whore your way around the Clan. I'll lose what I have with Tomas, and you'll be fine, because you won't even remember what happened between us." She stared into his blue eyes and said, "The only one that will get hurt by this is me."

Their eyes locked as he caressed her cheek. She closed her eyes. Grey whispered, "He doesn't even know who you are." Closing the space between them, he kissed her tenderly on the forehead, pulled away, stared into her eyes and whispered, "I can wait." He walked over and grabbed the menu off the bedside table. "Are you hungry? I'm starving. Let's watch a movie."

And just like that, their first big argument was over...

They spent weeks shadowing the nameless girl before finding out her name was Emma. She seemed nice, had a lot of friends, and appeared to be a half decent student. They only had to sit outside in the truck and watch her house for a few nights to figure out her schedule. Emma had a single mom. Her mother worked nights and she left at seven o'clock. She came home at two o'clock in the morning. Emma watched her younger siblings, while her mom was at work. Her brother and sister were five-year-old twins. She really needed to turn her bedroom light off, or at least close the curtains at night. This kid was completely oblivious to what was coming.

Grey handed her a bag of chips and said, "What do you think?"

Lexy watched her putting the twins to sleep from the lit-up bedroom, they were in a truck parked outside. "The kids are really cute. I think this one is going to be over in a few minutes. She's so trusting, and completely oblivious. Even I feel guilty watching this go down."

Grey teased, "Do you feel guilt?"

Lexy did feel guilt. Now, she did. This Correction would be like watching someone kick a baby kitten. Hell, three of them.

He sighed, "I want to write her an anonymous note, telling her to close the damn blinds and lock her front door. I bet it's unlocked right now." Grey got out of the car and snuck up the path to the front door.

Lexy was sitting in the car laughing as he danced up to her stoop and turned the doorknob just to see. He was joking around dancing in front of her door being a goof ball, when she opened it. *Abort! Abort prank!*

Grey always had the ability to think on his toes. He was face to face with the girl they were supposed to be inconspicuously watching. *Shit Greydon. What in the hell?*

Emma said, "Can I help you?"

Lexy thought of ducking, but realised she'd already seen her sitting there. She waved at her. *Grey, you bloody idiot.*

Grey replied, "I hope you don't think this is creepy, but I told my sister you were by far the hottest girl in the school. She dared me to look you up, go to your house and ask you out."

Emma grinned at him and taunted, "And the dancing?"

"I was just trying to make her laugh?" Grey gave her his most charming grin.

Smiling, Emma enquired, "And you turned the doorknob because?"

He replied meekly, "She told me you'd think it was creepy if I came to the house to ask you out. I thought it would be funny?" There was an awkward silence. Pretending to be embarrassed, he laughed, "I should just go. I'm an idiot." He started walking away.

Emma agreed to go out with him, "Yes…Sure. We can go out. I can't go out till the weekend. My Mom works nights, but you can come over tomorrow, if you want to. As long as I let her know, I'm sure it'll be okay."

Grey grinned and said, "I'll see you tomorrow then." He calmly strolled back to the truck and got in the driver's seat. They kept smiling sweetly and waving until they drove away. Once they turned the corner, Lexy started smacking him. Grey laughed, "Stop it…you have to stop. I'm going to drive right off the road."

She scolded, "What are you going to do? You can't be sitting on her couch, when they come to kill her whole family."

Grey was staring at the road as he chuckled, "Well, I obviously didn't think I was going to get caught."

"Nobody ever does," Lexy sighed. They pulled up at her hotel. Grey grabbed his bag from her feet. She asked, "Why don't you just get rid of your hotel room?"

He sparred, "Well, I might need it now."

She smacked him and bantered, "I'm sure if we're not supposed to speak to her, sleeping with her would be frowned upon."

They walked into the room. He chucked his bag on the bed and provoked, "A guy has needs Lexy."

Lexy sighed, "Some more than others." She grabbed a pillow and playfully beat him with it. They wrestled around, he flipped her over and pinned her beneath him on the bed.

His lips hovered a breath from hers and everything inside of her screamed for her to kiss him. *He knew she wanted him to.*

He whispered, "What do you want for dinner?" He cracked a giant grin and got off of her.

She squeezed her eyes shut and remained where he'd pinned her to the bed. *Her resolve was faltering. Maybe, she could just do it. Grey wouldn't remember, she didn't have to tell Tomas. Nobody would have to know...*

Grey laid down beside her and said, "I don't want to be the reason you cheat on your first real boyfriend. I told you I can wait, and I meant it. We've got nothing but time. Me and you, it's a forever thing. I'm sorry I was such an ass. I'm not used to sharing you, and the revelation that we've slept together was a lot, but it made sense. I know I've hurt you with my behaviour, I swear I didn't know. If I'm going to forget what happens, maybe if we don't push our luck, what I'm feeling right now, won't be erased?"

Lexy shifted to face him, balanced on her side and divulged, "I think I'm better equipped to deal with the hurt. How am I supposed to be with Tomas, when I know you're feeling like this?"

He trailed one of his fingers along the soft curve of her hip to her thigh. "What kind of selfish bastard would I be if I slept with you to erase the fact that I want you and left you to deal with the fall out? Tomas isn't a bad guy and he seems to really care about you. I'll do better with him. I'll be nice when we get back."

"If we're not both entombed for blowing a Correction," she taunted.

Grey stared at the ceiling and sighed, "Tell me you don't want to go over there to lock all of her doors and windows."

"And shut her lights off," Lexy chuckled.

Grey added, "I'd close all of her curtains and kidnap those two cute kids to get them out of that house."

They would always be like this if they didn't wreck it.

Lexy woke up in the morning feeling like things were going to be normal again. *Grey was singing in the shower.* She laid there giggling into her pillow at his off key soprano. *He was such a goof ball.* She got up and wandered in to brush her teeth, laughing as she brushed them.

He hollered, "You're about to see me naked. Either close your eyes or take a picture."

She dove out of the room, respecting the friend-zone. He danced out with a towel wrapped around his waist still singing in campy falsetto as he dug around in his bag for clothes.

Lexy shook her head and mocked, "A double threat, you don't just dance on doorsteps, you sing too."

Grey chimed in, "And I'm gorgeous."

She tossed his jacket at him and teased, "You're alright. We're going to be late for school. Less dancing, more dressing."

They rushed into their first class and sat down. *Emma's seat was empty.* Grey looked at her and she felt the weight on his heart. *She was better equipped to deal with this stuff.* Lexy raised her hand, told the teacher she wasn't feeling well and asked Grey for the key as she passed his desk. *Only one could leave, without it being obvious.* She signed out at the office, quickly made her way to their vehicle and turned the key in the ignition. *A part of her didn't want to know for sure.* Lexy drove to Emma's house and the whole street was blocked off with police tape. *It happened, but had she survived it? She needed to get a closer look.* Lexy got out of the truck and ran towards the house.

An officer blocked her route and asserted, "This is a crime scene. You can't go in there."

Lexy stammered, "But my friend!" *She didn't need to say anything else. She could tell by the expression on his face. They were all gone. They were already bringing out body bags.* She stood there, watching them carry out the body bags, before she walked back to the truck, feeling defeated. *There were four body bags. This was why she didn't want to know their names. This was why she didn't want to meet them and think they were nice. She had to be sure the girl hadn't survived.* Lexy waited for the ambulances to leave with their cargo. No lights, or sirens whirling, just a silent drive. She parked, watched them take the gurneys in through the emergency door and got to stealthily follow. Right away, she knew it was going to be tricky to get a good look at the bodies. The staff took all four gurneys directly to the elevators. Two by two, they were pushed inside. The doors closed. *Lily would have used her ability to convince the staff she was family. She'd be taken to ID them, without anyone batting an eye. Lexy had to be more creative. She needed access to the morgue. If these nurses were Trinity or Triad, she would have followed one of them into the bathroom and snapped her neck. ID problem solved. They were mortals, and she was supposed to protect mortals. It was inconvenient.* Lexy acted like she was supposed to be there, walking with a group of people, until she found someone's smock with a name tag, draped across a chair in the nurse's station. She made her way to the basement. The morgue was always in the basement. She'd woken up in enough of them to hazard a guess. The whole thing turned out to be way less complicated than she'd expected it to be. Nobody was in the morgue. Just four body bags side by side on gurneys. She unzipped the first one, it was the mother. *Her throat had been slit. They probably waited around to kill her before they left.* She opened the next body bag with a much smaller lump in it. *She didn't have to, but she was curious.* There was no blood, just broken vessels in the little boy's eyes. *He'd been suffocated.* She opened the next one. *The little girl met the same demise.* She unzipped Emma's body bag and zipped it back up. *She'd fought back, her Correction had been brutal. Emma was unrecognizable. For the first time, she wanted to bring one back. She knew she couldn't. Emma had probably gone through to the hall of souls already. She'd bring back something dark in her place. Emma had fought for her survival with everything she had, but she was gone.* Lexy snuck out and made her way to the parking lot.

She drove back to the school, to pick up Grey. They packed up their stuff, checked out of their hotel rooms, and stopped at a payphone on the way out of town to call, 'The

Aries Group.' They'd dispose of their paperwork, come up with an explanation for the school, and make sure there was no trace of them left behind.

They were both quiet when they rejoined the Ankh. They didn't speak about it. They just told them she didn't make it. Grey made good on his promise to be nice to Tomas. Lexy tried to relax and be content for a while. He'd eventually see her for what she was, but until then, she'd continue to pretend to be a semi normal, partially immortal girl.

Time slipped by so quickly and before she knew it, Lexy was waiting in the in-between for Tomas to return from his Testing. She'd been preparing herself for a while. *He wasn't coming back.* She'd sensed it in the days before the Testing. She'd felt his loss in every embrace, and in every time their lips met. *It wasn't pessimism, it was self-preservation. She'd known they were saying goodbye.* Lexy had been sitting in a meadow for hours, torturing herself with what she hadn't had the guts to say before he went in. The rest of the Clan began to appear. One by one, they solidified, and strolled over to the comfortable spot she'd found. She briefly locked eyes with Markus, and she knew the Testing was over. *He was gone.*

Grey knelt in the grass, he touched her arm and whispered, "Lex, you know we have to go."

She gently removed his hand and confessed, "I should have said it, at least once."

Grey plucked a tiny white flower out of the grass, handed it to her and replied, "Said, what?"

"I should have told him I loved him," she whispered, without taking the flower from Grey's hand. *She'd rarely experienced guilt, but she knew that's what she was feeling now.*

Stricken, he dropped the flower and asked, "Did you love him?"

In a hushed tone, she disclosed, "Not like he loved me."

Grey said, "Why lie?"

"I knew he wasn't coming back. It wouldn't have hurt anything. I feel like I owed him something after two years. Now, he's just gone," she whispered.

Markus interrupted them and asserted, "It's time to go."

Grey got up, looked at Markus and said, "Are you sure?"

Markus placed his arm around Grey and wandered away with him as they spoke, "Triad and Trinity made it out. Even if they somehow manage to make it to end of the Testing now, they won't be allowed to leave."

Grey looked back at Lexy as he asked, "What happens to them?"

Markus whispered, "Their souls are absorbed into the walls of the Testing, and their energy will be used as a power source. They're gone. There's nothing we can do about it. It sounds like a horrible thing to say, but you'll get used to losing people. This is why you shouldn't get involved with anyone until after they've survived the Testing."

Lexy heard the entire conversation. *She didn't say anything. A part of her knew it would be best if she turned her emotions off for a while.* Grey turned to look at her as they walked away with their somber Clan, to stand in the sand, and wait for Orin to summon them home.

Grey didn't give her a chance to say no as he embraced her. Holding her head against his heart, he whispered, "I'm still here. I will always be here."

She closed her eyes, allowing him to hold her as the scenery flashed with blinding white light. She felt his absence as her tomb solidified around her. Lexy laid there with her eyes squeezed shut as the light pulsed. Then came the humming sound of the rose quartz interior of the tomb. *She was back in the land of the living.* Her tomb slid open; she felt the grinding vibration of stone. Orin's face appeared.

Visibly upset, Orin held out his hand and said, "I'm sorry. I know you cared about Tomas."

He'd put her feelings to words. She may not have loved him, but she'd cared about him. He'd been important to her. He was a steppingstone in her evolution. He'd helped heal her, and she was going to miss him.

Time sped by, days became weeks, and weeks turned to months. The seasons changed and they added a few new faces to the Clan. Lexy kept her emotions off. She did a lot of Corrections during this emotionally vacant time. When Lexy was sent to do a Correction, there were no long-winded speeches, about the greater good. She gave no choices to those meeting their demise by her hand. Grey would try to make it nice for the random innocent, but most of the time it was done in seconds. She'd cut her hand, say the words as she marked their foreheads with her blood, and unceremoniously snap their necks. Life was simple when you took your emotions out of the equation.

Lexy didn't love much, but she could honestly say, she loved bumping into her nemesis, Tiberius. The Clans only crossed paths, while surveying, or stealing Correction survivors. She rather enjoyed their random encounters. It usually meant there'd be a fight. She'd stroll past him, and accidentally slam his face into something. It would always look like an accident. Sometimes she would lure him somewhere, by making him believe he could have her. After she suckered him in, she'd tie him up and leave him in embarrassing places.

Often, they'd go to the funerals of the teens that hadn't survived their Corrections. Tiberius frequented those funerals and he'd do his best to corner her somewhere. He'd push every button she had, knowing they were supposed to be flying under the radar. Grey would always be close by, with the sole mission of calming her down.

Over the years that passed by, they each had insignificant flirtations with other people, but their large attachment was always to each other. That never changed. Eventually, that attachment would start to grow. They'd spent more nights than they should have, wrapped in each other's arms, loving each other to the point of desperation, until the morning. Grey would always forget what happened between them, with the rising of the sun, and she'd be alone in loving him. After thirty years, she realised, she'd always be alone in loving him. He would never be permitted to remember. This would not stop her from willing those moments to happen again, with every breath of her being.

Wake up Lexy…Wake up Lexy…

Chapter 27

Waking Dragons

2014 Present Day

The year 2014

The alleyway was dimly lit by light that trickled in from open curtains in the windows above. There was a hissing sound as steam rose from a pipe near cracked cobblestone. It resembled a set from an old horror movie. Other girls would be disturbed by this scenario, but not Lexy. This was her element. Tonight, the girls of Clan Ankh were the lure for the most diabolical of beings. Serial killers could always be counted on to do their best to inflict pain in creative ways. This was her favourite kind of job. She loved to rid the world of dark things, but only after she'd had a chance to play. She longed to crawl up inside of their demented psyche to find out what made them tick. To do this, she was more than willing to take a stroll into the abyss. She would allow her Dragon out on these occasions. Lexy believed the punishment should always fit the crime.

She was being followed by Zach this evening. She'd been messing with his head for an entire year. The night he'd been taken from Triad. He had been the one to finish her off in a fight between the Clans. *The little shit had run her over with a truck.* She still smiled whenever she thought about it. This was only further proof of her epically twisted sense of humour. She was a Healer. She hadn't stayed down for long that night. Markus had made sure to entomb her long

240

enough to calm her offended ego. It hadn't subdued her wounded ego, but it had been long enough for her to see the bigger picture. *The kid had been Triad, and now he was Ankh. She would have plenty of time for revenge.* She had never done a thing to Zach, but everyone knew it crossed her mind on a regular basis. That little spark of uncertainty in Zach's eyes was enough payback for her. A part of her was secretly impressed by the balls it must have taken for him to come after her in the first place. She was infamous for her rage, and skill as a warrior. She listened to her heels as they clicked along the cobblestone. Walking on cobblestones in heels was a feat in itself. This was a brilliant setting for serial killers hunting grounds. In this winding maze of dimly lit cobblestone alleyways, it would be difficult for his prey to escape. *This was going to be fun.* Lexy stopped walking again and leaned back against the building. She could picture the sordid deeds that had gone on in this alley, perhaps against this very wall. The wall she was leaning against, *Sick.* She moved away from it and smiled. She thought of Kayn. *She was one of the new girls. She'd be trying to hose her down with hand sanitizer right now if she'd seen her lean against that wall.* Lexy thought about Melody and Kayn. Both were wandering the streets in search of the same evil man. Melody was a Healer, she'd be fine. Kayn was supposed to be a big deal, but so far all she'd seen was a dorky extremely likable teenage girl that spent an unusually large amount of time tripping over her own shoelaces. Lexy liked Kayn almost immediately. She didn't usually like people, at first sight. There was something about this girl that always made her smile. She hadn't wanted to become attached to any of these new Clan members. She knew better. It had been forty years since anyone survived the Testing.

Lexy looked in each dimly lit direction. She turned around, glancing behind her. Zach was just like every other man on the planet. Lilarah was supposed to be walking the streets in search of this psycho too. The Clan was attempting to subdue a serial killer tonight. Zach wasn't paying attention.

Lily placed Zach on her detail. *It was an epically ignorant move. She'd given him another opportunity to screw up.* The rule of thumb was that because young Zach was not paying attention, it would most certainly be her. A part of her felt like she should stroll back down the alley and beat the crap out of him to make a point. She was amped up for the hunt, it was a good enough excuse to smack him around. She smiled as she watched Zach hanging on Lily's every syllable. *She couldn't blame him. Nobody was impervious to Lily's charms. Lily knew exactly what she was doing. She was distracting him from his duties.* Lexy strolled down the alleyway, a stunning vision of long toned legs, and crimson hair. She felt like grabbing Lily's shoulders and shaking her senseless. *That girl had a one-track mind. Grey should have been the one following her tonight. He was still pissed at, Princess Lily. He wouldn't have allowed himself to fall for any of her crap. At least she would have had someone entertaining to talk to.* She picked up a rock, held it in the palm of her hand and stared at it. She could whip it at Zach's bloody head, then he'd be paying attention. She could chuck it at Lily. She grinned, turning around to do just that. *She was alone.* Lexy started to laugh, running a hand through her wavy scarlet hair. *Oh, you've got to be kidding me.* She leaned up against the stone wall, sighed and tossed the stone into the air, catching it in the palm of her hand. She'd just wait here. They'd realise they were idiots soon enough. She chucked the stone back up into the air and caught it again in her palm. She cursed under her breath, as she gazed down the empty alleyway. It occurred to her that Zach could be hiding so she would appear to be all alone. She opened her purse, took out her mirror, and applied a fresh coat of brilliant red lipstick. *This was her war paint.* She pressed her lips together and raked her fingers through her vibrant crimson mane. *He'd better be watching her.* She snapped the mirror together, placing it in her purse along with her lipstick. Lexy ran her tongue over her pearly white teeth, to be certain they were free of lipstick. *She was bored stiff.* Lexy sighed as she strolled down the alley. She shivered, as she felt the temperature drop a touch. A familiar voice whispered, *be careful*. She took a couple of steps. *Be careful*, her internal voice whispered again. She grinned, knowing the fun part of her evening was about to begin. The Clan would be relieved. In these situations, it was best if it was her that was taken. *She wasn't the least bit afraid.* Lexy smiled again. Serial killers were all the same. They were the most twisted, sick version of humanity. She was usually quite in tune with their thought process. Physically, they were no match at all for her. One may take her down, but not for long. She heard tires rolling on cement and prepared for the inevitable as she casually turned around.

A car rolled up beside her. In the driver's seat was an unassuming middle-aged man with glasses, he asked, "How much?"

"Well, that depends on what you want," Lexy teased, smiling seductively. *Oh, did you ever pick the wrong girl tonight.*

Thinking on his toes, he enquired, "Are you a cop?"

He was smart. If she'd been an officer, she would have had to admit it.

She sweetly replied, "Not even close, hun." The serial murderers she'd had the displeasure of keeping company with in the past had been quite homely looking, and indefinable. Just like this guy. His dark side was easily detected by her. *There was always something missing in their eyes.* He smiled at her innocently. He was almost attractive when he tried to flirt. *This emotionless abomination had a helpless quality. This was his mask. This was how he'd lured the others in.*

The unassuming man whispered, "I want everything. Will you give me everything?"

He wanted to look into her eyes as she struggled to take her last breath. That is what he'd meant by everything. Men like this would always find her. He touched her arm and her skin crawled. *Yes, this was the guy.* This was his little ritual. He was nothing more than a spider slowly making his way across the web towards his prey. It would be easier for him if she got into his vehicle of her own free will. Once he had her at his layer, he'd wrap her in his web of silk and take his time with her.

He wasn't going to kill her right here. Continuing her Oscar-worthy performance, she continued to wriggle in his web. She'd allow him to believe that she didn't see anything but a harmless middle-aged man. *Two could play at this game.* Lexy leaned through his window provocatively. He made a comment about being drawn to her beautiful hair. *He was a trophy keeper. He was telling her up front that he was going to keep a lock of her hair. Was he making a wig? Did he want her to look like his mother or first girlfriend? That was usually the deal. If he liked killing redheads, one of the two had been a red head.* She'd been sent to lure him out tonight. Part one of the job had been accomplished. Now, the Clan needed to creatively dispose of him. It would only be painful for her if he managed to take her by surprise, or if he managed to get the upper hand. She had an advantage the other women didn't have. She knew he was coming. "Where do you want to take me?" Lexy seduced as she glanced down the empty alley. *These sickos always had a second location for their messed-up rituals of depravity.* Her heart began to palpitate. Lexy wasn't afraid, she was excited.

He motioned for her to get into the car and replied, "Get in, I'll take you there."

Anyone else would have subdued him in the car. Lexy was far too curious. *This was an opportunity. Was he really a trophy taker? Was he ritualistic? She needed to see the real him. She wanted to see the evil behind the docile mask. She wanted him to run his whole routine from the capture to the kill, in its entirety. She needed to know what he'd done to the others. Those women hadn't had the ability to fight back. She'd need a moment alone with this one. She couldn't die. What did a little pain matter to her?* She looked back again at the empty alley. They were carrying on a conversation in the distance. *Had they noticed her situation? Were they just pretending to be in conversation?* Lexy wore a fingerless glove on her hand as they all did. They could still feel the heat from their glowing Ankh symbol, even if they couldn't see it. Once she was wounded, it would set off her symbol and signal her Clan. She climbed into the car. Lexy casually took off one of her earrings, and squeezed it in the palm of her hand, as the crappy little car's engine purred. He smiled at her. His eyes flashed with excitement. *She saw it coming. She imagined this was also the moment the others knew they were in the wrong car.* He covered her mouth with a cloth. Lexy inhaled the scent of the ether. The world shifted and whirled as she used her final moment of consciousness to squeeze the earring again, as hard as she could, driving the sharp end into her hand. This time it pierced her flesh. Her last sensation was the warmth of her own blood as it trickled a path down the lifeline on her palm. Her peripheral vision flickered, and she was overcome by the drug on the cloth, her captor clasped tightly over her mouth. She'd been drugged once before by a man like him. In her memory, Lexy travelled back to the moments before her own Sweet Sleep.

Wake up Lexy...She didn't open her eyes. She knew better. Lexy wasn't sure how long she'd been out. She kept her eyes closed, knowing the deal behind these sickos. He'd wait until she woke up to begin his torture. He would want to watch her squirm. He'd want to place his hand on her chest to feel her heart as it palpitated with fear. The longer she kept her eyes closed, the more time she'd buy. Lexy could opt out of the pain, but she was far too curious. She desired the full experience. She wanted to know what he'd done to his victims. *This was going to be fun.* She used her other senses to prepare herself for her surroundings. *She was lying on a cold floor or table.* She knew this without opening her eyes. She felt a light breeze; goosebumps rose in response. This gave her the knowledge she was naked. *What did she smell?* Lexy filed through the list of foul scents, in her memory. She recognized it as the tinny scent of blood, combined with paint, and gasoline. *Was she in a garage?* That was a place that may contain all those scents, minus the blood. These were all things she could tell without opening her eyes and giving away her return to the land of the coherent. One fragrance haunted her subconscious mind. The metallic aroma of blood had always stimulated her inner Dragon. *She knew Ankh would come. When was the question? She was trying to buy them time by pretending to be out cold for as long as possible. She was buying them time to save the serial murderer from her. If she killed him before they arrived. They wouldn't have the opportunity to mark him and send him to where he needed to go. Markus would be furious with her.* She hated disappointing her surrogate father figure but knew once their game began, it would be difficult for her to play nice. *Skippy the serial killer had chosen the wrong girl to play his wicked games with tonight. He wasn't going to buy it much longer.* She could feel him there. Without opening her eyes, she could sense his excitement. *She loved this part. She had a seriously warped sense of humour, but at least she owned it. Ah hell.* Lexy opened one eye to take a little peak as curiosity won the battle over her attempt at good behaviour. The room was covered in plastic. She tried to contain her smile. *He was one of these guys.* Lexy tried to shift her hands, they were only bound with duct tape. *This was going to be hilarious.* To her left, there was a sterile looking metal table full of silver instruments. She could smell a hint of bleach. *He took the time to bleach them between murders, isn't that sweet. His murder table was such a cliché. This tool had been watching too many late-night horror movies. His prior victims would have been terrified. Lexy found predatory monsters amusing. This is going to be fun. Some good old-fashioned vengeance was in order. She would settle the score for all those, who'd laid on this table before her.* A smile burst through her cheeks, and she began to chuckle aloud. The contemptible excuse for a human being appeared. She rolled her eyes and sighed. *It always drove these ones insane when you didn't react appropriately.* She casually glanced in his direction. His curiosity was peaked. She could see it in his eyes.

"You're not afraid of me?" He questioned, standing before her with his knife glinting in the stream of light that beamed in through the taped-up window.

"Surely, you're not serious?" Lexy taunted. She coolly met his eyes and provoked, "Why would I be afraid of something like you?"

Intrigued, by her lack of fear, he moved closer gripping his knife. He was perspiring, it caused his glasses to slide down his face. Her supposed assailant slid his glasses back up on his nose. He pressed his blade against her collarbone and watched her reaction. She gave him nothing. He shuddered as he traced his blade along the tender ivory flesh between her breasts, lightly slicing her flesh. A sliver of blood seeped from the cut and trickled almost artistically across the gossamer palate of her skin. Lexy didn't flinch. "What do you think you can do to me with that tiny knife? Please explain, and don't leave out any details. I'd like your punishment, to fit the crime," she taunted. She'd always had a hysterical sense of comic timing. Her wound had already healed. He was too busy acting out his sick little torture scenario to notice. He traced the blade down her leg from her groin to her big toe, on either side. She felt the burn of each slice, but it was only an irritation. She was a Healer, flesh wounds healed quickly.

Giddy with excitement, the hideous excuse for a mortal whispered, "In your worst nightmares, you've never imagined what I plan to do to you."

"That's what all my dates say," she sparred, wishing Grey was here to hear these comebacks. *They were priceless. She was on fire tonight.* She heard the laugh track from an old comedy in her mind as he slid the knife deep into her stomach. Lexy commentated on his murder skills, "My liver was a little to the left. You missed it by a hair. Do you need a moment to figure this out? Pass me my cell phone, I'll google it for you?"

He viciously knifed her twice more in the gut, and hissed, "Shut up you silly bitch."

It was always exciting in the moments before the psycho realised the tables had turned, and the hunter became the hunted. He began methodically picking up weapons, gaging her reaction to each.

Laughing, Lexy teased, "Oh sweetheart, you're going to need better weapons than those. Nothing on that table will keep me down for five minutes. Don't you have a gun? It's way more fun for me, when it's a little bit of a fair fight."

He whispered in his own special brand of mockery, "You are a piece of meat to me, nothing more. Speak again and I shall cut out your tongue, and eat it right in front of you."

Gross. Lexy grimaced as she shook her head. *This sicko talked a good game. That was an unnecessary visual, of this scrawny, creepy guy devouring her tongue.* She watched him choose his next instrument of torture. He looked rather pleased with himself as he turned around to find her sitting up on the metal bed, casually tearing duct tape off her arms. Bored, Lexy reprimanded, "You know duct tape sticks to the hairs on your arms. You have no self-preservation skills. How have you have gotten away with killing people for this long? You're not the sharpest tool in the shed. Think about all of that pesky D.N.A evidence you're leaving behind." His eyes wandered to her healed wounds. *There it was…Bingo.* He looked confused for a spilt second before running at her with his weapon of choice. She casually smacked it out of his hand, and then slapped him across the face. Lexy hissed, "Simmer down, cupcake. Trust me, you don't want to see me upset." He grabbed another weapon and came at her again. Lexy allowed him to stab her stomach. Her hand began to glow when he got creative and twisted his knife. He got sidetracked for a split second. She smacked his hand away, removed the blade and chucked it on the floor. Lexy comically ridiculed, "It's not that I don't find your psychotic rants, moderately entertaining. I really do appreciate your love of the kill, but once you've heard one serial killer's rants, you've heard them all." The pale, perspiring middle-aged waste of oxygen began to back away. She walked slowly towards him, past the table of weapons, without attempting to grab one. *Lexy didn't need a weapon. She was the weapon.*

He backed up until an axe was within reach. "What are you?" He hissed. He began swinging the axe in the air, in a laughable attempt at fending her off.

Lexy maneuvered out of the way, snatched it with one hand and provoked, "Okay muffin. Your twisted little deal is done. By twisted little deal, I mean, your mortal life, darling. We can do this the easy way or the hard way." He started throwing random weapons from the table. She swatted the objects away, without touching any using energy. *She wanted to snap his neck and be done with him. They'd better hurry up.* She paused and sighed dramatically. *He was quite the pathetic sight, cowering against the wall.* When he noticed she'd stopped moving, he stood up. *He wanted her to lose control. She could see it in his eyes.*

With dancing evil eyes, he whispered, "I did things to you. Things you haven't even dreamed of."

She took a step and he began rifling jars at her from the wooden shelf on the wall again. She grimaced, *that thought was disgusting.* Lexy coldly vowed, "I can think up a few things, you've never dreamt of." He tossed a can of paint, while her mind was still on his perverse admittance. It smoked the side of her head. She lost her cool and decked him. He dropped to the floor like a sack of stones. She stood above him, taking a moment to calm down. *Markus wants him alive.* The creep took a swing at her ankle, cutting the strap of her shoe. *He had another knife.* "You stinker," Lexy scolded. She peered down at Lily's destroyed shoe and spat, "I borrowed these shoes, you asshole." She stood on his shoulder to make him drop the knife. *He was pissing her off. He wouldn't let go.* She looked away to calm the Dragon who wanted to finish him off. *This was a bad idea.* It had the opposite effect. The blood stains on the plastic tarp told the sadistic stories of his past victims.

He wouldn't let go of the blade, he shrieked, "You whore! I'm going to cut you to pieces!"

"Well, we can't have that, can we?" Lexy answered coldly, stepping harder on his shoulder to shut him up. When that didn't work, she grabbed his wrist, and tried to pry the weapon from his grasp. He wouldn't let go of the blade. So, she stepped harder on his shoulder, yanking on the wrist clutching the knife. *He was ticking her off.* The ability to control her rage vanished. Lexy reefed on his arm, and accidentally ripped it off at his shoulder. *Whoops.*

He began shrieking, as his blood spurted across the room, "I've gutted dozens of whores! You're nothing! You are nothing!"

His contemptable words set the Dragon free. She saw flashes of the women he'd tortured in his plastic covered den of horrors. The terror they felt as they prayed for salvation. *Their prayers had gone unanswered. They would be answered in this moment, by her.* In a blind rage, she beat him with the wet end of his dismembered arm as vile images flashed through her mind. That was when the rest of the Ankh showed up.

They walked in to her beating someone with his own dismembered arm, screeching, "You sick! Pathetic! Twisted! Freak!" *She knew they were there, but she didn't want to stop. Why should she?* She caught sight of Grey standing in the doorway.

As stunned as the rest, Grey comically stated, "Well, this is new."

Melody walked towards her and calmly chimed in, "Honey… Hey, darling. You can stop beating him now. I'm pretty sure he's almost dead. We need to do a little ritual to make sure he goes where he's supposed to go. Come with me, Sweetie. Let's get you some clean clothes, perhaps a shower? I bet you could use a nice cup of tea?"

Lexy dropped the dismembered arm, and whispered, "That does sound lovely, but first, I need to see him go."

Lily cautiously walked over holding her clothes and whispered, "Grey and Frost have this covered. You trust Grey right? He'll finish this for you."

She looked at Lily's outstretched arms and saw that her clothes were soaked in blood. Their eyes met. Lily dropped the clothes on the floor. At the mention of Grey's name Lexy felt the tightly wound ball of rage within the pit of her stomach uncoil. Frost took off his shirt and tossed it to Lily, knowing Lexy wouldn't want to wear the blood-soaked clothing. *She'd forgotten, about her clothes.* Lexy peered down at her exposed breasts for only a second before Lily concealed her with Frost's shirt. Lexy allowed them to lead her out of arms reach...literally. They brought her to watch from the doorway. Melody knelt before her and unstrapped her one remaining shoe. She watched Melody collect her clothes and shoes from the floor and place them on the table surrounded by plastic.

Frost walked over to the man who'd finally calmed his screaming and cut his hand, causing it to glow. He placed the hand, dripping with immortal blood on the evil mortal's forehead.

In shock, the dying man murmured, "What are going to do to me?"

"You've done this to yourself," Frost replied. In Greek, he delivered his soul, just a moment before his shell died. With a last wheezy breath his mortal shell became still. The air in the room was clean again.

Grey motioned for the others to leave and offered, "I'll clean it up." He ripped the electrical outlet from the wall and placed his hand over it, heating the wires, until they caught fire.

It was always best to make the Correction look like an unfortunate accident. It was a shame to destroy the evidence of his crimes, but justice had been served. There was no mortal punishment worse than where he'd been sent. Grey finished the cleanup, his usual duty. His fire-starting ability only worked on small things. She knew they'd all seen this kind of blind rage in her before, but it didn't make it less of an embarrassment. Lexy knew she could get lost in the darkness. Grey was her tether to the light. Tonight, was one of those nights, she'd need him close. Grey walked out of the burning building straight towards her. He lifted her chin, so her eyes met his. She spoke to him without saying a word aloud, *I'm still here.* If there was a way fend off her Dragon and keep it as his own, he'd do it in a heartbeat. She was drained... emotionally vacant.

Grey whispered, "I should have stayed with you. I'll protect you from yourself next time, I promise."

He was blaming himself because she ripped someone's arm off. She understood what he meant. He wasn't going to leave her alone in the dark. He pulled her into his embrace. Her guarded stiff frame immediately loosened. She laid her head in the crook of his neck. He stood there with her rocking her back and forth. She whispered, "He broke my shoe." She was far too drained to explain why she'd done it.

Grey smiled, stroked her crimson silky hair and whispered back, "I'll get you new ones."

They drove straight back to the hotel that night. Grey got in bed fully clothed. She wearily curled up in his protective embrace. *He was her emotional attachment.* She felt him stroking her hair again. He softly kissed her forehead. Exhausted, she fell asleep in his arms. *She slept a dreamless sleep free of Dragons for she had slain them once again.*

Chapter 28

Uncomfortable Situations

Lexy awoke in the morning to find Grey still sleeping beside her. There was a time when she would have shut everything off after an experience like last night. He'd kept her with him this time. She fought the urge to wake him with a kiss. She stroked his hair, secretly relieved he hadn't left her side last night to be with Melody. Nobody else knew about them, but over the years, she'd always been able to sense the smallest touch of resentment when his duties as her Handler superseded his physical desires. Then all she'd have to do is guess who he was sleeping with. It had become a warped little game she played. Sometimes she wanted to hop on top of him and shake him senseless. *You're in love with me. We've slept together a hundred times. You just can't remember.* It even sounded crazy as a thought. They had no real secrets except for the ones that were pointless to share. It didn't matter how many times they confessed their love for each other, and spent the night wrapped in each other's arms. She was the only one that would ever be able to remember it in the morning. He was her Handler and she was a Dragon. He'd been spelled to forget. Dragons couldn't afford emotional complications. She wasn't sure how that worked because Grey had been her emotional complication from the moment they met. Melody wasn't going to be around long enough to be an emotional complication, in forty years none of the Ankh had made it out of the Testing. It was a reasonably safe relationship for him to be in. It stood no chance of being long term. Today however, she had the overwhelming urge to stake her claim on him.

He opened his eyes and teased, "Were you watching me sleep?"

Lexy stared back at him and answered with unfiltered honesty, "I'm just glad you're still here."

He questioned, "Where else would I be?"

Lexy rolled over to face the other direction and taunted, "I'm not stupid. Are we still keeping your booty calls with Melody a secret?"

Grey chuckled, "I'd never say you were stupid. I need both of my arms."

Lexy shook her head and bantered, "Funny."

He chuckled and ruffled her hair, "Awe Lex. Are you jealous?"

Her eyes widened. *No, shit Sherlock.* She spoke aloud, "Why would I be jealous? She'll be dead soon."

Grey pulled her into his embrace and whispered against her hair, "No, they won't. This group is going to make it. Let yourself believe it."

Lexy took it like a champ. *Ouch, that one hurt.* She allowed him to hold her. *She felt guilty. She wanted them to live. She was jealous.* She said, "I'm sorry, I don't want anything to happen to them. That came out wrong. Of course, I want them to come through the Testing. I'm just in a weird place in my head today." She shifted in his arms to face him. Grey moved closer until their noses touched. He gave her an Eskimo kiss before abruptly hopping out of bed and trudging to the bathroom. She'd held her breath, thinking he was going to kiss her, and only exhaled when he closed the bathroom door. Lexy sprawled on the bed, covering her mouth with her hand. She hopped out of bed and sauntered over to the dresser, glancing at her reflection. Her heart tightened. *He'd cleaned her up. She was blood free without a shower. It was these things that made her love him even more.* She was still wearing Frost's shirt. She pulled a few strands of her flaming red hair in front of her nose. *It smelled wonderful.* He'd even taken the time to shampoo her hair. She wandered over to the bathroom door, leaned against it and said, "Thank you." *He was in the shower, he probably hadn't heard her.* She turned the doorknob and entered the bathroom.

Grey's voice came from inside the shower, "Don't you dare number two while I'm in the bloody shower."

Lexy grinned. *Just in case she thought they were about to have a sexy moment. Leave it to Grey to wreck it.* She walked over to the bathroom mirror, unbuttoned Frost's shirt and let it drop to the floor. Staring at her reflection, all she could think of was how much he must love her to clean her up like this. *One more time, then she would stop loving him like this.* She pulled the curtain aside and stepped into the shower. He had his eyes closed rinsing his hair. When he wiped his face, he saw her there. He said, "What are you doing?"

With familiar confidence, she stepped closer and replied, "Tell me you never think of me this way." He didn't say anything. At a loss for words, his lips parted as his eyes took her in. Lexy pressed the length of her body against his, and seductively kissed his lips. He groaned, whispering her name as the kiss deepened. They became lost in each other. Grey always seemed to know just what she wanted him to do. It was as though he remembered where she wanted him to touch her. She gasped, clutching the shower curtain as she rode the wave of ecstasy, biting down on his shoulder. Anytime Lexy wanted him, all she had to do was push his buttons, just a touch. They stayed there in a torrid steaming shower of reckless abandon, moving from the shower to the bedroom. It was like this between them every time. In the end, as always, she lay in his arms, listening to his inevitable declaration of love. It was as though being with her in this way, allowed his heart to see her clearly.

Overcome by the emotion of what they'd just shared, Grey cupped her face with his hands and confessed, "I love you, Lexy." He grinned for this was the first time he'd ever said those words to her in his mind.

She kissed him again to shut him up. *I know you do.* Her eyes glistened with tears. *She wasn't a crier, for anything or anyone. This was the one thing she wanted. The one thing she could never have.* To have him holding her in his arms like this, telling her how much he loved her, it demolished her every time. Lexy took the opportunity to finish her fantasy. She whispered, "I love you more than you'll ever know." *This was the truth. Always.*

"Oh, I know now," he provoked, seductively tracing her hip with his finger.

This was one of his sexiest moves. She closed her eyes and tried to live in the moment.

He kissed her again and whispered, "I think I've always loved you."

Lexy blinked back her tears and caressed Grey's cheek. She whispered, "I know." *This was what she'd lived for.* It was these moments with him, entangled in each other's arms. At least they'd done this in the morning. She'd have a whole day with him before he forgot it happened, and they went back to being just friends.

He tenderly kissed her shoulder and enquired, "What's wrong?"

"I'm just happy, that's all," she disclosed, laying wrapped in his arms. She'd been cozy in his embrace gloriously content with sunshine streaming through the blinds for a few minutes when she realised he wasn't moving. *Awe Shit. You've got to be kidding me.* Sure enough, he'd fallen asleep. She got out of bed and went to grab his underwear off the bathroom floor. She snuck back into the room and attempted to put his underwear back on before he woke up, confused. She had his underwear up to his knees when he opened one eye and said, "What are doing?"

Knowing the drill, she replied, "You fell asleep with your underwear around your ankles. I know, I thought it was weird too. You must have been exhausted. Thank you for taking the time to clean me up."

He grinned as he got out of bed, pulling his underwear up. He teased, "If it was anyone else, I'd think they just took advantage of me, waking up with my ginch at my ankles." He winked at her and sauntered off to the bathroom.

Lexy exhaled, realising how close he was to the truth. *She'd taken advantage of him, in a way. She'd known exactly which buttons to push. They loved each other, but he had no memory of it. He always fell asleep; she hadn't thought he'd fall asleep in the morning. Now, she knew.* The bathroom door opened, startling her.

He hopped on the bed and laughed, "You should see yourself. You have naughty hair. I must have fallen asleep before I brushed it last night."

This was always so frustrating. She wanted to make him remember again. He started to run his fingers through her hair. She repeated, "Thank you for always taking care of me."

Grey ruffled her hair, winked and ribbed, "I'd do it even if it wasn't my job."

"I know you would," Lexy responded. She swung her long legs over the edge of the bed and ran her fingers through her hair. *Why did she have to love him this much?* She stood up and walked to the bathroom, closing the door behind her. She strolled over to the sink, gripping either side, she allowed only a few tears to escape then she wiped her face and smiled at her reflection. *Get your game face on. Come on Dragon. Where in hell are you when I need you?* She got back into the shower. By the time she came out of the bathroom, he was gone. Lexy stuck her head out of the room and whispered, "Seriously, Grey?"

Frost walked out of the room next door and baited, "Hey Lex. How was your morning? You look all bright tailed, and bushy eyed." He winked at her. He tossed a bag of stones at her and chuckled, "Did you forget to do something?"

Oh Crap. They might all know. She asked, "Did they go for breakfast?"

Grinning, Frost teased, "Hungry?"

Lexy sighed, "That's enough, Frost. He's already forgotten about it." Frost stopped teasing her. *He knew how she felt. He'd been there.* They walked towards the restaurant together.

"You have to stop. It will never get any easier," he disclosed.

Nodding, she didn't say anything. *She knew he was right.* They walked into the restaurant and their table was already ordering. *Grey was shamelessly flirting with Melody, the waitress, and anything that moved as per usual.* Lexy sat across the table and glared at him. *He didn't know what he was doing to her.* She watched him tuck Melody's hair behind her ear. *He used the same damn moves on everyone.*

Frost knocked over a glass of water in front of Melody, causing her to change seats. He glanced at Lexy and winked. He looked at Grey and declared, "You're an Asshole."

Confused, Grey said, "What in the hell did I do?"

Frost scowled at him and taunted, "Orin's daughter."

Grey sparred, "Freja's daughter?"

"Freja's not going to kill me for hitting on her daughter," Frost countered.

Grinning, Grey provoked, "I didn't sleep with Melody's father."

Frost chuckled, "I didn't sleep with Kayn's father."

"Mother, father…whatever. You know what I mean," Grey hinted.

Kayn piped in, "You guys know we're sitting right here."

Lexy took a deep breath and excused herself from the table.

"Good, now you pissed off Lexy," Frost scolded.

Grey stammered, "What in the hell did I do?"

Lexy couldn't help but crack a smile as she walked away. *Frost was never on her side. Today, he was her defender. He knew exactly what she was going through.* She wandered into the bathroom and closed the door. It swung open on the other side. *Well, that wasn't going to work. She should just go back to the table. She had to try to let it go.* Lexy, was standing in front of the mirror. The door opened. She saw Frost behind her reflection. Without turning around, she stated, "The symbol on the door is wearing a skirt not pants."

He grinned, strolled up behind her and teased, "Thanks for pointing that out. You were in here, I assumed it was a superhero cape. You know why I came in here to talk to you."

Lexy smiled back at her reflection and said, "I know what you're going to say."

He harassed, "Really? Before even I know, are you secretly an Oracle?"

She sighed and shook her head.

He came closer, explaining, "You've known me for forty years now. I actively try to stay away from her. You've watched me suck it up while she dates my friends, and even a few of my damn enemies. She'll never remember what we meant to each other. I've accepted that. How does Grey keep remembering, and forgetting? Is he doing this on his own, or are you making him remember? If he's doing this on his own, you should talk to Jenna. If you're doing this to him, you should still talk to Jenna, because you shouldn't be able to. They make Handlers forget for a reason. They make everyone forget for a reason. It's going to wreck your friendship. You'll never move on as long as you can still access the part of him that loves you. I'm saying this as a friend. You can choose to ignore me. I wouldn't blame you. Just know that I'm here for you if you want to talk, or if you just want someone to punch him in the stomach, and make it look like an accident. I've been where you are. I understand."

Lexy turned to face him instead of looking at his reflection. *Frost had been through everything she was going through. He wasn't wrong. She had to stop bringing Grey's feelings to the surface. It wasn't fair to either of them.* She whispered, "It was nothing. It didn't mean anything. I'm over it."

Frost winked at her and said, "I wish I could be a Dragon." He quietly closed the door as he left.

Lexy looked back at her reflection and whispered, "No, you don't."

Chapter 29

Partners In Debauchery

Days passed by, without further drama. Lexy did what she'd always done in the past. She forced her heart to get back into the friend-zone, where it belonged. The humming sound of RV's whirling tires was starting to sedate her as she drove down the highway towards their next stop. Kayn was sitting beside her while she drove, with the duty of keeping her entertained and wide awake. She'd fallen asleep. *Her co-pilot was out cold. The girl was so endearing.*

Frost wandered up to the front and whispered, "Do you need a coffee?"

Lexy smiled at him and replied, "I'll need at least three. Do we have time to pull over for a bit? I can barely keep my eyes open."

Frost whispered, "We can't stop, we're supposed to be there in a few days. I'll carry Kayn to bed. I'll be right back. I can take over for a few hours." He undid her seatbelt, lifted her up, against his chest, cradling her in his arms. He whispered, "I can't imagine her in the Testing."

Lexy was impressed as she watched Frost manage to keep his balance, while he carried a dead to the world Kayn, down the length of the moving vehicle. He slid her into one of the bunks, covered her up and went into the kitchen area for a second. He returned with two mugs of coffee. *He didn't want her to go to sleep. He wanted to talk.* She pulled over and he took the wheel. Lexy moved to the passenger seat and took a sip of coffee. She was pretty sure Frost was in love with Kayn. It was a truly complicated situation. He'd been with her twin sister Chloe. She was already dead when they met. Kayn survived her Correction, but the twins shared a soul. So, they all trained in the in-between together, unsure of what would happen when the twins joined. When their souls merged, there was almost no hint of Chloe. From what Lexy had seen, he'd fallen for Kayn while trying to find Chloe within her. If Kevin hadn't been in the way she was certain he would have ignored Chloe completely and fallen for Kayn. They'd met her as a child. Kayn had been a wacky little kid with a frog sticker on her face. She could still recall the chorus of, oh shits, when the group saw there were two little girls. The twins were Freja's. She was one of the original seventeen Children of Ankh. Freja was her friend. A friend she hadn't seen in thirty years.

Lexy looked at Frost and said, "It's been almost thirty years. Where in the hell is Freja?"

Frost shook his head and replied, "She was entombed, and then released to serve the third tiers. The king was obsessed with her. She escaped and then nothing. If Azariah knows where she is and hasn't forced her to come back to her Clan, there must be a reason."

Lexy took another sip of her coffee and remarked, "Kayn, sure looks like her, doesn't she?"

Frost grinned and answered, "So, much."

What had been left unsaid hung in the air between them as they travelled. Lexy drifted off to sleep, waking up on her bunk, next to Grey. They were still moving. *Who was driving?* Trying to balance on tired limbs, she walked to the front. Zach was driving.

He glanced her way and flirted, "You're even sexy with bedhead."

She plopped her behind down in the passenger seat and sparred, "It's way too early for pathetically executed pickup lines, Zach."

He chuckled, "If I ask you to get me a cup of coffee are you going to pour it on my lap?"

She looked in the mirror on the back of the visor and grinned. *She hadn't thought of that but appreciated the idea.*

Zach sweetly said, "Pretty please."

She heard Lily's voice say, "I'll get you one Zach." Lexy swivelled around in her seat. Lily was already wide awake, stunning as always. She petered around in the kitchen, brewing a fresh pot.

Within the hour, they were pulled over and everyone was awake eating breakfast. The truck was in front of the motor home. Melody had been driving the truck all night without relief. She looked a little worse for wear. With everyone squeezed into the small dining area at the same time, the confined space of the RV felt claustrophobic. *It was becoming difficult to listen to the three newbies laughing and joking around as though their lives weren't about to come to an end.*

They were back on the road before ten am. The two vehicles rotated drivers for the whole day, well into the evening. Once everyone inside the motor home had fallen asleep, all she could hear was a ticking clock and the vibration of the tires. With no music to play, Lexy sat there stewing, hoping she'd done a good enough job training these three. She'd gone hardcore on this group. Tomorrow they would be at the site where they'd regroup with the other Clans for their every five-year shindig. It was time for the Summit. After the older members of the Clans returned from the Summit, it would be time for the newbie's Testing. Against her better judgement, she'd grown to like these three. In one week, they would be dropped into the bowels of hell. They'd have to fight their way out to find Enlightenment. If they survived, they'd earn a permanent place in Clan Ankh.

She heard Lily's voice behind her, "If you pull over, I'll take over for a while. Go and get some sleep, Lex."

Lexy pulled over and slipped out of the driver's seat. "Thanks, hun."

"No problem, hun," Lily answered.

Lexy made her way past the kitchen area into the hall. She climbed onto her bunk, flopped down and was instantly dead to the world.

Lexy awoke hearing the rustling sounds of the others setting up the campsite. She dozed off again, and then awakened when she heard Frost and Kayn talking about going for a morning run. She pretended to be asleep until they left. *Frost needed a chance to be alone with Kayn. The other Clans would be here. She'd be running into Kevin today, for the first time.*

After she was certain they'd left, she cleaned herself up and headed down the familiar trail to the rodeo grounds. Lexy also needed some time alone. *It had a strange feeling, this place. There had been so many goodbyes.* Lexy waved her hands at the large gates, without touching them. They swung open revealing dusty vacant grandstands. This was where she came to pay homage to her fallen friends, forever trapped in the Testing. She climbed the rickety staircase until she found the spot where she'd carved his name. *Tomas… it had been such a long time.* She only had a few other names carved into the wood. *There were only a few others she'd allowed herself to become attached to over the years.* She traced Astrid's name with her finger. *Astrid had been her friend as well as Frost's. They'd both cared about her. She hadn't made it out.* She slowly, methodically began to carve Kayn's name into the wood of the bleachers. *She'd become attached to this one. She was endearingly weird, and goofy.* She'd watched Kayn go through the loss of her boyfriend Kevin to Triad. She'd barely known the kid, but it had affected her more than she'd been willing to admit. Frost cared for Kayn, and he never allowed himself to care for anyone. Perhaps it was because she was Freja's daughter. If she disappeared now Freja would never get to meet her. She was just so tired of losing people. Lexy jaunted back down the grandstand stairs to start her long walk back. *They'd all be up by now.*

They went into town for lunch, missing a few people. She was sent back to the campgrounds to find Kayn and Grey.

After almost running them over with the truck, they got in and drove back to the diner in town. Lexy glanced in the rear-view mirror, took in the devastation in Kayn's expression and didn't need to ask what happened. She already knew. She hadn't wanted that to be real. A large part of her had wanted Kevin to miraculously remember Kayn, but of course, it was real. She looked at the passenger seat where Grey was seated. He was living proof that once your memories were erased, they were gone. Grey had only had hours erased, not a lifetime. Tiberius would have erased everything for Kevin. He would have given him a clean slate.

They entered the diner and found a seat. Grey began regaling the comic events of the morning. It sounded like Kayn dealt with their first meeting reasonably well. She'd even managed to tell off Tiberius, by calling into question, his manhood during a well-timed comic duel. Lexy found herself staring at Frost, he was already emotionally vacant. *He knew all of the ground he'd gained with her, was about to be lost. She knew that feeling.*

The bells chimed at the door to signal someone's arrival. Markus and Arrianna were here. Lexy embraced Arrianna as a long-lost sister. They'd been a trio for so long. Eventually Arrianna ended up going with the other half of the Clan. It had been easier to separate herself from Grey in the end. She'd ended up with Markus. This was ironic, considering her initial hatred of him. Seeing them together now, it was clear she'd found the right person. Arrianna was in a blissfully content state of calm. The door jingled again and in walked Orin. She'd always loved Orin to death, he was a great guy. Well, except for that pesky year when he'd gone off the deep end after Jenna broke up with him for the opportunity to be Azariah's right hand. She embraced Orin. He sat on the other side of her and noticed Melody. *It had to be uncomfortable to bump into your offspring for the first time when you had never even attempted to contact them.* Melody was staring at her napkin on the table. She was obviously trying to avoid looking at the man who'd had a part in creating her. The door jingled again, and it was Jenna. With a gorgeous dimpled smile, she swept across the room stopping to hug people. It felt good to have them all back together. Jenna and Orin greeted each other with a strained polite, hello. *How awkward would it be to greet your ex of nearly a thousand years after she dumped you, and you retaliated by impregnating her mortal look alike, out of spite?* She couldn't help but feel like Orin was a little justified in his revenge. She loved Jenna, but after a thousand years Orin was owed more than the five second kiss off speech, she'd given him.

After they'd finished lunch, it became obvious they needed the newbies to leave to speak freely. Grey and Lexy caught the hints and brought the others back to the campground. The second the truck stopped, Kayn got out and climbed a barb wire fence, requiring a moment alone. Lexy watched her as she walked out to the center of the field and sat down. It was a little weird, but she was quite used to seeing this one doing strange things. They let her do her thing, understanding she needed a chance to sort out that first run in with Kevin in her head. Lexy glanced at Grey and whispered, "She's handling it quite well."

He smiled and replied, "On the outside."

Concerned, Zach said, "Are all of the other Clans going to be here this week? How's that going to happen?"

It was always a bit of a gong show. Lexy replied, "There's a cease fire, a temporary peace between the Clans as the older members go to the Summit. They should be gone about a week." Melody seemed relieved. Lexy took note of her peculiar reaction. Usually it was the fear of seeing your peers from your prior Clan again, if you'd been taken from another Clan like Melody had. Kayn caught up as they slowly walked away. Grey noticed the path to the beach, and the boys took off on a dead run towards the water, stripping off their clothes along the way. Always up for a swim, Kayn was down to her underwear in seconds, running after them. They bolted to the end of the dock and leapt off. Lexy stood there watching them splashing around, shrieking from the icy temperature of the lake. Melody excused herself to go to the bathroom. Kayn opted out of jumping in at the last second and followed her. Out of curiosity, Lexy snuck away from the group to see what they were doing. *Her instincts were on overdrive today.* Her feelings, and responses to situations, were impossible to ignore. She realised the girls were just talking privately and wandered back to the dock, allowing her memory to guide her footsteps down the trail. She'd been here so many times. Lexy stopped on the path as she noticed something carved into a tree. It read, Orin + Jenna. They'd been a permanent fixture for so long. Then came the twenty-year absence of both. Their final break up had been brutal, and harshly abrupt. Jenna had just up and left him. He couldn't do his job without her. He became so much of a gong show that he was granted a twenty-year partial leave. They only called on him in an emergency. When they had stolen Melody from Trinity, he'd been there to help that day. They'd allowed him to go back to his semi normal life for a couple years. He appeared to be back now. Grey shoved his way past and Lexy grinned. They were going to get Kayn and Mel.

Grey came out of the bathroom with Melody over his shoulder taunting, "Don't fight it sweetheart. I'm going to get you so wet."

Mel was fighting back laughing, "Let me take my clothes off first. Come on you guys."

"That's what she said," Zach chuckled as he grabbed her bottom half. The two carried a wildly squirming Melody to the end of the dock and tossed her into the water. She was still wearing her shoes. They all jumped in after her howling, shrieking and squealing. Kayn jumped in willingly. They surfaced and realised they were no longer alone. On the dock was Kevin who some of them already knew, another boy, and a petite brunette, standing between them with her hand possessively on Kevin's shoulder. Lexy immediately glanced at Kayn.

Kevin introduced his friends to the Ankh, "The blonde girl is Kayn. Apparently, we know each other. I met Grey earlier. I'm sorry, I don't know anyone else, but I'll hazard a guess that the hot girl with red hair is the infamous, Lexy."

Lexy grinned at Kevin. *The hot girl, that's funny.*

"You did pretty well. You also know Melody," Grey corrected.

Mel laughed, "I only brought you back to life once upon a time. It was no big deal."

Kevin grinned and replied, "I seem to have a few gaps in my memory."

"Yes... You seem to have a few," Kayn remarked.

The blonde boy who was a little chubby and not the usual Triad stereotype said, "I just have to say it. Are you all frigging insane? That lake has to be freezing."

"Don't knock it till you try it," Grey chuckled as he splashed the group with glacial cold water.

Kayn's lips were blue as she treaded water. Lexy could tell she wanted to sink under the surface and disappear. She met Kayn's eyes and nodded. They all swam to the dock. They began helping each other out of the freezing lake. Grey helped Kayn out. She saw his roguish grin just a second too late. "Don't you dare," Kayn hissed.

Grey shoved her back in and howled laughing as Kayn sputtered in the water. Lexy walked up and socked Grey in the arm. She didn't make a habit of hitting him, but that was a douche move. Kayn swam back to the ladder and began to climb out again.

Patrick extended his hand and vowed, "I won't push you back in again, I promise" He helped her out.

Kevin was only in Triad because of his grandfather, but this Patrick guy was a sweetheart. Kevin couldn't take his eyes off Kayn. Not even for the sake of being nice to the bitchy looking girl possessively clutching his arm. He was just standing there with a silly grin on his face. Kayn looked amazing with her womanly curvy frame, and subtle rounded hips. Kevin kept staring at Kayn's pierced belly button.

Patrick gallantly took his shirt off, and passed it to Lexy, "Your lips are blue."

Lexy would have thrown it back at anyone else. She took it and enquired, "Haven't you heard of me?"

Smiling, Patrick replied, "Of course I have. You're Lexy of Ankh. The one Tiberius is afraid of."

"He's going to kick your ass for saying that," Stephanie angrily scolded.

"It's the truth though," Patrick chuckled. He added, "You're cold. You can give it back to me later. Apparently, we're all staying at this campsite for the next week."

Lexy put the chubby kids' shirt on and smiled at him. *He was sweet.*

"You have dry clothes at the top of the dock Lexy. You just got that kids shirt wet for no reason," Grey reminded her.

"I'm sorry... I forgot," Lexy apologized. She took it off, handed it back to Patrick, and turned to walk back to her pile of clothes. Kayn followed her back up the dock, with her arms crossed over her chest as if she could hide what she'd been blessed with.

Grey said, "Nice to meet you buddy. My name's Grey." He shook Patrick's hand and gave him a giant smile.

Patrick stammered, "Patrick...My name's Patrick. I heard about you to."

"All good stuff I'm sure," Grey chuckled as they all walked up the dock together. Grey stopped in front of the girl. He blocked her stride and probed, "And your name is?"

"Stephanie," she snapped with attitude. Stephanie was pretty, but cold and unlikable.

Grey extended his hand to her and provoked, "Nice to meet you Stephanie. For the record, if you even entertain a single one of those thoughts running through your mind, I'll take it personally in the future when we meet without this cease fire."

Stephanie said, "I'm Triad and you are Ankh. It doesn't matter what you think. Your Clan is insignificant. We win against you, every time." She turned on a dime and strutted away.

That witch was rude to Grey. Nobody gets to be snotty with Grey, but me. Lexy walked up behind Stephanie mid strut and tapped her on the shoulder. Stephanie swung around to face her. Lexy hissed, "I've taken on your entire Clan, all by myself. That includes the fearless leader you so admire. He upset me, and when people are rude to my friends it makes me feel upset."

Stephanie's voice oozed with sarcasm as she sparred, "Is that supposed to scare me?"

"It should," Grey chuckled.

Kevin placed his hand on Stephanie's shoulder, squeezed it and warned, "That's about enough Steph."

Stephanie stammered, "You do not get to tell me what to do."

Lexy directed her attention to Kevin and remarked, "She's a bit of a handful."

Kevin was embarrassed by her behaviour. She could tell.

He coolly stated, "I said, that's enough. There are no sides this week. Try to smile and act like a reasonably sane person, or just do us all a favour and leave."

Stephanie shot daggers with her eyes at Kevin. She coldly replied, "You can't tell me what to do."

Kevin stated, "Probably not."

Stephanie mumbled something none of them could make out and stormed away. She tossed Kayn into the shrubbery as she passed.

Zach helped Kayn up and chuckled, "It looks like you made a new friend."

Kevin apologized, "I'm sorry about that, she's a little territorial."

"Also, a little certifiably insane, but she grows on you," Patrick added.

Zach brushed the dirt off her. Kayn looked at Kevin and asked, "Is she your girlfriend?"

Kevin chuckled, "Hell no, I'm not the girlfriend kind of guy."

Solemnly, Kayn said, "You really don't remember me?"

Lexy wasn't overly empathetic, but she felt Kayn's pain. Kevin didn't remember her at all.

Melody placed her arm around Kayn and urged, "Alright, we have a few things to do. See you boys later." She led Kayn away from the dock. Melody whispered, "You are doing well, hun. Just keep walking away."

Lexy let them leave without her, staying behind with Grey and Zach. Kevin seemed older, more controlled, than he'd been before he was lost to Triad. There was an aura of power that hadn't been there. Kevin hadn't been able to take his eyes off Kayn, watching her still as she walked away. His memory may have been erased, but he was obviously still drawn to her. It was more than that; he didn't appear capable of looking away. He still had feelings for her. She was willing to bet on it. Lexy was a little excited to see how this was going to play out.

Grey placed his arm around her, squeezed her and enquired, "Are you still cold?"

Fighting the urge to kiss his blue lips, Lexy replied, "No, I'm all good."

Grey embraced her, briskly rubbing her arms on either side to warm her up. He hugged her and whispered in her ear, "Thanks for not kicking her ass."

Lexy grinned and said, "Don't mention it." They said their goodbyes to Triad and walked back to the others.

As they strolled away, Zach remarked, "That insane girl was hot."

Grey started laughing with his arm around Lexy. He whispered in her ear, "Completely certifiable, but undeniably hot."

Lexy rolled her eyes. *Her best friend definitely had a type.*

They all gathered back at the RV. The plan was to roast wieners, over a campfire, make hotdogs and have a few beers. A casual dinner. Lexy sat directly across from Grey and Zach at the picnic table. She bit off an enormous mouthful of hotdog and listened to their conversation. Frost came and sat down with them at the picnic table. It looked like he had something he wanted to say. Lexy raised her eyebrows, swallowed her giant bite of hotdog, and took a drink of beer. *She knew what he wanted to ask.* Lexy cut to the chase and disclosed, "Kevin's memory's been wiped, but he couldn't stop staring at her. It might be out of curiosity?"

Frost grinned and admitted, "It's probably better if something does happen between them. She needs to tie up loose ends. Until that's happened, I'd have no chance with her anyway. Let's not talk about this."

Lexy stared into Frost's eyes. She didn't make a lot of eye contact with people, unless she was trying to intimidate them before a fight. It made her uncomfortable. It was a form of intimacy she'd yet to allow herself to embrace. She understood where he was in his head. He was thinking about what was best for Kayn. The same way she tried to think about what was best for Grey. Going with the urge to check on her, Lexy went inside and attempted to wake Kayn, but she was out cold. She needed some mental down time. Lexy left her sleeping in the motor home. They were going to the Ankh Crypt hidden in the forest. Frost had shown Kayn where it was earlier that day. They'd send someone back for the ones that stayed behind later. Once it was dark outside, it could be difficult to find. Frost put out the fire and a few of them walked through the woods to the Ankh Crypt.

Lexy lagged behind with Grey, doing their own thing. The sky was a miraculous mix of vibrant orange and fuchsia. It was a truly outstanding sunset. Grey stopped to stare at it, and she came to stand beside him. He held out his hand and she took it, as she always would. They stood hand in hand watching the fading expression of the day.

Grey squeezed her hand and whispered, "You'll be seeing Tiberius tomorrow. Do you think you can avoid killing him for a day? Just one day, and he'll be gone. I'd really like to go to this banquet."

Still staring at the sky above, she sighed, "I'll try, for you." Grey raised their entwined fingers to his lips, kissing hers tenderly as the sun flickered in the distance and descended. One last flash of light reached through the forest like it didn't want leave. Grey moved his hand through the final ray of light, filled with particles of dust and kept it there until it dissolved into nothing. *This was one of the million reasons why she adored him.* They began to walk through the woods towards the crypt in the dark. Just as they arrived, Zach leapt out of the bushes as a prank. With catlike reflexes, Lexy reacted and booted his head, knocking him out cold.

Running to his aid, Grey scolded, "Seriously Lex. You knocked him out. You'd better heal him before we go inside."

Still grinning, she knelt and laid her hands on his chest. When he didn't get up immediately, she started laughing.

Grey stammered, "Shit Lex. Did you kill him?"

"I believe I did. Be sneaky about it and go grab Orin. He owes me one," she instructed, giggling on the inside.

A moment later Orin appeared without Grey by his side. He snickered, "It's good to see some things haven't changed."

"He startled me," she explained, grinning.

Orin chuckled, "Let's move the body over there my slightly psychotic friend. Maybe they'll think he tripped and knocked himself out?" They towed Zach away from the entrance and hid him in the bushes. Then they knelt by him and laid their hands on his chest. Once they were certain he was alive again, they slipped away. Lexy walked into the crypt with Orin and found a place to get comfortable. There was an unspoken bond between Healers. Lexy had always felt it with Orin and Arrianna. She'd felt it with Melody, but she'd been a little standoffish because Grey wanted her. That wasn't Melody's fault. Lexy made a silent resolve to make more of an effort with Melody in the future, if she turned out to have one.

Orin leaned over and whispered, "You and I could get into a lot of trouble together, Lex."

Did somebody mention trouble? Drawn out of her thoughts back to Orin, Lexy teased, "We could also get out of a lot of trouble together."

"This is true," Orin baited. He tossed her a beer from the cooler.

Grey wandered over and sat down by the two of them. He shook his head and said, "I'm not feeling optimistic about the state of your anger management skills for the banquet tomorrow, my friend."

They heard the familiar scraping of stone on stone, followed by footsteps. Zach wandered in, rubbing his head, confused. He declared, "I think I just passed out in the bushes."

Orin piped in, "To much beer and not enough water? I've been there kid."

"Maybe?" Zach replied as he sat down with the three.

Orin tossed him a bottle of water from the cooler they'd lugged to the crypt. Zach opened it and began to drink it. Jenna, Markus and Arrianna appeared with another whoosh and grinding stone, followed by the steady click of descending footsteps. Arrianna hurried over to sit with Lexy. Embracing her, she said, "I've missed you."

Their reunion was cut short as Jenna summoned Lexy away. Expecting to get in trouble for the accidental murder, she looked back at Orin as she walked away and winked. *Shit, Jenna's good.*

"Please go collect Kayn from the college track. I need to speak to her," Jenna instructed.

Grey got up to come along and Jenna clarified, "Just Lexy."

Lexy sighed and glanced back, Grey was always worried she was going to lose her temper and do something crazy, like five-minutes ago. It was his job to keep the Clan's weapon from being entombed for naughty behavior. She left the flickering candlelight of the crypt and started on another journey into the darkness. *She'd never been afraid of the dark. She could barely recall the sensation of fear.* The college was quite far down the highway and the truck was nowhere in sight. *Great, this was going to be a crazy long walk after she'd just healed Zach. There's karma.* Lexy closed her eyes for a second and rubbed her Ankh symbol, instinct would show her a faster way. She cut time off by taking an overgrown path and forcing her way into the brush. Without wincing, she walked through prickles. Small wounds were always inconsequential to her. She'd be healed in moments from insignificant little scratches. She noticed the uneasy feeling in the pit of her stomach. Every noise seemed amplified. The hooting of owls and steady chirping of crickets were more entertaining when there was nothing else to see. After an excessively long jaunt to the college, Lexy found Kayn exactly where Jenna said she'd be. She watched the two, having an emotional exchange in the center of the lighted track. Lexy strolled out of the darkness into the lit area, "Hello again, Kevin. Kayn, you need to come with me. I'm sorry, Oracle's orders."

Angry, Kayn took a long last look at Kevin, and coldly said, "Goodnight...I'm sure we'll see each other again."

Kevin responded, "It's a small campground. I'm sure we will." He disappeared into the darkness as he stepped out of the beam of light.

They walked in uncomfortable silence. *She didn't know what to say. His memories were erased. It didn't matter how much history or love was there, he was gone.*

Kayn attempted to explain, "I didn't go looking for him."

Lexy replied, "I know hun. You got to see him, and he's all in one piece. Winnie has his back. You need to trust she'll take care of him."

"How do I just allow him to be this person? This isn't who he was. How do I just let him go?" Kayn questioned staring off into the black, almost starless night sky then back at the empty lighted track.

"He's already gone," Lexy decreed. She felt guilty as Kayn's expression altered and she stared down at the ground as they walked. *Kayn knew that he was gone. She hadn't needed her to say it aloud.*

After a moment of awkward silence, Lexy tried to make her feel better by adding, "Everything works out, just as it's meant to. He's probably already moved on, and now you can do the same." Kayn nodded and stared at her feet again. *Damn it, she was an idiot sometimes. She was trying to help, but her matter of fact way of thinking, always came out sounding cold. Kayn had tears in her eyes. It felt like she was kicking a kitten, but there was nothing she could say, that was going to make this situation easier.* Lexy decided to keep her mouth shut. *Yes, that would be the best move.* She reached over and squeezed her shoulder to be supportive. Kayn responded with a weak smile. Sometimes it's better to succumb to that moment of silence. The song of the crickets appeared to have a soothing effect on her devastated walking partner. *Why hadn't Jenna sent Grey? He would have had her petting squirrels, birds would be singing, and landing in the palms of their hands. He would have had her skipping back to the crypt singing happy songs. She had no people skills. She knew this about herself. Well, she had killing people skills, but that wouldn't help anyone deal with a broken heart, or would it?* They entered the crypt with the scratching of stone and descended into the flickering glow. In the soft calming flicker of torches, Kayn walked away from her and the rest of their carefree Clan. They were still lazing around, reminiscing about days gone by. Jenna peered up and smiled as Kayn walked past her. Lexy exchanged a look with their Oracle. Jenna got up and followed Kayn down the hall. Having delivered Kayn safely to the crypt, Lexy turned to leave.

"Where are you going? I've been waiting for you to get back," Grey teased.

She was so bad at peopling. Lexy sighed, "I think I only made things worse. I need to get out of here for a while. I'm mentally exhausted, for various reasons." She winked at Orin, her secret healing buddy from the accidental murder earlier.

"I'm coming with you," Grey remarked as he followed her out with a six pack of beer in his hand.

They walked in silence through the winding pathway strewn with roots, and other broken ankle traps. A branch was blocking the trail, Grey held it out of her way and asked, "Can we go to the rodeo grounds for a bit and talk?"

He hip-checked her and she nearly lost her footing as she replied, "Sure, sounds like a plan." They entered through the large wide-open doors and climbed the grandstands to their usual perch. He tossed her a beer. She opened it facing away from her, knowing it might fizz up and froth over the top. They each took a drink and gazed up at the brilliant stars above. She hadn't been able to see the stars, earlier as they walked to the crypt under the cover of branches. They began sharing almost forgotten tales, reminiscing about the people that had been lost in the Testing.

Out of nowhere, Grey said, "Are you going to tell me why you're mad at me, or do I have to continue to guess?"

Lexy met his eyes with confusion. *She wasn't sure how to word it.* Tempted to tell him, she asked, "Do you love her?"

Thrown off, Grey replied, "Who?"

She clarified, "Melody...Are you in love with her?"

"I didn't know, you knew about that," he answered.

She always knew about everything. Lexy replied, "Let's just say, I'm extremely observant."

Grey took another drink and said, "No, I'm not in love with her and she's not in love with me either."

Satisfied with his answer, she put her drink down, and rested her head on his lap. As he lovingly caressed her hair, their gaze locked and she felt the undeniable tug of her soul, enticing her to ignore ration. *Be with him. Make yourself happy. One more time.*

Grey whispered, "You're incredibly beautiful."

He seductively traced her jawline with his fingertip and leaned in. *He was going to kiss her. No, no.* She moved out of the way and got up. *She couldn't do this anymore. The morning after would kill her, and she needed to keep her cool tomorrow.*

She wasn't going to be able to if she was distraught because he'd forgotten he loved her for the thousandth time. She suggested, "We should get back." Lexy started down the stairs and glanced back, he hadn't moved a muscle. *Once a hint of his true feelings surfaced, he'd never been able to ignore them.* She kept walking. *Don't look back, Lexy.* She was almost at the entrance. She heard him coming but didn't stop. *She couldn't, she wanted him too.*

Grey laughed during his pursuit, "For heaven's sake, slow down for a second. Why are you running away from me? Just stop."

Shit, she knew what happened next. Lexy allowed him to catch up with her. *Damn it, Grey.* He stepped closer, her breathe caught in her chest as he kissed her gently on the forehead instead of the lips.

He tucked her flaming hair behind her ear and whispered, "I may not say this enough, but you're everything to me. You must know that by now. This thing with Melody, isn't going anywhere. I'm just the relief pitcher. Nothing has happened between us in months, it's nothing."

Lexy smiled and teased, "You don't need to explain anything to me. I was just curious, that's all." *This Handler, Dragon situation was bullshit. Their obligation was always to each other, and when one of them stepped away for anyone else the other one panicked.* She stared into his eyes, knowing if she pressed her body against his, the forgotten emotions would come flooding back. *They were trying to come through, even now. He was on the cusp of remembering.* Her heart ached, whispering to her between every beat, *one more time. One more night in his arms.* Her head scolded, *you have to stop the insanity.*

Grey whispered, "I can't stand it when I don't know what you're thinking. I can usually hear it loud and clear. You know I'd never do anything to hurt you, not intentionally. Just tell me what's wrong."

She decided to just say the words, "I can't keep doing this."

He said, "Doing what?"

Lexy paused and confessed, "Loving you."

Grey's eyes softened as he took her hand and probed, "You've been jealous? That's what this is all about? I get jealous when you're with someone too. She doesn't mean anything to me Lex. You know I love you." He towed her into an embrace and kissed her on the cheek.

He was missing the point completely. With the length of her body pressed against his, he kissed her again close to the soft tendrils by her ear. The warmth of his breathe caused her to shiver in response. He pulled back to look into her eyes, for only a breath. His lips closed the distance to hers. The instant their lips met, as always, his memory sparked. It all came rushing back and he remembered how much he wanted her. Familiarity and instinct took over. Grey backed her up against the edge of the railing, kissing her until her lips were swollen, and her body ached with need. She placed her hand against his chest and whispered, "Not here."

He kissed her neck playfully and whispered, "Where then?"

She took his hand and led him out of the rodeo grounds towards a patch of soft grass in the shadow of a large tree. He tripped, lost his footing and tumbled into the grass, towing her down with him.

When they stopped laughing, Grey sat up and naughtily ordered, "Get over here." He tugged her onto his lap.

She was straddling him. It was reminiscent of their first time together. He kissed her passionately as his hands travelled under her shirt in a sensual dance, causing her to gasp and forget how this scenario played out. She loved him so much, she couldn't stop her instinctual reaction to his kisses and wandering hands. It took everything she had to pull away and speak ration, "You'll forget about this in the morning."

"That could never happen. I love you, Lex," he whispered, tenderly cupping her cheeks in his hands, gazing into her eyes.

Lexy whispered, "We've always loved each other, but you'll forget about this. You've forgotten so many times before."

Looking confused, Grey said, "How many times?"

"Too many to count," she responded, touching his cheek lovingly. "You're my Handler. This isn't allowed to happen. It's to protect our friendship. You tell me you love me every time, and for you it's always just like it's the first time you've ever said those words aloud. I always say them back. Even though I know when I wake up, you won't remember what happened between us. I'm always having to adjust my feelings for you. That's why I've been so weird lately. It's hard to let this part of us go in my heart. It takes a while to see you as just my friend."

Looking like he'd been kicked in the chest, Grey whispered, "Do you know how it feels to know that I've hurt you?" He was silent for a second before asking, "Tell me about the first time."

In the grass beneath the stars, she decided to tell him as much as he wanted to know, "We were in the in-between. You were upset, and there was a lot of ash and soot. We were absolutely covered in it. You were the first person I'd ever chosen to be with in that way."

Grey's eyes teared up as he whispered, "I'm honoured you chose me. I wish I remembered that."

Her vision blurred with tears as she whispered, "Who could I ever trust and love more than you?" *She didn't cry.* Sprawling in the grass next to each other, Grey slowly traced a path on her delicate ivory freckled arm with his finger. *He was using his sexy move. Ignore it, keep telling the story.* Lexy disclosed, "That first time was pretty confusing for both of us. It just happened. I was glad you didn't remember that first time."

He whispered, "And what changed the next time?"

"We were dancing to Love Bites. Do you remember that song by Def Leppard? We were alone when we left the pub. We kissed outside and you chased me back to the room. We laughed and made love all night. It was beautiful. You told me how much you loved me before you fell asleep. I said it back. I told you everything I'd always wanted to say. The next morning when you didn't remember anything, I knew that your memory loss wasn't going to be a one-time deal."

He asked, "Where was Arrianna during all of this?"

"She was on a job with the other half of the Clan, you'd broken up," she explained.

Grey nodded and kept gently touching her hip as he deduced, "This is why you haven't dated anyone since Tomas? You were so determined to be with him, even though I knew you didn't love him. I was insanely jealous. I remember feeling more for you back then. I don't ever recall it going any further between us though."

Lexy smiled and clarified, "I let the fact that we'd been together slip out in one of my thoughts. You were furious with me. We fought for days. You came to my room and told me how you felt about me. I told you we'd been together and that you'd been spelled to forget about it as you slept. I told you I was happy with Tomas. I knew it wasn't going to last long. I wanted the experience of being loved in that way for longer than one night. You understood and you told me you'd wait. You spent a large amount of your time flirting with me back then. It drove Tomas crazy. After he was lost in the Testing we gave in, both knowing you'd forget. Your feelings were reset that night. You forgot everything I told you about being together before, and we were back to friends."

He took her hand and apologized, "You've been in a relationship with me. I just didn't know it. All those infatuations I've had with people over the years. It must have been killing you. It kills me to know I've been hurting you. This situation can't be making you happy? This is holding you back from finding someone. This isn't fair to you."

Looking up at stars that would never align in their favour, Lexy agreed, "It's not fair to either of us, Grey. I love you too much to say no. I do it to myself sometimes. I kiss you, or I get in the shower with you, because I miss you in that way."

"If I'm hurting you, then you have stop. I can't take control of this, if I don't remember anything. It has to be you," he prompted, squeezed her hand. Grey grinned at her, winked, and teased, "You might have to opt out of seducing me for a while."

In this moment, Lexy could have saved herself from the pain of another morning of Grey's selective magic induced amnesia. Wanting him still, she whispered, "If it were only that easy." *He was being selfless and that made her love him even more.* She was going to get up and leave. She kissed his cheek. *It was both that easy and hard.* She pulled away, gazed into his eyes, and kissed his lips. Carnal energy flickered as their lips parted and the kiss deepened into an erotic submergence of souls. The ability for reason was lost as the barriers of clothing, were torn hastily from their bodies. They made love in the grass until they were spent and fell asleep in each other's arms.

Lexy awoke feeling his skin against hers. She was naked in his arms, as suns first rays began to slink through the branches of the trees. *Shit, she really had to stop doing this.* She quickly gathered up her clothes and paused during her escape to look at him. *He was smiling. What had happened between them was only a dream.* She put her clothes on and watched the dust particle filled streams of sunlight until they stretched across his naked form. Lexy snuck back into the RV in the wee hours of the morning, pretty sure nobody had seen her. She kept her eyes closed as Grey did the same. He snuggled up into the bunk next to her. She grimaced. *There was a guy for you. Wake up in the forest naked. You have no idea what you've done or who you've done it with, but you get into bed to snuggle with your platonic girlfriend, without showering. Gross Greydon. At least she knew it had been her.* She grinned, before succumbing to the sedating rhythm of his breathing, and drifting off into a deep slumber.

Chapter 30

Watching Them Dream

When she finally woke up everyone had already left for breakfast. Lexy darted into the bathroom to get ready. She giggled as she looked in the mirror. She was humorously dishevelled. Once she was ready, she strolled out of the stuffy RV into the fresh morning air. *She'd broken her own heart this time. There had been every opportunity to stop last night from happening. Grey would have no clue what he'd been up to the night before.* She took a deep breath as she walked to the dining hall. *Friends, he's your friend. This can't keep happening. You have to move on Lexy.* She entered the hall to find the rest of her Clan finishing breakfast. She snagged a few pieces of bacon and toast, devouring it as quickly as she could.

Grey gave her a funny look as he picked some grass out of her hair and whispered, "Do you know where I ended up last night? Who did I end up with?"

She wasn't sure where his memory cut off. Lexy craftily enquired, "What's the last thing you remember?"

Leaning in like he was sharing a secret, he whispered, "We were walking back to the motor home from the Ankh Crypt. You said you were tired, but I convinced you to go to the rodeo grounds. Then it gets kind of foggy. I woke up naked in the grass by myself."

"I left you by the rodeo grounds and went to bed," she quietly answered. *It was sort of the truth.*

Looking confused, Grey whispered back, "Who in the hell did I end up with? Did you see anyone else when you were leaving? Why can't I remember anything?"

Lexy whispered, "You were drinking. I'm not sure what you did after I left." Lexy was aware that Grey kept staring at her like he knew she was lying. She'd been more omitting than lying.

Melody gave Grey a funny look and she said, "You seriously woke up naked in the woods?" She teased, "Maybe you went streaking?"

Good one Melody that made perfect sense.

Grey met her eyes and exclaimed, "Maybe I did?"

"Grey, you're my new hero," Zach chuckled as he ate a piece of bacon.

Lexy noticed Grey sneaking glances at her. *He suspected she wasn't telling him the whole truth. She wasn't worried about it. He'd always let it drop in the past.* She followed the group of Ankh out of the buffet area and back into the crisp oxygen rich morning air. They made their way to the Ankh crypt as a group. When they arrived Jenna and Orin were already waiting. They followed Grey down the long corridor to the end. There was a wall of stone, with no grooves, or ridges. *They had to walk through the wall. The newbies didn't know this, it was a trust thing.*

Zach ran his hand across the wall. Grey stood back and allowed him to try to figure it out. Zach chuckled, "I'll bite...How in the hell do you open the wall?"

"It doesn't open," Orin hollered from down the corridor. He added, "You have to run through it."

Zach backed up and ran at the wall, smoking into the stone.

Orin doubled over in a fit of raucous laughter, "That never gets old."

Jenna scowled at Orin and reprimanded, "That was completely unnecessary."

"Oh, I had to, at least once. Come on princess, admit it, that's always funny," Orin chuckled. Holding his hand out to help Zach up off the floor as a peace offering, he clarified, "After we make it so you can. Way to jump the gun kid."

Zach brushed himself off, scowling at Orin, a little embarrassed. Orin put his hand on the wall. Grey placed his next to it. Lexy did the same. The wall became almost transparent. Even after forty years, the magical things were always truly impressive. "Do you want a redo, Zach? One where you don't look like an idiot?" Lexy taunted.

Zach put his hand in first, then edged his body through the hazy wall. They all followed him into the large open room on the other side. In this room, there were four much larger than normal tombs. They easily fit three or four people, side by side. Lexy was grinning. *She couldn't help it. Kayn kept attempting to touch everything. They'd have to work on that after her redo. She'd never been able to grasp that concept.* She enjoyed watching the newest of the Ankh experience each first. *Hopefully, this wouldn't be their last.*

Kayn observed, "Obviously those tombs are made for more than one person?"

"These are the original offerings from Azariah," Orin explained, "There are four giant tombs at each crypt, hidden over a thousand years ago. These are at each site for travel, to and from the in-between. These tombs are only accessible by the hand of an Ankh. They can never be moved, or used anywhere, but right here."

Jenna began to speak, "This training you're about to have is incredibly important. This is your chance to see what you would do if you had a chance to redo your original, Sweet Sleep. Call it a quiz for the final test. This will show us what areas you still need work in."

They were all aware of what had happened on that day, their humanity began its steady descent into immortality. This was always an intensely private subject. None wanted their savage mortal ending to be witnessed. Lexy could remember the humiliation she'd felt, knowing Jenna had seen her fall and rise. Lexy rose from bile and she'd been born again with an act of brutal vengeance. She'd become a

Dragon after the slaughter. She met the panic in Kayn's eyes, with understanding. *What was this strange connection she felt with this girl? A girl she shouldn't care about at all. She was going to be lost in the Testing, just like all the others. Nobody had survived since she'd gone in with Arrianna and Grey. They were the last survivors, forty years ago.* She stared at Kayn. *This girl was important. She wanted to believe she'd make it out. She needed to feel like she'd given her the ability to save herself.*

Zach mumbled, "I'm guessing this isn't optional?"

Orin didn't bother responding. He placed his hand on each tomb and opened them up. They all looked at each other one last time, and they each climbed into one of the tombs. Without one word, they lay down in silence. The lids shut ominously. The four stood there for a moment, staring at the closed tombs. They'd known the horrors the newest of the Ankh were about to endure. She'd been there with Arrianna and Grey not long ago in the grand scheme of things.

Grey suggested, "Orin, maybe you shouldn't watch this. You'll see everything that happened to her, hear every thought."

"It's not optional," was Orin's response.

"Grey, are you sure you want to watch these?" Lexy asked, "You're the only one of us that can opt out. Jenna's running the show. Orin and I need to run the tombs, you don't need to be here. Do you really want to see what happens to her?"

Grey glared at her with wide eyes, Melody's father was standing right beside him. His trysts with his daughter were still a secret. He assured, "I'm fine."

Lexy was giggling on the inside. *That cattiness had been completely uncalled for, but it sure felt good.*

Orin whispered, "Enough messing around. You know they're in limbo right now. They're probably scared to death, lost in a sea of dark things. Don't leave my daughter in that place any longer than she has to be."

Lexy met Orin's eyes and realised she was being insensitive. *He was her friend and he had a serious adversity to dark places.* She touched Melody's tomb and it orbed twice. Mel would be the first to find her way out of the darkness into her worst nightmare. In front of the tombs there was a pool of water from an underground spring. They all submerged their hands in the liquid to create an emotional and physical link between them. Jenna knelt and ran her hand over the water's surface. They would be there with her, witnesses to her execution, passengers within her being. They would relive Melody's Sweet Sleep together.

Melody's Sweet Sleep

Melody winced as she yanked the car's back door open. *Her stomach had been hurting all day and she'd been plagued with this weird nervous energy.* She chucked her school bag on the floor in front of little Stevie's car seat and avoided his swinging legs. She bent over and kissed her baby brother's pursed lips and his face illuminated with joy. She lovingly greeted the toddler, "How's my sweet baby today?" Her other brother was ten years old and also in the back. Both boys were adorable with ash blonde hair and deeply set dimples. Melody smiled as she asked, "Did you have a good day at school Kevin?"

Obviously attempting to push her buttons, Kevin scowled at her and rudely baited, "You'd know how my day was if you ever came home after school."

They had the token sibling love-hate relationship but she really wasn't in the mood for his crap today. Her stomach cramped again. Little Stevie was laughing and wildly swinging his legs, kicking the back of her seat, trying to keep her attention focused on him.

Her mother complained, "Must you always slam the door?"

"Sorry," Melody apologised, meeting her mother's frustrated gaze. Even when she was angry her mother was stunning, with her vibrant auburn hair and wide gentle smile, framed by deeply carved dimples. She was a beautiful woman with the softest green eyes, so gentle her soul looked almost breakable; you just wanted to give her a hug and protect her. Melody looked almost identical to her mother except her chestnut brown hair was shoulder length with a natural, whimsical wave which she always wore tucked behind her ears.

It was pouring, when her mother announced her father was going to be late tonight. She succumbed to the chanting chorus of ice cream coming from the backseat and they made a unanimous decision to stop at the diner on the way home where they each ordered giant ice cream sundaes, even little Stevie; who had it literally everywhere by the time they were done. Melody smiled as her brother Kevin entertained the table with his outrageous sense of humour. She took a moment to fully appreciate her mother's easy laughter and calm demeanour even during Stevie's ice cream face painting episode. Her mom, all smiles, chose that moment to tell her they had another baby on the way and that she was well over four months along. It was a happy surprise. "Can you feel the baby moving yet?" Melody enquired as she ate another mouthful of ice cream.

Her mom replied, "Yes…I can."

Melody asked, "Can I feel the baby?"

"You can give it a try." Her mother answered sweetly.

It was fluttering around as Melody laid her hand on her mom's slightly rounded stomach. *It was truly miraculous.* She didn't want to take her hand off but she did.

As they stood up to leave, her mom whispered a secret in her ear, "It's a girl."

She watched her mom walk away from the table to pay for the sundaes. Once again, she felt a strange wave of apprehension ripple through her. Melody clutched her stomach and grimaced. She was a little worried but her little brother started to squeal and he winged his empty sundae cup on the floor. Melody crouched down with a napkin to clean it up and mumbled, "Seriously Stevie?" She heard her mother rustling around above her at the table.

Her mom said, "Thank you honey."

Melody grinned as she rose to her feet and replied, "No problem." As she followed her family out to the vehicle, her little brother's footsteps were humming in her ears. She shook her head. *I must be over tired? Maybe I'm coming down with something?* She was grinning in the car as they drove home thinking about how much she'd always wanted a little sister, while staring out the window watching the trees whirl by. She had to turn away. She was feeling a little dizzy. Motion sickness had never been her friend. The car swerved on the road. Startled, she laughed, "Mom, what the hell?" She glanced at her mother. *She'd passed out in the driver's seat!* Melody panicked and with no time to think, she took off her seatbelt while attempting to reach for the steering wheel. The car swerved in one direction and then in another. It happened so quickly. It lurched into a shallow ditch, leaving the rear of the car exposed to oncoming traffic. Melody felt an instantaneous explosion of pain as her body flew through the windshield. She toppled limply down a steep embankment coming to rest in high grass. Stunned, she tried to comprehend the severity of her situation. *What had just happened? That didn't just happen. This wasn't real.* She lay bleeding in the foliage by the side of the road, taking small laboured breaths, unable to move. *Did that just happen?* She could hear her baby brother's desperate, haunting cries, "Mommy! Melody!" They crackled through the eerie silence in the frigid night air. She began to fight her way back to reality. Smoke was billowing above the car. She lay there twitching, completely incapacitated. Her wrist was in her line of vision; a bone had pierced through her skin. She felt the hot, sticky sensation of her blood as it left her body pooling beneath her. Her head lay twisted sideways and she could see the car through the curtain of blood. She attempted to blink it out her eyes. Melody could see her little brother's face. He was sobbing with his hand against the window, imploring her to help him. He seemed to be staring right at her. She tried to move but her lack of pain let her know that she was in shock. No matter how hard she struggled, she couldn't move. A voice inside of her mind kept whispering, *go to sleep Melody. It's time to go to sleep.* Her little brother's cries kept her eyes straining to stay open. *She had to stay with him until she was sure he was safe. She couldn't allow her eyes to close. She couldn't succumb to the voice in her mind. Not until she knew somebody was there to help him.* Melody focused on his tiny outstretched palm on the window. She could remember what it felt like to hold it and how the feeling of her baby brother's hand in hers made her heart surge with love. *She felt no pain. She was only thinking about him.* Melody was silently praying as a big rig turned the corner and ran directly into the back of the vehicle. She lay there in horror as her little brother's cries were silenced by the sound of crushing metal. What was left of the vehicle made a high-pitched scraping sound as it tumbled down the road as a sandwiched pile of rubble. There was a moment of complete quiet before an echoing explosion, followed by the crackling of fire but there was no screaming, not a single cry for they'd all been crushed on impact. Melody began to scream from within her broken being. She screamed over and over until she finally succumbed to her mind's chanting, *go to sleep, just shut your eyes…Go to sleep Melody.* A final thought trickled through her broken mind riding on the last current of life as she bled out into the frigid unforgiving earth, *if they are gone, please let me die. The heartbreaking vision ended and faded to black.*

She was so cold. Where was she? Her eyes opened and the foggy images came into focus; leaves were all around her. *Where am I?* She could hear the steady humming of passing cars. She sat up and as she took in her surroundings, she realised that the sounds of the vehicles were coming from above her, up the grassy hill. She looked at her hands and touched her face, confused as to how she'd come to be lying in the grass down a ravine. Morning dew was still glimmering in small droplets on the tips of the tall grass surrounding her. It was strangely magical; it looked like daylight stars in a sky of lush green foliage. Her hands were smudged with mud, as were her clothes but she felt alright. Melody racked her brain trying to remember what she was doing by the side of the road. She began to get flickers of memory; the ice cream, the baby sister and her little brother's hand pressed against the car window. But nothing solid was coming to her. *Had she gotten lost? Had she been kidnapped or attacked on her way home walking from somewhere?* She wiped the dirt off her hands onto her clothes. She felt a little woozy as she tried to stand up but quickly found her balance. She stood there at the bottom of the hill in moist thigh deep grass thinking, *what happened?* As she tried to remember again, she was met with a piercing headache that throbbed and pulsated beneath her scalp. Her mind seemed to be saying, *just leave it alone; you don't want to know.*

She climbed up the side of the hill on all fours holding on to the long thick strands of grass as though she were a wild animal, with an unexplainable feeling of strength rippling beneath the surface of her skin. When she reached the top, she rose to a standing position by the side of the road with her feet half on gravel, half on cement and noticed she was missing a shoe. *That's weird, why would I only have one shoe on?* Thoughts raced through her mind, *there was something she needed to remember.* She had a flash of memory...*There were diamonds in the sand. She was standing barefoot in the sand with her toes in the warm luxurious silky grains.* As she recalled brilliant light and a beautiful woman, she felt more than a little bit delusional. *She must have hit her head?*

She could see teddy bears and a memorial around a tree by the side of the road and she slowly walked towards it feeling like it mattered to her in some way. She felt a sense of foreboding as she approached the shrine. Pictures of her family were on the tree, surrounded by flowers and toys. A cheerleading picture of her was also on the tree, as well as a picture of her on her horse. *Did I die?* She thought, still unable to remember anything solid. Melody stared at the pictures of her in confusion and picked up a bouquet of flowers from someone named Michael and read it…*Great loss of Melody and her family…My condolences…Was she a ghost? Had they all died in a car accident? That's why people made these shrines by the side of the road.* She dropped to her knees in front of the makeshift shrine, looking like an angel kneeling at the bottom of a perfect ray of light that shone through the dense forest as though it had extended from heaven to guide her way home. *Why was she still here?* A car pulled over but she didn't hear it because she was trying to process everything.

Her father spoke her name in disbelief, "Melody?"

What? She turned around and her heart leapt as she looked up at him. *Maybe angels came to guide you to heaven in the form of someone you love.*

Her father shook his head in disbelief as he took a step closer. His voice cracked with emotion as he gasped, "Is that really you?"

Angels wouldn't cry. Her heart leapt. "Daddy?" She whispered, "Can you see me?"

Her father knelt before her and she was afraid. *What if this wasn't real, just a cruel taunting nightmare.* He reached out and touched her shoulder. *He was real.* Her father opened his arms and she sprung into his loving embrace.

He cradled her, sobbing, "How…How are you alive? How are you here with me?"

Tears blurred her vision as she whispered, "Are mom and the boys with you?"

"No," her father choked out, "They're gone…I thought you were gone too?" They clung to each other and sobbed.

They were still crying in each other's arms by the side of the road when a police car pulled up. An officer got out and exclaimed, "Oh My God!"

Melody's father looked up with his eyes overflowing with tears of joy and replied, "Exactly."

After experiencing Melody's first death and resurrection as a Healer, they moved through her immortal experiences to the day of her Correction. When the Correction had come for her, Melody had been afraid, but instead of succumbing to her fear, she had blown up her house while blinded by fury. None of them had seen the dark side of Melody but now, they knew what she was capable of. When it was time to redo the events, they all watched as she made the conscious decision to remove her seatbelt once again and allow the scenario to unfold just as it was meant to. She was ready to battle in the crypt. She'd chosen to keep everything the same. Melody grasped the concept of immortality. She was emotionally advanced far beyond her years but this was a common trait for a Healer to possess. Just as they were finished a few naughty flashes of Melody in the in-between came through involving Grey. Jenna whooshed her hand over it, hoping Orin didn't see anything. He didn't appear to because he said nothing about it as they moved on to Zach.

Zach's Sweet Sleep

The school bus dropped Zach off, temporarily blinding him with dust from the rural road they lived on as it pulled away. His three younger siblings were walking behind him with backpacks in tow. They knew better than to accost him with chatter. He'd smack someone with his bag in a heartbeat. School wasn't easy for him and home life consisted of a house load of siblings with not a speck of personal space. Zach hadn't even come close to learning to appreciate what he had, before it was taken away. His yard was a scavenger's dream, adorned with shells from trucks amidst thigh high weeds. His younger siblings raced past him into the front door as Zach chucked his bag on the sundeck and made himself comfortable on the porch swing. Treasuring silence, he began to slowly swing. All there was for miles was cornfield and blue sky. *Chills crept up his spine followed by a nagging sense of foreboding. Something felt off. What was that scent in the air? He'd felt strange all day.* A murder of crows took off from the center of the field. *Was something out there? Maybe he should go check it out?* He decided against it and continued enjoying the peace and quiet. His mind prodded, *murder of crows. Anything could be hidden in that field. It was probably just their dog. Wait a minute...Usually their dog met them at the bus.* He stopped the repetitive creaking of the swing. *Where was their dog? It was too quiet. There was no commotion, no familiar laughter, his siblings weren't squabbling. There was usually something to irritate him but today there was not a sound. It was both wonderful and unnerving.* Zach had three older siblings. He was a middle child. *He was never in charge of anything. Why did he have this nagging feeling like he should be paying attention today? It was weird...His younger siblings never left him alone for his porch swing ritual.*

Zach spent a good hour on this rickety old porch swing each daydreaming of his future. Right now, he was just a scrawny built sixteen-year-old boy with moderately passable grades who dreamt of getting on a greyhound bus and leaving this place forever, but a part of him secretly feared he'd be stuck here with no options for the rest of his life watching this empty cornfield. He lived with six siblings, his grandparents and his single mother. He was the only unattractive one. Even his grandfather was better looking than him. A girl at school today said it best. She told him he could get an afterschool job standing in people's yards scaring off crows. A dozen crows suddenly lifted off in flight from the field. *Again? That was a weird thing to happen twice. It was probably the dog.* He thought about calling the dog's name but decided against it. If he made it known he was out here relaxing the silence might stop. Once again, he noticed the lack of noise coming from the house but chose to ignore it. The phone started to ring. It rang ten times. *Nobody was picking it up? Frig, there is ten people inside and not a damn one can get off their asses and walk five feet to answer the damn phone.* It stopped ringing and then started again. *Oh, Come on!* He let it ring out of sheer stubbornness as he began to swing again with the steady creaking sound. *I'm such a rebel.* The phone began to ring again. The quiet murmur in his mind whispering something isn't right became louder. As he got up, an ominous wind whistled past whooshing through the field of corn. An empty juice box tumbled across the wooden deck and hit the front door. *One of the kids left the door slightly ajar…That was strange.* As the phone began to ring for the fourth time unanswered, he ran inside and answered the phone on the table, "Hello?" *It was his mother's boss wondering why his mother hadn't shown up for her shift at the diner.*

He looked around the empty living room as he responded, "I just got home from school. I'll check and see if she's here." *She must be deathly ill. She never misses work.* Zach carried the phone with him calling, "Mom?" as he ran up the stairs they creaked under foot. He pushed open his mother's bedroom door. *She wasn't there?* He placed the phone to his ear and said, "She's not here. I have no idea where she is, but she'd never miss work unless it was an emergency." *Her boss seemed genuinely concerned, not angry.* He asked Zach to call back just so he'd know she was alright. Zach kept walking through the house. *Where in the hell did everyone go?* He checked each room. *Nobody was there. Where are they?* His mother's purse and car keys were on the counter. The house was ominously empty.

He ran back outside and walked around the back of the house. The field rustled. *Could they be hiding? His mother wasn't skipping work to play a prank. What was the other option? They all disappeared for no reason? Her car was there and her purse. She could have forgotten her purse. Maybe one of his grandparents had to go to the hospital? The car was still here. Where was everyone? This didn't make sense.* The cornfield rustled again in the distance. *There was someone out there, he was sure of it. There had to be a logical explanation. Carbon monoxide leak? There was a logical explanation for everything.* Zach felt sick to his stomach as shivers raised every hair on his body. *Oh no...He found us.* He sensed someone behind him but before he could turn, he was hit over the head. His vision wavered, his ears rang, and it all went black.

He was being dragged into the cornfield by his legs when he came to with his head bouncing in the dirt. He remained limp as survival instincts kicked in from his years of abuse. *Play dead. He'd lived this moment before. He wasn't strong enough to fight back. Play dead.* He heard shrill screaming but kept himself from stiffening in response to the pleas. *One of the older stronger ones would help. His job was ugly whipping post, not savior. No matter how far they moved. He'd always found them. His father despised him.* The older three and younger three were his, but Zach was sired by another during a time when they'd successfully escaped. Once the adorable baby vanished, the child that wasn't genetically his became visible. *He was a constant reminder that she could find freedom.* Things escalated until they ran again. He found them again. *This became a cycle. They never stayed hidden for long.* His mother was six months pregnant the last time they ran. *He'd learned to play dead, for this was the only road to survival.* He'd been pulled deep into the field and remained limp as he was kicked into a hole. He rolled into it, still playing dead, for if he moved it would only bring pain. He'd come to rest on his side. *There was the scent of rich manure. He'd been tuning out something else, smoke so thick it burned his nostrils. The screaming had stopped. He hadn't allowed himself to think about why they were screaming. It was only now in the silence that he wondered if his father could be heinous enough to burn his own children alive. He wouldn't do that. Why search for them and then kill them all?* Something heavy was thrown in the hole with him. The weight of it and size was jarring. He was paralyzed with fear. *This was no longer the stealthy wisdom of survival. Someone else's body had been thrown in. If it was one of his older siblings, they might be playing dead. The beatings were usually reserved for Zach and his mother. Something light was thrown over them. A blanket perhaps? Maybe his father just didn't want to see what he was burying.* Under cover of the blanket, he opened his eyes. *He was facing away from his grave companion.* Zach felt the trickling weight of the earth and the repetitive sound of the shovel. *Oh god, please help us,* he prayed while trying to remain calm. *If he moved his chest or breathed too heavily the grave digger would know someone survived under the blanket. He was being buried alive. They were being buried alive.* His mind whispered, *don't move. No matter what…Do not move. He doesn't have time to do anything more than cover us up. If the house is burning someone will see it and come to save us.* The dirt hushed the outside world. *Voices. Was there more than one voice? He was sure it was more than one. He had a headache…They were almost out of air. Nobody would find them until it was too late. The house was too big a distraction. If he didn't dig himself out, they'd die anyway.* He whispered, "Who's in here with me?" *There was no answer, no answer at all. He could smell cologne. It was Johnny. A year older, he was the only one who wore it. Why would he hurt Johnny? He was his favourite. Maybe Johnny tried to save him? He tried to stay positive. He was out cold. It was up to him.* He'd count to one hundred before moving. At about forty, panic set in. *Please be gone.* Zach reached the edge of the blanket and began clawing at the earth. Shielding his face with the material he vigorously clawed the ground. *Help us! Please help us!* He was going to have to move the only thing keeping the pocket of air. *It had to be done.* Zach peeled the blanket from his face and dirt slid into the gaps, smothering him. He was attempting shallow breaths but there was no air. He was breathing in the putrid soil. *This was it. He tried.* Right as his head was about to explode from lack of oxygen, a savior himself broke through the dirt and tugged him out. Zach was gasping for air, sputtering out soil, choking out his brother's name, "Johnny." Covered in mud, Zach saw the group of strangers that saved him. He didn't have time to discover if they were friend or foe as he frantically dug his brother out and pulled him free from the shallow grave. The whites of Johnny's eyes were open and speckled with the putrid smelling earth.

His brother was gone. Zach began shaking him, begging, "Wake up! Wake up! No! Please no!"

It was Triad that saved him from his grave. Tiberius asserted, "He's gone kid...Long gone. We need to get out of here if you don't want to join him."

"I can't! What about everyone else?" Zach panicked.

In an almost sensitive voice, Tiberius revealed, "They're all dead. Trust me, even if they weren't, you'd be coming with us."

"No, they can't be...No," Zach stammered as shock set in. He stared at Johnny's body and asked, "Why did you save me? Who are you?"

"We're Triad," Tiberius explained as he tore open Zach's shirt and branded his chest with his ring.

The sensation of melting skin stunned Zach momentarily but he didn't scream. *He could turn most pain off, for sadly he was used it. His oxygen deprived mind reeled through the horrific events. Dead...They can't be.* Dazed, he mumbled, "Is Triad a biker gang?"

Amused by the biker gang comment, he smiled and disclosed, "Sorry kid...No such luck." Tiberius unceremoniously snapped Zach's neck like a brittle twig. *The vision faded to black.*

"Call this a hunch but I have a feeling he'll attempt to redesign these events and blow it. He's never had closure," Orin declared.

Once they had all experienced the end of Zach's life, they each knew that the boy had endless possibilities if given the proper guidance. The survival instincts from his years of abuse would come in handy down the road.

Jenna looked at Lexy and declared, "He might be the sleeping Dragon."

"What do you mean by that?" Lexy enquired.

Jenna smiled and explained, "I have it on good authority that if one becomes a Dragon during the Testing, they'll come home."

"I'm betting on the dark horse. I'll change my vote. I say the boy lets it all happen as it went down," Orin wagered.

Zach had seemed unimportant until they'd seen the end of his life. He did as Jenna suspected. During the redo of his Sweet Sleep Zach tried to change it all. He would find out that even if you endeavour to revise a few of the chapters, the ending to the story always remained the same.

It was Kayn's turn now...Lexy placed both hands on the tomb and it burst two times with brilliant light. She instantly returned from the void to the safety of the tomb. Jenna ran her hand through the puddle of water so they could all witness her original Sweet Sleep.

Kayn's Sweet Sleep

As they pulled up in front of her house, she leaned across the seat and thanked Kevin's dad with a hug. She opened the door and took a deep breath. *The air smelled like wet cherry blossoms. It must have been raining while they were eating dinner.* She stepped out of the car into a puddle and twisted her ankle. *Of course.* With a soaked foot, eggs and school bag in hand, she hobbled up the steep driveway towards the front door.

They lived in a wooded somewhat isolated area. Normally she would have darted from Kevin's dad's car into the house, but her ankle stung each time she put pressure on it. As she came closer, she noticed the door was partially open. *It was a little windy out and quite normal for the door to be unlocked. Maybe it was left ajar and opened by the wind?* She heard tires on gravel and turned just in time to see Kevin's father driving away. Kayn felt off, apprehensive as she made her way up the long gravel driveway to the door that seemed to have a life of its own, shifting from cracked to closed with the breeze. She dug out her phone to look at the time. *Quarter after eight. She was fifteen minutes late.* The door moved again. She shook her head and laughed. *This was obviously a prank. They'd left the door open, and entrance lights off to freak her out. Chloe was probably hiding around the corner. Practical jokes were a daily occurrence in their household.* Slivers of light from the moon flashed through the branches as they swayed in the wind and for a moment it felt like they were waving her away. *She was being silly.* She shoved her cell into her pants, pocket dialling Kevin by accident.

"I'm home!" Kayn yelled as she kicked off her shoes and dropped her school bag. She flicked on the light, and nothing happened. *The power wasn't out. She'd seen the lights on upstairs as she walked up the driveway. It's just a burnt-out light bulb.* She massaged her ankle. *Great, there goes the track meet.* Kayn tried to take off her wet socks, but a stab of pain from her freshly twisted ankle caused her to place a hand on the wall while attempting to balance. Her hand slid off the wall, as she struggled to tug off her sopping wet sock. "Kevin's mom gave us eggs," she called out quietly, suddenly aware she was alone in the house. *Where would they go at this hour?* Her mind sorted through the possible scenarios. *Something wasn't right.*

"Mom…Dad?" She called out…answered by silence. She went to close the front door and felt something wet. A faint sliver of light was streaming through the doorway. She stepped into it and held out her hand. *Her palm was covered in blood.* Ripples of adrenaline coursed through her. *Whose blood was this? It felt like thousands of spiders were running on the surface of her skin.* She froze, paralyzed by fear as shivers of terror crawled across her flesh. She gingerly stepped backwards. A dark figure loomed at the end of the hallway. *Who was that?*

She heard her sister's voice scream, "Run Kayn!" In a pitch so raw, primal and shrill that it lit her survival instinct on fire. She spun around and ran, bringing the eggs with her. She could sense someone chasing her but knew looking back would only slow her down. Kayn ran with no rhyme or reason in the direction she was pointed in. Halfway across the back lawn she threw the bag of eggs behind her hoping to slow her attacker. She slipped in the wet grass and scrambled forward, knowing someone was mere seconds behind her. She spotted the overgrown opening to the trails and raced towards them, knowing from her childhood that there were a million places to hide. Fuelled by the animalistic instinct of survival she burst through the blackberry brambles blocking the path, ignoring the pain as they tore at her flesh for it only heightened the survival instinct which now possessed and drove her forward. She barrelled through the overgrowth, where instinct prompted. The crunching of leaves and twigs in the trail behind her told her he was close; far too close to do anything but react. She slipped in the mud again, skidding yet not falling. Kayn had now lost her precious half a second lead, allowing her hunter to close the space between them. Her heart pounded wildly in her chest, threatening to burst right through her skin as her tired legs propelled her body through the winding trail. The rocks on the path brutalized her feet as the sharp reaching branches and twigs slashed at her legs.

"You have to run faster Kayn, run faster," her sister's voice screeched inside Kayn's terror-driven mind. The ground was

crunching directly behind her. He was so close that she could feel his breath on her hair and neck as he panted. *He was almost touching her. He was fast, inhumanly fast.* A rush of adrenaline edged her ahead. *She could see lights from the neighbour's house peeking through the trees. She was going to make it. She was almost there.* The darkness that pursued her was keeping pace. *Almost to safety...just over the creek.* Her bare feet hit the small wooden bridge... *Almost there. She was going to make it.* Kayn felt the elation of victory, she was about to burst through the bushes when something hot was driven into her back. Her eyes widened in terror as the knife plunged into her again. The blade seared a molten trail of excruciating pain through her body. A sweaty hand muffled her gasp of shock as she sunk to her knees in disbelief. Her captor's arms, slick with perspiration, constricted around her neck crushing her larynx with the strength of a python. Screaming and pleading for her life was now impossible. He continuously brought her to the brink of strangulation and then harshly revived her. Each time her eyes slipped shut, she felt the slicing, searing pain of his blade as he brutalized her stomach and chest until her eyes remained open in terror. Blood sputtered from between her parted lips as she attempted to speak. She could see a shadow on the patio through the trees in the luminescence of the porch lights. *Someone was out there having a cigarette. They were so close. Help me, oh, God, please help me; see me, please, I'm right here,* Kayn's mind screamed. He continued to plunge the knife into her. *He's killing me...Please,* her soul pleaded as her vision blurred from her tears. She gurgled as she choked and sputtered out blood. *Why, why are you doing this to me?*

She felt the competing rhythms of their hearts, as his hot sweaty torso pressed intimately against hers. Her stomach churned with revulsion as she felt the warmth of his rapid excited breathing against her neck. His quiet laughter echoed in her mind as a raspy male voice began whispering things she couldn't understand. Her blood had soaked through her clothes and it was trickling down her arms. *She was going to die.* He released her. She slumped forward and tried to grasp the ground with her fingertips, but no matter how hard she struggled from within the confines of her mind she couldn't move. Her breath came in short laboured attempts as a soothing voice whispered, *Sleep, it's time to go to sleep.* As she closed her eyes, she heard Grandma Winnie's final words to her, '*You survive. You fight hard.*' She screamed from within, clawing at the soil and forcing herself up to her knees. Suddenly, there was a blinding explosion of pain across her head and face. The lights flickered and went out. *In the woods lay a bleeding angel in all her glory. Her arms posed gracefully above her head, her hair soaked in the mud, blood and feces in which she lay. Dying, fading into the other realm, her form was christened by the rain, as the trees had begun to weep upon her for the brutality she had endured.*

Kayn awoke in frigid darkness to the fragrance of damp moss, tree sap and the sweet metallic taste of her own blood in her mouth. Images from her childhood flickered through her mind as the pain recycled in waves until it began to slowly dull and become a tolerable numbness. *She was so cold. Where was she?* Her body gave an involuntary shudder as her mind fed her slivers, flashes of the inhuman savagery she'd endured until she understood where she was and how she'd come to be dying in the forest all alone. *If she kept her eyes closed, he might believe her to be gone. She could slip away peacefully and become one with the forest.* She could hear the soothing sound of raindrops as they tapped on the branches above her. *Maybe, he was gone?* She opened her eyes and imagined the lush green branches of the cedar trees above as giant arms, capable of offering her protection from the elements. At first the image was nurturing and beautiful, but then the trees came to life. They cackled and mocked her, "You're going to die you silly bitch," as they waved their branches to the haunting sound of rattling raindrops and the howling of the wind.

Kayn's consciousness snapped back to reality. *She'd lost a lot of blood…None of this was real.*

The forest floor was alive with a dancing mist that seemed to add a thickness to the tapping sound of the raindrops. Writhing in the mud as her essence moistened the ground beneath her, Kayn willed her body to move; her fingers clawed at the soil until she was spent. For a moment she lay still, feeling like a half dead animal waiting to be finished off by its hunter. With her eyes gazing towards the heavens, she'd been watching a stream of light from the moon that had made it through the cover of rain clouds and branches. It felt like she was breathing through a pinched straw. She concentrated on each breath...*in and out...a little air.* The glimmer of the ray vanished, leaving only cold isolating darkness and the flickering of blurry confusing images. *Help me.* The only answer to her soul's plea was the crackling quiet sound of the rain. What little vision she had clouded with tears, and she screamed from the confines of her mind as the blindingly excruciating pain abruptly returned. As the wave of agony passed, she sensed his presence. She tried to focus through the glossy film of her tears. His dark shadow ominously loomed as it had in the hallway. *Please, please...No more.* Now only a few feet away, he was watching her. She willed herself to grasp at the moist cold earth with her fingers, but she was unable to move. *Her body was now nothing more than a broken shell. How cruel for her mind to still see; to still desire life at this point.* As his form loomed above her, Kayn looked into his eyes with a desperate plea, *why are you doing this?* Her body gave an involuntary shudder. Kayn realised she was naked, completely exposed to the elements. *Why was she naked?* Her eyes filled with tears again. She felt instant, overwhelming shame.

The dark mass of her violator knelt beside her and leaned in. She could smell his putrid breath as it moistened her face. There was an electrical current between Kayn and the man in the dark, it was like a charge. Every hair on her body stood on end as he ran a finger over her exposed breast and said, "You were never to be born; this situation had to be corrected."

His knife glinted in the light from the moon as it was raised above her chest. *Yes,* she thought. *Let it be over now.* She closed her eyes as he sliced into her flesh and opened them with acceptance. She felt no more pain. She stared deeply into his eyes as hers filled with tears.

With a voice thick with emotion he said, "From this life unto the next." He slowly carved a symbol into the flesh above her heart.

She lay limp in his arms, still conscious of what was happening, as he pulled her close and cradled her naked body like a baby, rocking her broken violated flesh in his arms, stroking her blood-soaked hair. He began to sob as if he were repentant in some way for how he had tortured her. As her vision flickered one last time, the man was gone; it was her mother looking into her eyes. Her mother's eyes were filled with so much love that it seemed to release her from pain and fear as it had when she was a small child. Her mother cradled her as a baby, rocking her back and forth. She was safe now in her mother's arms. She was at peace. *Mommy,* her heart sang, *you're here to save me.* The warmth of her mother's love enveloped her tortured soul. She looked into her mother's eyes. Her mother lovingly touched her face and started to sing a song that she had sung to her every night when she was small…

Sleep, sweet sleep till the morning.
Just dream away and close your eyes.
My love, you'll be safe until the morning.
Sleeping in my arms, all through the night.
Although bad dreams come to scare you.
My love will scare them all away. My heart…
The lights flickered, the pain went away, and her mother was holding her, singing: "Sleep, sweet sleep."

They sat in silence with no words. Kayn Brighton's redo began without a pause to catch their breath.

Kayn was standing in the shower at her old high school with water pleasurably beating down on her. Covered in suds and slightly confused, she rinsed herself off. She found her clothes, put them on and stopped to look at her reflection in the mirror. She noticed a bobby pin on the counter, tried to move it with her mind and couldn't. She glanced down at her hand, there was no scar. *Interesting, this must be her redo. Lovely, she was in this day.* She shoved on the change room door and there Kevin was with his mouth open wide, looking up at the sky. Her heart felt like it was about to explode. She wanted to say, catching flies as she had in the past but instead, she decided to change things up a bit. She'd always wondered what would have happened if she'd just walked up and broke their friendship façade while he was still the dorky, stubborn yet endearing version of himself.

He gave her a strange look as he asked, "Is something wrong?"

"No," she replied. "I didn't realise how perfect everything was until now."

Kevin looked a little concerned as he grinned and teased, "Meaning me, of course. I know my perfection has always been utterly overwhelming."

"That it has," Kayn replied as she looked down at her feet instead of into his eyes. She wanted to stay with him but she couldn't go lay in the grass and watch the clouds knowing her family was being slaughtered. *She'd felt it when her twin was being stabbed. That's what that sharp pain in her stomach had been. Maybe there was still time to change it.* Kayn stopped midstride and gave him a partial truth, "I can't come for dinner tonight. I need to go home, it's a Chloe emergency." Everything inside of her screamed, *kiss him! Kiss him just once!*

As tempted as she was, she stopped herself. *No, he'll follow you home. Just tell him you'll see him tomorrow.*

"Alright, you'll be missing out," Kevin teased as they strolled away from the school.

This was one of her last moments of peace. It was hard to know that and enjoy it. Kayn took a last look at Kevin, wanting to remember him like this. *How had she not seen him clearly?* Under her breath, she gave him a response, "Not this time." She was about to walk away when she realised it didn't matter what she did, everything had already happened. Unable to help herself, she gave him a quick kiss on the lips before walking away. When she looked back, he was still standing there with a shocked expression. Hopefully, he wasn't going to follow her home like a confused puppy in search of an explanation. *There was no time to worry and it didn't matter anyway.* She jogged till she reached the alley before the woods and then sprinted through the trails to her house, slowing her pace to text her sister four important words, lock the bathroom door. She pressed send. *Maybe she'd have the chance to see her twin one last time. If she didn't have a plan she'd just be showing up in the middle of the slaughter. Brains before brawn.* She grabbed a sturdy stick from the trail and chucked it, shaking her head at herself. *That would never work. Think Kayn. Think. Chloe was killed in the bathroom, her mother in the doorway and her father in the carport.* She suspected by only one man. Almost there, she walked. *What was she capable of changing?* She doubled over in agony. *It was too late. The Correction of her family had begun.* For a moment, the nervous energy paralyzed her. She fought to see through the fog of her mortal emotions. *She was going to be sick. Just breathe.* She crouched behind bushes to conceal herself. *Just breathe.* She heard her mother's car pull up. *She wanted to see her mother again so badly.* Her emotions were all over the place and they couldn't be. Her mother would be killed two seconds after she walked in *It had already happened. This was a test. The past had already happened. It couldn't be stopped. What did she need to move on? She needed to see the face of the man who destroyed her life. She needed to look into the eyes of the man responsible for the excessively brutal Correction.* She snuck through the backyard alongside of the house and noticed an open window. *That's how he got in.* She stealthily climbed through it without a sound. She heard her mother's voice as she announced she was home. Instinct began screaming for her to try to save her. *Brains before brawn, use logic Kayn.* She heard the struggle at the front door and then eerie silence, followed by the creaking of the assailant's footsteps on the stairs. *He was going to finish her sister off.* Kayn tiptoed against the wall down the hall to the kitchen, knowing exactly where to walk so the floor didn't creak. She slid a medium sized knife silently out of the holder and crept back down the hallway. *She couldn't stop anything that was meant to happen, but she could use this opportunity for good old-fashioned vengeance on the being who murdered her family and cruelly tortured her without reprieve before violently ending her mortal life.* She was not going to pocket dial Kevin this time. As she entered the living room, she dialed 911 on her cell and whispered, "3131 Falls Rd. He's killing everyone. Help us." She ended the call, cranked her dad's eighty's metal on the stereo and harnessed her inner Lexy. *She'd make him come to her.* Kayn clutched the knife as her heart pounded vigorously. She allowed the rage to swell inside until she felt the energy of her fury crackling beneath the surface of her skin. He'd appeared to her the first time as a shadow in the darkened hallway. This time there was no lurking in the shadows. He walked into the room with an intrigued smile on his face. Chloe's voice whispered in her mind, "Let's kill him Kayn."

"What do you think you can do to me child?" He chuckled as he leaned up against the china cabinet, with eyes as black as night. *There was no visible white at all. Her Correction hadn't been done by Clan. The Legion of Abaddon had done her Correction and this revelation changed everything. She wasn't strong enough to fight this being. She hadn't been Enlightened. She was going to be brutally slaughtered all over again. Crap! She was going to have to run, but that hadn't worked the last time…Had it?* She needed to contemplate her next move. *She couldn't beat him. He had the strength of ten of her.* In her mind, she heard the words, *brains before brawn.* She had to make it past him to the kitchen so she amped herself up. *He killed your family. Think about your mother, your father, your sister...Think about Chloe. What would Chloe do?* Kayn met his black pool eyes and vowed, "Someday I'll kill you but today, I'll settle for pissing you off." She began rifling everything in the room at him. Laughing at her show of strength, the devious being didn't even try to stop her as she darted past, down the hall into the kitchen. He casually strolled after her like a killer from a horror movie. *Brains before brawn.* She grabbed the heavy bag of salt from beside the sundeck door. Its purpose had been to keep the doorways from getting icy but today she was changing shit up. Kayn slit it open with her knife and spun around as she tore it spraying salt all over the Abaddon. He shrieked as it scalded his flesh. Like a badass, she plunged her knife into his liver, booted him in the stomach and sent him flying backwards. Buying herself a few precious moments, her shaking hands fumbled with the lock as the demonic entity in mortal disguise struggled to his feet. He was losing a lot of blood. She caught the scent as she slid open the door and ran. She leapt off the sundeck like a superhero and sprinted across the back lawn, tossing what was left of the bag of salt at the mouth of the trail for old time's sake. He staggered after her to the sound of approaching sirens. Her eyes kept darting back to her mortally wounded foe. She smirked as she kept her eyes on her snail-paced assailant while pressing redial. She dramatically gasped, "Help, I'm in the trails behind my house." He paused for a second and started shaking while hunched over. *She'd beaten him.* He straightened up and she realised he was laughing. *Well, shit! She'd stabbed him in the damn liver, how was he still alive?* He grinned and began chasing her at full speed. *Crap!* She sprinted through the trails and across the bridge, this time with shoes on. Her heart was pounding wildly with the knowledge of how this played out. Kayn saw the light of the man's porch. As she was about to break through the bushes, she braced herself for the inevitable burning explosion of pain. The knife plunged into her back. She saw the flashlights flickering through the trees and heard voices. He had her in his arms, brutally squeezing the breath from her chest. She could feel her ribs snapping. *How was this asshole still alive? She'd stabbed him in the liver. His shell should have died before he made it off the damn sundeck.*

The dark being whispered in her ear, "Until we meet again," as he released her, yanking the blade from her back.

The fire that lit a path through her core ceased. She harnessed her rage, kicked back and booted him in his shin. His knife dropped as she swung around and drop kicked him in the groin with everything she had. He doubled over in agony and staggered backwards. She fell to her knees with a giant grin on her face and as he ran away, she whispered, "You can count on it." She felt the warmth of her blood as it soaked through her shirt. *He'd made that one wound count.* Kayn knew what he was now and she would count the seconds until the next time he crossed her path. When she was Enlightened, they would be fighting on even ground. The lights flickered and went out.

Grey smiled as Kayn's redo ended. He looked at the others and whispered one word, "Wow."

Jenna spoke aloud, "We may have underestimated Miss Kayn Brighton. She was Corrected by Abaddon and in her redo, she fought back knowing she couldn't win. Go into your training knowing the two girls are close to being emotionally prepared but Zach needs a few lessons in anger awareness."

"Maybe the redo was enough," Grey piped in. He climbed into one of the remaining tombs with Lexy. They'd help them lick their wounds first before putting them through the ringer one last time.

Jenna peered into the tomb at the two and ordered, "Work them hard. This is the last chance to help them conquer those fears."

As the tomb ground closed, Lexy and Grey stared at each other and smiled. *Sometimes it didn't seem like much time had passed since they went into the Testing with Arrianna. They'd also been three Ankh against six in each of the other Clans when they'd earned their tombs.* Lexy took Grey's hand as she whispered, "This group might survive the Testing, just like we did."

"I'd be willing to bet on it...Now," Grey replied as he took her hand.

Chapter 31

Famous Last Words

The tomb pulsed with blinding light and they were shot up into eternity. The experience of travelling to the in-between via tomb never got old. They hooted together in their excitement. Every second was amazing and each trip was slightly different than the last. Lexy's heart pounded with anticipation as their rapid movement upwards began to slow. She took a deep breath as they paused before the stomach-churning descent. In a matter of moments, she felt the wind rippling across her skin, the dampened air of the clouds as they passed through them. There was this sensation as the wind rippled through her crimson hair. It felt like the tickle of fingers running through it. Grey was falling beside her. They'd ceased to fear this part of the ride long ago. They both found it equally exciting. Their descent began to slow and they landed on their feet in the warm silken sand of the in-between. This moment always felt like returning home. Lexy wiggled her toes and turned to find Grey staring at her. Lexy plunked herself down in the warm sand and glanced up at her best friend, signalling him to join her. Grey sat down beside her and they both began to trail their fingers through the luxurious feeling sand. Grey wrote Arrianna's name in the sand then wiped it away by passing his hand over the area without touching it. Lexy understood how he was feeling. She felt the same way. *It always felt like they were missing someone. They'd gone into hell as a trio. They'd survived it and for ten years they'd been together before Arrianna left*

311

with the other part the Clan. She suspected they'd removed her from their trio on purpose. Arrianna and Grey's relationship had become messy. It was difficult for them to work together and she'd been removed from the situation. Lexy picked up a handful of sand. She watched it trickle through her fingers.

Grey remarked, "Don't you wish we could just stay here together for a while? Just hang out, and build sandcastles, without a care in the world."

Lexy started to try to dig a moat with the palm of her hand. The sand was so dry and slippery, that idea was not going to come to fruition. She grinned and said, "Sorry Greydon. It doesn't look like it's going to happen." She glared at him as he thought about them needing water. "Seriously Grey, you know better." They both leapt to their feet and checked the horizon in every direction for the wall of water they knew he may have summoned by even thinking about it. They stood frozen in place for a minute or two longer, prepared to run.

Grey chuckled, "I think we're safe."

Lexy grinned at him. He shouldn't have said that aloud either. He was off his in-between game after witnessing Kayn, Melody and Zach's redos. Her mind also kept travelling through the excess of information and emotions not her own.

"Do you remember the first time we came here together? Grey asked as he held out his hand.

She took it. *She would always take it. Grey was going to try to do his job, even though he was a mess himself. He was going to attempt to calm the Dragon. The reality of their situation was that he was her Handler. He was both her wings and chains.* He pulled her to him and started to dance with her even though there was no music.

He whispered in her ear, "Once you've seen someone's darkest moment, it's difficult to distance yourself. I know you try to keep yourself free of emotion. The odds of their survival are seriously crappy, but I also know you care, even though you try to act like you don't."

Lexy rested her head against Grey's shoulder. *She had to keep her mouth shut. The Clan couldn't separate them if things went wrong. He was her Handler. He couldn't ever be replaced, not for her. Damn logic, it was wrecking her fantasy. It had never gone past the first day romantically. Maybe it would have never lasted longer than a week, given the chance to play itself out. She had to get her head on straight. They were supposed to be running the three through their last bit of training. They weren't supposed to be dancing in the sand barefoot.*

Lexy closed her eyes. She thought of Zach and the kinship she felt towards him after witnessing the abuse he'd suffered as a child. *He'd come from a dark place. Jenna said they would need a Dragon in the group to make it out of the Testing. Maybe, it was Zach?*

Grey dipped her and enquired, "How do you feel about having another Dragon in the Clan?"

Lexy laughed, *he'd been listening to her thoughts.* She baited, "I'd love it if there was another Dragon. To have someone who understood me, somebody else capable of doing the dark deeds."

They continued to slowly dance to no music as Grey looked into her eyes and professed, "I understand you."

"Most of the time," she provoked.

He twirled her and chuckled, "Almost all of the time."

Lexy laughed, he'd just reworded the same thing. She whispered in Grey's ear, "Your girlfriend Melody is a badass. I'm officially impressed. She's an incredibly talented Healer."

Grey spun her around and laughed, "I guess the cats out of the bag with that flash of us in the in-between? Orin didn't say anything about it, but for the record, she's never going to be my girlfriend. She doesn't want that either."

Lexy winked and teased, "Right, famous last words."

He grinned and whispered in her ear, "She's really not that into me." Without warning he pushed her away and twirled her around again. Lexy lost her footing, as he let go of her hand and she landed in the sand with a not so graceful thud. She started to laugh, as she wiped the grains off her face, and spit the desert floor out of her mouth. She gave Grey the dirtiest look she owned and scolded, "You did that on purpose, you stinker."

He held out his hand. She took it reluctantly, partnered with a venomous glare. He chuckled as she swept his foot. Grey fell flat on his back in the sand with a similar sounding thud. He started laughing and said, "You want to rumble, don't you?"

She always wanted to. Lexy grinned and helped him up.

He didn't let go of her hand as he assured, "Melody and I are just convenient. We're just friends with benefits. It will be an awkward thing to explain to Orin when he calls me on what he saw in her flashes of memory. I'm honestly a little bit flattered that I was included."

Lexy sighed, "Orin is a thousand years old. He'll forgive you. Maybe, he didn't see it?" They started to walk through the seemingly endless span of desert together. Lexy tossed out, "Kayn obviously went into her redo with the sole purpose of seeing her killer's face."

"That appears to be what she did," he remarked.

It took a lot to disturb Lexy. *The man who had slaughtered Kayn's family had been Abaddon. Kayn and Chloe's Correction had been done by Abaddon, but why? Her family hadn't been murdered they'd been slaughtered. This had been an extermination of her family line. How had she survived? She had seen where the knife had gone in and how many times she had been stabbed. It was impossible. She'd been around long enough to know that some situations could only be fully understood once they played out. This would be the last chance to help them understand the concept of the Testing. They'd been through this before.* Lexy glanced at Grey and prompted, "Time to get started?"

Grey replied, "Might as well. We've got a lot of ground to cover."

They thought of Kayn, Melody and Zach, and in an instant, they were strolling through a grassy meadow towards them. They were perplexed to find the three Ankh fresh from their emotional re-enactments of their Sweet Sleep rolling around trying to face wash each other with grass. Their green smudged faces were extremely comical looking.

"Seriously kids, this is not very mature of you," Grey teased.

That sentiment coming from him added to the hilarity as they tackled Grey to the grass. Lexy just stood there shaking her head. They carried on the grass fight for another ten minutes while Lexy stood there watching. *Grey was always going to be a big kid.* Lexy cleared her throat. Grey stood up holding a handful of grass, looking guilty. The others froze mid grass toss. Lexy proclaimed, "I was certain we'd appear to find the three of you sobbing, distraught over the redo of your Sweet Sleep, but instead the three of you are wrestling in the grass like a pack of sugar loaded children." Grey tossed a handful of grass at her. She waved her hand in front of her face to block it without touching a blade of grass, it spread out travelling away in the wind. Lexy glared at Grey and sighed, "Make that four kids." She stared at her immature Handler until he brushed himself off with an enormous childlike grin. "Okay, enough shenanigans. Get up and brush the grass off. We have a lot left to cover," Lexy ordered in her most domineering tone of voice. Zach grinned at Lexy. You could tell something naughty was going to slide from between his sly lips.

Zach provoked, "Do I get a spanking from you if I misbehave?"

"Get up," Lexy ordered. She made a valiant attempt to avoid succumbing to the laughter that bubbled up behind her tightly pursed lips. They scrambled to their feet. The mismatched group of grass covered, messy-haired playmates all attempting to keep a straight face. They'd been through the ringer. They were in obvious need of a mental break. They hadn't had the opportunity to process the redo of their Sweet Sleep yet, so with their minds numbed and exhausted, they'd be capable of little until they had a small mental vacation. Kayn raised her hand and slapped Zach on the forehead.

Zach stumbled over, hand on his head and hissed, "What in the hell?"

Kayn grinned and said, "Mosquito."

Zach shook his head and stood quietly for a second before hauling off and smoking her rear. Kayn cried out, cupping her nearly bare butt cheek with her hand. She glared at him.

Zach casually baited, "Mosquito."

Beaming like a mischievous kid, Grey remarked, "You know it's going to be pointless. They need some time to recharge their unhinged brains."

Grey was right. Lexy sighed, "Why don't you three take the rest of the day to think, dream, and have a good scream. Do whatever you need to do. We'll come back for you. We need you to be ready to train with your sane brains on." Grey and Lexy turned around and began to walk away. Grey smacked her on the behind as hard as he could. She scowled at him. She was already annoyed. That wasn't a bright move.

Grey chuckled, "Mosquito."

They walked about ten more paces before Lexy snatched Grey's legs out from underneath of him, wielding his entire body in the air as effortlessly as a blanket, whirled him in a circle and smoked his whole body against the ground. Grey lay there gasping with the wind knocked out of him. Lexy leaned over and whispered, "Mosquito." She casually rose, glanced back at the three newbies and strolled away. A few seconds later, Grey scrambled to his feet and caught up with her. She was laughing as they disappeared and the scenery altered. They were now standing on the shore of an endless ocean. Lexy chuckled, "Apparently you want to go swimming."

Clutching the small of his back, Grey complained, "I was aiming for a hotspring."

Lexy took his hand and prompted, "Well, let's go then." They both closed their eyes and thought about hotsprings, opening them to find themselves standing by a series of caves. Looking around, Lexy admitted, "I've never been here before, have you?"

Grey responded, "No, I haven't been here. Let's go inside and check it out. We might as well have a little adventure while we wait for the others to come back to reality."

They climbed through the narrow opening on their hands and knees. Lexy did not like enclosed spaces. She was doing this for him and no other reason. She was quite aware that she'd probably slide down a five-hundred-foot-long ice ramp bare assed if he asked her to. She'd jump into a pool of lava without a second thought if that's what he needed from her. The entrance narrowed until they had to crawl on their stomachs to fit through. *She didn't like this. She really didn't like this at all.*

Grey was ahead of her. He called out, "Are you alright?"

He knew of her adversity to tight spaces. She replied, "If this doesn't open up to a larger cave in about five seconds, I'm backing my ass out of here."

He laughed from up ahead, "Duly noted." There was a brief pause as they continued to crawl into lord knows where. He loudly urged, "I see light up ahead, we're almost out."

"Good thing, because I was just about to back the hell out of here," she sparred. She saw the light glinting up ahead as Grey vanished from view. *Where in the hell did he go?"*

He reappeared and extended his hand to her. She grabbed it, he dragged her out and helped her stand. She felt a touch of sanity as she took her first unrestricted breath. It was then that she became aware of her surroundings. It was breathtaking. This was a reward worth the discomfort. It was a rose quartz cavern with chunks of amethyst and jade underfoot. There was a large bubbling hotspring set in rose quartz.

Grey climbed into the heated pool and lounged with his arms stretched out on the ledge. He sighed and urged, "Get your behind in here Lex you're missing out. This is truly amazing."

She gingerly climbed into the pearled pink pool of steaming water, feeling an instantaneous calm as she submerged herself in the liquid heaven. Lexy rested her head on the ledge and let a sigh escape. *It felt amazing.*

He whispered, "Wow, this is awesome."

Lexy met Grey's eyes and agreed, "It's incredible." They both smiled. The cavern went pitch black for just long enough for them to make an attempt to scramble out of the water. Suddenly, the rose quartz pool illuminated, and the ceiling came to life with the reflective glare of thousands of glittering diamonds.

"It looks like constellations on the ceiling," he gasped.

Lexy watched him smiling, staring up awestruck. With her heart full of adoration, his joy was contagious. He was ridiculously delighted. It wasn't the beauty of the place that made her happy, it was Grey's appreciation for the beauty of the moment. Most of the time she responded to situation's in refection to what she saw in him. She watched his eyes sparkle with joy and wished she could feel things as deeply as he did. The only thing she felt with that kind of certainty was her love for him. She loved him enough to stay on her side of the pool even though this was one of the most romantic places she'd ever been. The sparkling diamonds lit up the ceiling like stars in a clear summer night sky. While submerged in the calming influence of the steaming water of the rose quartz pool, Lexy made a decision, *she loved Grey enough to let him go. She had to attempt to move on.* She wasn't sure how long they stayed in the heavenly pools. She looked at her pruned hands and started to laugh. She held them up and he did the same.

Grey chuckled, "And that my friend is the universal signal for, get out of the water."

They both reluctantly exited the wondrous pools of relaxation, expecting the light to come back on as they stepped out of the water. *No such luck.* Grey went in first. Lexy followed as they endeavoured to crawl back through the tight space between the stones in the dark. *This sucks, it really sucks,* Lexy chanted in her mind as she squirmed in her water logged thigh high toga through the snug space between the stone. Grey tugged her out on the other end. Outside the cave's entrance, he held her against him for a second to long. Lexy placed her hand on his chest between them to stick to her newfound rules regarding the status of their friendship. *Platonic, they would go back to being platonic friends. There would be no anger over what he couldn't remember. The complications would end. She had to love him at arm's length.*

Grey enquired, "How long do you think we've been gone?"

"Not a clue, but we'd better get back to work," Lexy responded as they held hands and took a few steps together, thinking of the trio they'd left alone. Suddenly, they were standing in the jungle. She cracked a grin, "I did not see that coming."

Beaming like a fool, Grey declared, "I know where we are. Miss Melody likes me more than she pretends to."

Let it go Lexy. Let it go. Lexy sighed and shook her head as she admitted, "How could she not like you, Grey? You're the best guy on the planet."

He playfully shoved her and teased, "You're my best friend. You have to say stuff like that."

No, she didn't, but it was the truth. He was the best guy. They came upon the three newest Ankh, still joking around. Not much had changed since they'd left them earlier. They heard them before they could see them.

They heard Melody say, "Bibbidy boobidy boo."

"There's no such thing," Zach chuckled as he bumped into Lexy.

As they strolled up to the trio, Lexy asked, "No such thing as what?"

"Witches," Zach replied.

Letting go of her hand, Grey laughed, "Of course there are witches."

Melody asked, "Vampires, dragons and zombies?"

Grey chuckled, "Don't even get me started. One form of necrophilia should be outlawed, the other one is a lot of fun, right Lexy?"

Lexy choked as she laughed. Grey hit her on the back. *He'd made a dig at a short-lived fling. Funny.* Lexy got sucked into Kayn's inner dialogue. She was thinking without a filter again.

Kayn thought, *'the premise behind vampirism was sort of hot. She was even trying to think about zombies in a sexy way. She pictured one with missing chunks of flesh hanging off its face, and the nasty scent of decomposing flesh. It wasn't a sexy thought. Dragons...would be sort of a bestiality thing?'* Kayn was still tossing around messed-up thoughts when Grey asked her what she was thinking about.

After listening to Kayn's thoughts, Lexy looked at her Handler and teased, "Grey, you've known Kayn long enough to comprehend the depravity of her messed up sense of humour. Trust me; you don't really want her to answer that question."

Kayn winked at Lexy and chuckled, "No offense but theoretically if we had sex wouldn't it be necrophilia?"

She wasn't sure? Grey boldly took Kayn's hand and placed it on his chest. Lexy shook her head at her friend. *He'd flirt with a damn telephone pole.*

Her ridiculously naughty Handler toyed, "We are alive. We're living, breathing beings. Our hearts beat just like any mortal. We just heal a little faster, a lot faster if it happens to be your gift. That is why some of us can't end up in the hospital without freaking everyone out."

"I accidentally freaked someone out so badly they died the last time I ended up in the hospital," Zach remarked.

Grey grinned and rolled his eyes at him and said, "You know what I mean."

Kayn had been avoiding eye contact with Grey since he'd placed her hand on his chest. He hadn't missed her response. He wouldn't be able to resist teasing her now.

Taking her hand, Grey seduced, "Every reaction to stimulation is precisely the same as a mortal." He rubbed his finger slowly, rhythmically in circles on the soft flesh of Kayn's wrist, looking at her with his intense blue pools of seduction.

With sandy blonde hair swept across his brow, Grey looked like the male version of an angel. A naughty angel that threw temper tantrums with a sexy accent. "Oh, for heaven's sake Grey," Lexy hissed. "We have things to do, focus please."

Kayn exhaled slowly and yanked her hand away. Still staring her down, Grey stepped away grinning. Lexy was dying to expose him. *It was the pool of water by the apple tree that was making her feel romantically funny.*

Melody poked Kayn's arm and taunted, "I bet Grey comes and hangs out by this pool of water every time he comes to the in-between, hoping to find an emotionally distraught pliable girl."

Kayn lunged and punched Grey in the arm. He started laughing. She asserted, "I forgot where I was standing. You my friend are a jerk." They continued to walk away from the tidal pool of seduction. Kayn grinned and glared at Grey who was still most impressed with himself.

Melody poked her again and said, "You couldn't have reminded me of that tiny tidbit of information before you left? You left me alone with Zach."

Howling, Grey provoked, "Did you seriously fall under the tidal pool's spell again?" He winked at Mel and tried to mess her hair. They wrestled as she swatted him away. Grey threatened, "You better be good to her Zach or you'll have me to answer to."

Zach looked at Grey with wide innocent eyes and said, "I know better. We're friends. I never touched her."

Lexy smiled at Zach. *He was a much better guy then she'd given him credit for.*

Kayn put her arm around Melody and whispered in her ear, "I think Grey's jealous."

Mel whispered, "He's just a big kid splashing girls with water. I have a feeling he's never really serious about anyone."

Lexy placed her hand over her mouth to stop herself from laughing. *Melody wasn't remotely serious about Grey. She had him pegged like she'd known him for years.* Lexy glanced his way, he was a little wounded by Mel's words. She placed her arm around Grey and whispered in his ear, "Stop flirting with the girls, it's time to get down to business." Lexy threw a cold bucket of water on the conversation with her words, "So, what do you all think your Testing will consist of?"

Zach answered promptly, "A coliseum old school style, with the grandstands full."

Grey stepped back into the conversation and enquired, "Tell me Zach…Do you like video games?"

"I will have you know, I was the Halo champion of my family," Zach replied as he shuffled through the long grass.

Kayn was listening to their conversation, not watching where she was walking and almost bailed in the thigh high grass. Lexy grabbed her and gave her a disapproving look as she released her grasp. *She'd never known anyone this uncoordinated.*

Kayn piped into the conversation, "I was never much of a gamer but I did alright with a lightsaber playing Star Wars at Kevin's house. Trivial Pursuit Unhinged was my family's game night thing. I have amazing deductive reasoning skills."

"I'm good at board games." Melody added.

Grey carried on speaking, "As you know, fear can stifle your abilities. There is no need for fear. You can die repeatedly during your Testing. It will be just like playing a video game. You will be healed and sent back into the game. No death, no matter how violent, will be permanent. You need to leave your sentiments outside of the Testing. Emotional connections will only leave you vulnerable…Kayn." She slowly nodded without looking at him.

Zach stopped walking aimlessly through the grass. He sighed, "No matter how violent. Great. I was right, wasn't I?

It is an old-school coliseum, isn't it? Are we battling people? Third tiers? Will the three of us be together?"

Lexy stopped walking, turned to face the group and proclaimed, "We aren't permitted to tell you everything. Melody, you'll be able to heal quickly, this is an advantage physically but a disadvantage mentally. Zach and Kayn, you'll most likely be Enlightened during the game. You'll have to attempt to stay on task and I assure you, it won't be easy. When you are first Enlightened, you'll find yourself reacting as an addict would, craving whatever fuels your ability. You'll need to help each other through this."

With sympathy in his eyes, Grey addressed Zach, "Your pain level may need to be heightened to an absurd point to trigger your Enlightenment because of your tolerance as a mortal."

Lexy met Zach's gaze. *She'd seen his Sweet Sleep. He had an incredibly high pain tolerance. It was both sad and impressive. She was a Dragon and the ability to withstand a large amount of pain was a gift all on its own.* Wishing she'd understood this about him sooner, Lexy drew her attention away from Zach as she addressed the group, "There will be weapons for you to use. You'll find them in random places. There'll be swords, knives, clubs, arrows and salt. So, our first lesson today is on arrows. Trinity will have an advantage over the other Clans. Arrows are their Clans preferred weapon. Mel should be alright but there isn't enough time to even you two out with their skill level, but we can teach you how to evade them. The arrows will be drugged as I'm sure you all know. If one hits you, it doesn't matter if it only nicks your arm. The poison will take hold and you'll eventually go down." A bow appeared in Lexy's hands.

The scenery flashed with brilliant white light and they were now standing in the forest. With a comical tone, Grey announced, "We're counting to twenty...I'd run if I were you."

"Are you serious?" Kayn questioned.

Lexy began to count. Melody and Zach ran instantly, but Kayn took a second to embrace the reality of the people hunt. Once Kayn took off running, they shot off a few arrows and then sat down on a log together. They would give them some time to hide. This was the part of training Lexy loved to be a part of. She knew this was also Grey's favourite part. In Clan Ankh the whole bow and arrow thing was a part of the training they glazed over. They concentrated more on sword play and one on one combat. Neither Grey nor Lexy had any skill with a bow, but they could fake it. The whole point for the three was to run, which was an important part of the Testing. To be able to think on their toes and make split second decisions. The sounds of the forest were soothing. She closed her eyes to take in the chirps of birds, and gentle pitter patter of the rain, as it trickled through the branches and hit the leaves on the forest floor. She opened her eyes just in time to watch Grey close his. He was smiling as he felt the raindrops hitting his face. He was a remarkable guy. She'd always wanted to feel things as he did. She would watch him with wonder, enjoying the fact that he was having a moment. She closed her eyes and the raindrops that hit her face were just wet. She tried to leave them there instead of wiping them away. It was driving her crazy, she grimaced.

Grey teased, "Oh just wipe them off Lex. You know you want to."

She scrunched up her nose, wiped it off and confessed, "I wish I could see things as you do. To me, rain is just annoying."

Grey squeezed her shoulder and taunted, "That's why I'm me and you're you. Maybe, I wish I was capable of ripping off a serial murderer's arm and beating him with it?" He started to chuckle before she had a chance to find a clever reply. *He'd been joking.*

"Oh, come on. It was a serial murderer. It wasn't like I tore Bambi's leg off and beat him with it," Lexy mumbled.

Grey chuckled, "Thanks for that visual."

"It was an accident," Lexy countered. "He cut the strap off my shoe and he wouldn't let go of the knife. I borrowed those, they weren't mine."

Grinning, he provoked, "Well, that explains it. I understand now, not excessive violence, he should have known better. Nobody messes with Lexy Abrelle's shoes."

He'd used her mortal last name. It had been a long time since she'd heard it spoken aloud. Every time she heard the last name on her birth certificate, she wondered who that girl would have been if she'd been raised by her mother. Who was her father? He must have been immortal. Why had he never made himself known? She was a bit of a loose cannon, this was true. Hence, the accidentally severed arm. Why was she thinking about this? It didn't even matter.

Grey asked, "A penny for your thoughts?"

Her thoughts were too scattered to tell him what she was thinking. Instead, she brought up something she'd been curious about, "Was Kayn's Correction excessively violent or was it just me?"

"It wasn't you. I noticed that too," Grey answered, continuing his zen rain worshipping.

Watching him with wonder, she prodded, "Did you notice anything else?"

He responded, "The Abaddon thing?"

"The Correction was done by Abaddon," she clarified.

"It's strange that they did a Correction for someone who didn't end up with them," he remarked, still in his own little world.

There were peculiar things running around in her mind. She had a difficult time attaching to others yet wanted to attach to these three kids. It was more than that with Kayn. This girl had intrigued her from day one. Even more so, now that she knew Abaddon had done her Correction. There were Abaddon on the dark farm that gave birth to the Dragon residing within her. She'd seen so many Abaddon soldiers over the years. Some appeared to be mortal, until you took a closer look. They'd given them enough of a head start. "We should go hunt those kids down and try to look like we know how to shoot these bows," Lexy announced as she got up and cracked her neck.

Grey stood up, stretched and got all mushy, "I was just enjoying some down time with my favourite person." He put his arm around her and gave her shoulder a squeeze. He released her, as two quivers full of arrows appeared on the ground. He tossed one at her.

She grabbed it in midair and baited, "Back atcha, Greydon." *He hated being called Greydon but it was time to be feisty.* He taunted, "Cute."

Only he would think she was cute. Together, they walked into the forest of the in-between as they'd done a thousand times before. They chased the trio, pretending to know what they were doing, but neither had ever been even a half descent shot with a bow. They did fake the ability to near miss on purpose. They even managed to hit a few moving targets and kept up the facade for the rest of the training, even though each time they took one of them down it was by random fluke. By the time Lexy was finished the final act of training, she was more than a little bit ready to stop chasing three teenagers through the woods. It was always fun for a little while, because it was time spent with Grey. It was time to go back to the land of the living. Tonight, they would get a chance to witness the dynamics between the Clans. Only once every five-years did they come together under strict rules to behave. This was always an inconvenient situation for her. She had to control her violent urges instead of acting upon them and it was easier ordered than done.

Chapter 32

Flirting With Disaster

She applied her signature cherry red lipstick to her full pouty lips, pressed them together and ran her fingers through her hair. Outside of their cabin, she heard scurrying feet and the chattering of voices. Lexy accidentally dropped her lipstick on the floor, and it rolled under the dresser. When she crouched and attempted to grab for it, she couldn't quite reach. So, she sat cross-legged on the floor and tried again. Her hand brushed against one of the envelopes taped under it. They'd been hidden there many decades ago. She tossed around the idea of reading them. In envelopes were the notes she'd written with Grey and Arrianna. They were like time capsules. They'd each written a list of secrets and dreams, while drinking, so they ought to be good. They weren't allowed to read them unless one of them was entombed, or until 50 years had passed. *She knew what she'd written in hers. She'd promised Grey she'd behave herself tonight, but sometimes that was easier said than done. He'd always wanted a chance to go to one of these Clan banquets without having to leave.* Lexy picked up Grey's sweater and smelled it. Realising she may be seen, she shoved it back in his bag. *She really had to stop doing things like sniffing his sweatshirts.* She heard familiar voices outside and smiled. Each time something caused her to smile, she took note of it. *This was thanks to Grey.* The least she could do was grant him a night to cut loose. Lexy wandered over to the window and pulled back the blinds.

Zach was standing outside with Kayn and Melody. During Zach's Sweet Sleep, he'd been abused and buried alive. She was always impressed when someone endured a version of hell she hadn't experienced. She found herself staring at him, wondering if it was time to let him off the hook about the whole vengeance thing before she sent him into the Testing. A part of her even found him attractive now. *She should hit on him. That would confuse the hell out of him.* She stepped outside into the woodsy fresh air, inhaling deeply. She spotted Triad packing bags into a cabin directly across the path. *There he was, the supreme master of all douchedom. It was the one and only, Tiberius of Triad.* Out of the corner of her eye she noticed Frost and Grey chatting as they came up the stairs to the cabin.

Grey snuck up beside her, poked her side and provoked, "Oh look, it's your boyfriend."

Lexy spun around and walked back into the cabin. *She wasn't going to dignify that crap with a response.*

"He's staring over here, Lexy," Grey teased.

She glanced in Tiberius's general direction, and sure enough, he was staring right at her. *What a pathetic loser.* Lexy glared at her Handler as he tried to poke her again and hissed, "Do you want me to pluck all your toenails out and force feed them to you? Is that really how you want to spend your day?" She sensed the dig coming, he was always ready with some form of annoying, slightly pervie commentary.

"I think the lady doth protest too much," Frost provoked.

She swung around and socked Frost in the stomach. He dropped to his knees on the cabin floor. Grey was howling laughing as Frost valiantly struggled to catch his breath.

Frost choked out, "No fair, you never hit Grey."

Hugging her from behind, Grey taunted, "Well, if you cuddled with her once in a while maybe she wouldn't hit you either?"

Lexy swatted Grey away and shot daggers at Triad's cabin with her eyes. Her pulse began to race. She had to burn off some of this negative energy before attempting to be civilized this evening. She was going to have to hurt herself and heal. That would take the edge off. *Tiberius had always made her crazy.* Lexy casually leaned against the doors frame, feeling the urge to inconspicuously observe him. She wanted to rip Tiberius's arm off and beat him to death with his own severed limb. *That would be so much fun. This cease fire was inconvenient.* Tiberius was carrying a bag up the stairs. He put it down on the deck and blew her a kiss. *Asshole.* The older members of the Clan were going to the Summit, where somebody usually had to fight for the entertainment of the third tiers. *He'd be gone by tomorrow.* Lexy was kind of jealous. She'd always wanted to go. She strolled out the front door and down a few stairs, without saying a word. Tiberius was far overdue for his yearly beating. She secretly loved to hate him. He was the most disgusting vile excuse for a man on the planet. He'd done horrible things. She despised him with every fiber of her being. He slowly removed his shirt on the deck. *She should look away.* He made eye contact and arrogantly smiled. *She hated him.* He nodded, motioning like he was perfectly willing to undo the zipper of his pants and give her a show. She scowled, he winked at her and she looked away so he wouldn't see her smile. Grey was standing by the door.

He scolded, "As your friend, I'd be personally disappointed in you."

Lexy climbed the stairs, gave him a hug and whispered, "Hell would have to freeze over for that to happen."

Grey kissed her head and chuckled, "Yet, somehow everybody still does it."

This was the truth. She'd heard the stories about his many dalliances with higher ranking members of the feuding Clans. She wasn't sure how they'd done it because, he repulsed her. He made her skin crawl.

Grey chuckled, "As your best friend, if you're ever finding yourself tempted to go there, allow me to set you up with anybody else on the planet."

Unable to help it, she teased, "Any suggestions?"

He sparred, "Hell, even Frost is a better idea."

Frost joined in, "I keep offering my services, Grey. She keeps turning me down. It's starting to hurt my feelings."

"You don't have feelings," Lexy chuckled. Frost grabbed her as she giggled, swung her over his shoulder and tossed her on the bed. She landed ungracefully, bouncing on the mattress. She tried to explain, "He took his shirt off and caught me staring. He started taking off his pants like an idiot. He hates me too. The feeling is quite mutual. He only flirts with me because he knows it makes me uncomfortable. I've killed him in many embarrassing ways."

Frost stretched out on the bed beside her and said, "I heard he's afraid of you. You intimidate the hell out of him. That has to make you smile."

She knew he was afraid of her. It did make her smile.

Grey sat down on the other side of her and the three began thinking up funny revenge plots. Frost chuckled, "If he thought you wanted him back, it would totally mess with his mind."

Lexy smiled as an idea popped into her head. She crawled over Grey, grabbed the bottle of sunblock and replied, "Great idea, we should mess with him." She hopped up and strolled over to the door. Frost followed her to the deck. Grey trailed behind the two. Lexy stretched and sighed, "I think I might want to go swimming." She removed her shirt. Wearing nothing but a string bikini top, she made eye contact with Tiberius. He was standing there attempting to pretend he wasn't watching her every move. She felt his eyes on her as she slowly unbuttoned her shorts, seductively slipped them over her rounded hips, revealing string bikini bottoms underneath. She glanced in his direction, stretched her arms above her head, and faked a yawn. She bent over the railing, making eye contact with Tiberius, she requested, "Frost, can you put sunblock on my back...Please?"

Frost chuckled, "This is downright mean. Are you sure you want to be toying with him like this? You are aware of what dogs do to their chew toys?"

Lexy smiled and sighed, "Dragons don't lower themselves to rolling around in the mud with dogs."

Frost sucked in his breath and said, "Okay, contrary to popular opinion, I do in fact have a heart and it's going to get stomped out if Kayn doesn't come back from the Testing. I'd like to keep things all warm and fuzzy until then, if possible."

Lexy sighed, "Don't be a silly Frost. It's just sunblock. Kayn won't care." He shook his head as he applied the lotion. She kept smiling and staring at Tiberius. *He was openly ogling her and had forgotten to play it cool.* She took the opportunity to wave at him, just like he'd done to her. Tiberius openly laughed.

"Frost move out of the way," Grey directed. "I've got this. Hold up your hair, I'll get the back of your neck. You always burn your shoulders."

"My shoulders stay burned for all of five seconds," she laughed. She'd forgotten to hide her reaction to Grey's fingers as they massaged sunblock onto her shoulders and the back of her neck. *What did it matter? He was completely oblivious. When his emotions were freshly reprogrammed, it usually worked for a while. If she was standing here naked, he'd probably look right through her and ask her for the time.*

He gave her a pat on the head and remarked, "There, you're good to go." Grey disappeared inside. *That brotherly pat on the head had rather effectively snuffed out her ego.*

Leaning against the railing, Frost commented, "It's always all fun and games until you involve your heart."

"Don't I know it," Lexy mumbled. Frost smiled, squeezed her shoulder and passed her a towel so she could cover up. *What was she doing? She was intentionally flirting with Tiberius. Had she gone insane?*

Grey appeared in the doorway. He stood there for a second before asking, "Are you feeling alright?"

It was his job as her Handler to know when she was off. He sensed her volatile state. Stripping in front of Tiberius was not something she'd usually do. She nodded and confessed, "I'm going to have to impale myself and heal before I go anywhere. I need to be taken down a notch. I feel aggressive, frustrated. Yes, I'm off, but I always feel this way when that tool is around." Grey knew the drill. She had to heal herself or heal somebody else to calm down. He walked over to the counter, grabbed a knife, brought it to the doorway and called her inside. Lexy closed the door behind her and Frost pulled the curtains closed. She held out her hand so Grey could pass her the knife. He didn't give it to her. Instead, he sat on the bed and sliced his thigh. His face contorted in pain. She shook her head and came to his aid, pressing her hands on his wound, she felt the warmth of her healing energy as it travelled down her arms into his leg. The volatile edge dissipated, and it was replaced by a sense of overwhelming love. She whispered, "You didn't have to that. You know I don't feel pain like you do. Why would you do that?"

He embraced her and whispered against her hair, "I love you. I'd do anything for you." He kissed her cheek and patted her hair.

Yes, she was still in the friend-zone. Lexy whispered, "I know you would, and I love you back." Lexy grabbed a sundress out of her bag and slipped it over her bikini clad body. She sat down on the bed beside him as she slipped on her sandals. He moved closer. She stood up and tried to walk away.

Grey grabbed her wrist and teased, "You're going to let me stab myself, heal me and then just leave me here? Where are you off to in such a hurry?"

She shook her head and disclosed, "I should get away from Triad's cabin. I'm amped up again and you can't keep stabbing yourself all day."

Grey rubbed his thumb on the pulse point of her wrist and suggested, "Perhaps, we should go talk to Orin? He might know a few tricks."

Lexy smiled and said, "Orin's a Healer, but he's not a Dragon. I just feel anxious. It's not a big deal. Don't worry about me."

Grey whispered, "It's sort of my job to worry about you. Let's just hang out for a while. We can go for a swim? Maybe go for a walk? We'll find something to do to burn off that excess energy."

She had a few suggestions, but she'd promised herself she wasn't going to do that anymore. She recognized that look on his face. *He was concerned, he had good reason to be. Did he still look at her and see a wild thing, he'd tamed? She'd been cleaned up and she made a conscious effort to fit into the Clan, but under it all she would always be a Dragon. Her humanity forever teetering on the edge. A reckless moment away from the creature that dwelled in the woods.* Lexy sat on the bed next to him and asked, "When I'm feeling like this. What do you see?"

Grey tenderly stroked her cheek with his thumb, gazed into her eyes and teased, "I'm afraid to answer you. This whole conversation feels like one of those girl traps."

She cracked a smile. *Whenever he behaved like this, she usually seduced him. He'd forget and they'd start over from scratch the next morning. She wasn't going to do that anymore.*

"Maybe you shouldn't play games with Tiberius while you're in this agitated state? It could be irritating your situation," he suggested.

Lexy flung herself back on the bed and sighed, "You're probably right." Grey climbed up beside her. They both curled up on the pillows and stared at each other. *She was his safe place and he was hers. In his mind it was that simple. He didn't want to wrinkle up his security blanket.* She fell asleep, gazing into her best friend's eyes.

Chapter 33

Dances With Assholes

Lexy stirred to the sound of Grey's voice. He caressed her cheek, and whispered, "Wake up beautiful, it's almost time to go." He kissed the spot where he'd touched her face and her pulse raced. *Calm down, she had to calm down.* She kept her eyes closed. He lovingly stroked her hair, allowing it to slip through his fingers. *Stop it Grey. He had to stop. Why was he doing this today of all days? She'd made a deal with her heart. She couldn't love him this way anymore.* She kept her eyes closed, knowing he'd see the darkness in them and refuse to leave her alone. *She needed to be left alone.* The short nap in Grey's protective embrace had done little to subdue her overwhelming need to release the Dragon within her. *The situation hadn't been caused by Grey, but that didn't matter. It couldn't be stopped by him either. He was her Handler, but today, she felt like a ticking bomb. She was in a dark place and she was so bloody sick and tired of being controlled. Everyone was always trying to tame her. They were always trying to tone her down, unless it suited their needs.* She got up, without making eye contact and wandered to the bathroom. *Grey was good at his job. He knew she was avoiding him.* He knocked on the door, without waiting for her response, he barged in. Lexy scowled at him and complained, "Can you please give me five minutes? I'm trying to get ready."

"Only if you promise you're not going to go off the bloody rails tonight," he bartered, intently watching her.

Lexy didn't bother to respond, *it was a given. She'd try, but with Tiberius here, anything could happen. He was going to spend*

334

the whole night pushing her buttons. She stared at his refection behind her in the mirror and remarked, "Fine then, Greydon. You're about to get an eyeful." She slipped off her sundress, unlaced the strings of her bikini right in front of him and casually discarded it on the floor. *Why should she care if he didn't?* It never took her long to get ready. Naturally stunning, all she really needed to feel complete was her crimson red lipstick and a short skirt. Tonight, she wore a tight dress. He didn't say anything about the stripping naked in front of him stunt. Her crass unruly behaviour just seemed to make him try to ignore her sexuality even harder. She looked in the mirror, feeling powerful.

He whispered, "You look absolutely stunning. They'll be lining up to hit on you. If you ignore Tiberius, maybe you can have some fun tonight?"

Her eyes glinted with the promise of mischief. She glanced at Grey. *He was worried. He should be, she had every intention of allowing her freak flag to fly tonight.* Grey sighed as they strolled out the cabin door side by side and shook his head. He had the ability to understand where she was in her head, without her saying a word aloud. He knew any speech he had planned would be ignored. Grey held onto the railing as they took the few steps from wood to dirt. Lexy descended in four-inch heels with the agility of a tiger on the prowl. She heard his thoughts, *'Shit.'* Lexy almost cracked a smile. They wandered down the root strewn path towards the motor home. It was a feat in high heels. She heard Grey's thoughts again, *'Come on, just let me finish eating dinner this year.'* She grinned and responded to what he hadn't spoken aloud, "I'll try." They arrived to find Kayn not even close to being ready. Lexy didn't blame the kid. She wanted to avoid the whole situation this evening. Her feelings were hurt by Kevin's ignorant behaviour the night before. Grey was blocked at the door by the other girls.

Zach chimed in from his seat at the picnic table outside, "Kayn's not ready. They're dressing up Brighton."

Still standing, Grey advised, "Let's go. They can meet us there. I have a sneaky suspicion I should take the moment of peace before the shit hits the fan tonight."

Lexy heard Grey's comment before the door closed. *With her excessively hostile demeanour this evening, it may be prudent to have his panties in a twist out the gate.* The others were racing around, trying to find something for Kayn to wear. She'd spent a great deal of time making young Kayn over in the past, but tonight, there was no time. They found an outfit that fit, applied her makeup and scooted her out the door. It had taken Lexy a good forty years to begin to understand the rituals of womanhood. It didn't feel like every conversation was alien, anymore. They were a little late. She heard the humming of music and buzzing of conversation before they reached the door. *Intuition whispered, be careful, watch out. Something is coming.* Lexy looked at the others. Kayn squeezed Melody's arm, as a show of support as they entered. *She'd learned to read between the lines. Kayn was upset about Kevin. That was obvious. Melody was upset about? Was it Grey? She really didn't know that much about her. She was curious. If she paid attention, she'd figure it out.*

Standing at the entrance to the hall were the infamous Brothers of Prophecy, Tiberius, Thorne and Frost. Markus appeared to be the referee. *She'd always been intrigued by the brother's dynamics. Thorne was the good one. When his eyes met Melody's, the anguish was visible. They'd obviously been more than friends, when she belonged to Trinity. Intriguing.*

Tiberius chuckled, as he leaned closer to Thorne and provoked, "You, my brother, have the worst poker face I've ever seen and it's been a long damn life."

"I can think of worse qualities than the inability to lie," Thorne countered, he stepped away from his younger brother, as though Tiberius had tainted his air space.

"Touché," Tiberius jousted with a knit brow making it obvious he hadn't missed his older brother's body language. With a wry little smile, Tiberius casually pushed his buttons by baiting, "I bet Frost tapped that."

Under his breath, Thorne uttered, "Quit trying to fluster me you jackass."

"Who even uses the word flustered anymore?" Tiberius ribbed.

"Keep it up and the next time we capture you I am going to shoot a dozen arrows up your ass little brother," Thorne vowed.

"Promises, promises," Tiberius teased as his gaze travelled to Lexy, he smiled and winked.

She despised him with every inch of her being.

Reading her mind, Grey squeezed her shoulder and whispered in her ear, "You look beautiful tonight, Lex."

He was placating her, it wasn't real. Her heart constricted as she flashed back to prior confessions of love. At some point he'd always told her she was beautiful. *Her emotions were heightened to a dangerous level tonight. Calm down. Let it go. You are choosing a different road.*

"You promised Markus you'd behave," he reminded.

He had to stop whispering in her ear. If he didn't stop with the intimate gestures, the part of her that was Dragon would shut her emotions down for self-preservation purposes, and the shit would hit the fan. She curtly said, "I'm aware of that." Lexy walked up, politely shook Thorne's hand and said, "It's nice to see you, Thorne."

Always the gentleman, Thorne smiled warmly and replied, "It's nice to see you too, Lexy."

There, she'd been nice to Thorne. Markus wasn't stupid. He knew she wasn't going to be able to behave for long. She glanced at Tiberius. His gaze was travelling appreciatively up the length of her legs. Her green eyes glinted. *If she were a girly girl, he may have enticed a blush with his overtly lewd behaviour, but Dragons don't blush.* Lexy strolled right past Tiberius and taunted, "Charmed as never."

Tiberius called after her, "Satan, it's so nice to see you again. Glad you could make the trip to hang with us mere mortals."

She stopped walking and turned around to glare at him. *Why must he always poke the damn Dragon?* Grey had her arm right away. *She wanted to storm back over there and knock him out cold.* "Well, isn't that the pot calling the kettle black?" Lexy sweetly sparred.

Markus appeared at her side, taking her hand, he leaned in close and whispered in her ear, "Do try to behave tonight. Might I politely suggest that you sit as far away from Tiberius as you can? He always tries to mess with you."

Lexy grinned and remarked, "If he behaves himself, I'll make a genuine attempt to behave myself." She watched Melody take Tiberius's hand. He whispered in her ear, and she stomped on his foot.

He abruptly yanked his hand away and scolded, "A cease fire means you're not allowed to do that sweetie."

She liked Melody. She turned to the banquet hall full of Clan. *Grey had been wrong when he'd suggested she could have anyone she wanted. They were all afraid of her.* She turned back and caught Tiberius getting touchy feely with Kayn, trying to intimidate her. He took the pins out of Kayn's hair. Again, she wanted to march over and punch him in the throat.

Tiberius teased, "Now that's much better. You look like the lion that you were always meant to be. You are not meant to be a mouse."

She was a mother lion and he was messing with her cub. "Touch her again and I'll show you what a Dragon is capable of," Lexy threatened.

Tiberius glanced at Lexy and provoked, "I dare you."

Lexy met his gaze with a fiery one of her own as she took Kayn's hand and whispered, "I'll fix your hair, it'll only take a second. Ignore Tiberius, nothing he says is important." She pinned her hair back up and pulled a few tendrils down around her face. She smiled and released her cub into the wild, "See you inside." Kayn almost had an extremely sexy moment as she strutted confidently away from Tiberius. Until she awkwardly stumbled in her heels and fell into Frost's arms. *She could only do so much.*

Frost whispered in Kayn's ear, tucked a ringlet behind her ear, propped her back up and advised, "Ignore my brother. Tiberius knows nothing of lions. Sheep are his cup of tea."

Tiberius teased, "Don't knock it till you've tried it brother."

"I'm hot enough to stick with my own species," Frost declared.

Thorne rolled his eyes and muttered, "Oh, for the love of everything sacred, you two are a thousand-years-old. Your immaturity level is actually painful."

Grinning, Tiberius jousted, "Mr. Monogamy doesn't find my shenanigans funny. Oh, thank god. If you did, I'd have to chuck it all and join a monastery."

"You'd never be able to stop talking long enough." Thorne bickered.

Frost boisterously laughed and piped in, "He'd light on fire as soon as he stepped through the gate."

"Right alongside of you," Tiberius provoked, patting Frost's shoulder.

"Touché," Frost chuckled. "You have me there."

They stopped laughing. *Lily must be here.* The group became silent as Lilarah cleared her throat. *She always had a way of making an entrance.* Grey grabbed her hand and towed her into the reception hall. *She was grateful Grey and Lily ceased to be a thing. That had sucked so badly.* They strolled over to Ankh's seating and he pulled out a chair for her. She felt her hostility dim. *He'd always been the perfect imaginary boyfriend.* She slid into her seat. Grey sat down beside her, placing his hand over hers on the table. She looked at him and he smiled. She sensed her Dragon's calmed state. *Her hostility had subsided.* She clasped her other hand on top of Grey's. *Their connection was an intensely spiritual one. Most of the time, they didn't need to use words.* She heard the clinking of glasses, and the faint buzzing of voices. *It wasn't overwhelming her anymore.* The décor was minimalistic white themed wedding reception with crystal and ornate candlesticks. Once everyone was seated, there was the high-pitched squeal of a microphone. Jenna and two others were standing at a wooden podium.

Jenna began to speak, "Some of you are probably wondering why you are here. I'm sure your Clans have already made you aware that your authority figures will be leaving you alone for the next week. There has always been a prearranged cease fire between the Clans while the leaders go to the Summit. The older members of your Clans that have already gone through the Testing are permitted to leave. The new untested Clan members must stay within a five-mile radius of this campground. This happens every five years, for one week. Anyone who disrupts this one-week term of peace will be entombed. This event is brought to you by The Aries Group. Enjoy your dinner and spirits."

Grey left the table to get them a drink. He'd only left her alone for a minute but Lexy had killed enough people in this room to make it more than a little awkward for her. She went to find Grey. As she made her way to the bar, someone's legs blocked her path. She looked down. *It was him.*

"We should finish what we started this afternoon," Tiberius flirtatiously provoked.

Lexy smirked and baited, "Oh honey, you couldn't handle me even if I came with blow by blow instructions."

He lowered his voice to a seductive whisper, "Sweetheart, five minutes alone with me and I'd have you screaming my name so hard you'd lose your voice for a week."

Where normally she would have had something clever to say, she froze as her pulse raced. *What was wrong with her? Oh yes, she was forcing her heart to put Grey back in the friend-zone, and Tiberius had brilliant timing.* He brushed his thumb suggestively against her inner thigh, it gave her the shivers. Her throat was dry as she swallowed. *She'd reacted to his touch. He'd seen it with his own eyes. Now, no matter what she said or how much she pretended to despise him, he knew different. He knew a part of her wanted him to touch her. She couldn't have that.* Lexy hauled off and cuffed him. Grey towed her away, a second too late. She glanced back at Tiberius. He was smirking and rubbing his jaw. *He'd loved it.* She bit her lip. *Tiberius was a Dragon too.*

"Seriously, you hit Tiberius five minutes into the damn banquet," her Handler scolded.

Lexy sat down in her seat, still smiling, but confused. Adrenaline was coursing through her body. *Were her cheeks warm?* She raised one of her hands and touched her cheek. *She was hot. Way too hot.*

Absolutely livid, Grey interrogated, "What in the hell did he say to make you have selective amnesia? We are in a cease fire and you bloody decked him? You could be entombed for that stupid move."

Lexy sweetly toyed, "Do you really want to know what he said? I'll tell you, but I'm sure you'd prefer to leave this one alone."

Grey took a drink of his wine and prompted, "Tell me what he said."

She started to explain, "I went to look for you. He blocked me with his leg and suggested we finish what we started this afternoon. I told him he couldn't handle me even if I came with instructions. Then, he told me he was going to make me scream his name until I lost my voice for a week. He touched my thigh. I liked it so I hit him."

Baffled, Grey repeated her words, "You liked it?"

He was making way too much out of this. She whispered, "I'm not sure why I'm defending myself. He touched me and I hit him."

Grey's tone became dead serious as he said, "Not Tiberius Lexy, not Tiberius."

Shaking her head, Lexy replied, "You can't seriously think that would ever actually happen? He was just teasing me. Why is this bothering you tonight? He always messes with me. It wasn't a big deal." There was a long pause in their conversation as a slow song they'd always enjoyed began playing in the background. He tenderly caressed her face and gazed into her eyes. *What was he doing?* He leaned in and kissed her lips, softly. Lexy was stunned. *What was he doing?*

Grey whispered, "Please don't…not him."

That had come out of nowhere. Now, she was confused. Had that been a real kiss? It felt like one. It was wishful thinking; she knew that. It had only been a matter of days since they'd been together, not even forty-eight hours since he'd last been erased. She knew the drill. Her heart was seeing things that weren't there. It didn't matter if he'd meant to kiss her. She wasn't doing this with him anymore, she couldn't. Lexy stood up, and excused herself, saying she needed to go the bathroom. *What she needed was space. What in the hell was he doing kissing her on the lips like that?* She made her way through the crowd without bumping into anyone, slipped down the hall and quickly closed the bathroom door behind her. *The only person on the planet that had the ability to reduce her to a pile of mushy goo was Grey.* She stared in the mirror, touching her lips where he'd kissed her. She closed her eyes and took a deep breath, before leaving the safety of the bathroom. The dance floor was full, with barely the wiggle room to get by the partying Clan. She maneuvered her way back to the table to find Jenna and Orin chatting with Grey. Markus had seen her hit Tiberius. *Judging by the expression on his face, he was not impressed.* She sat beside Grey, and he placed his hand on her knee, her heart began to flutter. *Her platonic boyfriend was making things quite confusing for her this evening. It's all in your head. It's only been a few days since you crossed the line with him. Quit reading more into everything he does. These urges for something deeper from him will pass. It always does.* The voices in the banquet hall began to echo. She could feel the blood as it rushed through her veins. *It felt like everyone was out to get her, and it was beginning to cloud reality. It wasn't Grey, it was everything. These were all signs something awakened the Dragon within her. Something was coming.* She peered up and met Grey's concerned expression.

He leaned over and whispered, "Are you okay?"

With a confused look, she responded truthfully, "I don't know?"

Grey reached over, sweetly tucked her hair behind her ear and whispered into it, "Don't worry, I've always got your back…Always. Ignore what I said earlier, we can just leave." She gazed deep into his eyes and replied, "I know how badly you want to stay. If it doesn't stop, I'll leave before anything happens."

"I'm with you, whenever you need to go, just tell me and we're out of here," he vowed. They didn't look away from each other, they just continued to stare. He touched her thigh and whispered, "Your skin is so soft, and that dress is the sexiest thing I've ever seen you wear."

He kept seductively stroking her thigh. She placed her hand on top of his to stop it from travelling any further. *Why was he doing this to her tonight? He'd tricked her into believing he wanted her back a thousand times by behaving like this. She couldn't allow herself to fall for it. He was staring at her lips. He was going to kiss her again and she was going to let him. What was she doing?* His lips moved towards hers.

Jenna interrupted, "I need to talk to you about something important." She took Grey's hand, tugged him out of his seat and towed him to the dance floor.

A waiter placed another glass of delicious tripped out Clan wine in front of her. She'd consumed a few already. *Maybe it was a potent batch? That wasn't the explanation for her altered state this evening. Her Dragon had started to growl earlier in the day, but it could be the reason she was dealing with touchy feely Grey. He was trying to distract her.* The group at the table began to talk about who they knew around the room. They spoke of past exploits and other entertaining things. Lexy sat there listening. She was afraid to speak, with her mind, a jumble of amped up emotions. *Worried about what she'd reveal.* She placed the glass of wine down and shoved it away. Markus was staring at her from across the table. *He knew something was going on. She was his token unruly child.* He was always trying to pre-empt her bad behaviour in inappropriate situations. *This wasn't the time or place for her to go all silence of the lambs on anyone.* She glanced over at Markus and asked, "Is the third-tier wine stronger than usual?"

Markus replied, "It's the same as it's always been. Why do you ask? Is something wrong?"

She leaned across the table and quietly responded, "I think there might be. I'm feeling extra volatile tonight."

Markus whispered, "You have to rein it in. Stay as far away as you possibly can from anyone that triggers those feelings. You know who I mean."

The group started talking about the Summit. *She'd always been curious. The idea of going to another realm full of immortals and having a Clan on Clan gladiator fight in an arena was ten thousand levels of awesome.* She asked Markus a question, suspecting he wouldn't be allowed to answer, "Which Clan has to fight at the Summit?" A peculiar expression passed across her leader's face. *Markus knew something he wasn't allowed to say. She'd guessed that much.* They were never allowed to give out the details. Frost fought many times. Lilarah was always stuck with the royalty and rarely had the opportunity to do anything else. *Maybe Triad had to fight and Markus was afraid she'd spill the beans? She might. It was probably better if he didn't say anything.*

He changed the subject, "We are under strict cease fire rules. Try to have a good time tonight. Drink a little more of that wine and have fun. Please, just stay as far away from Tiberius as you can."

"I have no plans to go anywhere near him," Lexy replied. *It was the truth.*

Markus winked at her and sparred, "You never do."

That was also the truth. He excused himself from the table and began to circulate around the room. Frost was making a show with Melody on the dance floor, trying to tick off his brother, Thorne. Lexy scanned the room for Grey. Jenna and Grey appeared to be having a deep conversation. *Grey was probably being told to do his job as her Handler and nothing more. That was what the timing of her interruption would suggest.* She took a drink of the wine she'd shoved away earlier. *He'd probably only kissed her because he was afraid that she was going to do something stupid tonight.* She took another sip and allowed her eyes to travel to Triad's seating. *Tiberius was watching her. There he was...something incredibly stupid.*

Orin caught their exchange of looks and taunted, "Trust me, you don't want to go there."

"What is it with everyone tonight? How would that even happen? We hate each other. We aren't even in the same Clan. I don't just hate him, I despise him. I'd welcome the opportunity to kill him with my bare hands...Again," she sparred, glaring at Tiberius.

"There's an extremely thin line between love and hate," Orin countered with a nudge.

She nudged Orin back and teased, "I bet you just sit around all day thinking up creative ways to throw overused clichés into conversations?"

He chuckled, "They are overused for a reason. I once slept with Glory from Trinity during a fight. Don't you remember that fiasco? It was hotter than hell, but it caused serious shit."

Lexy grinned and confessed, "Years ago, Glory kissed me. She's hot, I don't blame you."

Fascinated, Orin smiled and probed, "Care to elaborate?"

"There's nothing else to say. It was a memorable kiss," Lexy disclosed. They both glanced over to Trinity's seating. There she was in all her glory. She smiled at the cliché she'd thought up, opting out of saying it aloud. Glory waved at them and they both waved back. *They'd totally been busted.*

Orin moved his seat a touch closer to hers and whispered, "I've always thought you were one of the hottest girls in our Clan."

This was the weirdest night ever. Lexy teased, "Are you hitting on me Orin?"

Orin gave her one of his giant adorable grins and flirted, "Is it working?"

She took his hand in hers and replied, "If your intention was to make me feel better, you have." He hopped up, still holding her hand, yanked her to her feet and she laughed. *He wasn't taking no for an answer.* A man with a mission, he pulled her against him and whispered, "Let's make both of the people we're in love with crazy jealous."

"Damn it, Orin, I thought you were serious," she provoked.

Moving seductively to the music, he wagered, "In one year if we don't have them back, I say we stir up a shitload of drama and get together."

Lexy laughed, "It's on."

"I hope you know I'm holding you to that," he chuckled.

Resting her head on his shoulder, she admitted, "I hadn't realised how much I missed you until now."

"I'm not sure how to take that? It's been over twenty years, and you didn't know you missed me until now?" he taunted, pretended to pull away. He spun her instead and when he pulled her back in, he whispered in her ear, "I had to go. I couldn't be here without her. It's been twenty-years, my pouting sabbatical is over and it's painfully obvious Jenna has no intention of giving me another chance."

"Well, you did impregnate her human double five minutes after you guys broke up," Lexy teased. "Jenna was probably sitting with Azariah in the in-between going what in the hell Orin?"

He chuckled, "I was a train wreck, I imagine it looked pretty messed-up, but it's not like I can take it back."

Lexy prodded, "Speaking of surprise children. Have you even spoken to Melody?"

Orin glanced at Melody and said, "I'm a thousand years old. I know that there is almost no chance they make it out of the Testing. I can't know her yet. I can't do that to my heart. Not until it's real."

Lexy laid her head on his shoulder and felt the agony he was in. *Was this empathy?* The lump of stone residing within her chest cavity related to his plight. *This would be inconvenient.* A voice in her head kept prompting, *turn this off. She had to get out of this deep conversation. She couldn't think about the three headed into the Testing. The next week would be a difficult for everyone. She'd been staying away tonight; it was time to keep them at arm's length. That was the smart thing to do. In one week, she may never see any of them again.*

Orin whispered in her ear softly, "You like these ones, don't you?"

Lexy didn't answer. She changed the subject and suggested, "You should go home with someone else, take the intensity down a notch or two."

He teased, "Are you offering?"

Lexy cracked a grin and said, "Ask me again in a year."

He laughed as they continued to dance. It felt good to be with someone without the emotional baggage that comes from an overly involved heart. Lexy noticed Glory from Trinity staring in their direction. Orin had been gone for a long time, but he must have made an impression, she obviously still remembered him. She whispered in his ear, "Glory's staring at you."

Orin whispered in her ear, "We could take off together tonight and shake the whole Clan up."

Lexy giggled, "I knew you were secretly a badass."

Laughing as he spun her around, playfully lured her back in and whispered, "I'll deny saying this if you tell anyone, but you know you could do the same thing. I bet Tiberius would be a ton of fun if you didn't let your heart get involved."

Lexy asserted, "He's the biggest asshole I've ever met. I actually despise him."

"That's what they all say," Orin chuckled.

She wasn't just any girl. She was a Dragon and Tiberius was worthy of nothing, but her contempt. Lexy whispered back, "If this were any other day, I'd pick up a knife from the table and slit his throat rather than listen to him speak."

Orin swayed with her to the music as he provoked, "Such hostility, now there's the Lexy I know and adore. You were being too sentimental earlier. It was scaring me a little. Dragons aren't meant to be tamed. I'd hate to find out you'd lost your edge."

Lexy teased, "What do you know about Dragons? You're like a fluffy white toilet paper commercial kitten."

Orin winked and flirted, "That's badass fluffy white toilet paper commercial kitten to you."

What was wrong with her? Everything anyone said sounded sexy tonight. Orin just called himself a badass fluffy white toilet paper commercial kitten and she was seriously contemplating the merits of finding out why Glory was still interested after two decades. Her senses were heightened. *She'd been off all day.* After forty years she knew any form of oversensitivity meant something was coming. Something, she had to be prepared for. The song ended so they went back to their seats. They'd been taken. They sat across from Kayn and Zach. Lexy whispered to Orin, "Frost is dancing with your daughter."

"He wouldn't dare," Orin chuckled.

Zach imitated what he imagined Frost was saying to Melody, "Just relax, go with it. You know what would make my brother certifiably insane? If we slept together, he would be absolutely furious."

"It's for the good of the game," Kayn ribbed, imitating Frost's game.

"I'm sure Kayn would be fine with us hooking up. We have an understanding," Zach chuckled.

They were immaturely joking around, when the empty seat next to Kayn squealed as Thorne slid up beside her.

Leaning closer to Orin, Lexy suggested, "We should go dance again." *Orin was about to find out his old friend Thorne had a thing with his daughter.*

"What? This conversation is just getting good," Orin whispered.

With a knowing smile on his face, Thorne sighed, "My younger brother's immaturity level can be astoundingly toddler. He doesn't really think I'm buying this, does he?"

Kayn answered honestly, "He's just trying to help her feel better."

Intrigued by her response, Thorne said, "Well aren't you a breath of fresh air. Not a lie in that whole sentence."

Kayn kept the brutal honestly going as she replied, "Why bother making a half-assed attempt to lie to you. Honestly, I think Frost figured the two of you out five seconds after you saw each other. It was obvious to everyone."

Here we go.

Admitting nothing, Thorne took two glasses of wine from the tray as it passed by and placed one in front of Kayn.

"I'm missing something here," Zach admitted.

Lexy whispered to Orin, "Hey, we should really go and dance." She was trying to avoid the awkward moment that was seconds from happening. They were oblivious to who was sitting there. *The cat was about to come out of the bag. Why would they think of Orin as a concern when he'd barely spoken to any of them? He'd been sitting in the background for days.* Lexy grimaced as Kayn spoke.

"Thorne and Melody had a thing when she was with Trinity," Kayn disclosed.

Taken aback, Zach looked at Trinity's leader and quietly pressed, "Melody and you were actually together in the biblical sense?"

Thorne was watching the show his brother and Melody were putting on. He sheepishly glancing at Orin, who hadn't had the opportunity to reign in his mortified reaction.

Lexy shut her eyes. *She should have warned him. She'd been dancing with him all that time and it hadn't even crossed her mind.* She reached over, gave Orin a reassuring squeeze on his knee, and whispered in his ear, "I should have warned you. I'm sorry, I didn't even think about it."

Thorne didn't answer, aware Orin was listening to every word. Changing the subject, Thorne glanced at Kayn and said, "She looks happy. Has she been happy?"

Kayn looked into his eyes and teased, "She hasn't been with anyone else if that's what you're beating around the bush about."

Lexy stopped herself from smiling by taking a drink. *Drama.* Thorne didn't reply. He just smiled as he took another sip of his wine and glanced over at Orin again.

Thorne had knowingly slept with his daughter. Orin didn't say anything. Lexy couldn't help but wish she had been a fly on the wall a thousand years ago. She'd heard the Children of Ankh story. Frost found seventeen immortal children hidden in a crypt, saved during the first Correction in Rome by Azariah. Orin was one of those children, and so was Jenna. The twins, Freja and Frey were also original Children of Ankh. Orin had known Thorne for a thousand years and he'd slept with his daughter. *That wasn't cool.* In that moment it clicked, two of their newest Ankh were offspring of the original Children of Ankh. Again, Lexy felt a strange sensation. Her stomach flip-flopped as everything in the room slowed to match the beating of her heart. Every moment, each voice…*Something big was coming.*

Orin leaned over and whispered in Lexy's ear, "You appear to be more disturbed than I am, and you knew about it."

Lexy whispered back, "Do you feel that? Look at my arms. Something's wrong. Can't you feel it too?" Her arms rippled with adrenaline and goosebumps appeared on the surface of her skin. Her heart palpitated with warning.

Orin took her hand beneath the tablecloth, squeezed it and assured, "It's not happening to me. Whatever you're feeling must be a personal warning."

The song stopped and Frost scooted up a chair beside his brother. Thorne scowled and remarked, "That was a little mean-spirited. Going after the girl your brother wants is so unlike you."

Orin was sitting protectively close, holding her hand. He leaned over and whispered in Lexy's ear, "Just breathe slowly and allow the feeling to pass. There is a cease fire between the Clans tonight. Nothing is going to happen."

She felt Grey coming before she saw him. He pushed a chair up beside her and placed his arm around her possessively. He glared at Orin, who laughed and let go of her hand. Orin winked at her. Grey's touch had an immediate calming effect. With the ball of stress unwound, she picked up her wine and drank the entire glass.

Grey teased, "Wow, slow down rock star. Are you sure that's a good idea given your volatile state this evening?"

She hadn't said anything. He'd known she was still feeling off. It was instinct. Lexy whispered, "Do you feel it too?"

Grey baited, "You mean Orin's anger over Thorne's fling with his daughter?"

"At least it wasn't Tiberius," Orin sighed.

It took serious balls to throw someone else under the bus, you also had tickets to ride. He was intuitive enough to know she was feeling off, that was all. She tucked the warnings of impending doom away and decided to have a good time, enjoying the Brothers of Prophecy comedy channel. *It was always entertaining when they got together.*

Frost chuckled, "Oh, come on. That was my good deed for the day. You needed a push. She went to the bathroom. If I were you, I would go talk to her. You can be alone in there."

"That is the last thing I should do. You've always been a troublemaker," Thorne mumbled while watching her walk away.

Tiberius slipped into a seat on the other side of the table, "I was feeling left out of the brotherly bonding moment."

Lexy glared at Tiberius for violating her airspace. Orin touched her leg under the table and she giggled. Grey had his arm around her and Orin was also trying to calm her down behind the scenes. *It was hilarious, and honestly a little strange.* She looked up and even Markus was staring at her now.

"I just was pointing Thorne in the right direction," Frost said, taking the wine Thorne put down.

The leader of Triad provoked, "Well, isn't that nice of you. You should find me a date while you are offering up your Clan." Tiberius met Lexy's glare from across the table and sighed, "No means no Lexy. I don't want to date you."

Without hesitation, Lexy threw a knife from the table directly at his chest. Tiberius caught it, completely impressed where another would have been traumatised. In absolute awe, he seductively baited, "You really have not one single bit of self-control, do you? That may be my new favourite thing about you."

She was in shock herself at what she'd just done. She was insanely amped up tonight. Orin had been right. *There was a thin line.* With unveiled distaste, Lexy scowled.

Tiberius gave her unwanted advice, "Next time, distract me before you throw the knife. You might take me by surprise and hit your target." He stood up and threw the knife back.

Lexy blocked it with her hand, it went through her palm. Without flinching, she yanked out the knife and held up her hand as the wound vanished before it had a chance to bleed. Both Grey and Orin tried to restrain her, afraid she was going to stand up and kick his ass. *She wasn't going to though. It was exactly the opposite. This didn't feel like an attack. This felt like foreplay between Dragons.* Tiberius gave her a knowing smile. *He had her number. He knew exactly how to push her buttons.*

Grey took her freshly healed hand and prompted, "Let's go get some fresh air."

Lexy replied, "Yes, the air smells a little bit off in here."

Tiberius pointed at Frost and mouthed, "I think he farted."

Lexy couldn't help it, she smiled. *She wanted to hate him, but that was funny.* Grey was grinning as he dragged her away from the table. They almost jogged through the dancing people and burst out into the lobby. They both howled laughing and sat on opposite sides of the couch. Fresh air was drifting in through the propped open door. She closed her eyes and let the cool breeze dance across the surface of her skin.

Grey booted her and giggled, "You threw a damn knife at Tiberius during a cease fire. Are you completely insane? Granted, it was bloody hilarious. The look on his face was priceless." He mimicked Tiberius, "That may be my new favourite thing about you. What in the hell was that douche talking about?"

She knew. Lexy stretched out. He was staring at her legs, instead of looking at her. She could tell he had something more to say. She smiled and sighed, "Spit it out Grey."

Resting his hand intimately on her silky leg, he suggested, "Orin might be a good guy for you, if you like him in that way. I'd be okay with Orin."

Lexy shook her head and closed her eyes. *Everybody was pushing her buttons tonight, even Grey. He'd be okay with Orin? Was he trying to offer her an alternative to Tiberius? It had only been a few days since his declaration of love, since she'd given herself to him, against her better judgment.* She kept her cool, looked at her friend, nodded and said, "Good to know." He kept looking at the dance floor. Lexy sighed, "I'm fine, I promise. I'll hang out with Orin. Go have fun. I'll see you later."

Her Handler grinned and baited, "You just threw a knife at Tiberius."

"It was just a small knife, and I promise I won't throw another one. Go have some fun," she urged. Lexy held up her pinkie and whispered, "Pinkie swear." Grey locked pinkies with her, shook his head, stood up and disappeared into the crowd. She stayed on the couch for a good ten minutes, contemplating her options for the evening. Her mind kept floating back to the hatred she felt for Tiberius. *The all-encompassing overwhelming disgust. It was foreplay between Dragons. It would be better if she left before she did something stupid. Foreplay between Dragons. She had to get out of here.* She went to the bathroom to fix herself up. She'd planned to sneak out and make her way back to the cabin to get some sleep, but she bumped into Frost in the hall and he dragged her out onto the dance floor. *He wouldn't let her leave.* Tiberius walked past her a few times. Each time he obnoxiously told her to stop flirting with him. After many more drinks she ended up dancing with Patrick, the nice kid from Triad.

Chapter 34

The Journey To The Summit

Someone was hammering on the door. Rather epically hungover, Lexy opened her eyes and realised Grey wasn't sleeping beside her. She touched the empty pillow where his head should have been. Their relationship was undeniably strange. *Friends with benefits he'd been spelled to forget. Why was she questioning this state of halfway together now? That was what they were, halfway to the finish line. They slept side by side, spent all their free time together, but had relations elsewhere. He'd obviously hooked up with someone last night.* Someone knocked loudly on the door again. *No, she was too hungover to people.* She buried her face in the pillow and screamed into it. *She didn't remember a thing. What happened last night? She'd gone to the banquet.* She grinned as she recalled Tiberius greeting her in the receiving line as Satan. She recalled her response to his touch. The way he'd teased her before she'd attempted to stab him and vice versa. *She'd loved it.* She looked at the palm he'd thrown a knife at, with fond memories. *This was so messed-up.* She had her face buried in the pillow as the door opened. She heard footsteps and felt the pressure of someone sitting on the bed by her.

Frost whispered, "Wake up sweetheart. I left a note for the kids. It's time to go. Where's your sidekick?"

"Probably deflowering the rest of the camp," Lexy mumbled.

Frost chuckled, "The last girl I saw him with was far from an innocent flower."

The bathroom door opened, a young guy from Triad wandered out. Frost teased, "Or was it you who was deflowering the camp?"

Confused, Lexy looked up at Patrick. *He'd been sweet. He gave her his shirt. How had he ended up in her room? She was drawing a blank.*

Patrick smiled and said, "Thanks for the conversation and thanks for everything else. I know what I have to do now."

Without knowing exactly what he was talking about, Lexy replied, "Glad I could help?" *It came back to her. She'd given him somewhere to hide out and they talked. He had things he wanted to hide for a while longer. It had been nothing more. He must have passed out in the bathroom.*

Sprawled on the bed next to her, Frost baited, "Alright, spill it young lady. You were quite obviously fraternizing with the enemy. Did you actually make him sleep in the bathtub afterwards?"

She rolled on her side, met Frost's eyes and disclosed, "Trust me, I'm not his type."

"I should warn you. I know where Grey ended up and it was sort of my fault. Someone had to defuse our friend Lily. I thought you might like a heads-up."

Lexy dramatically sighed as she flipped on her back, "Why in the hell would you get him of all people to do that? He just spent the last year getting over her." She was still a little ticked at Grey, but she didn't want his heart demolished.

"It couldn't be me," he replied.

Annoyed, she flung off the covers and went to the bathroom without saying anything. *She had to sober up. Grey was going to be smitten and her life would be full of drama for the next month.* She got in the shower, yanked the curtains closed and turned on the water. She heard Frost come in and saw his outline leaning against the sink.

He started to speak, "Listen, I know you guys sleep together and he doesn't remember. I know how that feels. If what I had him do last night causes you a second of pain, I want you to know I'm truly sorry. I have no excuses, it was a selfish thing to do. I just needed one more night with her."

She rinsed off, turned off the water and asked, "Can you throw a towel over the top for me?" He draped a towel over the top of the shower curtain. She quickly dried herself off, wrapped it around her, opened the curtain and stepped out. Frost moved out of the way so she could get to her makeup at the sink. He stood there quietly as she got ready. *He wanted her to answer him. He wanted to clear things up before he left for the Summit. She needed a minute to process it.* She put on the final touch, her signature cherry red lipstick. *This new stay on brand she'd discovered was amazing.* She made sure none was on her teeth. Lexy announced, "Alright, let's go sit and talk. Just look away for a minute, so I can get dressed." *Frost wasn't his usual cocky brazen self this morning.* He didn't even attempt to peek at her as she put her bra and panties on. She slipped on a white cotton dress. Frost handed her a coffee and they both sat down at the little table across from each other as civilized people.

Frost started, "I know I come off like this insensitive idiot that doesn't care about anyone. It's just easier than allowing myself to be hurt. My story sort of relates to your situation, I think. It could help you if it does. I haven't really talked about this in a long time and I would appreciate it if you never told anyone what I'm about to tell you. I know you've heard the whole Brothers of Prophecy story. I'm not the hero of this story. I'm the villain. I was the brother that showed up for a wedding and stole Thorne's bride. Tiberius was her best friend. He was her Kevin. They were together when her father decided she should marry Thorne instead of him. Tiberius has always been a loose cannon, but he loved her. I know she loved him back. Both of my brothers loved her, I'd been gone for years. I came home for my brother's nuptials and destroyed everything. I didn't know she was my brother's future bride when I first saw her. I was gone the second our eyes met. I was hers, she was mine and it felt like there wasn't another way it could have played out.

We didn't know how to control our abilities yet, and we were similar creatures. I was selfish. I could have walked away when I realised what I'd done, but I didn't. I alienated both of my brothers. They were already furious with each other. They both directed every ounce of their anger and aggression towards me. Well, as we know happiness gained at another's expense always has karmic repercussions. We were in love in the most beautiful soul altering way and then, every one of her memories of me was erased and in their place, the ability to want me physically, but never love me back. To make things worse, I became the only cure to a pesky affliction she has. I could never leave her side. Nearly a millennium of not having her and never being able to let her go, trapped in my own personal purgatory. There have only been a few people I've cared for. Each time, I was forced to do my duty and save her from herself, I lost the happiness I'd managed to find. I have been punished for what I did to my brothers by fate for a thousand years. I just want a chance to be happy. Just for five minutes, or five years. However long it takes for her to go off the deep end and for me to be forced to follow her in to save her."

"Why can't you just say her name? We all know who it is," Lexy probed.

Frost smiled as he explained, "Lily believes she is only a few centuries old and it has to stay that way. There are parts of her ability that must be suppressed. We can't allow her to remember."

"I was only teasing about you not having a heart Frost. Anyone can see you have feelings for Kayn," Lexy admitted. *She could tell what he was thinking by his expression.*

Frost solemnly replied, "She's not ready for me, the timing is all off."

Lexy finished the mug of coffee and was dying for another. She got up and grabbed Frost's half empty mug along with hers. She filled them both up, glanced back and said, "Maybe the Kayn thing will happen once she turns the page on Kevin?"

He replied, "I may seem like an insensitive player, but it's out of necessity. You have to get back out there. Get back in the saddle and let yourself fall in lust if you can't have the love you want. That's the only way you'll get out of the vicious circle you've found yourself in with Grey. Maybe it's time to take your heart out for a stroll and see what it's capable of?"

"I'm not sure I can," Lexy whispered. *He didn't come out of the Testing. Grey always remembers he loves me. These were all excuses.*

He teased, "Hey, my last serious relationship was with a dead girl and I've been trying to get into her live twin sister's pants ever since. I'm no expert on relationships but I am an authority on having fun. It's time you gave your heart a break. If you don't, the resentment you're feeling will kill your friendship with Grey. Take a chance on someone else. You guys have an eternity to end up together."

She knew he was right. Lexy smiled and sparred, "Is that why you never made a serious play for me? Was it because of Grey?"

Frost chuckled, shoved her like a brother and playfully provoked, "I never made a play for you because you're stone cold crazy and you can kick my ass. Hell, you kick my ass a few times each week and we've never even slept together."

True. Lexy teased, "I'm sure you mean that in the nicest possible way."

He winked and replied, "I wouldn't want you to be any other way. You are one of a kind Lex."

"I know you're not just trying to get into Kayn's pants, it's more than that for you. It must suck to leave her here with another guy, she cares about," Lexy affirmed as she drank her coffee.

He replied, "When I backed away from her, it wasn't by choice. It was an order. There are important events that have to play out in the evolution of Kayn."

"I figured as much," Lexy commented.

They sat there in silence for a moment longer before Frost probed, "You watched the redo of their Sweet Sleeps, tell me they have a chance."

"I can tell you what I saw and then your guess is as good as mine," Lexy answered. "Melody opted to keep her Sweet Sleep the same during the redo. Her mother and two little brothers die in a car accident. Her pregnant mother passes out behind the wheel, and Melody takes off her seat belt to try and stop the vehicle. She's launched out the window, down an embankment. She witnesses her family's death before she dies herself. When she reached the moment during her redo, where she has the choice to take off her seat belt and keep things the same, or keep it on and endeavour to change things, we knew she was something special. She understood the situation had to happen as it was meant to. That girl is going to wake up quickly each time she dies during the Testing. I know what that's like. Her biggest problem will be mental exhaustion. She doesn't have my ability to turn her emotions off." Lexy paused before continuing, "Zach's Sweet sleep was a surprise. You can't tell by looking at him but he's a survivor of incredible proportions. His father beat him almost to death and buried him alive. He was probably possessed by Abaddon, but the family had been running from him for years, he might have done it anyway. Zach clawed his way out of the ground only to find out his family had been burned alive in their house. He opted to change everything during the redo of his Sweet Sleep. His lesson was simple, you can't alter what has already happened. There's anger inside of Zach, he hasn't set free. If he can manage to do that, he'll be an asset in the Testing." Lexy met Frost's eyes and knew what he was looking for. He wanted her to give him hope.

Frost asked, "How did Kayn do?"

She wanted to tell him they were going to make it out but she knew the odds were against it. She divulged, "The events leading up to Kayn's Sweet Sleep were so violent. During her redo she did something nobody's attempted to do before. She understood it already happened and she couldn't change anything. She allowed her family to die just as they had in the past. It looked like her soul purpose was to see the face of the man that murdered her."

"Was it Triad who did her Correction? It was far too brutal to be Trinity," Frost enquired.

Unsure of how much she should say, Lexy revealed, "The Brighton twin's Correction was done by Abaddon. It was a hard-core extermination. There is no way she should have made it to the hospital alive. I know we got to her and helped, but we're missing something big about that night. I paid attention to where each wound was inflicted. I'm telling you, there's no way she should have survived. Freja is her mother, but who is Kayn's father?"

Frost replied, "Nobody knows who he is?"

"It's not you, is it? That would be awkward," she baited.

Grinning, he countered, "We were long over when Freja got pregnant. More than twenty years, over."

They stopped talking abruptly when Grey walked through the door and sheepishly said, "I'm just going to go shower."

Lexy tried her best but the joke was sitting there on the tip of her tongue. Her friend was at the bathroom door when she innocently provoked, "Feeling dirty for some reason this morning?" They both attempted to stop themselves from smiling.

Grey glanced back and muttered, "Funny, you two are frigging hilarious." He slammed the door.

She wanted to keep making light of his shenanigans but the joke wasn't as funny when it was on her. *He'd slept with Lilarah.*

Frost touched her arm and advised, "Do yourself a favour and just move on. There is nothing more painful than loving someone incapable of loving you back."

Lexy met his concerned expression and she replied, "I know." *She needed to go elsewhere with her heart, and quickly.*

After Grey unsoiled himself from last night's debauchery, they began walking in a group to Ankh's crypt. Lexy only intended to see them off and embrace the week of relaxation. She wasn't going to cave on her resolve to keep Grey in the friend-zone. *Not now.* She was going to send him out on the town to have fun with a smile on her face. She'd plant herself on the bed in their motel room to chain watch a season of a show on Netflix. She'd have a bubble bath, some wine, order room service. If she felt adventurous, she'd wander down to the pub and be social. *Nobody was talking. Something still felt off.* They were walking in silence like they were headed for the firing squad. If that's how Frost looked at it, she wouldn't blame him. She was the only one who thought of a fight as a good time. Grey stopped walking and held out his hand, having a zen moment with a ray of light through the trees. She wished she saw the world as he did. He was the only one that was happy most of the time. This was a gift. He knew how to find happiness in the little things. A cold burst of air rushed through her, Lexy shivered. She knew better than to ignore this. *Maybe something messed-up was going to happen after the others left? It was something.*

Once they arrived at the crypt Frost ran his hand along the inside of the tiny opening to the burrow like cave and the ground opened revealing the flight of stairs. They descended into the flickering darkness. The torches were already lit down the long dingy hallway. The others were already there. They passed the carvings on the wall of the Brothers of Prophecy and the beautiful prize otherwise known as Lilarah. She glanced at Grey. He was staring at her, wondering when the lecture was coming. *She wasn't going to give him one. There was no point in being angry at him for something he couldn't change. He'd already slept with her. She'd already decided to stop the insanity. Bringing it up would be creating drama, she despised drama. She was a Dragon. She deserved to be coveted, feared and, revered.* They met up with the others. The room became silent. *They'd obviously been talking about something they weren't supposed to hear.*

Markus looked directly at her and announced, "Alright everyone, are you ready to go?"

Grey echoed, "Everyone?"

Lexy shivered as another pulse of adrenaline moved through her body. *Were they coming this time?* Her mind warned her again with a shiver and she understood. *This was a day for Dragons.*

Her Handler repeated his sentence, "We're going with you this time?"

"Yes, you're coming with us," Markus answered.

Grey looked at Lily, then at Markus and questioned, "And why would we be doing that?"

"They didn't clarify," Markus replied.

Grey stopped cold and said, "Are we fighting?"

Markus looked away, and Grey moved to her side. She was his comfort and he was hers. Lexy didn't need comfort for this. She hadn't even flinched at the news. She'd already known on some level that something big was coming for her. She had always been more than a little excited at the prospect of seeing what the Summit was all about. She was a unique individual. Most people would be utterly terrified at the prospect of fighting the other Clans, but not her. Lexy offered herself up, "I want to fight. Can I volunteer?"

Markus chuckled, "You my dear have quite the unquenchable thirst for chaos."

Her Clan was in utter awe of her reaction. She always appeared to roll through each twist and spiral that fate tossed at her emotionally unscathed. They knew that she had battle wounds. Hidden ones that remained a secret to all, but the few who'd been present during her redo of her Sweet Sleep. The members of her Clan who'd been privy to her mortal end, understood how the flames of her inner fire had been fanned.

"It's usually me," Frost sighed.

Lexy met his eyes and announced, "I'll volunteer to fight for you. I say bring it on."

Frost chuckled as he flung an arm around her and teased, "I'm so glad you're on our side."

Grey was standing just a little too close to Lily. The lingering looks were beginning to piss her off. She needed to feel strong. Right now, that meant getting the hell away from him. Logic had explained her turmoil. It had been Frost that had her back this morning. She needed to feel emotionally void, hardened by strength. This meant Grey had to steer clear of her. *He was her kryptonite. It wasn't personal.*

The group stood before the back wall of the Ankh crypt. They were all together in the same place, at the same time. Arrianna was standing beside Grey. She had a flashback to the moments before they'd entered Testing. *It felt like this. She'd been excited and they'd been terrified.* Orin would be their tether. He was all stocked up. He'd have to live in the crypt until they returned. Jenna would be going as their Oracle. They walked directly through the shimmering back wall into the chamber where the tombs were held. The tombs were already open, ready to go. They would all be fitting in three tombs together. One needed to be left open in case of an emergency. The Ankh they left behind always needed an escape clause. Lily and Frost climbed into one, Lexy, Grey and Arrianna in another. She felt a sense of warmth with the three together again. Jenna and Markus climbed into the other one. *This part of being Ankh never got old for her.* It was a euphoric feeling, travelling via tomb to an unknown destination.

Grey embraced her from behind and whispered, "I'm sorry I disappeared on you last night. I hope you're feeling better today?"

Lexy replied, "What feelings? Nobody in this tomb thinks I have those." *She'd given a hostile response. She hadn't meant to.*

Arrianna whispered, "Did something happen last night?"

Lexy quietly replied, "Let's not have this conversation right now."

"Why are you ladies talking in code?" Grey asked as he squeezed Lexy's arm. *She couldn't move away. There was nowhere to go.*

He felt her stiffen to his touch and whispered, "You know it didn't mean anything."

In a hushed tone, Lexy baited, "What didn't mean anything? Kissing me last night or ditching me to sleep with Lily? I'm confused it could have been either one. You had a busy night." *Where in the hell had that come from? Crap. She'd lost her filter.*

Grey whispered, "I did kiss you, didn't I? I'm not sure why I did that, I was pretty wasted."

Had he seriously just used, I was wasted, as his explanation for kissing her? That was just insulting. This wasn't the time or place for this conversation. Arrianna lying next to them. Grey and Arianna's relationship had broken up when he'd slept with Lilarah.

Arrianna leaned across Lexy, smacked Grey on the side of the head and hissed, "What in the hell is wrong with you?"

"Lexy, that's not what I meant," he backtracked.

She'd picked that fight for no reason. The kiss had been nothing, a quick peck on the lips. That wasn't why she was feeling hostile towards him. If it had been some random girl from another Clan, she knew it wouldn't have affected her like this. She whispered back, "I know." He squeezed her arm.

Markus loudly chastised, "We can hear everything you're saying. You have five seconds to make up. We don't have time for drama."

They snickered as Orin began the process of sealing and joining the tombs. The sound of stone grinding closed above them, excited her. Lexy's blood pulsed, shivers of adrenaline coursed through her body as her mind prepared for the adventure. *Her adventure...This was what she'd been feeling. The third tiers wanted to watch a Dragon fight.*

Chapter 35

The Summit

Lexy felt the familiar rush as the tombs were launched into the air. Grey let out a cat call as they spiralled upwards, and her stomach churned. The tomb paused. Her insides lurched as the free fall began. Lexy rode an intense rush of adrenaline, knowing in her soul that she'd been summoned with the others for a reason. The group plummeted through the multicoloured fluffy visual of clouds during their rapid descent into the unknown. Lexy narrowly missed an enormous scaled creature as it soared past. Her eyes followed it, as it flew off into the backdrop of pastel clouded sky. Her heart almost burst within her chest. *It was miraculous.* A real dragon with teal, crimson and shiny black scales soared off into the distance. *They were real. They were not only a figure of speech or a description of one's being.* She spread her own arms to either side of her, smiled and closed her eyes, attempting to mirror the majestic span of its wings with her semi-mortal limbs. It disappeared from her line of sight, into the cover of the clouds.

She heard Grey's voice call out, "We've missed you, Arrianna!"

Arrianna screamed back, "I've missed you guys too!"

Lexy didn't bother adding to the sentiment, after feeling the intensity of the dragon's presence. Lexy's inner voice whispered, *shut it down.* She heard a chorus of excited hoots as the sky turned into a foggy blur of colours beneath them.

"I have a feeling this is going to suck!" Grey shouted.

The foggy blur solidified and now, they could see the rapidly approaching scenery. They were falling directly into a full coliseum full of cheering people. The ground appeared to be red in colour, for as far as the eye could see.

"You always think everything's going to suck Grey!" Arrianna hollered.

When dealing with Third Tiers, if Grey thought something was going to suck up front, it would be a pleasant surprise if it didn't. *He needed to believe his state of mind altered scenarios already set in motion. She didn't.* They slowed themselves, like old pros, landing solidly on their feet. The other Ankh had landed slightly before them. Lexy looked down at her attire. Grey and Arianna were also wearing the white sarongs from the in-between. They looked like sexy peasants in comparison to Lilarah and Frost, who were dressed in royal gold armour. Lilarah smiled at her. *She wanted to be mad at Grey for sleeping with her, how could she? Who wouldn't? What did it matter now?* Lilarah was in her element. She noticed Jenna and Markus were also wearing gold armour.

Grey put words to her thoughts as he asked, "Markus, how come we aren't all duded up?"

Markus replied, "That's easy kid, you have to earn the armour."

How long were they going to refer to them as kids? The Ankh in gold armour were all original Children of Ankh.

"This is a little intimidating," Arrianna whispered, as she slowly spun around, looking at the full stands.

The cheering crowd looked like normal people, wearing loose sarongs and most were shirtless. They were all shapes and sizes. *Were they all third tier?* The coliseum had a mix of people similar to what you'd find at a concert in a stadium. She searched the faces in the stands. *There was a surprising number of children. Who would bring a child to watch a blood bath?* Lexy whispered back, "At least they are cheering for us."

With pride, Markus clarified, "They are cheering for you."

She did always prefer it when someone just ripped the band-aid off. Markus knew that. The others hadn't heard him. They were still gawking at the crowd.

Arrianna looked at Markus and enquired, "For fear of sounding stupid, where are we exactly?"

Smiling, Markus answered, "You were here once before, after your Testing."

"Not Earth then?" Grey questioned as he looked down at the crimson sand beneath his feet.

"Not exactly," Frost replied. "It's better if you don't know the name. The penalty for saying it aloud is entombment. It doesn't exist."

"Alright then, it doesn't exist, we're not even here, got it," Grey whispered.

Lexy hadn't bothered to ask questions, she didn't care. She took in the vibrant sky. *It was like the in-between.* The colours rippled across the horizon like a watercolour painting that was still damp. The whole skyline was a tangerine and fuchsia sunset with only a faint haze of blue. The sand beneath her feet was an ominous mix of rust and crimson. A voice summoned the group. *It felt like it had come from everywhere.* They were led through open gates and upstairs to balcony seating. She sat beside her Handler.

Grey leaned closer and whispered in her ear, "Are you still mad at me?"

She didn't care now. She'd already begun the process of shutting down her emotions. It was time to fight.

Grey poked her and teased, "You're not even paying attention."

She whispered back, "Don't worry about it. What's done is done." The crowd started booing as the first group of Triad landed brazen and barefoot in the center of the coliseum.

Sitting on the other side of her, Markus casually stated, "I take it I don't need to tell you what's going to go on here."

Lexy's eyes lit up as she grinned and responded, "No, I've got this." *He knew she could handle it.* Arrianna was anxiety ridden. She'd seen that look on her Handler's face before, Grey was about to toss his cookies. The crowd cheered for Trinity and they were led to their seating next. The Legion of Abaddon arrived and there was silence. They didn't have six or seven like the other Clans brought. Abaddon had a small army of thirty or forty black-eyed, soulless looking warriors, along with a half dozen long-clawed creatures. The first row of men had urns. She imagined those were filled with black mist. Once Abaddon filled the coliseum, they were led out through the large intricately carved arches.

"I guess none of you remembered to bring salt," Markus taunted. He smiled as two of the three in white sarongs, patted themselves down as a joke.

Arrianna teased, "Where would we hide salt?"

"I would have gone full airport smuggler if I'd been warned there might be one on one combat with demons," Grey mumbled.

Lexy whispered, "Cut the comedy routine, I need to psyche myself up."

Grey looked at her and said, "What do you mean by that?"

"It's all good. She's got this," Markus decreed.

A man materialized out of nowhere and announced, "Miss Lilarah, your company has been requested."

Lily stood up to follow, glanced back and assured, "Don't worry; they just want me to sit with the royal family." She followed the man away.

Arrianna nudged Frost and baited, "They're not taking you too?"

Frost scowled and remarked, "I'm sure they'll come and get me later."

Court jesters began a comic duel in the center of the coliseum. Lexy had a few flashes of the banquet after the Testing. She glanced up at the balcony and saw him with his family. Amadeus was staring. It had been forty years. He'd allowed himself to age, appearing to be in his late thirties.

The royals she didn't recognize, could be his adult children. For Lexy time stood still.

Jenna leaned over and whispered in Grey's ear, "This is sort of a who's who of the savage planet earth."

She felt someone else's eyes upon her, instinct prompted her to look up. The culprit was a fine specimen, with bronzed muscles in gold armour just like the others in her Clan. *She knew him. He'd been in their Clan when she'd first arrived, she was sure of it.* She looked at Markus and enquired, "Who is the guy sitting by Lily again?"

Waving, Markus chuckled, "Don't you remember him? That's Silas, he's their best warrior. He's Ankh; he was with us when you first arrived in the Clan. Long story short, he opted to stay. It's usually Silas against Abaddon. They like to study us. They want to know what our partially mortal short comings are. Only the royal family and our Oracles get to watch the Testing. The public gathers in the coliseum to bet on which Clan will make it out. Everyone can come to the coliseum during the Summit, to watch us fight."

Lexy gazed up at the Testing grounds, hovering ominously in the distance. *They must move it above the coliseum after they drop new Second Tiers in there.* She'd been avoiding it with her eyes. *She'd succumbed to her Dragon and gone so dark; she couldn't recall a large portion of it. The giant grey mass in the sky had imprisoned every Ankh that went in, since her group made it out. They hadn't brought a Dragon along. The crypt hovering above the city was a fifty-foot-high, twenty-mile-wide floating stone slab of guilt. A place of magic, its walls were alive with the souls of the lost. Kayn, Zach and Melody would be dropped in there to race the other Clans to the Amber room. They'd have to stay together, while retaining their sanity. It could take weeks or months to make it out. The endless violent scenarios made short work of one's sanity. You become lost, an apparition of sorts, your soul is forfeited to an energy source. Forever lost in the game.* She felt Grey and Arrianna looking at her. *She was the reason, they'd survived. She was a Dragon, and Dragons are never afraid.* She looked up at the crimson sky as one swooped overhead and came to perch on a tower. Three others were perched on towers circling the ring. *Her family was here to watch. It was time to start.* She'd been so busy watching dragons, she hadn't noticed the guard's approach. Knowing they were here for her, Lexy rose. Grey attempted to go with her.

Ankh's leader stopped him cold and explained, "Lexy has been chosen to fight for us. We don't have a choice, but they couldn't have picked a better candidate."

With unwavering belief, Arrianna praised, "You've got this, Lex."

"With her hands tied behind her back," Frost declared.

Grey lost the ability to speak. Her Handler was nervous. He should be, they hadn't had a chance to make up.

Grey mouthed the words, "Come back."

No longer able to summon mushy pointless declarations, Lexy was escorted away by guards. They briskly ushered her through the majestic arches of the coliseum and ordered her to keep walking. Without a hint of emotion, she strolled out to the roar of the crowd and stopped dead center of the coliseum. *Bring it.*

Chapter 36

Born Of Light Created In Darkness

Lexy looked up to the stands where her Clan was seated and smiled. It wasn't a brave smile, nor a kind where one secretly feared what was to come. It was the smile of a warrior primed and excited. Some girls have fantasies of marrying their prince, wearing a flowing white silk gown and in a magical moment, white doves are released into the air above as they say I do. Lexy's fantasies were always more about kicking asses. Her aspirations were about strength and autonomy, oneness of self. She was a breed all her own born of light created in darkness.

There was absolute still. Not a peep from the crowd as tension filled the air. Lexy stood barefoot in the rust-coloured sand as the Dragon they told scary tales of before tucking in their immortal children. She allowed perspiration to trickle down her brow into her eyes, for even the wipe of a hand may be interpreted as weakness. A sudden breeze coated her moist flesh with red grainy war pant. It was a symbolic moment. This battle would define her in their eyes. *She would show them what a Dragon was capable of.* She felt the layer of crimson sand as a reminder of her strength. She couldn't wipe the smile off her face, as a half dozen Triad appeared in the entrance to the coliseum. Her predatory heart pounded the war drum as adrenaline rushed through her veins, with anticipation. The brazen pack of almost dead Triad strode towards her. *Tiberius free of course. That chicken shit.* Triad had swords and she had no weapon. She noticed weapons hanging on the coliseum's walls and calculated the distance she'd have to run to acquire one. *It was always a matter of choice.* She surveyed her surroundings, not remotely concerned. Sure, she was outnumbered, but Lexy had something else in her arsenal more powerful than blades or swords. She had the apprehension these men felt as they edged closer. The anxiety in their subconscious, triggered by tales they'd been told. That was the first weapon she'd use to her advantage. Fear was a powerful deterrent. The Triad walked towards her. They appeared confused, glancing at each other. Lexy read their thoughts. *They were wondering why she hadn't attempted to run for a weapon. Why hadn't she brought one?*

You could hear a pin drop in the coliseum. The crowd held their breath believing she was going to be slaughtered weaponless. A woman alone in the center of the coliseum, no armour, no weapon, just a feisty redhead standing there, deep in thought. She rolled her neck and causally stretched her arms above her head with her fingers clasped together. As always, she would remain calm, until the right buttons were pushed. *Once someone made her angry, she wasn't responsible for her actions.* They watched her, grinning as they inched closer. Only the Triad holding swords appeared unnerved. *Time to shut it down.* Lexy exhaled, releasing her humanity, she allowed her mind to remember. She travelled back to the dark farm and heard their voices, demeaning and harsh. Her flesh recalled the depravity that crushed her adolescent spirit. Bile rose in her throat as unspeakable acts surfaced. She evoked each humiliating blow and depraved violation. Her mind filtered through events kept hidden until needed to fuel her Dragon's fire. The scent of submerged decomposing flesh. Charlotte, floating in the well. She felt the stone beneath her fingertips as she climbed the side of the well. She experienced her being surging with power, and then the slivered wooden handle of the axe grasped tightly in her hands. The axe had been her weapon of redemption. She glanced at the axe clenched in one of the Triads hands. *That's convenient.*

Looking into the Triad's eyes, Lexy coldly menaced, "First, I'm going to chop off both of your hands and feet, right at the joint. I'll stand there, enjoying your shrieks of agony, as you squirm around helpless, before hacking off your legs at the kneecap. Next, I'll hack off your arms at your elbow. While you're begging me to end your agony, I'm going to take your own severed hand and stroke your face gently so that I may have a moment to ponder which appendage I'm going to chop off next." Visibly shaken by her calm words of insanity, the Triad closest to her almost dropped his axe. The others were frozen in place, encircling her. None made a move, knowing it was only a matter of which one was going to die first. A predator by nature, it was easy to spot the weakest links. The unskilled would assume it was the Triad who'd shown obvious fear by almost dropping his axe. *Fear makes you weak but cocky makes you stupid.* Only two, appeared to be excited, *they were who she'd take out first. The others would be too terrified to move. She could take them out easily, once she'd dealt with the loose cannons.* A loose cannon swung and missed as she easily maneuvered out of the way. Lexy signalled for the Triad to come at her with her fingers. She sacked the cockiest in the junk, snatched his sword and used it on three like they were standing still, only incapacitating the Triad, having promised a much more creative demise. She registered useless flesh wounds from swords swung frantically around her and felt the warmth of her healing ability before blood had a chance to seep from the wounds. With the blade of her sword and a few powerful kicks, they were all down. Void of emotion, she dropped the blade on the coliseum floor. Dust rose as she wiped the sweat off her brow, picked up an axe and stood above the Triad least afraid. Eyes begged her for mercy. *Dragons do not give mercy. Dragons do not understand the concept of empathy. Dragons always keep their promises.* She swung the axe and chopped off the Triad's hand at the wrist. High-pitched shrieking enticed the crowd. The Triad would feel each limb severed. *To induce fear, following through wasn't a choice. She had promised it. It must be done.* One by one, she publicly cut off each foot and held them above her head for the silent crowd as a prize. She did the same with each hand, up to each elbow, then to each knee. The blood spraying from their arteries covered her in a fine mist of red and she became lost in the dark. The axe clutched in her hand was now slaying inhabitants of the farm where she'd been held captive. She was drenched in Triad's blood. Christened by it, empowered by its sticky warmth. She saw an opportunity and smiled as she knelt before the deceased, wiped the tears from their faces and rubbed their salty agony all over her body.

To the crowd it looked like Lexy was rubbing their blood all over her and enjoying it. The Ankh knew what she was doing, eventually they would send in Abaddon. She was using the salt from the tears of the Triad she'd systematically dismembered to protect her. The crowd was disturbed, confused and silent.

A vision of red, she knew what she wanted as she rose to stand in the center of the coliseum. She hollered, "Send me Tiberius!" She heard hands clapping. *One set.* She glanced up at the stands. The lone applause was from the warrior Silas. He was howling laughing. He got up and mock bowed to her from his seat in the stands. This enticed scattered clapping from the mortified crowd. *She knew Tiberius was scared shitless of her. It was far past time she had the opportunity to hard core kick his ass. She'd earned it.* She surveyed the stands and caught sight of Tiberius. He stood up and made his way from the stands down the stairs, disappearing for a moment before emerging through the arched entry of the coliseum. He strolled towards where she was standing.

A voice bellowed through the coliseum, "A challenge has been made. Tiberius of Triad must fight with Lexy of Ankh." A long dramatic pause ensued, the voice then continued to speak, "Against Trinity."

He was about ten feet from Lexy, when the third tiers added the twist. He started to laugh. *They wanted her to fight with Tiberius, not against him. It was evil genius on their part.*

Tiberius teased, "Looks like your evil plot to dismember me has been thwarted young lady."

"Oh, I can put it off for a few minutes for the sake of public entertainment," Lexy sparred.

Tiberius's eyes lit up and he provoked, "Bad ass psychotic chicks have always turned my crank. By the way, you look unbelievably sexy in red."

He was referring to the blood she was soaked in. Lexy taunted, "I look sexy in everything."

A nervous group of Trinity marched through the open arch and methodically spread out around the coliseum, encircling them, and began preparing their bows.

Tiberius complained, "Drugged third tier arrows, shot from a distance. Alright, queen of all macabre situations. Do you have a plan for this scenario?"

"There's only six. We can manage to avoid a few arrows. Once I get close enough, they're done," She coolly decreed.

Grinning, Tiberius explained, "I'm not sure you understand. These are brilliant marksman. If we're hit once, we'll go down. Five minutes later, they'll have our heads on spikes in the center of this arena."

Lexy smirked as she surveyed the stands. *She wasn't concerned. She'd been shot by many Trinity arrows before.* Lexy met Grey's eyes, quickly looked away and disclosed "If I yank them out quickly, I can take a half dozen direct hits and heal before I go down. This isn't even a challenge."

Tiberius grinned at her as he slowly shook his head and explained why her idea would never work, "You've always been a cocky one. There's a problem, one of these arrows is the potency of three from back home. So, you've got one, possibly two direct hits in you. Even if you manage to yank it out immediately, it's going to take you down. I must avoid them all together. Once that first drugged arrow hits me, I've got roughly sixty seconds before I'm out. This isn't my first trip to the rodeo."

There was a way to win. She just had to see it. Lexy observed the Trinity. *She'd taken many more than six on random occasions but only after recently feeding her ability. She should have taken energy from Grey before she left his side. She hadn't thought of it. Their bows all appeared to be aimed directly at her. They were going after her first. Smart marksman.* "If we avoid the first arrows. I can kill them while they prepare the next. If you're hit, kill as many as you can in that sixty seconds, then just go down and don't worry about it. I'll make sure neither of our heads end up on spikes."

"If I sacrifice myself to beat Trinity, you allow me to use my ability on you before the Abaddon round, so I can recharge it. I get to see how you were created. That's the deal," Tiberius bartered.

If the poisonous arrows were as lethal as he claimed, she didn't have a choice. If she went down right away, she'd look weak. Her stomach tied in a knot, as she agreed, "Alright, it's a deal." Lexy glanced at Tiberius. *She'd just made a deal with the devil, but the devil was going to trust her.* Confused, she asked, "Why would you trust me, knowing it would make my decade to dance around your head on a spike?"

He met her gaze and responded, "Honour between Dragons."

Anticipating the announcement, they were both poised to dive out of the way. Adrenaline coursed through her veins. Goosebumps of anticipation prickled her flesh. *Maybe, they would just start shooting? It was like waiting for someone to take a picture.*

The sworn enemies braced themselves, as the announcer's voice boomed, "The round will begin in five minutes. This is your last chance to grab a snack from the vendor."

What in the hell? Lexy glanced at Tiberius and probed, "Honour between Dragons, even though I slaughtered your men?"

"They needed a lesson in humility," he admitted, with a flirtatious wink.

"Oh, I didn't know you guys taught lessons in your Clan. I assumed you sat around burping, drinking beer and throwing your food on the floor, with a little caveman sex thrown in there from time to time," Lexy sparred.

A trumpet played a tune, followed by the announcer's booming voice, "Clan Trinity versus Lexy of Ankh and Tiberius of Triad!"

An arrow whizzed past Lexy's head on the last syllable. She dove into the crimson sand. It gave her cover as it clouded around her.

Tiberius sprinted at one of the men, darting side to side, narrowly avoiding arrows. "Quit hitting on me!" Tiberius yelled as he dove into the sand for cover, causing a cloud of earth to explode.

Crawling like a wild thing through the sand floating around her, she kept moving so they couldn't pinpoint her location. She crouched in his fresh cloud, creating enough of a haze to give her a second to plot her next move. *Time was up.* She rolled away, narrowly avoiding a shower of arrows and jumped up. "Get over yourself!" She hollered back. They separated, running in opposite directions, forcing the Trinity to concentrate on one or the other. They dodged the arrows until the shooting paused, to reload. They each ran at the closest Trinity and snapped their necks, thinning the number of poison arrow shooting assailants to four. The two dodged whirling arrows till the next reload, and then there were only two. Lexy was hit in the back. *Crap. She couldn't reach it.* Tiberius saw and raced over to help. His attention was focused on her as he yanked the arrow out of her back. *Their plan faltered.* His attention was on her for a second and that's all it took. He staggered away. *She was drugged.* In her peripheral vision she saw Tiberius go down, leaving behind a cloud of crimson sand. *He wasn't coherent enough to pull the poisonous arrow out of himself. Damn it Tiberius.* Lexy ran at the Trinity, closest to her, tackled her, and unceremoniously snapped her neck. *She was still disorientated from the arrow. Why hadn't she healed?* She glanced down and noticed she'd taken a second arrow in the stomach. *Shit. How long had it been there? She hadn't felt it.* Lexy tugged it out of her abdomen, while the lone Trinity reloaded. *She thought she had more time.* Lexy staggered as the world shifted around her. Instinct told her she was going down. *There wasn't time. Shit. She pictured their heads on spikes. She had one play left.* She staggered to Tiberius' semi-conscious body. With scenery wavering around her, she collapsed a few feet away, and clawed through the rising crimson sand towards him. Her vision flickered with white flashes of light. She tore the arrow out of Tiberius' shoulder, covered his body with hers and whispered, "Wait until the last moment to take him out." She used the last of her energy to heal Tiberius.

The Trinity cautiously walked towards the crumpled bodies. He pulled back his bow and stood above his seemingly defeated enemies.

The crowd went wild repetitively chanting, "Snap their necks!"

The last Trinity was a second from snapping Lexy's neck when Tiberius stopped playing dead. He reached out from underneath Lexy's body, wrapped his hands tightly around the Trinity's throat and squeezed, beating him to the punch. The Trinity's neck snapped and he crumpled to the ground. The crowd went insane. Lexy's ability to heal had begun once the arrow had been pulled out of her stomach. Tiberius was standing above her when she came to. He extended his hand. She took it and he helped her up.

The voice boomed, "Mortal enemies, united against a common cause!"

The crowd cheered so loudly it was deafening. Tiberius laced his fingers through hers and held their joined hands up in the air.

"Together in victory!" the announcer bellowed.

It was all about the show.

When Tiberius released her hand, she scowled and wiped off his cooties on her blood-soaked attire.

He whispered, "You went into this wanting to kill me and you saved me. How did that happen?"

She gave an honest answer, "I still want to kill you."

Tiberius began to howl.

The voice barked out, "We will have a short break for the feast, and then we shall return for the main event! Abaddon versus Lexy of Ankh and Tiberius of Triad!"

Lexy watched the crowd make their way out of the seating. They funnelled through the arched doorways. Four identical copies of the same man began to remove the Trinity's bodies from the coliseum. She noticed Thorne standing off to the side, he waved the identical men over and the remainder of the Trinity carried their people away. She glanced up at the stands and more copies of another man swept the isles. *The workers were all copies of the same two men. They looked familiar.* Holy crap, the all looked like copies of a well-known comedy duo from earth. *Were they cloning people?* They were led away from the coliseum, through the grandiose archways. "I'm starving," Lexy confessed.

Tiberius teased, "Mass murder always makes me hungry too."

Lexy glared at him. *It was funny but it felt like she needed to get her game face on.*

The guard leading them out of the stadium commented, "That was an impressive round. Hope you've got another one in you. Trinity is nothing compared to Abaddon."

She knew that. They were ushered into a room with a table full of food, the door was closed and locked behind them. *The door was locked, and there were no witnesses. They were completely alone.* Lexy stared at the locked door and questioned, "Why would they bother to lock us in here?"

Tiberius took a deep breath as he looked around and replied, "People try to run."

It seemed like a ridiculous idea. Why would you try to run? Where would you go? Lexy smirked and baited, "Who'd run?"

Switching subjects, Tiberius remarked, "I saw you staring at the cleaning crew. The third tiers kidnap people from earth and clone them. The clones usually have no idea they're clones. They return the original to earth with missing time and do crazy things to the copies. They also kidnap and clone cattle. You saw the dragons, right? Well, this place was solely inhabited by dinosaurs when they settled here. That's why the immortals choose to live in the desert. If they keep the dinosaur population well fed and occupied with human clones, they don't attempt to leave the green space."

That made sense. It was seriously messed-up, but it made sense.

Tiberius chucked a hunk of bread at her and urged, "Eat up, this next part is going to be a blood bath. Our blood that is…You saw the amount of Abaddon. We have no chance."

"There's always a chance," Lexy responded.

"How Ankh of you," Tiberius provoked, standing behind her.

He was so close, the energy between them was humming. *She shouldn't turn around.*

"They drop off thirty clones of famous entertainers in the green space. If the clones manage to survive for seven days, they're retrieved and used as slaves or entertainment. They give the clones numbers, mark them, televise the event and people bet. I watched one of my friends be cloned, as punishment. She got to watch herself be devoured by dinosaurs for days."

That was impressively dark. "You have friends?" she provoked.

He hovered his palm above her arm and playfully countered, "Shocking I know, but yes, I have friends."

She spun around and hissed, "Don't touch me."

He whispered, "We have a deal. I'm going to have to touch you." He motioned to the table and prompted, "We should sit and have something to eat first."

She followed him to the table. He poured them both a glass of wine. *How was she going to fuel his ability? If he planned to read her mind, he'd find out how much she despised him. He had to know.*

Grinning, Tiberius raised his glass and saluted, "To unexpected allies."

She glanced into the goblet, knowing they'd drugged her in the past. *There were no yellow flowers floating in it, but that didn't mean they hadn't drugged it. Tiberius didn't appear to be concerned.*

He dropped something and it rolled on the floor. *The acoustics in the stone dungeon were amazing. It looked as though they should be chained to the wall, not enjoying a fine dining experience.* She caught site of her reflection in his silver goblet. *She looked like an extra from a horror movie.* She started to laugh.

He popped a fig in his mouth and asked, "What's so funny?"

"I just saw my reflection in your goblet of wine," she replied.

"I'm sure we both look equally hideous," Tiberius teased as he walked over, picked up the basin full of water sitting in the corner and carried it back to the table. He submerged a washcloth and rung it out to remove the excess water. He leaned closer, wiped her cheek with the cloth and showed it to her.

She stiffened and asserted, "I can wash myself." He threw the soaking wet washcloth at her face with a splat. She scowled but didn't retaliate. She methodically washed her face and arms.

He teased, "Are you really that afraid of me? I thought you weren't afraid of anything?"

"I'm not the least bit afraid of you," she sparred.

"Prove it. Let me help you clean up, you're missing half of it," he dared. Tiberius winked as he held up another cloth and suggested, "I could use some help too."

She allowed him to take her feet and place both on his knee. He thoroughly washed her feet. He continued using the damp cloth up her calf towards her thigh. *He was playing a game with her. He told her she was afraid of him so she'd feel like she had to prove she wasn't.* As he moved the cloth towards her inner thigh, her lips parted, but she didn't tell him to stop. She whispered the words, "Why do you keep trying. You'll never have me."

He paused with the washcloth, stared into her eyes and teased, "Maybe not today, but we both know it's only a matter of time. You want me back even if you don't have the guts to admit it. By the way, you promised me something, it's time to pay up."

He wanted to see the memories that made her the Dragon she'd become. He would regret it. He looked at her like he wanted her now, but once he saw those memories his perception of her would be, forever altered. "You don't want to see my memories Tiberius," she whispered.

"Trust me there's nothing you can show me I haven't already seen. I've been seeing what's in people's heads for a thousand years. This is a matter of pride more than anything else. They put us together after a request to battle against each other, it's only fair we win this whole damn thing. I need to use my gift to have the energy do it."

Tiberius held out his hands, she shifted closer so he could watch the horror movie in her mind. The horrific acts that led her to every reaction and dark moment since. The moment his hands contacted her skin, she felt them warm. His eyes grew pale, then solid white and rolled back into his head. He was struggling to breathe. He held his palms there for only a short time before fighting to pull away. He dropped to his knees on the stone floor and began to heave. His body lurched as he struggled to bring his mind out of the horror he'd witnessed. He stayed on his knees, staring at the stone floor for a minute. She was certain he'd never witnessed anything as horrific as what she kept locked away inside of her mind. He'd seen every mortifying event she'd lived through, within the walls of the dark farm. He'd floated with her in a well of rotting, half grotesquely bloated submerged corpses. The child beaten beyond recondition she'd cared for. Her, praying Charlotte would die before they came back to hurt her again. Being shot like an animal by the sickest of men, and finally, the freedom as she died. She awoke as a Dragon, in the well of children lost with fury so powerful, so volatile that she was able to scale the walls like the monster she was, to seek her revenge with an axe in the farmhouse. He would have seen all the moments after. *He now knew everything about her. She was never afraid because there was nothing worse than what she'd survived.* He got up, walked over to the table and took a giant swig of wine. He poured another glass, put it down, and began to drink the whole bottle. Lexy walked up behind him, touched his shoulder and suggested, "Put the wine down. We don't need you hammered. You have to be able to fight."

He placed it on the table. Without looking at her, he said, "You are an emotionally wounded, savage and unbelievably brave girl. When this fight is over, come to me. I'll take those memories away. Please, let me erase them, so that horror never has to cross your mind again."

He still couldn't look at her. She was disassociated from those memories, most of the time. She kept them locked away, until she needed them. She'd never used them as an excuse. She used them to fuel her Dragon. Lexy stated, "That dark place created me. Those memories played an essential role in my evolution. I've became stronger than I'd ever thought, I could be. It's where I draw my fury from." Tiberius faced her, tenderly cupped her cheek with his palm and she didn't shrug away from his touch. *He knew her in a deeply intimate way. He had all the ammo he'd ever need against her.*

He whispered, "What did you learn as a child from them, that humanity is evil? That kind of darkness is all-encompassing. I can make it so you can have a relationship with a man. You can fall in love and be loved back. Don't you want that?"

Lexy responded, "Maybe my path is to learn to overcome my past, to learn to love anyway, to trust anyway." *He didn't believe it was possible.* She could see it in his eyes. Her soul was stripped naked, fully exposed to her enemy. It was as though they were in a strange parallel universe where it wasn't about the name of their Clan. They were both Dragons, they'd fought together. She caressed the prickly stubble on his face, pain still registered in his eyes. He teared up, overwhelmed by what he now knew was her truth. It created a connection. A unity of souls touched by darkness. She had nothing left to hide from him. Raw, passionate, primal need swelled within her as they gazed into each other's eyes. Her lips parted as they inched closer, drawn by the magnetic pull of wounded souls. Their lips met and as they provocatively kissed, she was rocked to her core. As their lips parted, shock registered in both of their eyes, exposing the undeniable truth. *They wanted each other. It couldn't be denied.* He kissed her temple. It was an intimate loving gesture that tugged at her heart. *He'd offered her freedom from her memories, and shown he was capable of compassion. It was possible they both weren't who they seemed to be.* Her mind whispered, *what are you doing? This is Tiberius.*

He groaned, his hot breath against her hair, "I've wanted you for so long, but now isn't…"

She'd spent all these years despising him with every breath of her being. She hated him, but now, she was blinded by all-consuming need. Lexy moved her hands across his rippling muscular chest, kissed his neck and nipped at the tender flesh with her teeth. He responded by cupping her bottom, lifting her up, and carrying her across the room. He pressed her back against the wall and kissed her until her lips were swollen and her body ached with need. His hands never ventured beneath the blood-soaked material that barely covered her. *She'd started it, she wanted him to finish it.* She kept touching him, until he grabbed both of her wrists and pinned them on the wall above her.

He choked out with a raspy voice, "You're making this really difficult. You got me ready, I have to get you ready to fight." He kissed her hairline, her cheek, and her neck softly, then bit into the soft flesh of her throat hard enough to cause blood to trickle down the ivory pallet of skin.

She felt the healing energy fire up inside of her. Her heart began to race and the adrenaline pulsed through her. He was getting her ready to fight as only another Dragon could. She felt power surge beneath her skin and the warmth as she healed. She needed more of it. Lexy whispered, "There's a knife on the table."

He released her wrists and followed her obediently across the room. He brushed the food aside, the plates smashed on the floor. Lexy laid on the table. Tiberius groaned, "Oh, the things I'd do to you if we had the time."

He took the knife and sliced a thin line along the surface of the skin on her exposed thigh. She arched her back in response to the warmth of the healing energy. She met his eyes as he wiped off the blood with his thumb to reveal freshly healed skin. This turned him on. He kissed her thigh and climbed onto the table, feathering kisses down her shoulder, and neck. Lexy stroked his hair and forced Tiberius to look into her eyes as he sliced her shoulder. She gasped as she healed and he dropped the knife. He wiped the blood off her skin and kept touching the area where she'd healed.

"You have the softest skin," he whispered, gently stroking her collar bone and the surface of her skin above her heart. *She allowed him to. This was an act of intense intimacy, for both.* He kissed her again and slipped his hand under the thin material. She arched her back again and moaned loudly. *She wanted this so bad.*

Tiberius groaned, "That's it, your mine." Their lips met and tongues intertwined, hands travelled until they both succumbed to the waves of pleasure. The resolve to prepare for battle vanished. There was nothing, but the here and now.

She breathlessly anticipated what came next, without a thought of the repercussions. *Don't stop.*

He pulled away, touched her cheek and whispered, "We won't do this, unless you want me too. You have to say the words." This kind of intimacy had never been in his game plan.

She pulled him back to her, and whispered, "I want this." Their lips met as the lock on the door jingled. They scrambled off the table and away from each other to look like they were still at each other's throats. Lexy slapped him square across the face.

The guard stammered, "You have about twenty minutes before we begin."

He shut the door and Tiberius chuckled and rubbed his jaw. She pushed him up against the wall and kissed him again, this time with an almost volatile intensity.

"Keep it up and I'm going to shove that table against the door and make that coliseum full of spectators wait until we're done," he groaned against her hair. He nipped the soft skin behind her ear. He was wearing something that was going to take him a lot of work to get out of, but she wasn't. He brushed the fabric and held her against him. He groaned, "I can't believe I'm saying this, but we have to stop now. We have to come up with a plan."

She shouldn't tell him what their Clan had discovered but knew it was a necessity. She grabbed the salt from the table and instructed, "Come over here." She drenched a cloth in the water and motioned for him to sit beside her. Her hands cupped the water, trickled it over his skin and she applied the salt. Another strangely intimate gesture. *She was giving away an Ankh secret. He wasn't her enemy on this day though, he was her ally.* They'd been covered in blood their whole naughty makeout session. They'd become sidetracked and hadn't finished wiping it off.

Tiberius whispered, "Even with not an ounce of makeup on, you're crazy beautiful."

"Stop being nice to me," she teased, smiling. "I'm going to have to punch you again." She scrubbed off the blood caked on his ears and told him to close his eyes. She salted his face, without getting any in his eyes and he did the same for her. He appeared to be deep in thought. Lexy asked, "What are you thinking about?"

"Nothing we have time for now," he tempted.

"This is the only time," she countered. "It's not like we can meet up to have coffee together or hook up after the Summit."

"True," he answered, caressing her thigh. He thought about it for a second and said, "It will happen though." He pulled her in for one last salty kiss.

She'd become dark out of necessity and then because it was what felt natural to her. She had made a choice when she came to Ankh to slip into the darkness only when it was required. She stayed in the light living in laughter and humour because of Grey. She felt guilty as she recalled his words, *'Not Tiberius.'* Suddenly, she found herself concerned he'd tell her secrets.

Tiberius winked at her and teased, "Don't worry honey. Now that I've had the chance to read your mind. I'm more afraid of you than I was yesterday." He laced his fingers through hers and stared into her eyes. *'Damn it, she's gotten into my head, my heart and my pants.'*

She heard his inner dialogue and smiled, a little proud of herself. "That's good, you should be," she sparred. *Tiberius would be a horrible boyfriend. Imagine the person you love knowing every deep dark desire. How intensely you would obsess about them if their every thought was literally under your skin. She shouldn't be thinking about these things right now. How was she going to summon her inner Dragon when all she really wanted to do, was take him up on his offer to push the table in front of the door and make the others wait until they were done.* Tiberius was laughing as the door opened. *He must have heard her inner commentary too.* She followed Tiberius out the door, knowing under any realm of logic they stood no chance. *With their body's covered in salt, at least they'd taste nasty when they were eaten.* "Maybe we'll at least give Abaddon heartburn," Lexy commented. *He'd put a chink in her armour. They were similar creatures, feelings destroyed them. Life was much better while reptilian cold-blooded. Tiberius of all people had broken through her wall of hatred for everything in general by surprising her with random kindness. He had hurt her in battle. He had made her heart feel something. Damn it Tiberius.*

Grinning, Tiberius whispered, "You have to shut them down. I can hear your thoughts. This really isn't great timing for an emotional breakthrough."

It was horrible timing. She was trying. It wasn't working. They were going to be slaughtered. They strolled out into the center of the coliseum. She looked up at the stands and saw her Clan.

What was she doing? He was going to bring this up every time the Clans bumped into each other.

With ice cold resolve, Tiberius blurted, "I lied, by the way. I'm going to tell everyone. Your memories make you look weak. I was thinking maybe I should go online, buy myself a farm and give it to Abaddon. I'll send you an email occasionally with a picture that says, wish you were here."

What in the hell was he trying to do? Asshole! Sparks of rage lit up her pupils, she plowed him a good one.

Blood trickled from his nose. He smirked, wiped it away and pushed her further, "You loved everything that happened and frankly that's a little sick in the head. Some twisted shit went on there. I saw some hanging racks, whips, chains and ropes. What didn't they do to you, Lexy? I bet that's an easier question to answer?"

*Son of a B...*Lexy dove on top of him and strangled him with her bare hands. She felt her grasp on reality slipping away. Adrenaline began to blind her with rage.

He grabbed her face as she choked him, and gagged, "I had to. I had to make you angry." He gasped as her grasp loosened and declared, "Look into my eyes. Those people on that farm, weren't human. They were demons, it was a settlement. So, when you killed them, you didn't really kill them. I bet some of those men are here right now. They'll be standing out there grinning at you, because they know you biblically. When you kill a demon, you must use a special blade. You know that. They have those blades here. You can kill them all right now if you want to. We can kill them together."

Lexy was gone. Her humanity had shut off as a form of self-defence. She understood what he was saying but she was removed from what was going on around her. The place was full of Abaddon. They were surrounded by Demons with eyes of night and hollowed cheeks of stretched flesh. *It was two Second Tiers against at least thirty Abaddon. She had this.*

"Snapping their necks will only take them down momentarily," Tiberius explained. "They'll keep coming at us like rabid possessed zombies. Only the blades on the walls of the coliseum will work. You need to get to the Abaddon blades."

Lexy had the ability to do the impossible if she was backed into a corner, so Tiberius had backed her there and hoped for the best. The horn sounded and they ran right through the crowd of demons. They were burned by the salt as they attempted to grab hold of them. They made it to the walls and they each grabbed a blade, swung around, and sprinted back into the crowd of demons. They were amped up warriors, shrieking in rage as sharp nails scratched and knives stabbed their flesh. They kept swinging at their targets. A fine spray of blood showered them both with a sickening crimson mist as they dove, twisted, leapt and rolled through the hoard of putrid creatures. Their weapons hitting their targets, as each demon was impaled by the end of a silver blade, they exploded into a black mist and dissipated into the air. What they'd accomplished together was impossible. They had rid the coliseum of demons in record time and only the essence of black mist lingered.

They were only given a moment to recover before the gates opened and the next batch of Abaddon's worst took their turn. Two long clawed, slimy tar black demonic creatures came through the open coliseum gates, with the black mist swirling before them. They both had salt on them, but it had been covered in blood. This had the creatures extra excited, their jagged fangs, dripping with saliva in anticipation. *They'd probably been starving the demons for this occasion.* Lexy thought about breaking Tiberius's legs and leaving him there. *They'd be distracted, while they ate him. She could kill both.*

"You know I said those things to make you furious, so we could win the last round," he clarified as the demons approached.

She didn't bother to respond, she didn't care. "I have an idea, but you're not going to like it," she announced.

"Do tell," he laughed, as he swung his blade at the last of the swirling black mist.

The mist would have subdued them, had it not been for the blades. They would have been a feast for the beasts that slowly meandered across the coliseum. "Pretend to be incapacitated by the mist. Keep the blade in your hand, when they come close, lift it towards the sun, and try to catch a beam. If you blind one, for a second. I can get behind it and take it out. We can take the last one out together."

Clutching his blade, Tiberius agreed, "I can do that."

Their tails as sharp as swords on either side. They were slow moving, but their tails were lightning fast. They could slice a man in two, in a heartbeat. They had tunnel vision and nocturnal beings in bright glaring sunshine, were at a disadvantage. Getting beside or behind them unseen was the key. Tiberius fell limp to the coliseum floor, the crowd gasped. They hadn't even known he was wounded. The creatures salivated excitedly as they sped up and hobbled towards where Tiberius lay. Lexy sprinted to the side, making sure to use her sword to reflect the light. They couldn't even look in her direction. *She might not even need Tiberius.* Lexy circled around behind them, took a deep breath and ran at the closest creatures back. She sliced his tail off, in one stealth movement. With its main means of self-defence severed. Lexy dove on its back, positioning herself over the back of its neck. With a mighty thrust of her blade the monstrosity disintegrated into fine black grains of sand. She fell through it, landing in the crimson sand with a thud. The pile of black sand, that surrounded her, turned to a black mist and blew away in the breeze.

Tiberius held up his sword to the sun, temporarily blinding the other abomination. It staggered backwards, disorientated. Lexy sliced off his tail. Stunned, it looked up to the sky and Tiberius knifed it in the throat. The creature turned to black sand and covered Tiberius. He panicked at first, hacking and coughing, as he brushed it off himself. In seconds it floated away in the air as a black mist, which then turned into nothing. The crowd roared and they both collapsed flat on their backs on the coliseum floor. Tiberius laughed hysterically, "That was amazing."

Glancing at Tiberius from where she lay, Lexy felt the urge to smile. *They were enemies again.* She bit her lip as images of their steamy time together flickered through her mind. She stood up and he was beside her. He looked at her and laced his fingers through hers. They held hands one final time, raising them into the air in victory.

The announcers voice bellowed, "Lexy of Ankh and Tiberius of Triad." The crowd went wild.

They lowered their hands. Tiberius squeezed hers before he let it go. *There would be no point in reminiscing about those kisses. They shouldn't have happened. It was either despise him or want him and wanting Tiberius of Triad would lead to nothing good. Well, maybe one good thing.* She glanced up at her Clan and they were all clapping except for Grey, who was visibly upset. *Good, it was his turn to feel that way.* Pulling off the band-aid. She turned and said, "Liked it my ass." In one fluid cat like movement she swung her leg around and kicked Tiberius in the side of the head, knocking him out cold. She casually strolled out of the open archway of the coliseum as the crowd roared. She glanced back and smiled at the sight of him lying unconscious in the rising dust of her footsteps.

Chapter 37

Introducing The Winners

Lexy walked out of the main part of the coliseum and nobody tried to stop her. *They wouldn't dare.* She scaled the staircase covered in blood and strolled up to Ankh's seating. *They hadn't even had a chance to leave. That sexy stranger Silas was sitting with them.*

He stood up smiling, "You are truly meant for this." Silas held out his hand to shake hers.

"I'm covered in blood," Lexy cautioned.

"I don't care," Silas countered, keeping his hand there until she took it. "You'll be my guest for the celebration. Come with me. I'll arrange to have you bathed and properly dressed."

"Are you saying this isn't a good look for me?" Lexy teased. Her clothing was caked in blood, ash, dust and unidentified matter.

"Not at all, as a matter of fact it's a bit of a turn on," Silas flirted as he led her away from the group.

"That's a little twisted, even for me," Lexy sparred as she followed him.

Grey yelled after her, "Hey, when your date is talking about blood being a turn on. You should run!"

Grey sat back down still chuckling to himself.

"Those two were made for each other," Jenna commented.

Grey looked at her and questioned, "Are you being serious?"

Their Oracle smiled. Knowing what may come to pass, Jenna baited, "Don't worry, there's always more than one option."

"Who is mine?" Grey whispered. Come on now, it's been like forty years. Can't you just tell me?"

Jenna laughed, "You have to figure these things out by yourself. Don't worry, I'll warn you if you're going too far in the wrong direction."

Grey looked up at Lilarah with the royal family and admitted, "Even though a part of me once wished it was, I know it's not her."

With his hand laying on his shoulder, Frost cautioned, "Try to remember that while you're having fun."

Grey stared at the doorway Lexy disappeared through and complained, "She didn't even speak to me before she took off with that Silas guy."

Jenna kept smiling and said nothing in response.

Lexy followed Silas through long flowing silk curtains into a room with a large teal marble group bath. There were servants, scurrying around with scented flower petals, throwing them on the surface of the water. They ran up to her and began to remove what was left of her morbidly soiled attire in front of Silas. Lexy laughed, "Can I take my own clothes off?"

Silas cocked his head and taunted, "Are you ashamed of your body?"

"No, I'm not ashamed of my body. I just prefer to bathe privately," Lexy countered, as she struggled to hold onto what was left of her blood-soaked sarong.

"That's cute," he provoked as he passed her a fresh short sarong. "You can wear this after the bath." They scurried around and removed his armour. He dropped his bottoms.

Lexy turned away so fast she didn't even see if he had anything on underneath. Curious, she peeked as he stepped into the large community bath. He was wearing a loin cloth, with rather limited coverage. Lexy was led to a private bath with just a few women. She climbed in and submerged her aching muscles under the surface of the heavenly liquid relief. She lay there concealed by scented flower petals, closed her eyes and had almost drifted off to sleep, when someone cleared their throat.

"Don't you dare go to sleep yet, it's going to be a long night," Tiberius's voice commented.

Lexy wrapped her arms around her chest. Even though she knew she was covered in petals and he couldn't see anything, she scolded, "Get out of here, I'm naked."

"You killed me, after all I did to help you. You actually did it... bravo," Tiberius jeered. Chuckling to himself, he knelt by her and put his hand in her bath water "It's perfect," he toyed.

She looked up, with her arms concealing her chest. She shook her head.

"I meant the temperature. I should climb in there with you. Do you want me to?" Tiberius probed, as he moved the petals with a wave of his hand.

He'd already had a bath. He was clean. He was Triad but if he hadn't been wearing that difficult to remove armour, it would have happened. He wasn't wearing any now. Her breath quickened as she whispered, "You probably shouldn't, you're all clean."

"Are you still feeling dirty?" He tempted as he flirtatiously scooped up a handful of petals. "You know I prefer you that way. I'm going to be picturing you lying on that banquet table every time we run into each other."

Damn him. Her pulse raced and she bit her lip. *She was going to be thinking about the look in his eyes and the wreckless abandon she'd felt.* Fighting against the alluring dark magnetic pull, Lexy denied her desires, "Our situation has changed."

"Have I told you how adorable your accent is?" Tiberius seduced as he ran his hand over the surface of the water, shifting the petals again.

Another male voice piped in, "Well, what's going on in here?"

She looked behind her. *It was Silas. He was enjoying her predicament.*

Silas sighed, "This is why you were taking so long. Tisk, tisk, two timing me already."

The men were sizing each other up. Lexy splashed them and scolded, "Seriously, can you both get the hell out of here?"

Grey walked in next, "Oh, sorry Lex." He covered his eyes, peaked through his fingers and teased, "Lexy, now this is a little bit naughty. How many men do you need for bath time?"

She splashed him too, moving the petals and revealing more of herself by accident. She stammered, "Alright, I've had it, you three, get the hell out of here. If I have to get out of this tub, you'll regret it."

Tiberius chuckled, "Probably not."

All three of them left laughing. She sunk her head underwater. *Would drowning herself after winning the battle be frowned upon?* A couple of women came in and she got out of the tub. They dried her off and gave her two tiny pieces of material with ties made of exquisite white silk. They helped her put it on, did her hair and chatted for a while. *Since when did guys aggressively flirt with her? She was both flattered and confused.* They pulled the curtains and led her to the full community bath. Her sparsely clothed Clan was relaxing amongst wealthy third tier, the other Clans and scantily clad men and women in communal bath, drinking heavily. *This wasn't going to go well.*

Tiberius causally placed his goblet of wine on the ledge and taunted, "How's your girlfriend?"

Frost laughed at his brother's attempt to provoke him and replied, "She's spending the week with your grandson."

Tiberius sparred, "Is that why you're going buck wild? I thought you had real feelings for this one?"

"I haven't done anything wrong yet," Frost coolly countered, surrounded by a flock of adoring women, some massaging his shoulders, others hanging on his every word. "Well, not biblically," he couldn't even keep a straight face as he said it. "I told her I wasn't going to behave myself and that she shouldn't either. She needs to figure out her feelings for him before starting something with anyone. I haven't been asleep for a thousand years, you know."

With a playful shove, Grey scolded, "Oh, come on. You know Kayn wouldn't just sleep with Kevin. Not this version of him, anyway. There's no excuse for this."

Triad's leader started an argument between friends for his own entertainment. The conversation was becoming heated. He was just watching it unfold with a big grin on his face.

"Seriously, you too Grey? By the way, how was your night with Lily?" Frost dropped a bomb in the pool.

Taking an imaginary dart to the chest, Tiberius sighed, "Brother, bad form, her father's sitting right there." He shook his head at Lily and taunted, "You are such a naughty girl, flirting with me brazenly all night and bedding somebody else."

Markus sighed, "Grey, why would you do that to yourself?"

"Dad, that was uncalled for," Lily argued, embarrassed.

"Seriously, honey? You know I didn't mean that in a disparaging way. It took a year for you two to get back to some semblance of normal," Markus clarified

"Don't pee where you sleep," Frost baited. Lily punched his arm.

Pretending to ignore the sparring match, with a girl hanging off his arm, Thorne started coughing, to cover up laughter.

It drew Frost's attention, he provoked, "Oh, by the way brother. I made sure Melody was alright after you left last night."

The gloves came off as Thorne stiffened, turned and vowed, "I'll kill you, if you ever even think of touching her. If it even crosses your mind. Do not tempt me. I might just kill you for sport."

Tiberius was laughing at what he'd started as Thorne's lady friend stormed away, and it was difficult to storm away dramatically in water. Thorne hadn't noticed, because he was in a drunk pissing match with Frost.

"But I slept with her last night," Frost provoked.

"You did not, I can tell when you're lying. You've had the same tell since you were a kid," Thorne bantered.

"It was innocent, she slept in the same bed as us. She was passed out cold. We thought we needed a Healer after what our dear brother did to Lilarah," Frost maneuvered the whole thing back to Tiberius.

"Bravo my twisted siblings, our little chats are always hysterical," Tiberius sparred.

Lexy was standing above them, listening. *They'd yet to acknowledge her presence.* Tiberius looked her up and down appreciatively. She glared at him. *Don't you dare.*

Tiberius grinned at her, winked and said, "Markus, do you mind if I make out with your girlfriend? She's the only one of your Clan in the pool I've missed."

Lexy's eyes burrowed into the back of Tiberius's skull. *She was going to kill him.* Grey stared at her in shock, then back at Tiberius. Lexy knelt by the edge and summoned Tiberius over with her finger Intrigued, he obeyed. She lured him closer, and it looked like she was going to lean in and kiss him. Swiftly, her hands clasped around his throat and she began strangling the life out of him. She lost her balance and fell into the water, with a giant splash, releasing him for a second.

Running away, Tiberius choked, "In the pool! I said in the pool!

In a split second she had his head underwater, trying to drown him. The Ankh pried her off him as Lexy swung and clawed, enraged.

Markus got out of the water. Standing on the marble floor barefoot and furious, he commanded, "That's enough! All of you! You're acting like a pile of friggin' children!"

Thorne pulled himself out of the water and walked away from the group, laughing as the Triad joined the bathtub fight against Ankh. Thorne passed some Third Tiers in the corridor and huffed, "Classless animals, just a bunch of wild hooligans."

They were all trying to drown each other when a voice came over the loudspeaker and barked, "Enough! You should be ashamed of yourselves! Get out of the bath, dry off and get to the commons!"

The dishevelled inhabitants of earth sheepishly got off each other and climbed out of the enormous bath. Grey and Lexy strolled side by side in silence. *Perhaps, he just didn't know what to say. She honestly didn't know what to say for herself. She had no excuses. Dragons shouldn't need excuses.* She grinned while she walked. *It had been fun though, and Tiberius hadn't added her to his list of conquests, she'd added herself by her overreaction.*

Grey grabbed her arm gently and whispered, "I don't know how far it went and I know you think I'm going to give you shit, but I'm not. You had some fun, it's not a big deal. I do reserve the right to tease you mercilessly for the next ten years." He winked at her as they parted ways.

Lexy was dressed in gold, adorned in jewels and led to a room that hadn't been altered in the last forty years. She smiled as she strolled over and touched the luxurious velvet curtains. She knew why she was here. She sat in the same chair, picked up a carafe of yellow flower free red wine and poured some into a silver goblet. She didn't look up as she heard the door open.

Amadeus declared, "That was a long five years."

Lexy grinned and replied, "It definitely was." She glanced up at her still handsome yet aged princely saviour and said, "You look good."

Amadeus walked towards her with outstretched arms. She stood up and they embraced. He squeezed her, laughed, "You're a liar." They sat down at the little table across from each other. "Impressive fighting skills by the way," he praised, raising his goblet for a toast. They clinked glasses. Lexy chuckled, "I try."

The conversation paused as servants brought their meals in. *Servants that looked like the comedians from earth that were cleaning up the stands and towing bodies out of the coliseum.* Lexy waited until they left and she asked, "How come the servants all look the same?" *She knew, she just wanted to hear his side.*

Amadeus chuckled, "It wasn't a planned thing. Every week we put one of each cloned celebrity from earth and other places into the green space. We give them numbers and televise it. These two guys are insanely entertaining to watch. If they survive for seven days, they are granted options. For six months now Seth Hogan and James Tanko have been the only survivors. It's just a freak thing. It wrecked the whole betting part of the show."

Lexy started to laugh, *that made her week. That, and getting to murder a mass amount of Clan in a coliseum.*

Amadeus took a bite of something that resembled a pastry and said, "I'm not going to bother asking you if you want to stay. I already know what the answer will be."

Lexy smiled as she picked up a pastry and bit into it expecting to find fruit. It was meat. It was delicious. She enquired, "How's the wife and kids?"

He grinned, took a swig of wine and disclosed, "Sleeping with my father behind my back and the kids are all grown up."

That was uncomfortable. "That's got to suck," she mumbled and joined him by guzzling her whole glass of wine.

They sat in awkward silence for a minute or two before Amadeus casually probed, "How's Grey taking your fling with Tiberius?"

Lexy winced and questioned, "There were cameras in that room, weren't there?" *Oh, shit.* Her mind replayed the steamy, intensely private moments they'd shared.

Amadeus nodded and whispered, "It was seriously hot and incredibly disturbing. The whole royal family saw it. They might be showing a few clips of it at dinner. It's going to be a pay per view event. I'd like to think of myself as a friend and I thought I'd save you from sitting in the banquet hall while they watch the promos."

Lexy nodded and pursed her lips together. *Her whole Clan could be watching her have a kinky moment with Tiberius right now, even worse…the other Clans. This was going to be humiliating. She would never hear the end of it.* She looked at him. He had a giant shit eating grin on his face. *He was full of shit.*

Amadeus started chuckling, "You should have seen the look on your face. That was amazing. There's no pay per view event. I was just messing with you."

"You jerk," she scolded, throwing food at him from her plate.

Doubled over laughing, almost in tears, he laughed, "You totally went for it. How was he?"

"I didn't do it," Lexy hissed. She couldn't help it, she started to laugh, partially out of relief.

They spent the night together as old friends, talking about the years gone by and what they wanted for the future. This time they didn't stay sitting at the table. They laid in bed next to each other, as nothing more than friends, laughing hysterically every time he brought up the pay per view event, until they fell asleep.

In the morning she woke up and he was already gone. There was a note on his pillow that read, 'See you in five years.' Lexy made her way back to the red sand of the coliseum, to meet up with the rest of her Clan. Grey was standing there with his arm around Lily. *Great, this ought to be fun.*

The first thing out of her best friend's mouth was, "Where did you end up last night?"

"Wouldn't you like to know," Lexy baited and strutted away.

Grey left Lily standing there. He chased her down, tackled her, pinned her in the sand and messed her hair.

"I'll kill you," Lexy laughed as she squirmed, trying to get away.

Grey pinned her shoulder to the ground, kissed her on the cheek and said, "No, you won't."

Lexy stopped struggling and sighed, "Probably not."

He teased, "You're not going to tell me what happened, are you?" He got off her, stood up, and extended his hand.

She took it and sparred, "Maybe someday." *She felt different now. Acknowledging that she wanted Tiberius back had given her a sense of power. It was something new, something she'd never felt before.*

With his arm warmly around her, they wandered back to their group as he vowed, "We have all the time in the world."

They returned to the in-between for a breather before going back to collect the three newbie Ankh for their Testing. Standing in the white sand of her true home, Lexy watched her Clan members joking around and laughing together. *She adored these crazy people.* Grey was wrestling with Arianna and Frost was standing there with his arm around Jenna. Markus was deep in conversation with his daughter, Lily. *These were her people.* She gazed at her symbol, raising it to her lips, she smiled and continued to watch. *Her soul tingled and she felt the pull.*

Jenna announced, "It's time to go."

Orin was summoning them back to the land of the living. They took their places side by side, standing in the silken sand, under a brilliant water colour sky.

Grey grinned at her and said, "You were amazing in there."

She smiled back, without speaking, because she didn't need to say a word. The tingle became a prickle, and her heart surged with warmth as they dissolved into the air. With a flash of light, followed by the sensation of falling. Suddenly, she was back inside the tomb, next to Grey and Arrianna. Lexy exhaled and smiled as the tomb ground open above them to flickering candlelight.

Orin's face appeared, looking in at the trio, he questioned, "How was it?"

Grey grinned and replied, "It was epic."

"Lexy was epic," Arrianna added.

It was epic, now that was the perfect description. The other two climbed out of the tomb. She heard them telling Orin about everything that happened...every sordid detail. *That had taken five seconds. She was never going to hear the end of this.* Lexy remained in the tomb for a minute longer. *Not hiding, never hiding...Dragons never hide. Dragons do epic things.* Lexy sighed and got out of the tomb to join the others. Orin glanced at her and winked. *Sometimes it was difficult for Lexy to tell the difference between an ending and a beginning, but this time she knew...*

The Beginning

Biography

Kim Cormack is the always comedic author of the darkly twisted epic paranormal romance series, "The Children of Ankh." She worked for over 16 years as an Early Childhood educator in preschool, daycare, and as an aid. She has M.S and has lived most of her life on Vancouver Island in beautiful British Columbia, Canada. She currently lives in the gorgeous little town of Port Alberni. She's a single mom with two awesome kids. She has a son in grade 8 and a daughter in University at VIU. If you see her back away slowly and toss packages of hot sauce at her until you escape.

A Personal Note From The Author

I began writing this series shortly after my M.S diagnosis. I had many reasons to fight. I had incredible children, a wonderful family, and amazing friends but this series gave me a purpose. Whenever things become dark, I use my imagination to find the light within myself. No matter what life throws your way, you are stronger than you believe. My hope is that the character's strength becomes an inner voice for the readers that need it. Stand back up and if you can't stand... Rise up within yourself. We are all beautiful just as we are. We are all immortal.

All heroes are born from the embers that linger after the fire of great tragedy...

She slept a dreamless sleep free of Dragons for she had slain them once again...

Behind The Series

One thousand years ago, procreation with mortals became illegal under the immortal law. Any suspected immortal offspring will be allowed to live until the age of sixteen. At this time, a Correction will be sent to erase their family line. The suspected immortal and their immediate family will be executed. If the partially immortal teen manages to survive their Correction, or they have impressed the Guardians of the in-between with their bravery, they may be granted a second chance as a sacrificial lamb for the greater good. They must join one of three clans of immortals living on earth. Clan Ankh, Clan Trinity or Clan Triad. They will then have the symbol of that clan branded into their flesh and with this mark, their souls will no longer be permitted through the hall of souls when they die. Once they have reached the age of eighteen, they will be sealed to their clan. The next step is to train their partially mortal brains to survive the stresses of immortality. The next feat will be the immortal Testing where they will be dropped into a floating crypt the size of New York City. This Testing is fuelled by your worst nightmares. It is a place of magic. A personal hell, where anything can happen. Here you must die a thousand times if need be, in increasingly violent ways until you understand what it is to be immortal. All three Clans go into the Testing. They must remain together and search for the Amber room in order to survive. There is a catch…only the first two clans that find the Amber room will be allowed out. *The third clan will remain trapped in the nightmare forever…*

A sexy dark comic romp through the afterlife with three clans of naughty certifiably insane antiheroes who battle each other for shits and giggles while collecting human teenagers as they survive bloody gruesome exterminations of their family lines. If they have demonstrated an impressive level of badassery they are granted a second chance at life as sacrificial lambs for the greater good. They must join one of three clans of immortals living on earth and can be stolen at random by any other clan until their eighteenth birthday.

Plot twist...To prove their partially mortal brains are capable of grasping immortality, they will be dropped into an Immortal Testing which is basically a simulation of their own personal hells. Like rats in a maze made of nightmares and other ghastly depraved thoughts best left locked behind those mortal happy place filters, they must come out mentally intact after being murdered in thousands of increasingly creative ways.

Drop by the series website childrenofankh.com and say, hi. We'd love to hear from you. XO

Table Of Contents

Warning

The information contained within this series is not intended for mere mortals. Reading these books may inadvertently trigger a Correction. If you survive or have shown great bravery during your demise, you may be given a second chance at life by one of the three Guardians of the in-between. For your soul's protection until your 18th year, you must join one of three clans of immortals living on earth... Ankh, Trinity or Triad. You are totally still reading this, aren't you? Good luck mortal friend.

Made in the USA
Middletown, DE
09 October 2021